OzHouse Reopened

The Curse of Budistiltskin

Other books by Dennis Anfuso (DennisAnfuso.com)
The Winged Monkeys of Oz
The Astonishing Tale of the Gump of Oz
A Promise Kept in Oz

Other books by Alan Lindsay (Alanglindsay.com)
Ambaguam, Beginning at the End
A, a novel
The Burzee Rose, a Christmas Carol

Also by Alan Lindsay and Dennis Anfuso
OzHouse

Forthcoming by Alan Lindsay and Dennis Anfuso
Intruder in the Realm

OZHOUSE
Reopened
The Curse of Budistiltskin

Chronicled by
Alan Lindsay
& Dennis Anfuso

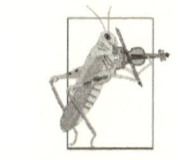

Interset Press
2018

OzHouse Reopened, The Curse of Budistiltskin by Alan Lindsay and Dennis Anfuso

Text Copyright © 2017 by Alan Lindsay and Dennis Anfuso

This is a work of fiction. Any resemblance of characters in this book to actual persons, living or dead, is unintentional and purely coincidental.

9 8 7 6 5 4 3 2 1 /0 1

Interset Press

35 Burns Hill Road

Wilton, New Hampshire 03086

Interset Press is a registered trademark and "Fiddler," the Interset Press colophon, is a trademark of Linda Anfuso.

Book design by Dan Fuso and Geimle Burzeen.

Cover Art by Dan Fuso

Many thanks to Tom Benson for his proofreading prowess.

Printed in the United States of America. First Interset Press edition: June 2017

Library of Congress Cataloguing-in-Publication Data: Lindsay, Alan and Anfuso, Dennis

OzHouse Reopened: The Curse of Budistiltskin

Summary: Ten years have passed. Charlie fears his love of fairylands has ruined him. Jessica needs to save her sister from following the path of her lost and alcoholic mother. Doug Robbins' marriage is coming unraveled, and the state almost never sends children to OzHouse anymore. Should they look to fairylands for help? Or do fantasies just make things worse? No one has dared the magic doorway in years, but maybe there are answers there. Can Charlie renew his art? Can Doug renew himself? Can Jessica find a better place for her sister and her sister's doomed children? Perhaps the answers are tied to the fate of the one they left behind, poor, little Buddy Samson. Perhaps they need to find him. But first, they'll have to face the devil.

[1. Fantasy. 2. Fairytales. 3. Oz. 4. Anfuso, Dennis. 5. Lindsay, Alan.] 1. Title [Fic.]

ISBN: 1-978-57433-048-9

For Matte

~Alan

For Michael, Corinne, and Kayla

~Dennis

PROLOGUE

"I'LL HAVE ANOTHER PINT of the house ale." Charlie slid his empty glass across the well-worn varnish of the bar.

As he crossed back to his table, he snuck another glance in her direction—the woman with the short red hair. She was still watching him, following him with her eyes. She'd been doing it for a while. He'd tried to convince himself that she wasn't really interested in him as he sat at his table sketching the room. Maybe it was someone behind him, or something out the window. He tried to pretend she still wasn't. Sure, she was pretty. But her undisguised gaze his way every few seconds made him uncomfortable, as though his shirt was inside out or his head must be on crooked or something. Why else would she be doing it? The obvious explanation—that someone as attractive as she was would be interested in him—that was hardly likely. Random women did not scope out Charles Emerson in pubs. And he'd been in a lot of them. (This was one of his favorites. It was called *The World's End*; it was in Camden, the best part of London. It was built on the site of the home of an ancient witch named Old Mother Red Cap, which may have been why he was drawn to it.)

He looked up again as he sat down, vaguely, so she wouldn't know he was looking at her. She was still doing it, watching him. Perhaps *ogling* would be the right word. She really was unnecessarily pretty, wavy haired with large eyes in a close-fitting patterned top. She reminded him a little of Cinderella. But even if he was interested in catching her eye, she was with two friends—and that was enough to put him off. Speaking to women was hard enough when he had an introduction, and doing it with an audience—that just wasn't going to happen. Years of rejection and the sounds of snickering as he walked away made him gun shy. He could set up at a show and chat away about art for hours with anyone looking at his work, but selling himself was a different story.

He put down his ale and picked up his pen. Not a minute later the woman was standing beside his table, not saying a word, taking a hard look at the scene he was drawing. Charlie could smell her perfume. He smiled nervously and tried not to fidget as he continued to draw. When he reached for his ale, she said, "Nice work."

Small talk was another of Charlie's underdeveloped skills, but she *was* attractive, so he glanced up and acted startled. "Thanks. This is not my usual stuff, but I am trying to keep sort of a journal of my comings and goings while I'm here."

"Yank, then?" she smiled. "Or are you Canadian? It's hard to know the difference with your accents."

"But we don't have the accents, you do," Charlie grinned.

"Definitely a Yank," she laughed a little. She sat down without his asking and took a sip of his ale. Her numerous bracelets jingled. "Well, at least it's not lager."

"If I wanted piss I'd have stayed in America."

She laughed again. "So you came all the way across the pond for an ale?"

"Wouldn't you?" he chuckled. "But since I'm here anyway, I thought maybe I'd do some sketching and a little painting."

"Of English pubs?" She brushed his hand as she turned his sketch so she could get a good look.

"Not pubs, specifically. I'm here more for the countryside."

"Oh, I see." She gave him a look like a mother gives a child daring him to misbehave. "You mean like we did in primary school? Going to press leaves too?" Harsh words, but her smile was infectious.

"I brought my sketchbook along, if you're interested."

"Busman's holiday, I suppose."

Charlie didn't follow.

"I work in a gallery. I spend my time reviewing people's portfolios."

"Oh, well, then don't bother. It's not important, I thought you might like to see my stuff."

"Oh, no, I'll have a look. I don't mind. That's why I came over, actually. I saw you sketching. And it wasn't like you were showing off. You were completely oblivious to the whole room."

"Well, I saw you." He waited, but she didn't seem to register the remark.

2

"I look at so many dull landscapes and twee still lifes. This'll be refreshing."

Charlie opened his portfolio and placed it on the table, careful to avoid his ale. She flipped rather quickly through several paintings that he was especially pleased with before muttering, "Or maybe not so refreshing."

"Excuse me?" Charlie's eyebrows flew high on his head.

"Sorry, I wasn't expecting children's drawings."

Charlie slammed the portfolio shut and almost spilled his drink. "My art is not for children."

"Not for adults, that's for sure," she said.

"Thanks for stopping by uninvited. Sorry you can't stay." He took a large gulp of his ale, dropped the glass down with a bang and stood up.

"Don't be so touchy. I'm sure you could do good work if you weren't drawing dragons and castles. You've clearly been to school."

He stared straight at her, prepared to tell her off in a way that would embarrass her in front of the whole room. But the profound indifference of the look she was casting disarmed him.

"Look, your pub sketch, that's got merit. But this stuff," she waved at the portfolio, "it's just not art, I'm sorry. You've got to grow up."

Charlie stalked out of pub, muttering. He needed to grow up, did he? Really? Well, maybe he did. Maybe he needed to get to a place where he didn't hold back telling a person off just because she was beautiful.

Anyone seeing the gangly young man with his shock of orange hair sticking up in all the wrong places and muttering things to himself might be excused for thinking he was crazy. People moved away from him as he queued for the bus.

CHAPTER ONE

Dear Gary,

You were right. I loved Stratford-Upon-Avon—all the phony Shakespeare stuff. One guy was actually selling Shakespeare's actual skull (alas, poor Yorick!)—but the great part was that it cost £10—two for £18. ROTFLMAO!!!! He may be the most honest man in all England!

I didn't have much luck in London. But as you predicted, I was really drawn to Camden Town. I met so many off-the-wall artists doing such great stuff—nothing like mine. I admit I didn't get as much work done as I hoped, but I have so many sketches, I plan to sequester myself at OzHouse for months and do nothing but draw and paint and figure this out. This trip was absolutely what I needed. I really think so. Yeah, maybe I thought I was going just to collect material, but sometimes you've got to get more confused if you're going to grow—right? I'm confident it's just a matter of working through it. And I think maybe I'm starting to see where I should be going. Just got to find my subject. Anyway, I think I made the first step by figuring out where I was going wrong.

Not much room in this card, so I will end, and tell you all the sordid details (though not as sordid as I'd hoped!)

when I see you.

I trust you got the message I left on the machine. My flight arrives in Boston at 5:30—but why am I telling you that in a letter that will surely arrive after I do? If my cell works (or "mobile" as the Brits say) I'll call from Logan, but I hope you will be there when I arrive because the trip to OzHouse will take almost three hours and I will be plenty jet lagged already.

See you soon,

Chuck

"I NOTICED YOU NEVER TALK ABOUT IT," Gary said as he pulled onto the highway.

"Well I guess I *do* think it must be weird, living in that house all these years knowing that thing is there." Charlie placed his fingertips lightly upon the plastic lid on his coffee cup—still too hot to drink. "Do *you* ever talk about it?"

Gary shrugged. "Among ourselves? No. Not really. I mean, sure, Doug seemed interested at first, but since we couldn't use it, well, I guess as time moved on we all just put it behind us and it sort of stopped feeling real. But then it didn't mean as much to us as it did to you."

Charlie exhaled audibly and raised and lowered his cup without taking a sip.

"Personally," Gary went on, "I'd let you use it if I could. It's all boarded up of course."

"Don't worry, Gary, really. It's not going to be a problem."

But Gary kept talking, "But after last time, you know, what choice do we have? We promised not to use it."

"Promised? Promised who? Glinda the Oz-Nazi? Doesn't matter. Really, I'm not interested." He paused. "But if I were, I don't think that promise would really weigh on my conscience."

"Oz-Nazi?" Gary made a face. "That's a little harsh, don't you think?"

"Okay, perhaps, perhaps a little, but still… Ouch." Charlie put his hand to his mouth as he lowered his coffee—scalding, bitter, bottom-of-the-pot. "Not that it matters. Like I said, I'm really not going to give you any trouble about the door. Last thing on my mind right now."

"Are you sure?" Gary glanced at the highway signs.

"God, yes. Not a kid any more, Gary. I wouldn't go back there now even if I could."

"Because if, like you said, you didn't get what you needed in England, I just thought…."

"No. Fairyland, it would be the worst place in the world for me right now."

"What about seeing your old flame?"

"Excuse me?"

"You know, Cinderella?"

Charlie laughed. "Did you know she's actually not even Cinderella in the oldest Grimm versions? She's got a different name—Ashen-something. And it's her mother instead of her fairy godmother and she's like a tree spirit or something. I forget. I'm surprised she even answered to 'Cinderella' when I saw her. She seemed to know just what I was talking about."

"Oh, I'm not surprised. Truth is, no matter what you've seen, those tales were already mixed up before the Grimm boys ever got their hands on them." Gary looked over at Charlie, slouched in the seat. "Okay. So if we're good about the secret room, we don't need to talk about it anymore. I can tell them I did as promised."

Gary took a deep breath and reached for the radio. But he took his hand away without turning it on. "So what's this about finding your subject? I thought that was the one thing you were always sure about."

"As I said, time to grow up."

"Folk tales are not children's tales. You know that."

"That's easier to say than believe. And easier to believe than to convince anyone of."

"Do you know how often the devil shows up in those old tales?" Doug gestured at Charlie's reflection on the windshield.

"Yes, I do. There's some real creepy stuff there, not child friendly at all. I studied all of that. But that's not how people see it. And what if just no one's interested?"

"Then you *make* them interested. That's what artists do."

Charlie stared out the window as the miles of dark trees raced by. Driving down this highway, Charlie almost always felt as though he was threading his way through an endless evergreen forest. He knew of course that he and Gary weren't really doing that. There were houses and neighborhoods just on the other side of the trees. But it was a pretty convincing illusion.

"Do you ever wonder what became of Buddy? I looked at a bunch of copies of Rumpelstiltskin in the Bodleian, and it wasn't changed at all. I sort of expected it to mention a small boy in the tale now. That would have seemed right to me."

"We always knew we didn't change the texts when we went into the stories."

"Yeah, but I was still hoping. Like I wonder sometimes if we did a good thing leaving him there. Is he really better off than he would have been if he had returned with us?"

Gary thought about this. It had never felt to him like a decision he'd made, more like something that had just happened. He wasn't tempted to second guess it. Besides, in his memory Charlie had been all in favor of Buddy staying behind in fairyland. "Well, in the end, it's just not worth worrying about, Chuck. The door took Buddy where Buddy wanted to go."

"Unless it just took him where it took him. I don't think we really understand how that all works."

"I suppose that's possible. But it's a question we'll never get an answer to. No one, not even me, has been in the room in ten years. We did a lot of damage last time. And a promise, even to an *Oz-Nazi*, is a promise."

Charlie dropped his bitter cup into the cup holder and reclined the seat a few degrees. He had a lot more to say about all of this. But that would require an involved discussion, and he could feel the jet lag pulling him down into sleep. He didn't want to talk about anything.

But Gary kept plying him with questions. "Seriously, what is this thing that led you to this sudden doubting of your subject matter?"

"It's just... The fairytales, they're not working for me anymore. Time to move on. I need to find out what I should be doing next. I'm just going to get in that studio and paint like a maniac till I find it." He closed his eyes. "Anyway, that's the plan. So, what's new back at the old OzHouse?" Maybe if he could steer the conversation to something easier, Gary would do the talking and he could doze off. "Have you got a good crop of kids?"

Gary rubbed his bald head. "In fact we have four kids staying with us right now. First we've had in a while—pretty much since the last leadership changed at DCYF. I don't think that's a coincidence either. Place seems downright empty most of the time. Two are siblings from Lebanon, and the other two arrived on the same day from up near Berlin. Quiet kids, one doesn't seem to know how to speak. Hasn't said a word since he arrived."

"Beth must love that."

"Actually Beth's in Spain."

"Yeah? With Doug and her parents? That must be interesting, I mean for Doug. The way they talk about him."

"Doug didn't go." Gary stared at the road. "Well, Beth wanted to see her parents. Yeah, I know, that's odd. But they are *her* parents and they're not getting any younger. And if she's ever going to have a relationship with them..." Gary was trying to make it sound normal, but

7

Charlie still thought it funny for Beth to go without Doug. He'd never remembered one of them going anywhere without the other.

Charlie pushed back into the head rest, and closed his eyes again. It was a signal to Gary that he was done talking. But Gary ignored it. He wanted to know what happened to the extra money Charlie had asked him to wire. He tried to sound casual.

"The exchange rate ate up a lot of it," Charlie explained. "And good ale ain't cheap."

They laughed. Gary kept his eye out for the exit.

"I'm only asking because, you know, Gwen was willing to help, but she wasn't thrilled when the price kept going up."

"Really?" Charlie always found it odd when wealthy people were tight with pocket change.

"You know, with the stock market and all, money's not quite as— well let's just say 'available' as it used to be."

Gary turned his head long enough to see the baffled expression written across Charlie's face.

"Nothing to worry about," Gary laughed, though perhaps not as convincingly as he had intended. "We all go through ups and downs. Doug's work isn't selling much these days. He hasn't placed a story in a while. I haven't got as many illustration jobs myself as I used to. Bad economy. It'll pass," he chuckled.

When they finally pulled into the long gravel driveway of OzHouse, all was dark. No moon, no stars. The bulb in the floodlight must have burned out and no lights were on in the front rooms. When Gary turned off the engine, the whole house disappeared into the kind of muddy darkness you hardly ever see in the electric world. Charlie poured his tepid, undrunk coffee on the grass.

"Gwen must have gone to bed," said Gary. He sounded surprised.

They groped their way to the door.

Gwen had not gone to bed. As they walked in the door, they heard kitchen cabinets banging and ceramic mugs clink, not in the small kitchen by the front door but in the large central kitchen they hardly ever used these days. She'd timed their arrival—which made Charlie smile, it was so like her, and so like home. She had a fresh pot of coffee brewed and ready. It was one of the quirks of the Robbinses to drink coffee at bedtime. Charlie should have expected it. He himself had fallen into the habit years ago. He tossed the airport cup into the trash and took a mug of the real thing.

"I'm not going to ask too many questions tonight," Gwen said as they hung up their jackets and Charlie dropped his luggage on the hall floor. "But I will want to see your photos and your artwork and hear all the stories tomorrow."

"Fair enough," said Charlie. Taking a sip form his mug of perfect joe and grabbing his carry-on, he headed up to his room. "It is empty isn't it?"

"That's *your* room," Gary quickly cut in.

Charlie dragged himself up the steps and muttered about the many ways people would die if they woke him in the morning.

"He's home," Gary smiled.

"But for how long?"

CHAPTER TWO

Chas   10:48pm

is back at OzHouse, where he never expected to be.

"Really?" Jessica glanced down to the corner of her screen. She mumbled to herself: "What the heck."

Jess   10:49pm

Are you really back at OzHouse, Charlie?

Chas   10:49pm

Got here a few days ago.

The words popped up so fast, it seemed he must have been sitting there waiting for her to find him.

Jess   10:50pm

That's so funny. I've been thinking about OzHouse a lot lately. You remember that Suzy who never came back, or Buddy.

While she waited for Charlie to respond, a message from her sister popped up:

Izzy R.   10:50pm

jess, you really there mom's been in touch with me again did you know she's on facebook should I friend her

Jess   10:50pm

NO!!!!!!!!!!!!!!!!!!!!!!!

If only there were a more effective way to chat a yell.

Jess   10:50pm

you crazy?! u know her

Chas   10:50pm

Figuring stuff out. You looking to leave this world behind—again?

Jess   10:50pm

my pregnant sister's thinking of running home to my alcoholic mother—again.

Chas   10:50pm

Remember: that door's closed.

Izzy R.   10:50pm

I know

Jess   10:50pm

I have an invite

Chas 10:50pm

Your psycho sister is having another baby?

Jess   10:50pm

She's not that bad She's had a rough life.

Chas 10:50pm

Jess I've met her, remember.

Jess   10:50pm

Oh, right.

Chas 10:50pm

You gonna save the world again?

Jess   10:51pm

I think I'm just gonna run away this time and stay away

Chas 10:51pm

Unlikely. I don't think OzHouse is gonna be here much longer.

Jess   10:51pm

WHAT!!!!!!!!!!!!!!!!!!!!!!?!!!!!!!!!!!!!

Izzy R.   10:51pm

she left Nick I think she's finally going to get her life together

Jess   10:51pm

she always does this

Izzy R.   10:52pm

You always want to save the whole world but you won't even talk to your own

mother

Jess   10:52pm

No, not after last time I've done everything I can think of already Some people

can't be saved.

Chas   10:52pm

It's like the bubble burst. Just hope I'm on my feet before they pull the rug out.

Jess   10:52pm

OMG!! Like a stock bubble? Like they lost everything?

Izzy R.   10:52pm

you don't know that

Jess   10:52pm

then some people I can't save

Izzy R.   10:52pm

Not all of us can live up to your standards jess don't you think we owe her

something for raising us

Jess   10:52pm

And the witch fed Hansel and Gretel, what did they owe her?

Jess   10:52pm

I can't believe it

Chas   10:53pm

Who buys art in a down market? And DCYF hasn't hardly been sending kids here for years. That ass Brinks he's the head of it now. They think he's behind the emptiness. The mood is grim.

Jess   10:53pm

I thought kiddie lit was safe from the recession

Jess   10:53pm

why would you even think it?

Izzy R.   10:53pm

I need a place to live

Chas   10:53pm

Books are dying, kid. And I don't think Doug and Beth are doing so well.

Jess   10:53pm

You mean like their marriage? No way. They were tight.

Chas   10:53pm

He's here and she's in Spain. Used to be if she went, he went too.

Jess   10:53pm

I'm coming right over

Jess   10:53pm

I'm coming right over

CHARLIE LOOKED UP FROM THE SCREEN. Just like her, he thought. Some people never change. Maybe nobody ever does.

Gwen and Gary and Doug were long since in bed when Charlie led Jessica and Isabelle and Isabelle's spirited little girl Amanda into the Persian Room.

Charlie and Jessica were catching up: "I went to England to just get away and find focus. I mean, I sold this painting a couple years ago for like seven thousand dollars, which was a fluke because," he laughed, "the tag said seventy dollars, but the old guy couldn't make out the decimal point. Well, I thought I was on my way."

"Seven thousand? That's way cool."

"Try living for two years on seven thousand bucks. Not gonna happen. Gary lent me some money. And I went looking for, you know, the key that was going to open it all up for me. Europe. Where fairytales

13

come from. But it didn't happen—because there isn't one. This stuff just isn't important anymore."

"You don't believe that."

"Yes. Yes, I do. And even if I didn't, I've done this for so long, the vein is empty. I'm just stagnating."

Isabelle wasn't following the conversation: "They won't mind us being here?" she asked.

"Nah, they're cool." Charlie scanned the armor and weaponry he had so often wanted to play with as a boy. The room had been converted back into something very like the Persian Room of his earliest memories: golden camel statues guarding the exit, swords and armor on the walls. He reached up to tug on a sword that he knew full well was bolted fast.

"Is that one of your paintings?" Jessica was looking at a canvas on an easel in front of the wall, beneath the swords.

"I did it years ago. I needed a sword in this warrior's hand. But Gary won't let me take them off the wall. So I had to paint in here, which is crap, but it's their house."

"Gary must like it," said Jessica. "He keeps it here on the easel like you're still working on it."

"I think he just liked to pretend I was still here painting."

"Don't say that," said Jessica. "It's beautiful."

Amanda, on Isabelle's hip, looked at the picture of the medieval knight in front of a landscape like colored clouds and said, "Sold'r."

"Warrior," Jessica corrected.

"Down," said Amanda.

As soon as she was on the floor, the little girl went straight to the golden camel.

"She knows what a soldier is?" said Charlie.

"Keith's doing."

"Her father?"

"Izzy's deadbeat boyfriend—who kicked her out when she got laid off," Jessica explained.

"It's not like I don't have a place to go," Isabelle quickly added. "My mother will take me in. Do you have anything to drink?"

"You're pregnant," Jessica reminded her.

"I just meant like water or grape juice or… You're so judgmental."

"Your mother's back in New Hampshire?" Charlie tried to diffuse the situation.

"I'm just trying to help. And you are not going back there," Jessica commanded.

"You call that help? It's not like I have much choice. I can hardly stay here. I'm not exactly a kid. And as for those people you rent a room from…" And then without finishing the sentence she said, "She's our mother, for God's sake."

"Meaning what?"

"Amanda, stay away from the camel."

"Camah," Amanda stepped back and pointed.

"She can't hurt it," said Charlie. "I've met your mother. I'm kinda with Jess here, if it matters to you."

"Amanda, don't climb on the camel."

"Camah," she jumped.

"Really, she can't hurt it," said Charlie.

"Camah," said Amanda.

Isabelle looked up at Charlie, a tall, goateed, rust-headed man. He may have wanted to look cool or artsy with his earrings and choker, but to her he looked too self-consciously artistic—and a little kooky.

"I'm sure you can stay here a while if we ask. There's lots of room."

Isabelle grabbed Amanda by the hand and pulled her over to a chair and sat down. "I don't have rich friends," she said.

"He's serious, Izzy. I've told you about these people."

Amanda struggled out of her mother's grip and headed out the door. Isabelle called her back, but she didn't come.

"Aren't you going to get her?" said Jessica.

"Can she hurt herself out there?"

Charlie looked around. "Absolutely."

Isabelle leaned back in the chair and closed her eyes as though to summon, past the fog of fatigue, the magic spell that would make it possible to rise. Jessica cast a look of disgust and took a step toward the door. A crash came from the hallway; Amanda screamed. Jessica darted into the hall.

"What did you do?" The stern tone shot back into the room.

"It brokt."

"Wonder what she broke," Charlie said.

"As long as she's not hurt," Isabelle said. "I'm sure everything's replaceable."

"Not in this house."

Jessica yelled at her sister from the hall to come get her daughter so she could clean up the mess. But almost as soon as Isabelle dragged herself out of the Persian Room Jessica walked back in with Amanda in her arms.

"Where's Isabelle?" Charlie asked.

"Why should I pick up the mess?"

"That's a pretty amazing sentence coming from you."

"Speaking of that," Jessica whispered, "listen. I have this plan."

"You can't use the door," Charlie said flatly. "It's locked for good."

15

Jessica exhaled. "I knew you'd say that." She pulled a folded up letter out of her pocket. "I mailed this to Gary as soon as I got it. But he mailed it back, said I should keep it." She handed him the worn and often folded sheet of vellum. It was a letter—from Sarastiltskin. Jessica continued her explanation as Charlie read silently, "of course Gary was right. Nobody who found this would ever think it was real."

Charlie looked up, in confusion. "How did she?"

"I have no idea how it got here. But it doesn't matter. Did you read it? It says right there, 'I hope you are as happy as we all are; if not, ask the nice people who care for you children to send you here and we will adopt you too. As for me, I will accept as many as will come.' I take that as an invitation. And that trumps anything Glinda ever said. And let me tell you, Amanda would be better off there than with my mother or Keith."

"So you've rethought the whole Buddy thing?" He had vivid memories of her anger at leaving Buddy behind.

"You take the best available options. Isn't that what Buddy did?"

"There's a few obvious problems with that plan—like it sounds like kidnapping for starters."

"I'm not going to…."

"Oh? Do you think Isabelle would let her go?"

"I just have to talk her into it."

"It's a dumb idea."

"Just because you've given up on…"

"I'm not giving up. I'm moving on."

"Which is why you're back here?" she asked.

"Sometimes you need to turn a corner. Besides, even if you could make the door work, which is not certain—Gary's the only true adult we've ever known that got through—but even assuming you could, they won't okay it. The door's all boarded up. You couldn't open it with a crowbar."

The sound of footsteps came down the stairs. Someone must have heard the crash. It was a cavernous house, but the sound of a child's scream travels. In a moment they heard a voice in the hall: "I'm sorry, I don't think we've met."

Jessica popped through the doorway. "Doug? That's my sister, Izzy"

Doug looked at Jessica. "Okay," he said. "But who would *you* be?"

Aside from a head that was now completely bald on top and a loosening of the skin around his eyes, Doug had hardly changed. The same could not be said of Jessica.

"Jessica," she said. "Sorry."

"Jessica?" said Doug with an uncertain expression on his face. Charlie poked his head out the door.

"Hi, Doug. You remember Jessica."

That seemed to help a little. "Jessica. I'm sorry. Did you…? I'm sure you must have spent some time with us. We've had so many, you understand."

And then another voice, coming the other way down the hallway, "Jessica Holton?" It was Gary. And Gwen was with him. Gary rushed forward to hug her.

Doug got a broom and he and Gwen cleaned up the broken vase. Gary offered to concoct some quick hot chocolate, and ten minutes later they were all in the North Pole Reading Room, huddled around a table, Amanda asleep on Gwen's lap.

"Anyone else would have put this off until morning," said Charlie.

Gwen's reply was a sympathetic glance.

Isabelle did not interrupt Jessica's telling of her story.

"You will be taken care of," said Gary.

"I don't need to be taken care of," said Isabelle.

Gwen stood up, cradling Amanda, "In that case, someone will drive you to your mother in the morning. Unless you don't need that either."

Charlie and Jessica shot a glance at Gwen. Doug smiled; Gary chuckled into this mug.

"She can't," said Jessica.

"How old are you, Isabelle?" Gwen asked.

"Nineteen."

"She can do anything she wants," said Gwen. "If you don't want our help," she said to Isabelle, "fine. I'm tired. I'm going back to bed. Charlie can find you a place to sleep." She swayed slowly back and forth as she spoke, not waking Amanda, perhaps giving Isabelle a chance to change her mind.

"You know my mother," Jessica pleaded.

"I met her briefly a long time ago."

Perhaps Jessica should not have been amazed that to these people, who had been so important to her life, she and the experiences she'd had in her short time here, which were so thoroughly burned into her brain, were just dusty memories. Did they even know, really, who she was? Gary remembered—but Gary had gone through the wardrobe looking for her. As for Doug and Gwen—well, you couldn't expect your favorite teachers to remember you the way you remembered them, could you? But still, Jessica was amazed. And saddened.

Isabelle seemed to read her sister's mind: "They don't even know who you are."

"Of course we do," said Gary. Doug shrugged. Gwen remained silent.

Isabelle looked around the room in confusion. No one was trying to talk her into staying because there was no lasting connection between them and Jessica that she could exploit.

"When you're dealing with Gwen, it's not good to pretend you want one thing when you really want another," said Doug.

"No," said Isabelle, "I'm not." Then she turned to Gwen, "Thank you," she said, "for treating me like an adult."

Gwen crossed the room and handed Amanda back to Isabelle. "Unless your mother has greatly changed since we last met—yes, I do remember the impression your mother made quite well.... It's true, I don't remember Jessica herself very well. She was not here long. But the events that transpired when she was here would be pretty hard to forget. But as I was saying, unless your mother has changed, I cannot believe you would want her to raise another child," then she cast a glance as Isabelle's stomach, "or two."

Jessica stared, incredulous.

"You can't help people who don't want to be helped," Gwen said.

"It's just until I can get a job and move out," said Isabelle. Amanda stirred in her arms. "I'm doing the right thing."

"No, you're not," said Gwen.

"I'm doing what's right for me."

"No, you're not doing that either. Don't deceive yourself. But you're doing what you've chosen. I wish you the best. I'm going to bed." Then she turned to Charlie, "the rooms on Doug and Beth's side are all free. You can put them over there for the night."

The next morning Isabelle hugged Jessica before Gary drove her and Amanda to Manchester.

"Why didn't you drive her—you're her sister?" Charlie and Jessica were standing beside Jessica's car.

"I won't have any part of her going back there. I can't believe they would let her go."

"She's an adult."

"They didn't even try to talk her out of it. What the hell are social workers for? Gary and Doug, they just sat there."

"They've got a lot on their plate right now. I told you. I think Beth and Doug might be splitting up. I don't know what that's all about. No one tells me. Maybe it's because they hardly ever have kids here anymore. Think of it, Jess. That's their life's work. Especially Beth." Charlie pointed to the hulking structure of OzHouse, a little like a mansion, a little like a castle: the great façade above the yellow brick road, the widow's walk over the main house where they used to hold barbeques in summer, the great barn-like addition where the gym and the swimming pool were. The black flags hung limp on the turrets shaped like witches' hats above the two giant columns that stood on the corners. Jessica's room used to be at the top of the near one, just under the long ribbon of the pointed hat: *The Little White Horse* Room. She'd probably have to duck to get through the little door these days. "It's their life's work, and it's not working right now. You think they're rich, I know. And they are rich. But it takes a lot of money to run this place. And their investments have tanked, and Gary is having a hard time getting work as an illustrator and Doug's books aren't finding a publisher. Who knows, they might have to sell the place."

"Who'd buy it?"

"Things aren't as cozy as they used to be. I don't think Gwen wanted Gary to give me the money to go to England even. I thought it was pocket change."

"Yeah, but they turned down a chance to help Izzy."

"They're not a foster home for troubled adults, Jessica."

"What about Amanda? What about that baby she's going to give birth to in January?"

"She's not an orphan or a foster child."

"I think Buddy was right. We all should have just stayed where we were happy."

"In Oz?"

"In Oz."

"I wasn't happy in Oz. I've been more places than anyone. I think you've got to be crazy to want to live in a fantasy."

"You really don't want to go back?"

"No. No, I don't."

Jessica wasn't sure she believed him.

"It's for kids. It doesn't help people my age. I got all I could from it back then. I went to England to try to relive it. Or come as close to it as I could. It didn't work. I couldn't tell Gary the whole story, not right out. He doesn't want to hear it. But I just don't want to do it anymore."

"You don't want to find out what happened to Cinderella?"

Charlie cast her a look.

"You told me about Cinderella. You visited her before she married the prince, remember?"

"She married the prince, that's what happened. She was reunited with her shoe and became a princess."

This time Jessica cast the look.

"I read it in a book."

"I want to take Izzy and her kids to see Buddy and maybe Suzy."

"Just forget that. That's not what it's for, Jess."

"No. No." Jessica looked up at the house. "No," she repeated. "It has to work. It worked before."

"Even if it was a good idea, you remember how it worked. If you

19

did take your sister and Amanda through there, you'd end up back in the hall with Isabelle, and Amanda would be lost in Mother Goose Land or something, like when we lost Buddy. It'd be the same thing over again."

"No." Jessica said again. Then she crunched up her mouth, slammed the door of her car and marched back toward the house with Charlie at her heels.

"What do you think you're doing?"

"I'm going to get Buddy."

"For what? You can't."

Jessica turned around at the door. "I can't help Izzy. And you can't help her. And they won't help her. So she has to go somewhere where she can get help. I'm going to get someone to come and get her and take her through the door."

Jessica took off. Charlie ran after her.

They met no one in the hall, no one on the stairs. The house seemed eerily empty as she walked through the darkened hall on the third story at the front of the house to where the old closet stood amid old books and boxes of storage unopened for years.

"They boarded up the back," said Charlie. "See," he pushed aside the coats. The back of the closet was painted with a mural of a snowy landscape and a lamppost. Across it, painted to be part of the mural, were three horizontal boards nailed to the sides and held to the back with carriage bolts. "Boarded up tight. The bolts on this side are affixed to nuts on the other side. You can't get them off," said Charlie. "You'd need a wrench on the other side, and there's no way to get to the other side. It's ingenious. I don't know how they did it."

Jessica stared up at Charlie. "You said you didn't want to get back."

"I don't. I was just hoping to see some of the things they boarded up. No one's been in that room for ten years."

Jessica pushed past him to see for herself. She grabbed the boards, ran her finger along the smooth round surface of the bolt. "If the bolt has to be loosened on the other side, it had to be tightened on the other side, which means there's another way in."

"At one time, perhaps."

"I thought you would at least try to help." Jessica sat on the floor of the wardrobe, her feet dangling in the hallway. "She's my sister."

"You can't fix everyone's problems. Didn't you learn that when you went after Buddy the first time?"

"Does anyone ever learn anything?"

That sounded too much like Charlie's own recent pessimism. It sounded wrong somehow, coming from her. "Maybe," he said. "Besides, you know, you grew up with your mother, you turned out okay. And Amanda has Isabelle…"

"…who's turning into my mother. Rotten boyfriend, two children by two different fathers."

"She's not doomed," said Charlie. "Look at you."

"Your standard of 'okay' is pretty low."

Jessica pulled her feet into the wardrobe and stared at the back of the box. Though she was hiding her face, Charlie was sure she was trying to prevent herself from crying. Without warning, she kicked the doors between the slats.

They swung open and just as quickly slammed shut. She turned to Charlie, her face wet and smiling: "It never occurred to you to push?"

"Of course not," said Charlie. "It's bolted."

"The bolts are fake." She pushed the doors wide with her feet and slithered between the slats.

"What's the point of that?" Charlie followed, headfirst.

A moment later they found themselves in a pool of the bright colored light that hung in the air on this side of Beth's big stained glass window. They were surrounded by the old books and toys and art of the Narnia Room that must have sat unobserved for years. Surprisingly, nothing had been taken out when the room was abandoned. When they were children, the mounted head on the wall always hailed their entry. But its batteries would have died years ago. The Gump head was now as still as the rest of the space. Immediately in front of them stood the huge, open, guest book still awaiting the signatures of adventurous children. The room was as still as a painting—and smelled of orange blossom.

Before either could register the oddness of the odor in the abandoned room, something moved. Their attention was drawn to the two couches roped together in the center of the room, behind the guest book. There, sunk deep in the depression of the body of the Gump like a man taking a bath, so deep that all they could see over the back of the couch was the bald crown of his head, sat Doug. He held a book up over the edge as though to make clear he'd been there idly reading. When Charlie and Jessica looked doubtfully at him, he raised his bushy brown eyebrows and waved, goofily.

CHAPTER THREE

Dearest Budy,

Your father and I will be visiting my sister for a few days. There is plenty of dried meat in the larder and enough coin for you to pick up any provisions you may need. Please try and finish up the venison pie. I know it is not your favorite, but it's a terrible shame to waste it, and I want to be sure you have some good food in you to make up for whatever you managed to eat while you were off on your trip.

If you could manage to split some of the firewood that is behind the shed, I know your father would be ever so glad to know it was done before the first snow. I hope your visit with Jack and his cousin went well and that the plans for an apprenticeship work out.

Keep warm.

Love,

Mama

BUDISTILTSKIN WIPED HIS ROUGH, DIRTY HANDS on his pants and folded the vellum into thirds. He placed the note on the desk near his bed and went outside. It was nearing sunset, and the nights were getting cool, and he needed to pump some fresh water for tea before dark. There had never been a lock on the heavy oak door, but a heavy brass latch had to be lifted to keep the door from swinging open in the wind.

The yard was, as always, immaculate.

Budy toted the wooden pail to the pump, whistling a tune he had known as a small child though he could no longer remember the words. He primed the pump and drew enough water for his drink now and possibly tea later on. Although he was nearly a man and had proven himself capable of taking care of himself, Mamastiltskin still worried about leaving him alone for a few days. He had to smile at her concern. He'd already made it to Jack's and back without supervision. And what did he have to do now except feed himself and keep warm? It would be good to show Mama and Papa how well he could manage. He had grown tall and strong in the wilds of Grimmswood, and, assuming this thing with Jack worked out, he was ready to make his own way in the world.

Giving up his mother's cooking would be hard, and he and his dad had so many fine memories of hunting and fishing and sleeping under the stars by the open fire. But his plans didn't call for him to be so very far away that he couldn't visit. Cousin Jack had recently been advanced to master furniture maker which put him in a position to take on an apprentice. Budy had been doing errands for him for years. Now, being a master, Jack would be opening his own shop. As Budy's folks aged, he knew they would rely on him more and more for some of the heftier chores. It was true that neither Rumpel nor Sarastiltskin looked a day older than they did on the day they had adopted their son, but that was simply a trick of the forest magic. They were both hundreds of years old, and the years did take a toll on them. They all knew Budy could manage work and family both. He wasn't really going anywhere.

He had grown to love woodworking and carving. His father was not adept at this art, and they all knew he would need to be apprenticed to a master, so it was fortunate he had a cousin in the trade. But then fortune had been pretty kind to the Stiltskins all in all. Rumpel had not at first taken to the idea of his son being a tradesman, but as the boy had shown no aptitude for magic, it did seem his only sensible choice.

With a fire blazing in the stone hearth, Budistiltskin picked up a book. The Stiltskins had precious few books in their home, but Sara had encouraged Budy's fondness for reading, and she had managed to gather a few old volumes that he could read and re-read. He had read all the fairytales over and over—or anyway, all the ones his father allowed in the house. He liked the ones about Rapunzel and Red Riding Hood. He didn't really know these girls, but he had met both of them along with many others at a big county fair many years before, and he was amused to learn what had *actually* happened to them when they were young— how Rapunzel had tricked the witch into hiding her in the tower, how

Red (as she told it) with the help of her grandmother had craftily set up an encounter between the woodman and the wolf who had been threatening the girls who wandered from the path in the woods. It would seem their well-known tales had been a little edited for print. Budistiltskin had laughed when he heard the clever girls tell the events as they remembered them. Oddly enough no copy of his father's story was to be found in his house. Rumpel forbade any copy of the tale to come through his door. Nor did he allow any mention of the tale in his presence. Sara had explained this to Budy when he was no more than ten, which only made him curious to know exactly what the tale said and whether it was true and why it upset his father so much.

After a hearty dinner of Mamastiltskin's warmed up, left-over meat pie, Budy got out his carving tools and continued working on the fancy top rail and splat on a chair he'd begun with Jack. It was going to be a gift for his mother. She always seemed to favor the kinds of flowers that grew in the meadows, so he carved a bouquet of daisies and buttercups into the beech wood. It would be good to have it finished before his parents returned from their trip. He wanted to surprise Mama when they arrived.

After a good hour of sanding, he got his jar of varnish, which was nearly full (he'd brought it all the way to Jack's and back but hardly used a drop), along with some rags Mama had set aside, and he started to polish and shine up what he'd already completed to see how the intricate carving stood out against the plain back. He'd never got to the varnishing stage with Jack but he didn't see how there could be any mystery in varnish. Jack always told him to wait until all the carving was done, but, as his parents so often said, he was a little impetuous. While he was giving the work a final rubbing, not paying attention to where his feet were, he kicked over the jar. He could hear the voices of his father and Jack telling him to take his time, not to rush, as he frowned and sighed to see the liquid pour out of the container and run across the floor. Before he could grab a rag, the varnish had spread to the edge of the fireplace. There was some danger in that. He reached for the jar. But just as he picked it up, an ember of pine erupted from the fire and landed smack in the center of the puddle.

Budy gasped as the flames erupted. The whole puddle went up at once in a hot, silent explosion. The heat and smell flashed Budy back to his oldest nightmare—when he had been trapped in a burning room, when his first mother and sisters had died back in that old world, nearly forgotten now, in a place that his father told him was called Manchester, in another place called New Hampshire, names his father had learned from a girl Budy was supposed to have known but could not remember. Budistiltskin told himself not to panic. The fire was hot but small. And he had water. He dropped the empty bottle and grabbed the bucket and tossed his tea water on the fire. Even before the water hit the flames, he realized his mistake. He gasped again to see the water spread the fire across the wooden floor. His next instinct was to call for help, but of course no one lived near enough to hear.

The flames flashed and grew around him. He should have run for the door. But in a panic he closed his eyes and wished the fire had not started—although he knew wishes at best were magic and magic does not work for mortal boys.

At least it never had before.

As suddenly as the fire had erupted, it died. His eyes remained closed, but he couldn't feel the heat or hear the crackle of the flame. They were just gone, like a cast-out demon in a story. He opened his eyes. Nothing. Not a hint of flame, not even in the fireplace.

"W...what happened?" he asked no one but himself.

The fire had stopped so quickly he almost doubted it had really been there. But there were scorch marks on the floor, a fading odor of smoke in the air, and the dropped jar of varnish.

Was it magic? Had he done magic? Could he do magic? His father had spent years trying to teach him, but he had never been able to light a candle with a word or spin one strand of straw into gold. Had he done this? He spun around expecting to see one of his parents in a doorway. Surely a word of magic from his father had saved him. But he was alone.

He made another wish—a wish to get the fire burning again where it belonged, on the hearth. Nothing happened. But that was not surprising. One burst of magic, if that's what it was, wouldn't necessarily mean he'd turned some magical switch inside himself. He would still never be a magic worker like his dad. As he pondered this, he tried to reignite the half burned logs in the fireplace. But he could not manage it. That *was* a surprise. He could not raise a flame with flint and steel, not even with his father's prized sulfur matches. He couldn't even make the smallest spark. He couldn't light a candle. No fire would burn anywhere in the cottage.

CHARLIE AND JESSICA STOOD SPEECHLESS, staring at the grinning face of Doug Robbins. Charlie had managed to think up two plausible lies to explain their being in the forbidden room, but before he could open his mouth, Jessica launched into an explanation.

"I know we aren't supposed to be in here but before you say anything let me explain. You saw that my sister is about to have her second child and you know she can't possibly raise these kids, and I am in no position to help her, really. Charlie and I started talking and we were wondering if Buddy had turned out all right growing up in a fairyland, so we just wanted to see how he had done, but we really weren't going to disobey the rules, not really, and well, okay maybe a little, but not enough to upset things like we did the last time and…"

Doug's face was still smiling, but the smile was a little smaller.

"Wait, wait, wait," Charlie jumped in. "I, myself…"

"What makes you think you would find him?"

"Excuse me?" Charlie gave an almost cartoonish head shake.

"From what Gary told me, if you use that thing, you don't know where you'll end up or when, if you can even get through at all, that is. And even if you arrive where Buddy went, you could get there before he arrived or after he died. Isn't that right?"

"Believe me," said Charlie, "no one knows more about going through that door than we do—the two of us."

"Which is how we know he's right." Even in her distress, Jessica would not let Charlie misrepresent their chances. "The time thing isn't usually so bad. It seems to go out of sync mostly for new people in my experience. But you're right, there's very little you can control. But there's some. If you know where you want to go and you concentrate on a specific incident…"

"There *may* be some things you can control, sometimes," said Charlie. "At least that's the assumption we've always worked with."

"So there's an algorithm?" said Doug.

"Hmm, no. I wouldn't call it that," said Jessica.

"Maybe as a metaphor," said Charlie. "Look, we really don't know. We just don't think it's random."

"Okay. Okay. So you really think you could do it?" Doug interrupted.

Jessica had to take a deep breath and rethink. This was not what she expected him to say, and she wasn't really done trying to explain what they were doing.

"Is that all you have to say?" asked Charlie.

"What else is there to say?"

"How about, 'What were you thinking?' or 'You know the rules.'"

Doug climbed out of the Gump Couch. "You sound like Gary." He slid his hands into the pockets of his jeans and paced a little in front of Alice's Looking Glass and Aladdin's Lamp. "Why would I ask you that? Am I some kind of idiot? You're here for the same reason I'm here. You want to use the magic. I have been trying for—forever and have never managed even a spark. If I didn't trust Gary so much, I'd feel like an idiot. But you two have made it work before, so I ask again, do you think you can do it?"

Charlie's face was all scrunched up as though he was trying to solve a math problem. Jessica's smile continued to grow as she realized that

Doug wasn't going to try to stop them.

"All I heard from my brother for years was how amazing it all is. How invigorating it was to his imagination. I know he told me the dangers, but hell, what isn't dangerous? We could die in a car crash driving to White River Junction. But it just wasn't in me. I might write books for children, but apparently this sort of magic died in me like it does in everyone—which is more disappointing than I can tell you, given who I thought I was—and nothing I did could re-kindle it. So much for the author who never lost his child-like spirit."

"What about the promise we made to Glinda?" Charlie found it odd to hear himself taking Gary's side in his absence.

"Shut up, Chuck," Jessica smiled.

"*I* never made any promise to anyone."

"Sometimes, a group can do what an individual can't," said Jessica.

"And sometimes no one can do something that isn't supposed to be done," Charlie replied. "Listen, Doug, I came here to talk her out of it. It's a bad idea."

"So then maybe Jess and I can do it without you," said Doug. "Doesn't matter to me."

"No," said Jessica. "We'll need Charlie. I mean, if I understand it right, the energy or the magic or whatever it is is stronger the more you've done it. The more you've done it, the more you understand it or believe in it—or whatever you want to call it."

"You really have no idea," said Charlie.

Jessica crossed her arms. "It's a theory."

"All right," said Doug. "So if we need your help, Charlie, why do you think it's such a bad idea? Why don't you want to go?"

"Because you'll be stuck there forever even if you come back. It happened to Jess. It happened to me."

"Did not," Jess shot back.

"It did. First thing goes wrong you jump to fairyland as the solution. Things have to be solved in the real world, Jess. And as for me, I haven't moved on in ten years. And I didn't even know it until recently. I've been there. I've done it. Now I have to move on. I can't stay stuck in fairyland. My art..."

"Oh, right, you have to grow up," Doug mocked, "you can't still be an adolescent when you're thirty. You need to put childish things behind you."

Charlie did a double take. "Well, yeah, something like that."

"Gary said that's what you were thinking. You're talking to a guy that writes children's books for a living. And here's my secret: I don't write them for children. My whole job is making sure no one does too much growing up. My art will be better if I get through. Have you thought maybe you need to be renewed instead of cleansed?"

"No, not really," Charlie huffed. "I'm stuck. I don't want to be stuck."

"Or are you just afraid you've lost your imagination? If you've lost that, you won't be any use anyway, I suppose. I mean that's..."

"That's not it, Doug."

"Why would you say that?" Jessica raised her voice.

"I was going to say, I sympathize. That's a terrible thing. I've been there myself. I'm just saying, maybe if you can't do this for yourself, you could try it for me and for Jessica."

Charlie put his hands in his pockets and stared blankly at the wall. "All right," he said, "fine, I'll try."

"Thank you," said Doug.

"It's not going to work anyway."

"There's the spirit," Doug chuckled. "Now, tell me everything you did to make it happen before. Don't leave out anything. I'll make a list."

"It isn't like that," said Jessica. "You can't organize and plan it. You just have to just accept it."

"That's pretty big, coming from you," Charlie almost managed a laugh.

"Don't be an ass. Life needs to be organized. But this isn't life. It's magic. Besides, there's only one step: think. Concentrate. If you're there in your head, your body will follow."

"So we try it together. Your belief boosts mine?" Doug wondered aloud.

"If that's what we're calling it," said Jessica.

"We could try anything," Charlie said.

"I thought you were the expert," said Doug.

"Like I said, there are no experts in this field," Charlie repeated. "To quote the wizard, I don't know how it works. Not really."

"Well Jess seems to. And you've done it before. That makes you more of an expert than I am."

"We need to think of going to find Buddy. To see how his life turned out. To see if maybe my sister should send her kids there too."

"Okay, let's concentrate on the Grimms' Fairytales," said Doug.

"That probably gives us our best shot. But you might want to be a bit more specific. Think Rumpelstiltskin. You don't want to end up in 'The Devil's Grandmother.'"

"Of course. That makes sense," Doug muttered.

"And don't think of him with the miller's daughter or in the castle. Think of him at home."

"And be very careful," said Jessica. "As we all know, the fact that you go in together does not mean you'll pop out in the same place."

"Any place is okay with me," said Doug.

"No, wait—just—look," Jessica had just thought of something. "If we do happen to all make it and end up in like three places, whoever comes back, leave a note, okay?"

"Why?"

"Because I don't want to have to chase all around fairyland looking for someone who's out in the yard raking leaves."

"That's actually a good idea," said Charlie.

The three held hands and prepared to pass through the doorway together. Each kept repeating the words "Rumpelstiltskin" and "straw into gold," and "house in the woods."

They opened the door and passed through the fur coats—and fell though the other side of the closet into the hallway. The second time it was the same—only Jessica was sure she had heard some birds singing and she assured them she smelled evergreen. On the third attempt Charlie was saying the name Rumpelstiltskin putting the accent on a different syllable each time. Jessica's thoughts had flittered back to Isabelle and Amanda before she caught herself and had another thought. Doug was becoming discouraged, but he tried to join Charlie in saying the name, and as he stepped into the back of the doorway he said with as much confidence as he could muster, "We want to be in Rumpelstiltskin's tale, not 'The Devil's Grandmother.'"

In a flash of light, he fell to the ground.

CHAPTER FOUR

mom threw mittens at frank
whos frank
moms new ex
mittens?
hr cat
hr cat?
yes
mom hurled a live cat at sum1
yes she was mad
no kidin did manda see
yes
call gary get out of there
u call 4 me
i cant u call
No response.
izy?

No signal.
Unbelievable!
No, no, actually quite believable. Predictable in fact. The only question was, why had it taken so long? Isabelle must have been there, what, ten, fifteen minutes before all that played out? Jessica could just picture it. Isabelle shows up at the door, "Hi, Mom. Here's Amanda." Mom, full of love, already drunk, "You'll be paying your share of the bills, little girl. I can't afford...." Then this Frank, whoever the hell Frank is, says something which could have been anything from a direct

insult about her mother to a tasteless comment about Isabelle. So mom just picks up the nearest object, which is a cat for the love of God, and throws it at him. Must've hit him too, if he's already an "ex." Yeah, but mom's exes don't tend to stay exes for long. Izzy had to get out of there.

But Jessica had "no signal" no matter where she walked. Amazing she'd had service at all here—probably some effect of being in some kind of proximity to the wardrobe. Even then she could only text, not call, which didn't make sense, but it had been a long time since she'd expected magic to make sense. This was a fairyland. Most of them don't make any sense either past a certain point. What fairyland it was, she didn't know. Warm, breezy. Nondescript. The air seemed to be full of the sounds of birds, though there were no birds to be seen.

Now, she'd already managed to lose her way to the wardrobe while she was trying to get a signal to respond to that first text of Isabelle and then running around looking for Charlie and Doug—though she knew very well how slim were the chances all three of them ended up in the same world. That was her final thought the moment the magic started to work. It happened very fast, as it always did, but it left, as always, a detailed memory: she crossed the threshold, holding Charlie's hand to try to keep them together, then she felt a breeze; she heard a bird that she thought for some reason must be a robin (though she wasn't that good at bird songs) and she saw the bright outdoor light flash, and then she was on the ground, alone. Hardly surprising. The wardrobe had hardly ever taken even two people to the same place as far as she knew, let alone three. That's how the whole adventure started last time, Buddy going to Mother Goose Land and her not able to get there. That was how the whole thing ended too for that matter: she and Buddy trying to get home. She made it. He ended up with Rumpelstiltskin—who she was sure was not the kind of character who ought to be raising a human child. Nasty, grumpy old dwarf. But then she got the letter from his wife.

Another maze of a forest this was turning out to be. It was full of rocks. "The first rule of wardrobe travel," she said to herself out loud: "don't lose the wardrobe." She could be stuck in the woods forever. And now she *really really* had to get back. Isabelle wasn't going to call Gary. Jessica would have to do it for her, as usual. Isabelle's M.O.: put up a strong front, then hang on to it until someone offers to rescue you, then push them away.

Jessica exhaled deeply and looked around to get her bearings. It was a typical sort of place for the wardrobe to leave a person: the very middle of the woods. It was nothing like the woods she was dropped in when she ended up at the Emperor of China, however. Here again there was a mixture of very tall trees. But it was dominated by oaks with small leaves. And there were no saplings at all that she could see, as though the woods were groomed—perhaps for hunting or something. And the ground was nearly bare. Why there was so little understory was hard to tell because the sun certainly penetrated. The ground was dappled everywhere. But the most outstanding feature of the landscape was the rocks: huge rock walls five stories high with little crevices running the whole height. Mostly flat too, as though a glacier had passed through here in the last ice age and smoothed out every surface. She certainly didn't recognize the place from anything she remembered reading. She had no idea where she was—so how could she have gotten here? She *should* be somewhere in the Grimms' forest. Charlie's repeated "Rumpelstiltskin" was in her ear as she entered the wardrobe. And she heard Doug mention "The Devil's Grandmother"—so that's probably where he was, unless he was in the hallway at OzHouse, which was actually the most likely thing, come to think of it, because despite his success with kiddie lit, Doug was a pretty down to earth guy. So maybe Charlie was alone in the Grimms' world looking for Buddy—whom he'd probably find, knowing Charlie—and she was the only one uselessly lost in Nowhereland. So not only wouldn't she be any help to anyone, she'd become part of the problem and would need to be rescued.

Why was it life went so smoothly for everyone else and so rough for her?

Well, if she couldn't relocate the wardrobe by herself, she might be able to find some sort of magic worker who could help her. Just her luck, she might be in Oz and Glinda would find her and—boy, she didn't want to have to deal with that.

She heard the hoarse laugh of what might have been a raven nearby and turned her head. The old bird must be in the rock wall somewhere. Then from the other side she heard a woman's voice cry, "Janey. Be it thou? Hast thou come back to us? We have waited long in hope thou wouldst return." Jessica swiveled her head and saw a woman probably not much older than she was in a long purple dress, possibly velvet, with a green sash. She had on a long, pointed hat with a deep green satin cloth hanging down from the top of it—an outfit completely out of place in the forest. It belonged in a court. Jessica's own clothes, her jeans and T-shirt, must have been the reason for the woman's confusing her with someone else. But who was Janey? And why had this woman been waiting for her? Experience had taught Jessica not to be too quick in revealing herself to the people she met in other worlds. It was better to process the moment first—at the very least, to figure out where you were and who you were dealing with. The well-dressed woman was smiling hugely as she hurriedly approached. She was glancing all around and even seemed to be trying to look behind Jessica, as though there might be someone hidden from her view by her body.

"And where is my love? Did he not come back with thee?"

"Your love?"

"And the king. Is not the king with thee? I was sure he must have joined thee, having left soon following the two of you."

"The two of me?"

"Be thou alone then? I never did think thou wouldst return by thyself." The woman seemed to be trying to remain strong after a big disappointment. "You left together, did you not? Where is he, what hath happened? No, no, no. Thou must tell us all together."

"So where am I?" she said too quietly for the woman to hear.

"Will, John, everyone—come hither," the woman yelled loudly, "'Tis Janey. She will have news for us." And then she turned back to Jessica, "Oh, I must get thee meet raiment. The men will look on thee in these strange undergarments."

Well, if a T-shirt and jeans looked like underwear to this woman, that was a clue. But then again, not a very helpful one. The woman took off her shawl and laid it across Jessica's shoulders.

"Oh, surely we must cover that bosom before the men draw nigh. I fear I was too quick to call unto them." Then she glanced down at Jessica's jeans. "Here, stand at my back."

As the woman pushed Jessica behind her so only her head showed over her shoulder, a host of men in Lincoln green with bows in their hands and quivers on their backs poured out of the rocks like ants from a stump.

Jessica, realizing where she was, understood why her clothes might cause some embarrassment and allowed the woman to stand between her and the men.

CHARLIE AND DOUG STOOD AT THE EDGE of the woods near a great cornfield. Doug brushed himself off and scanned the area. Charlie had already run, head low, some distance down the cornfield to see what he could see. Looking back at the doorframe a few yards from the cornfield, Doug understood at last what had happened. He leapt—he leapt as high as he could, spread his arms wide, made a fist, and let out a laughing victory whoop. Charlie threw his head back in Doug's direction and trotted back, at the same time motioning for Doug to keep it down, but Doug leapt again and cried out a second time. This time, Charlie threw himself to the ground and crawled in among the cornstalks.

Doug took no notice. "Jessica," he yelled.

Charlie stuck his head out from the corn, peered left, then looked back at Doug. With large demonstrative gestures such as someone might use across a room to prevent another guest from blowing the big moment at a surprise party, he tried to get Doug to quiet down. Doug ignored the sign language. "Where exactly are we?" he called out.

Charlie rolled his eyes, put his finger in front of his mouth, and waved Doug down with his other hand. Doug rolled his eyes in mockery of Charlie.

Head low, Charlie darted up to him as quickly as he could. "From the look of that corn," Charlie panted when he was close enough to yell softly, "I'm guessing we're in 'The Devil's Grandmother.' Thank you, oh, so very much."

"Hmmm," said Doug.

Charlie pulled the older man down low enough so his head could not be seen above the corn. But Doug immediately stood up and put his hands to his mouth as if to yell for Jessica again. Charlie threw his hand over Doug's mouth and pulled him back down.

"From what I recall there should be an army here with three deserting soldiers and, oh, yeah, the devil in the form of a dragon. And if they don't already know everything there is to know about us, I don't really want to draw their attention, if you know what I mean."

Charlie yanked Doug into the concealing depths of the cornfield.

Doug looked puzzled. "What could happen?"

"Well, for one thing, we could contract our souls to the devil for seven years."

"I would never do that."

"Or we could just incur the wrath of an army that mistakes us for deserters."

Doug contracted his brows. "What?"

"This isn't one of the fun stories, Doug. This is one of the ones where they use real swords and real bullets." Charlie did nothing to conceal his exasperation.

"No way," Doug laughed. "*We* couldn't die. It's a fairytale. We're not even part of the story."

"Nice theory, but pretty well untested."

"No one's died yet," Doug informed him.

"That we know of. This isn't an amusement park, Dougie. It's the real thing. It's Grimm; people die."

Doug looked skeptical, but he bowed lower. Looking back, he could no longer see the wardrobe. "Look, if you're so worried, why don't we just head back and go someplace else. I mean, now that we know how it works."

Charlie stopped and held his hand up as though he'd heard something.

"Not as easy as you think," he whispered. "Besides, we came to find Buddy. And we made it to Grimm first try. You know the odds against that? We go back, there's no guarantee we ever make it through the wardrobe again, let alone anywhere near the Grimms' Forest. Do you want to be the one to tell Jessica we got this close and gave up?"

Charlie listened for evidence of people, but he heard nothing.

"Hey, I'm good with staying. You're the one who was thinking we were going to die or something. Still," said Doug. "I should tell you, I didn't actually come to find anyone."

"You can tell me your troubles later," said Charlie.

"I'm just, I don't know, tired of OzHouse." Doug showed no sign he'd heard Charlie. "I'm tired of my marriage, which is terrible of me, I know. But there it is. I'm tired of not having kids to take care of. I'm tired of having kids I don't know how to take care of. I'm tired of writing books no one wants to publish. What's more, Beth is tired of me, too. She's tired of America in general in fact. You should hear her go on about right-wing, global-warming-denying, religious fanatics."

"So go away. Move to England. Rekindle your romance. You have enough money, don't you?"

"Sure, money solves one problem. And it brings on a bunch of others. And then there's all the just normal problems everyone has. Plus how am I supposed to revive my writing career from England?"

"Really broken up for you, Doug. Tell me all about it—later."

"So," Doug opened his hands wide, "*this* is going to solve it for me. See, that's why I came. I'm going to get away from my troubles for a while and renew my mind at the same time. Where's Jessica, by the way?"

"She wouldn't know this story. I'm surprised *you* know it."

Doug looked hurt. He peered over his shoulder in the direction of the wardrobe then looked back at Charlie. "Professional storyteller. It's my job to know these things. On the other hand, I don't actually remember it that well."

"Then how did you get here?"

"I remember there's a dragon who is the devil, as you said, and he has a grandmother and something about corn. Sort of a Hans Christian Andersenesqueness to it, wasn't there?"

Charlie stood up slowly and peered over the corn. "Maybe it's all right. I don't see anyone."

Doug followed suit, imagining an army across the corn spying out a shock of red hair and an egg-bald pate from across the field. He eased his way back to the edge of the corn.

"Either the army and the deserters are gone or the story hasn't happened yet. Just so you know, in the story, in order to escape the wrath of the army which they've deserted, the three soldiers sign a book and have to give up their souls in seven years unless they can solve a riddle. You still want to stay?"

"That's brilliant. Love Grimm. I should put a twist like that in my next book."

"Good, fine. Get inspired. But don't sell your soul to the devil, okay? I mean, if we happen to bump into him and he asks, you say *no*."

"Or, on the other hand, maybe I could do just that. I'll bet I'd learn something."

"Doug!"

"It's a cartoon devil, Chuck. What are you worried about?"

A shadow passed over their heads.

Before Doug could look up to see what it was, Charlie bolted past him in a kind of Ray Bolger gallop, flattening the corn in his path. Doug looked up. A great big, black dragon, its underbelly gold and red, had circled back and was now gliding noiselessly toward them. It had a long worm-like neck and an even longer, pointed tail. It flew low enough to look Doug straight in the eyes as it turned. Then it lifted its eyes and pinned them on Charlie.

"Man, that would be something for Gary to draw." Doug fumbled for his phone to get a picture as the shadow of the dragon passed a second time over his head. But he didn't have it on him.

Charlie made it to the edge of the field. The flattened corn opened a vista that made it possible for Doug to see the open doorframe of the wardrobe.

Helping Jessica was all well and good, Charlie thought, but there were limits. Besides, if he jumped through the door there was probably at least a fair chance he could get it to work again, maybe even closer to the cranky dwarf. In a few swift strides, he was almost there. But the dragon was closing fast. Charlie yelled for Doug to follow.

Doug was standing within the perimeter of the corn, still as a scarecrow. Maybe he was in danger, maybe he wasn't. Still, it was a big, powerful dragon. There was no sense running toward it.

The devil glided up to Charlie, then, surprisingly, kept going, flew right past him on a line. Charlie had just about made it to the wardrobe. But just before he could dive into the open doorway, the dragon puffed a little ball of fire. It fell upon the wooden frame like a giant handful of flaming jelly. It must have been extraordinarily hot. The whole thing was consumed before Charlie could begin his leap. The fire burned out as quickly as it started. Charlie's momentum sent him right through the already dying flames. He fell, unscathed, on the grass.

"No one would believe it," said Doug.

GWEN PASSED THE FIESTA WARE around the table: "Green for Debbie, blue for Trisha, red for Jennie, and orange for Caleb—which leaves boring old yellow for me."

"Yellow happens to be my favorite color," Debbie announced.

"Oh, then you can have the yellow," Gwen reached to take her green plate away, but Debbie's hands reached out to grab it.

"No thank you, Mrs. Robbins," she said.

Gwen decided not to press it. "I didn't really mean *all* yellow is boring," she corrected herself. "Just, well, this isn't my favorite shade."

"The sun is yellow," said Debbie. Trisha and Jennie looked on with interest. Caleb just stared at his plate.

"And so is spaghetti," said Gwen. "I hope you like spaghetti. We have so much spaghetti. I hope Gary gets back soon. It's just about his favorite…"

"I like brown spaghetti," said Debbie.

"Whole wheat? I wish I'd known." Gwen held onto the wide smile and cheery note like a hired clown at a party. "We have some lovely brown meatballs."

Trisha laughed. "Meatballs are red."

"I think they're green," said Gwen. Trisha laughed all the louder. Gwen's eyes went wide. "What do you think Jennie? Are meatballs green?"

Jennie's mouth opened in a huge "O," but no sound came out.

"What do you think, Caleb? Are meatballs green?" Caleb just stared at his plate. Clearly producing any glee in this group would require ramping up the easy laughter of Trisha.

"Green meat makes people sick," said Debbie.

"What about green eggs and ham?" said Gwen. "Would you eat green eggs and ham?" Trisha. "Would you, could you on a plane?"

Trisha giggled. "Noooooo."

"What about you Jennie? Would you, could you, down the drain?" Jennie's mouth went from an O to a smile.

"What about you Caleb? Would you, could you on a crane? On a crane fifty thousand feet up in the air? With birds flying all around it and a meatball the size of a pregnant watermelon?"

Caleb looked away from his plate and over at Gwen. Gwen got up and walked over to Caleb and squatted down to his height as she plopped a great big meatball on his plate. "A great big crane, full of spaghetti and one giant-giant, green meatball?" Looking up, she noticed Gary leaning in the doorway. "You could help," she said to her amused husband. The shift of her eyes said, "I'm *this close* to getting an actual word out of Caleb."

"That's not what cranes are for, Mrs. Robbins," said Debbie

"Snot green meatball," said Caleb.

Trish was about to laugh but Debbie groaned, "ewwwwww." And that seemed to take the air out of the moment.

"Isn't this where Julie Andrews bursts into song?" asked Gary.

"Know any?" Gwen was trying to patch the moment, hoping Debbie was too hungry to jump up, hurl some devastating insult at Caleb, and storm out.

Gary burst into song:

> On top of spagheeeeeeeettiiiii,
> All covered with cheeeeeeese,
> I lost my poor meeeeeeeeatbaaaaaaall,
> When somebody sneeeeeeeezed.

He grabbed the spaghetti bowl, started to dance as he let big globs of noodles drop onto the plates. Then he came around again, never missing a word, and splashed extra sauce on everyone's spaghetti. Gwen joined in, then Trisha joined in and finally Jennie too started to sing as Gary and Gwen held hands and danced and sang gracelessly and off key around the table.

> And then my poor meeeeeeatbaaaaaall,
> Went out of the doooooooor…

With a perfectly timed choreography, Gary finally sat down at his end of the table, grabbed a purple plate, piled it with spaghetti, sloshed it with sauce, plopped a giant meatball, grabbed his fork and repeated,

And then my poor meatbaaaaaaall,

as he pressed his meatball down into the bed of spaghetti,

Was nothing but mushshshsh.

Gwen clapped, Trisha clapped, Jennie clapped, Caleb let out a one-syllable laugh, and Debbie decided not to be contrary.

"Thank you, Ginger," said Gary.

"Thank you, Fred," said Gwen.

"But you're name's Gwen," laughed Trisha.

Raising his fork to his smiling wife, Gary said, in quotes: "To move wild laughter in the throat of death? It cannot be; it is impossible: Mirth cannot move a soul in agony."

"It's not getting any easier," said Gwen.

"It's not polite to make references people don't get," said Debbie.

"One day," said Gary, "I do hope I manage to live up to your exacting standards, Deborah Thomas."

Debbie dropped her fork, pouted deeply, and stalked out of the room.

"Fuss budget," said Caleb when she was gone, and everyone laughed.

"We were so close," said Gwen. "You guys are a lot of fun, you know. We've just got to get Debbie into the game."

"Her mommy died," said Jennie. "And they can't find her daddy."

"Where's Doug?" asked Gary.

"I know," said Gwen to Jennie. "I have no idea where Doug is," she said to Gary.

Gary's cell phone vibrated in his pocket. He pulled it out. "No phones at the table," said Gwen.

"It's a text from Jess," he said. He glanced at his phone. "Two words," he said and he held the phone up as though Gwen might possibly be able to read it from across the table. "Call Izzy."

CHAPTER FIVE

Doug,

    Couldn't find you, so Gary and I are taking the kids into town while we do some shopping. Not sure where you are, or when you will be back. We should be home in time to make dinner, but if we run late we'll take the kids out for fast food and you will have to fend for yourself. There are leftover meatballs in the fridge, and some chicken wrapped in tin foil somewhere behind the OJ.

    Beth called. She was a bit put out that you weren't here. She said she told you she'd be calling today and expected you to be around for it. I'd call her back if I were you. She said to tell you, "if you are interested," you can reach her at the hotel she's staying at with her folks. Guess you have the number.

    See you later,

    Gwen

    P.S. Why do you have a cell if you never turn it on?

"DID YOU LEAVE HIM A NOTE?" Gary asked.

"Yeah, I put it on the kitchen table. He should see it there," Gwen pulled the door closed and turned the key.

"Think I should call Isabelle?" Gary knew the answer but asked anyway.

"We told her that if she needs us, she can call us."

"Maybe I'll call her."

"STAND AND DELIVER," a strong, bass voice bellowed from the band of stern-faced men in deep-green gowns fast approaching. Clearly, these men had not heard the friendly tone of the woman who'd called them—either that or they didn't have the same opinion of Janey she had.

"Boys," the woman said, "'tis *Janey*," still shielding Jessica from the hoard, "you shall frighten her."

Too late for that. Jessica raised her hands and quickly explained that she meant them no harm. The woman's shawl fell from her shoulders.

The men turned their heads in every direction. The helpful woman stepped more directly in front of Jessica.

When the men detected no sign of any others, several of the men laughed. "We did not think so slight a thing as thou art, having no weapons, might enter our wood to harm us."

"I didn't," Jessica started to lower her arms.

"How could she harm anyone, John," said the woman.

"Wast told to lower thine arms?" The gruff man who seemed to be the leader waved a sword and peered at Jessica with his piercing blue eyes.

She quickly raised her arms again—at which the men laughed again. Jessica frowned and stared back. "Are you laughing at me?" She must certainly be right about where she had landed. "Or are you just being merry men?"

More laughter. She looked through the trees and watched more of the company scurrying about in their green tunics and deerskin boots. She was sure now she knew where she was, but how could she have gotten here of all places?

"Do you enjoy frightening young women?" She surprised herself at the level of anger in her voice. She stepped out from behind the woman. Immediately she felt the eyes of every one of the men upon her. Their smiles were no longer merry. Jessica picked up the borrowed shawl and stepped back.

"Where be our lord?" asked one. "What mischief hast thou done him?"

Before Jessica could speak another said, "Art thou in truth a woman?"

41

"Will Scarlet, such a question," said the woman shielding Jessica.

"Dressed thus? We cannot be sure. May hap thou art a eunuch or a frail boy." And then he looked directly at the woman who had first called them out. "Art thou sure this be Janey, Marian?"

"Thou hast quite lost thine eyes, Will Scarlet, if thou thinkst this could be a eunuch," said the woman Jessica now understood was Maid Marian. "Thou hast indeed seen too clearly otherwise."

Jessica tried to think of a good reason for her to be dressed in an odd "tunic" and pants. It seemed not even the men of this era had ever heard of pants. "I couldn't very well wander in thine woods in a dress now couldest I? I neededst to find you in all haste, and thoughtest it easier to travel thus berobéd-ly."

The men laughed again, and Jessica felt her face get hot with anger.

"Thou art dressed as little Janey. And thou speakest with such sureness for a woman—and yet with such foolishness of tongue," said the deep-voiced man who had first addressed her.

Jessica would have asked who this Janey might be, but she was wary of seeming ignorant.

"Be-eth Robin here?" she asked suddenly.

"Doth Janey ask after Sir Robin of Locksley?" From the tone of his voice, Jessica could tell he thought she'd asked an odd question. But why?

"What doth thou mean?" Marian addressed the question to Jessica.

But how could Maid Marian be confused by such an obvious question?

"Why doth thou ask," Marian continued. "Thou doth know, surely."

Jessica couldn't tell if she was making a statement or asking a question. In fact it sounded most like an accusation, which only served to confuse her the more.

"Yes, yes, of course I do. I…I…do truly know him, and he would be very unhappy to see you harassing his old friend in such a manner," Jessica stammered.

"Be this Janey? Perhaps it be some new witch from the Merica? Wouldst Janey not know the whereabouts of Sir Robin?" And then he turned to Jessica, "Didst thou not steal Robin from us?"

"Janey did *save* Robin," said Marian. "I do tell thee again, Will Scarlet, Janey did *save* Robin from certain death at the hand of the sheriff."

"Then be it not high time she did bring him back to us?"

A grumble went through the crowd.

The men all started laughing again, though the laughter was now more obviously nervous, as though some of the Merry Men were afraid of her, as though she really was a witch. The red-bearded fellow who had approached her first stood before her and frowned. "'Tis true, Janey was a friend of Robin. And yet," he peered over Marian's shoulder as though to see Jessica from head to foot. Marian raised her shoulders and threw them back, "art thou truly Janey, fully grown?"

"What's up with you people? You're treating me like I'm the bad guy here. I haven't done anything, I just want to see Robin," Jessica pouted. "It is very rude, and not at all the way a gentleman should conduct himself with a lady."

The laughing continued until the red-bearded man said, "Be it not rudeness to speak falsehoods? And what hath we done to tell thee we be gentlemen—though I do not say there may not be some few with titles among us? Nor do I believe thou art any more lady than we be gentlemen."

Did he just call her a liar and claim she wasn't a lady? Okay, maybe she *was* stretching the truth. But she *had* met Robin, very briefly, in the market at Nottingham where she'd boldly wandered on one of her first trips through the door, but this man couldn't know that, and how dare he imply she was a slut or God knows what they called women who were not ladies in this time. She wasn't even sure what year it was. Robin Hood? He was from a long time ago. Before Shakespeare even. When she realized how long she was taking to reply, she blushed and quickly said, "I'm not a liar. And I *am* a lady."

"Of what peerage?" said a voice in the group.

"Thou hath not given answer," declared another.

"Who art thou in sooth?" said a third.

Jessica blushed.

"See, Marian. This surely be not Janey from the Merica."

"Well, I am a lady, anyway," she quickly said.

More laughter.

"And who then is thy lord?" one of the men shouted.

"She hath somewhat the spirit of Janey," said another.

"But her speech be not of the kingdom. She hath surely learned her English from some county were it be but poorly spoke, as it is, if I recall, in the Merica," said the man with the deep voice and the red beard.

"It hath been a half score years no less. Janey would be grown now, much like this one."

"She doth dress the part, but her hair be too dark, and her face the wrong shape. And why would Janey come to us to seek Robin? I did see the child then, having been one whom she did lead into the castle. Who can these people be? Women who dress themselves in such shameless garments and yet show so little shame?"

"If I knew what you were talking about I would try to explain," Jessica said. "You're right. I'm not Janey. My name is Jessica Holton, and I'm not from your, uh, your country. I do not know this Janey you are talking about, but if she was dressed like me…" At this point she felt no need to pretend to understand their ways, though she doubted they'd believe where she had come from or how.

The blue-eyed man interrupted her, "Years ago a small child, she did call herself Janey, did show herself in this wood. Indeed she wore clothes like thine, and she did speak no better than thou doth. By her word, she did come from a place Ahs-house behight, in the Merica, through a magic doorway. Stuff and nonsense it did seem to us. But we could not reckon her clothing nor her speech. Now thou showeth thyself, in such dress, and must we believe from thy lewd clothing and poor speaking that thou cometh from this Ahs-house in the Merica." The man looked skeptically at Jessica.

Jessica fixed herself more squarely behind Maid Marian. But she did not hesitate to speak: "Oz-House," she corrected, "in Ah-merica. And, well, yes, I did. This is how we dress. T-shirt, jeans, running shoes." They looked at her feet as she tipped her toes forward. "And if Janey dressed like me, she must have come through the magic doorway too."

"Janey led us into the castle; she did know things no normal child would. In the end, she did prove herself witch or some cursed soul for she did vanish together with Robin, and we have seen naught of him nor of her in all this time."

"Have I not always said that Janey used her powers to help Robin escape the gallows?" said Marian. "That she did send him off with her to the Merica and that she must bring him back to us? The men once did believe this as well. Janey did seem so much like one whom one might trust. But when she did not come and she did not come, they did begin to call Janey witch, one who in the service of false-king John did come to steal Robin."

"And then she did come back and steal Richard as well."

"She came back?" said Jessica.

"Not that we did see. But Richard did come home from the Holy Crusade. But he too was caught by John and they did say he did vanish the same as Robin and Janey."

"Which means there's another door," Jessica said quietly. But some of the men seemed only to hear the word "which."

"Witch," yelled one man. "And have we then another among us." The glance the man cast in her direction would have torn her to pieces if a glance could tear.

"She wasn't a witch." Jessica exploded. "And neither am I."

"Sorry to hear thee say it," said Friar Tuck.

"Excuse me?" said Jessica.

"What doth thou mean?" Maid Marion asked.

"A witch might stand a better chance of defeating John and finding Robin or Richard," said the Friar.

"But the powers of darkness," said Marion.

Little John laughed. "Well I suppose being thieves already, we stand not far from the powers of darkness e'en now."

"Nor can we hold on against John many days without Robin or King Richard. The sheriff and his men grow more cunning each day."

CHARLIE KEPT HIS HEAD DOWN as the shadow passed once again over the corn. Even so, the wind from the dragon's great wings, blowing the stalks aside, briefly exposed his entire head before the corn snapped back. But had the dragon noticed?

Doug crawled over the sharp stalks which stabbed at his legs and hands and called too loudly to Charlie, "Do you suppose there's another door?"

"There is no door," Charlie whispered. "They were all carefully destroyed the last time we left."

"Okay. So what are our options?" Doug remained a good deal less concerned than he should have been.

"None," said Charlie. "We're stuck. The way in is the way out. But right now I think that's the least of our problems." He pointed to the sky.

"Oh, no," said Doug, "can't be as bad as all that. These things always work themselves out. Suppose we find our way into another Grimms' tale. Perhaps we can find your Rumpelstiltskin. He got a letter to Jessica. He may know a way to get us home. What we need is a plan."

Charlie put his finger to his lips and pointed his eyes at the dragon.

"I know," Doug said, "I know. Sounds pretty iffy. Of course, I'm not one of you seasoned travelers. If we can't find Jessica, and that dragon..."

"It's the devil," Charlie whispered.

"I don't believe in the devil."

"In this world you better start believing because that's who it is. And he better not find us or we really won't have to worry about getting home," Charlie sighed. "And maybe when you get the chance, you can tell me how I let you talk me into this."

"You wanted to come. You love this. You can't live without it."

"That some kind of Jedi mind trick?"

Doug cautiously raised himself up and took a peek over the stalks. "I think I hear soldiers. But no sign of Jessica. And that dragon seems to have gone."

"We should be so lucky to get rid of the devil so easily. And Jessica is probably in another story, good for her." Charlie rubbed his face and pulled corn silk from his hair.

"You don't think the dragon's gone? I don't see it anywhere."

"Maybe it is, maybe it isn't. It's the devil, not an easy creature to dodge. But if we can't see him, maybe he can't see us. I think the best plan would be to just run for those trees over there. We'll get more decent cover." He tried to recall the tale. Would the soldiers have guns? "Just follow my lead," Charlie whispered. "First we'll make our way to the edge of the field. If no one's looking, we'll make a run for the woods."

Doug raised himself high enough to judge the space. It was maybe forty yards of corn and then a wide open space between the edge of the cornfield and the trees. It had been a long time since he'd run that far.

"Once we start running, just don't stop for anything," Charlie continued. "The dragon may see us if he's still looking, and then we are toast, but we might be lucky and make it to the woods before he or the soldiers notice. Keep your head low and follow me."

Charlie stood up but kept bent over to be sure his hair didn't stick up over the top of the corn. No sign of the devil to the north or east. Oh, but there he was, shadowed against the sun in the west. "The devil is definitely *not* gone, but he's far away." An ink spot against the sky beyond the back of the long cornfield. Hurrying, they stumbled and tripped on the stalks as they made their way to edge of the field. Before they got there, faster than Charlie could have imagined, the devil was back. His shadow passed overhead. They froze. But the creature made no sign it had seen them. It flew on by and breathed no fire. Perhaps it was too intent on the soldiers to bother with them. Stooping, they hurried on to the edge of the cornfield. Charlie imagined the waving line of corn seen from above. That would be a dead giveaway if the devil was looking for them. But the dragon seemed to have disappeared again. Could they really outmaneuver the devil so easily? Perhaps the devil in a children's story might not be that clever. Weren't people always fooling the devil in old folk tales?

They heard the shout of what might have been a soldier not far away. Charlie's heart was already beating hard and he hadn't started to run. He didn't know how he could make it all the way across the open grass and into the trees. But if the devil wanted them and knew they were here, it was all over, so run he would—with Doug scurrying along beside.

And then the odor of smoke crept up on them. In a moment all around them a thin black fog began to gather. Turning, they saw the dragon was igniting rows of corn as though he were erasing lines of text.

"So he is after us," said Charlie.

"But he must not have seen us. He's trying to smoke us out," said Doug.

"He's trying to burn us out," said Charlie.

"Clever," said Doug. "I'd like to see him up close."

They were at the edge if the field. The corn was no longer tall enough to hide in. The woods seemed far away. And there was no cover between here and there.

"Do you believe in prayer?" asked Charlie.

"I guess if I'm hiding from the devil it would seem logical to pray."

"So start praying because we've got to run, and we could be caught as soon as we step onto that grass." He could see Doug smiling.

"Cut that out."

His smile only grew. "Let's see if we can outrun the devil." Doug took a step forward. But Charlie grabbed his arm. The wind or the dragon's flapping wings now sent clouds of black smoke billowing over their heads.

"Hang on." Charlie waited for the smoke to thicken. "Now," he said. Charlie dashed off towards the trees. Doug jumped up and ran alongside waving his arms with a sound like glee.

They reached the edge of the trees without slowing down, and they did not stop there. Coughing from the wind-blown smoke, they pressed on. They did not feel safe. Although there still was no sign that the devil nor had any soldiers spotted the two men sprinting between the tree trunks, they ran deeper into the woods. They finally got ahead of the smoke where the forest floor sloped downward into a ravine into which they jogged, stumbled, and slipped. They did not stop until they collapsed at the bottom.

"At your age I would have been able to do that and hardly break a sweat," Doug smirked, heaving on his back.

"I'm an artist not a gymnast," Charlie on all fours huffed.

"At least we're safe," Doug gasped. "Hell of a dragon, though."

Charlie didn't try to respond. He waited for a calm breath and let his temper grow. As soon he could get the words out, he exploded: "*We are not safe*, Doug." A bird fluttered from the branch of a tree. "Not even close. Without that portal we are stuck here. Not for a day or a week, but possibly forever."

"Unless we find a way into another Grimms' tale and locate Rumpelstiltskin." Doug refused to get pulled into Charlie's drama.

"Who may for all I know not be able to help us anyway, or, even if he can, will be unwilling since we can't pay him."

"Or unless we find Jessica. Would she not have another door?"

"You can't assume she's here. You can't assume she's anywhere. And even if she is, do you know how big this place is? We are not safe."

Doug rubbed his bald head and sighed, "You are such a drag, man. I know we got problems. But we made it into a fairytale, a lame fairytale, but we did it. How many people in the whole world can say that? We'll find a way out. I know we will. People always do."

"In fairytales, Doug. In fairytales. But we are from the real world. All bets are off. Those rules don't apply."

"But *maybe* they do, so let's assume they do, and have a look around. I used to love reading *Children and Household Tales*." Doug stood up and brushed dirt and pine needles from his pants. "Enjoy it, Chuck. Have an adventure, man. What the hell are you so uptight about, anyway?"

Charlie inhaled as deeply as he could. "That's the devil," he said, "the actual devil."

"You beat him. He's not here. He's way back in the corn. What else you got?"

"I don't want to be here. I do not want to be lost in the Forest of Grimm. England cured me of fairytales. I did the myths I did the folk tales, now on to bigger, better, you know...."

"No, actually, I don't know. And you don't know either. So let's just accept that we're here and explore. I'll be fun."

CHAPTER SIX

**kthx gary im good can handl
mom jus fine If u c jess
tell'r 2 facebk me
she dropt off face o erth**

GARY SHOWED GWEN ISABELLE'S REPLY to his voice mail as he lowered a bag of onions into the shopping cart. Gwen's impassive expression did not change. He knew what that meant: the poor girl was doing everything wrong, just as Gwen knew she would. "It's her choice. We have to let her make it," is what she would have said if she'd used words.

"I know," Gary replied.

It had been a long time since he and Gwen had strolled the aisles of a supermarket together, let alone done so with four kids in tow. Jennie was in the cart. Caleb, Debbie and Trisha were walking alongside. Gary felt a stab of nostalgia. It was a thing they used to do for lots of reasons back when OzHouse was routinely full. Sometimes there were kids that just needed time out of the house. Sometimes some of the adults needed to remove certain children for an hour or two so the others could work with the rest. Today the reason was nothing as big as that. It was Doug's turn to do the shopping. But they couldn't find Doug. Gary said he'd do it. He said it in front of Gwen and all the kids, and all the kids said they wanted to go shopping. "Well, why not? Absolutely. Let's do it," Gary said before Gwen could speak. And that meant Gwen either had to go as well or that she had to disappoint the kids because if she let Gary go alone with four kids, he might lose one of them.

But Gwen had things to do at home, so she was in a bad mood from the start, which meant she was calm and in control. It also meant she would maintain a very narrow range of conversation for the next several hours. Gary was used to that. To him, it still felt like old times.

"One less problem for us, then," said Gwen. "Do we need that many onions?"

Gary frowned and put the bag back. "Habit," he said.

"Some of us like onions," said Debbie.

Gary glanced back at his iPhone before deleting Isabelle's message. "You understand she's lying."

"It's not our problem. Do we need brie?"

"No one *needs* brie. I think we should help her."

"People should try new things," said Debbie.

"She's one tough girl," said Gwen. "She thinks she can handle herself."

"You mean stubborn," said Gary.

"I mean heading into a storm," said Gwen.

"I've never had brie," Debbie said.

"We did get apples?" asked Gwen.

"If she wants brie…" Gary started, but Gwen cut him off.

"Do you know what brie is, Debbie?" She was trying not to sound too skeptical.

"Never mind," said Debbie.

Gwen told the children to keep their hands off the food—which led Caleb to grab a bag of shaved almonds and scrunch his face at Gwen.

"Do you think we should help her because you're so fond of her or because you can't wait to see what the years have done to her lovely mother?" Gwen deftly withdrew the bag of nuts from Caleb and held so tightly the hand she took it from that he could not struggle free. Caleb's meekness had disappeared the moment he found his tongue.

"Because she needs help. That's what we do," said Gary, "we help troubled children."

"You're just bored. Paint a picture, build something, weed the garden. Are we out of peanut butter?"

"Don't you have a list?"

"I hate lists. You know that. I've never used a list. Your turn," with her eyes Gwen pointed to Caleb, who was still struggling. Gary picked Caleb off the floor and stood him up on the seat of the grocery cart so he could look him in the eye.

"I'll hit you," said Caleb.

"You'll hit me? Hitting people, that's what a baby does. I thought you were a big boy."

"You shouldn't let a small child say things like that," said Debbie.

"No hitting," said Jennie.

"I *am* a big boy," Caleb swung his hand at Gary's head. Gary caught it in flight and held it. Caleb swung with the other; Gary grabbed that hand as well and pinned both hands to the boy's hips.

"I'll kick you," said Caleb.

"No kicking," said Jennie.

"If you let him get away with that, he's just going to keep doing it," said Debbie.

"I thought you were a big boy," Gary repeated. "Only babies hit people and kick people. You're not a baby. You're way too big to be a baby. You're as big as mountain."

Caleb stopped struggling to process the remark. Gary turned to Gwen. "I never knew you didn't use lists." Suddenly Gary understood years of innovation in OzHouse cuisine. He felt he'd gained a new insight into his wife. She made it up as she went along, cooking, art, life. Was that why he'd always found her so interesting—and at times a little frustrating?

Caleb kicked the cart handle.

"I'll tell you what, Caleb, if you give up on the hitting and the kicking, I'll let you ride in the cart with the Juice Buddy Brand 100% Real Juice Boxes." He assumed Caleb had seen the commercial.

"If you reward him for bad behavior," said Debbie. But Gwen cut her off.

"Debbie, how would you like a Juice Buddy Brand 100% Real Juice Box?"

"You're patronizing me, Mrs. Robbins."

Gwen rolled her eyes and looked to Gary: "You've never known I don't use lists? We've had this conversation before."

"We have not," said Gary.

"A thousand times," Gwen shook her head in amusement or disgust. "Haddock or salmon?"

Gary didn't answer. Jennie held her arms out to Gwen, who picked her up and looked over the girl's shoulder to Gary.

"Haddock or salmon, Debbie?"

"Seafood is full of mercury, Mrs. Robbins."

"And Isabelle is not a child," Gwen reminded her husband. "We don't have to rescue her."

"But Amanda is. Why are you so unhelpful today?"

Gwen shook a bag of baby carrots in her fist. "I just don't think we should rescue the world to relieve ourselves of boredom."

Gary took the bag of carrots and placed it gently in the cart. "Why not? I mean, who cares? It's still a good thing to do."

"And anyway," Gwen went on, "is that even what we do? Rescue

51

people? Don't we just give them a place to crash on the way to their desperate lives?"

"We don't track them."

"Because we don't want to face the fact that we're not actually helping anyone?"

"This is really about Doug and Beth, isn't it?"

"It's about life," she said.

Gary was starting to wish she'd stayed home. Gwen's calm had devolved into the kind of bad mood she rarely allowed herself, and it cast him in a role he did not like; he was supposed to raise her spirits and tell her everything would turn around. But he wasn't all that gung-ho on the future right now himself, and he'd never been especially comfortable playing the role of life's cheerleader, not even when life deserved it, at least not with adults. And right now Gwen's mood solicited platitudes he knew she didn't really want. So why did she do this to him anyway? She had her own much more effective ways of getting over her emotional funks—she'd paint or make pottery or walk her labyrinth or redesign the garden.

Gary tried to change the subject. The conversation limited itself to groceries before it died out altogether. They drove back to OzHouse in silence and lugged the food to the kitchen.

A MAN COULD NOT JUST LEAVE SHERWOOD FOREST these days, Will Scarlet explained. One could not but carefully leave the safety of the part of the forest where the Merry Men had their elaborate and well-guarded encampment. False King John's spies and scouts were everywhere. His grip on the kingdom grew stronger every year Richard was away.

It was very bad, Little John added. In a move made easier by the absence of King Richard and Robin, the false king was colluding with mother church on a strategy that would secure his power permanently. They knew so from their loyal friends who remained in the castle. They had their own spies, of course.

"And for this plan of his to come to pass, he must needs capture the lot of us." Will pulled his hand through his wooly, red beard. "For he doth know no such plan may go forth but with public rite. And this we vow shall not come to pass while there be but one arrow in one quiver amongst us."

"Thus he must catch or kill or scatter us," said Alan-a-Dale without looking up from his lute.

"Aye to that," said Little John, "and those he doth catch he must cast to rot in the dungeon or stretch upon the rack like strips of kidskin."

"What, and lengthen you further, Little John?" said Marion. "The false king may be a skunk for wit, but even a skunk dare not make more of you."

Several of the Merry Men chuckled at the joke. But Will Scarlet didn't even break a smile. He went on in a mood so serious it was almost sad. And yet, he said, the Merry Men were by no means sure they would find out about this ceremony in time to stop it. Indeed, it was the false king's fear of their resources more than the truth of them that kept England safe from this scheme—for now. It had always been Robin, he said, who had managed to sneak in among the enemy and spy out the surest intelligence of the false king's plans. Their efforts without him had already more than once exposed them to the king, from which nothing but Mistress Fortune had rescued them. Only Robin was Robin.

"Aye," said Little John, "we do all know Lady Fortune to be a strumpet. Ours today, the false king's tomorrow."

"'Tis let out that the false king plans to swear Richard lost in the Crusades," declared Friar Tuck, "and to have himself crowned King Eternal."

"But there must be someone that saw him come back," said Jessica. "You said he disappeared in the castle."

"None of our men, or, at any rate, none that will say it. None that will dare John's hand without Richard or Robin to lead."

"Yeah, but, when Richard doth comes home again, he can just...."

"Will not matter," said Will Scarlet.

"Aye," said Friar Tuck. "As King Eternal, John will have all earthly power in the sight of God."

They explained that this plan had been proposed by the false king and agreed by all the knights at court out of fear of John and worse fear that Richard was indeed gone for good; even some who had come back from the Holy Crusades had agreed to it. Should the false king's plan succeed, not even Richard could contest it. "A kingdom cannot forever await a king's return," said Marian. "'Tis nowise practical."

"And if he doth win all of Richard's knights to his cause through bribe or fear, what hope hath we then?" said Alan-a-Dale. He was staring at the neck and adjusting the strings of his instrument as though he were getting ready to play it.

They all sat around a low, round table in a back room of a very large, tallow-lit cave that had been cut into the side of a cliff. Friar Tuck was gripping a book tightly to his robe. Jessica assumed it was a Bible. Alan-a-Dale kept adjusting and fingering the strings of his lute as though he were thinking about the structure of chords. But he had yet to play a single note. The table at which they sat came only to Jessica's knees. It was very awkward for eating on, but that was how it was designed. Sitting on a short stool, she had to keep both knees together and sit sideways and reach across herself to her plate of wild carrots, boiled egg, and roasted venison and her mug of very weak beer. She was dressed now in one of Maid Marian's long green tunics. It was much like the men's but floor length and closer fitting, though still loose enough so no one could tell that she had kept her jeans and T-shirt on underneath. At Maid Marian's insistence she also wore a long, funny, pointed hat. A lady did not present her bare head to men, she was told. The green hat was cone shaped. If it had been black it would have been a witch's hat, yellow, a dunce cap. It had no brim.

Friar Tuck opened the book he was holding and laid it beside her dish on the table. Jessica glanced from the book to the Friar without reading anything.

"False King John hath long since decried our hiding place," Will Scarlet went on, "but not even with his best rangers hath he thus far been able to shake us from it. Once before did he venture to lead an army of Normans to scare us out. But being forewarned we did scatter before e'en one ghastly Norman did fall upon the place."

In the absence of Robin Hood, red-bearded Will Scarlet had apparently taken over as leader of the Merry Men.

"But wander out there," said Little John with a laugh, "and thou wilt like as not be scooped like a corpse in a death wagon. Aye, and may *be* one as well." He emitted a wry laugh and took a long pull on his mug.

"Should any of John's spies be in choler," Marian finished the thought. "No friend dare say aloud two words about any hap that may befall any of Robin's men."

"Then I'll just have to go back the way I came," said Jessica. She'd given up trying to talk like them. "You have to help me find the door. My sister needs me."

An unhappy laugh went around the table. Jessica had the sudden impression that she'd missed the point of the conversation.

"Thou canst not just fall in amongst the band and seek our help, giving us nothing for it," said Friar Tuck.

"I thought that's what you guys did," said Jessica without thinking. "You help people. Rob from the rich, give to the poor."

From the looks of the men, Jessica expected another laugh.

Friar Tuck tapped his index finger hard on the open book, drawing Jessica's attention at last to the pages. It wasn't a Bible.

"So thou hast read the text."

It turned out that they'd read that motto about robbing the rich in the book and had laughed themselves out on the joke long ago.

"Be thou the rich or the poor?" asked Alan-a-Dale.

Jessica turned the pages. It was *Robin Hood.* She flipped through it, pausing at the color illustrations. The book was from the twentieth century.

Looking up from the page, she stared at the portly monk with the funny spot on his head. "Janey?" she said.

"Aye," said the Friar.

She had always pictured Friar Tuck the way he was often drawn, as a sort of Santa Claus-like fellow. But this stern fellow, though portly, showed no sign of being a jolly old elf. He was young and hard, his face browned with the sun. And he had small, distant-looking eyes. He stared hard at the young woman. It felt like a threat. "False King John taketh from the poor and giveth to the rich. We take what spoils we can from the false king."

While the others went on as though Friar Tuck had not placed the volume on the table, Jessica was trying to figure out why Friar Tuck had shown it to her.

What they did, Little John said, was just this: "we taketh from the oppressors and thieves—that they do have the courts on their side doth not make them any the less thieves—"

"—and we buy the loyalty of the peasants by returning to them a tithe of their former wealth," Will Scarlet finished the sentence.

"A tithe?" She wasn't sure what a tithe was, but it didn't sound like much. "What do you do with the rest?" She decided not to ask about the book.

"That would be our—our alms," said Alan-a-Dale fingering a silent chord and glancing at the friar.

Jessica frowned. This seemed complicated and political, just like the stuff in the real world she'd always preferred to avoid. "But you're not real life," she said out loud. These book people should be able to maintain the benign innocence of a children's story.

Everyone laughed again the same dry, mirthless laugh.

"You mustn't think we care naught for the poor," said Marian. "If we also do seek their aid by maintaining their subsistence, that doth not make us the less willing to help them in their plight. We do help them more by fighting to free them of the yoke of the false king than by risking our lives merely to steal them back their gold."

"I see," Jessica said even though she didn't.

"Whatever door thou hast lost in these woods, thou hadst good fortune to come from there to here unseen," added Will Scarlet. "And as thou doth not know just where this door be, I must say, Fortune alone will not do thee the good office to lead thee back to where it is again."

"Thou canst be sure that one of us will find it in due course, and we do assure thee we shall take thee safely to it when we do, only..."

"Only I have to help you first," Jessica finished the sentence.

"Thou art quick as a Merry Man," said Little John.

"They *are* good men," Marian replied to the look of doubt on

Jessica's face. "But they cannot do deeds for strangers without something in fee."

A whole caveful of Rumpelstiltskins, she thought, but she knew better than to say it.

"Surely not, when there be work the stranger may do for us," Will Scarlet smiled.

These were definitely not the men she remembered from the books. Jessica folded her arms in front of her chest.

"We sue no man for his blessing. 'Tis but honest, fair, and wise. And indeed, the times be fraught with harms," said Little John. "We do as we must. Thy sister is in no danger just now, or so thou hath said."

"'That I know of' is what I said," Jessica shot back. "You don't know my mother's choice of boyfriends..."

"'Tis one sister to thee or all Britain for us," Will Scarlet was unphased. "If thou seeketh our help, thou must first bring Janey's task to its close."

"And how am I supposed to do that? Bring back the broomstick of the Wicked Witch of the West?"

Will Scarlet and Little John looked at each other in confusion.

"No, no," said Will Scarlet. "Thou must needs find Robin."

"As we hath told thee, Robin himself didst bring Janey to us that time," said Marian.

"Having found her," Little John continued, "on the castle grounds on a day when he was looking for notice he had word of—of an archery trial."

"One in which he wouldst surely have bested all comers had he joined," said Will Scarlet.

"—as did happen again in this book," added Friar Tuck with heat in his voice.

"He did tell us of a girl he had spied one time before who did seem lost in the market, whom he did rescue from the sheriff's men."

Jessica jumped and banged her knee on the table: "*That* was me," she exclaimed. "That was not Janey. I told you I'd met him."

Everyone looked at her in surprise.

"Thou hast been here before?"

"It was very short. In and out. I remember the door left me off in some trees outside the castle. I saw the people selling stuff. And I was just walking around, and everyone was just sort of moving away from me like a crazy person."

"Dressed as thou wert when thou didst show thyself just now?"

"Yeah, I know now. It was one of my first trips through the wardrobe. I had no idea what I was doing. I think I yelled something like, 'What's everyone staring at?' and then I saw a guy that I guess must have been the sheriff point at me and these two men started coming toward me. Scared the crap out of me. Then there was an arrow, then another arrow, and then this other guy grabbed me. And he said, "'Don't be afraid. I'm going to rescue you.' And so it turns out that was Robin Hood."

"Robin would not speak thus," said Will Scarlet.

"Okay, so like 'be-est not fearfully, I willest rescuest thee,' whatever. He grabbed me and next thing I know I'm back outside the walls, and he's trying to talk to me but I'm running like crazy for the door."

"How didst thou know it were Robin?"

"Like I said, I'm not sure I did. Or maybe he said his name at some point. I think he said something about paying him back, too, now that I think about it." Jessica looked around the room at all the eager faces. "On the other hand, I probably just made that part up. We were talking about Janey, right? She must have come later."

A wave of awkward laughter spread around the table like a candle passed from man to man. "And so," Will Scarlet continued, "Robin, thinking it had been Janey he did see before, did bring the child and her book, this book, here to us, where she did stay a day or part of a day making us merry with strange tales of Ahs-house and the Merica. And so, going again to Nottingham, Robin wast caught and cast into the dungeon."

"Which doth not happen in the book," Friar Tuck exclaimed.

"Janey didst say she could help us to slip unmarked into the castle. She wast but small, and she wast strong in her craft."

"And that is the last we did see or did hear—nor of Robin nor of Janey," said Marian.

"And now thou must end the task Janey did begin. Draw Robin back unto us."

"Is that all? All I have to do is what the whole troop of Merry Men hasn't been able to do in ten years?" Jessica scanned the room beyond the table. There were easily thirty scruffy men between herself and the cave mouth, all of them at least half listening. And no one was laughing.

"Aye, and King Richard as well," added Little John.

"But didn't you just say it won't matter if they come back, if this John fellow makes himself king eternal?"

"Therefore thou must proceed apace," said Little John.

"And Robin mayhap may do what the true king by himself cannot," said Will Scarlet.

Jessica wondered what that could be, but before she could ask, Friar Tuck said, "Thou needs must make the things of this tale to be." He struck the page of the open volume hard with his open hand. "Only one from Ahz-house may do this."

So that was why he'd shown her the book. And it seemed he expected her to know that without telling her. She picked up the book; it was Paul Creswick's version, illustrated by N.C. Wyeth. She had started it herself in OzHouse many years ago but found the archaic language frustrating and didn't get far. Janey had apparently had it in her hand when she went through the wardrobe and had left it behind when she went back.

She did not find out until later that Friar Tuck had taken the volume and studied it like scripture, deciphering what he called, with some concern, "Norman-English." He'd given updates on his progress as he went through the volume and then weekly teachings once he'd finally deciphered the whole. Everyone in the room knew the story intimately.

"Thou must fulfill the prophecy," the friar whispered.

"But this is only one version of the story," Jessica told them. "You can't be sure that this is what was supposed to happen. There's hundreds, and that's just the fictional ones."

A groan traveled like another flame around the table.

"Richard isn't always the good guy."

"What doth thou speak?" asked the friar.

"This is one of the oldest stories in English. There's old folk tales and ballads and there's even movies. Errol Flynn and Kevin Costner and Mel Brooks, and even Russell Crowe. Even Disney. In that one you're a badger," she told the friar. "They're all different."

"But we favor this," said Little John.

"Yet not the corruption of the King's Speech," added Marion.

"Richard comes and False King John and the blasted Sheriff of Nottingham and all the wretched Normans fall. Long live King Richard!"

Whatever they were doing, all the Merry Men paused, raised a mug distractedly, and "Long live King Richard" echoed through the cave.

"I'm just saying, you can't assume because you have a book that you know what's supposed to happen."

"But Richard didst come back," said Little John. "We heard rumor. And by this book he wast to meet Robin and lead his men, with our aid, into the castle."

"But that did not happen because Robin cameth not," said Will Scarlet.

"So Richard wast taken and jailed."

"Enclosed in the very cell where Robin had been. And he wast taken by witchcraft, just as Robin had been," said Marian.

"Thou must make it happen," Friar Tuck repeated. "Thou must fix it."

"I can't," said Jessica. "I would if I could. But I can't. What happens happens." She was surprised to hear herself say it.

But it wasn't good enough for the Merry Men.

"Thou *wilt* fix it," said Little John.

Jessica screwed up her face—and decided not to reply. The silence grew thick as she looked from face to face and every one was staring hard at her. Finally, she said, "You don't suppose they were just beheaded in the middle of the night? People don't just disappear."

"Nor do they fall from doors in the deep wood," said Friar Tuck.

"Nor wouldst False King John behead Robin in secret. He wouldst make a show of it to affright all men—run his head on a pike and parade it seven times about the castle, set it up on his ramparts for the ravens to peck, which if we did not know it already is told for surety in this book," said Will Scarlet.

"I'm saying, you can't trust the book. What happened wasn't in the book," said Jessica.

"Because Janey the witch did magic the cell," said Will Scarlet.

"She's not a witch," Jessica was exasperated and a little frightened. Then she thought of something. "There doesn't happen to be a door or a door frame inside that cell does there?"

"Such as that which thou hath lost in our wood?" asked Friar Tuck.

"No one hath seen the inside of the dungeon since Robin," said Will Scarlet.

"Oh, but that have I," said Marian. "I wast there with Robin, the guard being an old friend of mine. He didst leave me in the cell for a time. There wast no door. 'Tis not unlike each several cell, stone walls and wooden rafters and fetid rushes."

"That's all I've got," said Jessica. "I'm really sorry. But I can't help you."

"As thou wisheth. And so Marian hath a bunkmate, and we hath ourselves a second cook," said Will Scarlet. "And thy lost door shall stay lost."

"That's blackmail," said Jessica.

Jessica looked around at the roomful of silent men staring back. It was quite clear they were not bluffing. They would keep her here as long as they thought she might be of any help at all.

"You say both of them went into the castle, and neither came out?" she said at last.

A ROW OF PINE TREES ERUPTED in flame not three feet from where Charlie and Doug stood. The two fell back as though they'd run into a wall. The flames roared. Before they could rise, a monstrous black dragon, tentacles streaming from his snout, landed with a ground-shaking thud amid the flames. As his wings beat the flames to a frenzy, with his two large forefeet he pushed two flaming pine trees to the ground like parting a curtain.

"What an entrance," said Doug.

"Shut up," said Charlie.

Smoke blew up from the burning trees. Sparks filled the air like incendiary snow, which, landing, ignited the leaves and needles strewn on the forest floor. The dragon glowered, but he seemed from the curve of his mouth a little pleased with Doug's praise for the theatrics of his arrival.

"You saw us?" said Doug. "We thought we'd got away."

"Curse my black scales, but you are brilliant," laughed the dragon. "How could I miss his red silk poking up through the corn or your cumbersome bones galumphing through the open field? Your legs are old sticks tied together with twine."

"Don't you need to catch the deserters?" Charlie asked.

The comment only made the dragon roar with menacing glee. He sent a rocket of flame up into the trees, igniting the top of a tall pine like a giant candle.

"You know about the soldiers?" The devil didn't seem particularly surprised.

"They're hiding in the corn right now, I'd say," said Charlie.

The dragon smiled. "Did you really think you could outsmart the devil? You are seven years too late."

"No. No, no. The army is there," said Charlie, "so the deserters have to be there."

"The army is always there," said the devil. "It's a regular stop on their maneuvers. And there hasn't been a single desertion from their ranks since I plucked those three in my talons exactly seven years ago. *There* was theatrics for you. I was like an osprey hauling three struggling fish up to my nest to pick apart their flesh to feed my young. Scared the crap out of everyone who saw it. You should see those soldiers in battle now. Fight like hell."

"Oh," said Charlie.

The smoke thickened. Doug waved at it and coughed.

"Seven years," Charlie too waved at the plumes in front of his face. "That means…"

"They got away," huffed the dragon. "Someone cheated me—gave away my riddle. No way they could have figured it out on their own. I was toying with them, like a cat. But they answered my questions perfectly." Then he paused and looked from Charlie to Doug and back to Charlie, "which means I'm looking for some replacements." The devil licked his chops.

Doug snickered. "This is a way better story than I remember."

Charlie looked at his companion sideways. "Is this why Beth is in England without you?"

"Excuse me?" said Doug.

"How many times have I got to tell you? When you're in it, it's not a story. That's real fire and real smoke and a real devil."

"*The* real devil," said the devil.

Doug waved his hand and laughed. "I should have brought my phone. I could get a picture. Look how that skin moves." The shiny black scales of the dragon caught the orange glow of the pine fires as he slowly moved his thighs, pacing the ground in front of the roasting trees.

"Don't we get a riddle or a magic whip or something before you drag us off to hell?" asked Charlie. The story was coming back to him in surprising detail.

"Made that mistake already," said the devil.

"Yeah, but you have to back us into a corner and give us the appearance of a choice when we don't really have one. That's the whole point of the story, isn't it?"

The devil looked down his snout, then he brought his whole head down so close to Charlie's face that the young man could feel the short hairs of his nostrils and smell the old sulfur of his breath. Up close, the dragon's scales were pocked and porous as a dog's nose.

"What do you think the fire's for?" the dragon whispered hoarsely. Then he slowly straightened up. He seemed to grow half the height of a tree. "Here's your deal: You can serve me for seven years as my slave and then be dragged to hell forever, or you can burn up right here right now and take your chances." The dragon blew a plume of fire over Doug and Charlie's heads to ignite the trees behind them in case they had any thought of making a break for it.

"That's your deal?" said Charlie.

"Take it or leave it," said the devil.

"Why aren't the soldiers helping us out?" asked Doug.

"No one gave the order. Besides, they don't get paid enough to risk their lives for strangers. Don't change the subject," said the devil.

Charlie looked around and coughed. The smoke was rising. He could not see the field beyond the trees. There were places where he could barely make out the trees beyond the circle of flame. And his eyes were starting to water. As best he could, he shouted: "In the great North Sea lies a dead dogfish, that shall be your roast meat, and the rib of a whale shall be your silver spoon, and a hollow old horse's hoof shall be your wineglass."

The devil's eyes grew wide, his nostrils flared. With a great, angry huff, he blew out the flames on all sides. Doug and Charlie stumbled to the ground gulping air.

"This is so cool," Doug laughed once he could breathe.

"You know my riddle?" yelled the dragon. "How?"

"I know how the deserters learned it."

"Tell me?" the dragon roared.

"If I do, you'll let us go?"

The dragon drew himself up to his full height and crossed his forepaws like great arms. He didn't like losing two more victims.

"You were right. Someone tipped them off," said Charlie.

"You?" asked the dragon.

"No. But I know who did. And if you don't find out, this someone will continue to help your victims. You'll lose more time and more souls. Seven years wasted already. Think of it."

The devil looked up to the cloudless sky and made a deep-throated roaring sound that might have been another laugh. Then he looked back down. "Mortal man," he said with lawyer-like calm. "Do you realize what you are doing? What you are proposing will help me catch more souls. Once I root out the informer, what is there to stop me? So you are trading your freedom for the souls of strangers—maybe lots and lots of strangers, maybe whole armies. You okay with that, morally speaking?"

Charlie hadn't thought of it that way.

"He's tricky," said Doug.

Charlie thought it over. Then he looked straight up at the dragon. "Yeah," he said. "I am. Each person's soul is his own, after all. Isn't that how every story goes?"

"I wouldn't know," said the devil. "Stories make me look bad. I never read them. So do we have a deal?" The dragon extended his long left forepaw.

Charlie extended his right hand but stopped just before grabbing the dragon's paw. "Well, you may find this hard to believe," Charlie wondered, now that he was on the verge of revealing the secret, whether the devil's anger upon finding out it was his own grandmother who'd betrayed him might lead him into a pyromaniacal fit. But on the other hand, would it be wise to toy with the devil? He put his hand on the dragon's paw and held it without shaking it. "But if I tell you this, do you promise…"

But Charlie didn't finish the sentence. Just at that moment a strong wind blew through the woods, extinguishing the remaining fire and clearing the smoke. Doug laughed.

"What the…" Charlie let go.

"Who's there," yelled the devil.

Just then a man hopped out from behind a tree, holding one of his legs in his hands. "That would be me," he said, as he slipped his leg into his overalls—it was not a wooden leg but a real flesh-and-blood leg. "I can't say I approve of the way you are dealing with these strangers," said the man. "I thought I'd interfere."

"I'll teach you to goad the devil," yelled the devil, and he flashed a plume of flame in the direction of the now two-legged man. But the man dashed out of reach of the fire. From the edge of the plume, the man yelled, "You'll have to do better than that if you want to catch me."

The strange man ran up to the devil, slapped him on the snout and, in a flash ran behind a nearby tree and stuck his head out, smiling.

As Doug and Charlie, watching carefully, backed slowly out of the way, the devil's eyes grew big. He roared to his full height and sent another plume of fire at the man. But the stranger easily dodged the flare, danced a quick jig by the side of the tree, then turned and ran toward the open field, yelling, "Come and get me."

The devil bolted after like a dog chasing a bone. In a moment they were both out of sight.

"Well, that was weird," said Doug.

"You kind of expect things like that in Grimm," said Charlie. "Kind of random."

"See, I told you," said Doug, "no real harm can come to us."

Charlie rolled his eyes. "I wonder how he put out the fire," he said aloud.

Just then five motley men stepped from out behind a tree: one nearly as tall as a giant, one who came to the tall man's knees, and three more normal looking men, one with a gun and one with a hat cocked awkwardly over one ear.

"Actually, that was me," said the short one. He laid a finger over one nostril and with the other blew a breeze that put out the most recent fire as it collaterally tore a sturdy branch off a maple tree.

"He can uproot a whole tree," said another man, the least distinctive among the five. "He doesn't like to show off."

"The Six Soldiers of Fortune," said Charlie. "Don't you recognize them?"

"Vaguely," said Doug. "Stay away from him when he's got a cold." Doug laughed at his own joke.

Everyone else merely frowned.

"Boy, that's the first time we've ever heard that one," said the man with the gun.

CHAPTER SEVEN

BEEP Doug? I wasn't going to call back. I mean I did tell you to be home for my call. I thought it would be important enough to you to be there for it. Seems I was wrong. Can't imagine what was so important that you couldn't be there for my call. And once again you are not home, and neither is anyone else. Fine. We'll be at the hotel in Madrid till Friday, and then we'll be back home. Assuming you still have the paper I left you with the phone numbers, just remember the 055 at the beginning of the numbers, not sure I wrote that part down. And I'll be 5 hours later than you, so don't call too late at night. This is assuming you plan to call at all. All my love to everyone at OzHouse. Ta.
BEEP

"SHE'S PISSED," GWEN SAID.

"You mean pissed as in British for drunk?" Gary placed the last of the groceries on the table.

"As in Doug will get his head handed to him when he finally returns her calls." Gwen placed a bag of celery it in the refrigerator.

"That's what I thought you meant. Where is Doug, anyway? What the hell is he up to? And Charlie? I haven't seen him since yesterday."

"Maybe they are up to something together. Jessica's car is still here," Gwen dropped a plastic bag of tomatoes into the drawer with the celery.

Maybe they'd taken Doug's car and gone somewhere. Neither could remember whether they'd noticed it in the garage, though they'd just been there.

Gary groaned. He picked up the phone, but then he put it back down.

He seemed more worried about his brother's marriage than Doug was.

Without another word, he left the kitchen and walked down the hallway. He felt funny, as though something was wrong, but what was it? He knew that Doug and Beth were going through a rough patch, and Jessica's mother and Isabelle and probably Jessica as well had plenty wrong with them, but it was more than that. Something felt out of place. He planned to go to his private den to see if he could make some progress on a painting he had been struggling with for weeks—or was it months? But as he rounded the corner and looked down the dimly lit corridor, he thought of the secret room.

Maybe they are up to something.

Gwen's words echoed in his mind. Not that she really meant anything by that statement, but with Jessica and Charlie back in the house, how could he not wonder? To prove himself wrong, Gary walked up to the old wardrobe and opened the hand-carved wooden door. It was slightly ajar, but that was not too surprising since it really didn't close tightly and any vibration on the creaky floor might nudge it open a little.

He looked inside. The coats were all pushed to the left. Is that how they'd left them? He wasn't sure, but he didn't think so. The back seemed closed up tight as a drum. Might someone have tested his fake bolts? Again, he didn't think so, but sometimes he trusted his cleverness too much—or underestimated the cleverness of others. He sighed and rubbed his face. This was ridiculous, but he had to know. He slid his hand past the horizontal slats and gave a push. The back opened easily. But that was supposed to happen. A familiar but unexpected odor wafted through the door. Was it fruit? Fresh? Canned? He crouched in and slid between the boards.

Inside, the room looked the same as always. Early evening sunlight filtered through the stained glass window. No one was there.

"Of course not," he said out loud. He was an idiot to think they'd try to use this room again. Doug couldn't. Charlie didn't want to, and as for Jessica, well you couldn't know what she would do after all these years. But the three of them were missing, not just her.

He smiled to himself as he ran his fingers over the jackets of the old and precious volumes. How foolish his suspicions had been.

But were they really foolish? What if they *had* been here and left? What if they *had* tried the door? Could he be sure they could not have managed the magic? Why not? He'd managed it himself as an adult years ago.

But after how Charlie had talked in the car, it was clear he at least didn't want to go back there. He had serious work to do.

Didn't he?

How would you know? He looked around the cluttered room, at the toys, the stuffed animals, the knick-knacks, the paintings on the walls. His hand fell on a volume of Agatha Christie.

What would Hercule Poirot think? What clues would he look for? What were Gary's own tiny gray cells telling him? The room wasn't dusty enough for a room abandoned for 10 years. That was true. And that was curious. He couldn't imagine Charlie dropping in after all this time and bringing a feather duster with him, and Jessica had too much on her mind. He couldn't imagine her swiping a can of air freshener and rushing to the Narnia room for a spritz-down. But then of course, there was Doug. Doug would do that. Doug would come in with a feather duster and a can of air freshener, Gary chuckled to himself. He could have been doing it for years for all Gary knew. Gary sniffed. Yes, that out-of-place odor. It was Beth's favorite air freshener—a cinnamon-orange he'd always thought smelled like soapy food.

So someone had been here. And it was probably Doug. But so what if he had? Doug liked to clean things. He wouldn't have disappeared on a routine cleaning. Even if he'd wanted to—and he'd never expressed to Gary any interest in going to fairyland—he wouldn't have the power to do it.

The mystery of the fruit-smelling air was solved for good when he found one of those plug-in things in an outlet behind the stuffed Aslan. It had probably been there for months. Though why Doug thought an empty room needed freshened air he could not say. But Doug was odd about such things. No, no one had been here recently. The window was closed and locked.

Still, he found himself a bit disturbed by the lack of dust. No doubt Doug had dusted when he'd installed the air freshener. Could a sealed room say undusty for months on end? There were no footprints nor was there anything obviously out of place on the tables. Nothing but the smell showed that anyone had been in the room since he'd put those fake bolts in—which he'd done just in case someone from the fairy worlds happened to want to come back, Suzy Bishop or Buddy Samson. They never did come back, of course. Why would they? But he'd slept better all these years knowing if they did, they wouldn't end up trapped in a locked room without food or water.

So there was no sign of disturbance. He confirmed it again. No one had been here recently.

No sign.

Except perhaps for the book on the couch. Yes, that was definitely a clue. Doug would have come in to clean, but a man who sneaks into an empty room to dust does not leave a book on the couch. And *he* certainly hadn't left it all those years ago. He was always careful to replace books in bookcases when he was done with them.

And what a book. *Lust for Life*. How odd. Not only was he sure this book would not have been in this room of classic fairytales, he didn't even remember owning the life story of Vincent Van Gogh.

Jessica wouldn't have it. Charlie? Who knew? Doug? Maybe Doug. Everything kept pointing back to Doug.

He approached the large leather-bound book at the end of the couch on the small oak stand. The last name written in blue ink was Douglas M. Robbins. Well, he was right about his brother. It was Doug. And so neat Doug forgot he'd left a book on the couch. It wasn't that crazy.

Mystery solved. He would have made a great detective. Doug came by months ago in a dusting frenzy and left a book on the couch. Yes, Hercule Poirot would have been proud.

But where was he now? Or Jessica, or Charlie?

Well, it didn't really matter. As long as they weren't in fairyland.

"HONEY, WE HAD NO IDEA YOU WERE BACK. Everything is so dark," Sarastiltskin saw her son in the moonlight wrapped in a quilt sitting in his father's big chair as she opened the latch and entered the cottage.

Budy was sitting in the blackness holding an unlit tallow candle in his hands.

"Don't just sit there, son. Light a fire and help your mother with her packages."

"Can't," sighed Budistiltskin twirling the candle between his fingers.

"What nonsense?" Rumpel put down the box he was holding as he crossed the threshold. "What's wrong, Budy?"

"I don't know. Everything is wrong. I did something."

Sara went to him.

"What did you do? What could be so terrible? Are you hurt? Are you sick?"

"No. I mean, yes, maybe," rubbing his eyes free of tears, Budy smeared soot all across his cheeks.

Hearing the sound in his voice, Rumpel and Sara, tired as they were, dropped everything and took a seat on either side of him.

"Tell me what it is, my boy," his father said.

"I don't know what it is."

"Let me make a fire," said Sara.

"No," said Budy louder than he intended. "You can't. I have tried and tried and…"

"Nonsense boy, you've been making fires for years. Why would it be a problem now?" Rumpel's gnarled hands took hold of Budy's smooth strong ones.

"It just won't burn."

The boy explained what had happened and how he had wished the fire to go out. From that moment on he could not relight the fireplace or a candle or the lamp. He couldn't light a fire anywhere in the house.

"Sounds like a spell," said Sara.

"Sounds like a curse," muttered Rumpelstiltskin as he made a few passes with his stubby arms and pointed at the wood on the grate.

For the first time since the days of the strange but brief confusion of the fairy worlds, when Glinda the Good of Oz had had to set things right, the little man failed to accomplish the simple task of making fire. He rubbed his hands together, the rough calluses sounding like a grasshopper calling to his mate. He made the pass again, and even Sarastiltskin tossed some silvery dust into the pile of wood in the fireplace, but no fire lit. Not even a spark.

"Seems impossible, but there you have it," Rumpel sighed. "You wished the fire to go out and it's out. Have you tried to make a fire in the yard and bring it in?"

Budy shook his head. The thought had not occurred to him.

"There is much to magic we have not taught you, mostly because we never thought you'd need to know, but there is usually a back door, so to speak, in getting an enchantment to take hold. Sometimes you just need to rattle a few knobs till you find it."

Sara took a few pieces of kindling outside and by the light of the moon she placed them in a teepee shape and tossed more silvery dust. With a woosh the dry wood burst into flame. Smiling, she picked up one of the twigs by the cool end and walked back into the house.

As soon as she entered the doorway the flame vanished.

"Oh dear," she exclaimed. Turning quickly she returned to the little fire outside and gently grabbed a pair of burning branches. They too remained lit until she entered the house. Again, the fire ceased to burn as she stepped across the threshold. "Seems the yard is fine but the house is cursed."

Budistiltskin approached her and said, "I'm sorry Ma. I don't know how I did it and have no idea how we can fix it."

"Hmm," said Rumpel. "God bless us if the back door here isn't a whole new house. Hate to have to build a whole new house."

The small fire Sarastiltskin had made was burning bright between the rounded rocks of the outdoor fire pit.

Budy said, "What if I bring in all the rest of the fire at once? All that fire might overpower the magic." He walked past his mother into the front yard. The moment he crossed outdoors, the fire went out. There was not a puff of smoke or any sign that the branches had just been burning. No, there wasn't even any heat. Only the blackened edges of the wood showed that any fire had ever been lit.

"Oh, no," Rumpel rushed past his wife and son. "This is much worse than I imagined. Ma, go inside and start a fire in the fireplace. Budy, you stay with me."

Muttering the foolishness of trying this again, the old woman hobbled back inside, and within seconds the fireplace was a blaze of light and heat.

"Go inside with your Ma," Rumpel had a look of fear on his old wrinkled face that Budy had never seen before. He did as he was told, and as his son stepped inside Rumpel saw the golden light in the windows die. This was worse than having to build a whole new house.

No fire would burn near Budy. The house wasn't cursed. It was his son.

JESSICA DIDN'T HAVE A PLAN. That wasn't like her at all. She always had a plan, even if it was a poorly thought out plan that had to be scrapped early on. But this time she had no plan. So she'd better form one, right away.

As she saw things, she had two options. She could try to convince these Merry Men to allow her back into the woods where they had met her so she could try on her own to find the portal that had brought her to Sherwood Forest, even if that meant dodging the king's scouts, or she could work with them to try and find some other portal that may or may not exist in the castle.

She sat with Marian and hoped that the two of them could see which of the options was more likely to work. It was easier to have access to the woods than the castle, and Jessica imagined she had at least a vague idea where to look. But Robin's men were not going to let her just up and leave them. And as for sneaking past them, that was not likely. Marian felt sure that the Merry Men wanted Robin back far more than they wanted her to go away. Once Robin was found they'd have no problem with her leaving, but she was their only link to Janey. And Janey was somehow responsible for Robin Hood's vanishing.

"Okay then," sighed Jessica. "The castle. Assuming there is a portal in that place, is there any chance it's not in the dungeon? You did used to live there, right?"

"Surely, many a year. And many a man and many a woman hath disappeared since the reign of the false king to be sure. But I know not of any doorway such as thou seekest, nor have I ever sought any such a thing. What, pray tell, would it look like?"

"Just a doorway. It tends to blend in with wherever it ends up. Usually it's made of wood. But you can't tell. I've seen a lot of them. Most of them are similar, nondescript things, sometimes whole closets. But they're not all exactly the same." Jess looked at the floor a moment.

"Someone said Robin was in a cell in the dungeon, right?"

"Heaven's truth. Thus did I say. Robin was placed in the false king's dungeon."

"There is a cell, in the back of the dungeon, hardest to enter, hardest to leave, where those prisoners are kept whom the king fears. In this cell Richard would have been put and, as you knowest, Robin as well. There I was led to see him with mine own eyes."

"When Robin did free himself from the cell," Will Scarlet interrupted, "it was said he had help from one among the guard. And not knowing which one it had been, they did torture and behead some few before one did confess."

"'Twas the same when Richard escaped. But then they did tell a story that an angel did visit him, one whose voice was heard in the cell by many a prisoner."

"An angel?" asked Jessica.

"Doth thou not believe it?" said Marian.

"Nor did we," said Friar Tuck. "Wast an angel? Or wast the witch Janey? None did see Janey come back, nor do we know for truth that the king was not moved in the night. But yet, it could well be that the witch in the show of an angel hath ta'en them twain. A powerful witch she was for one so young."

"She wasn't a witch," Jessica once again insisted. "But maybe... We may not be able to know for sure what happened. But it's the best theory I think we're going to come up with. What we need is access to that cell." Jessica looked over to the few men that were in the clearing with them. They had obviously been listening, but none made a sound.

"Well, can any of you get me into the dungeon?" she said with her hands on her hips and an angry look in her eyes.

"Getting thee into the dungeon shall not be so hard," Friar Tuck said. "And yet, if thou doth wish to come out again, that shall surely be a nut more tough to crack."

"Just get me in," Jessica replied. "If there is a door I'll have no trouble getting out."

"And if there be no such door?" asked Marian.

"Then you'll have to crack the nut, won't you?"

The group ate a sparse meal of cold boar and crusty bread while Marian and Friar Tuck discussed possible ways to get Jessica put not just into the dungeon but into King Richard's cell. It would not be as easy. Too minor a crime and they would simply give her a few lashings and release her, too harsh a crime and they might put her to death. What crime could she commit that would necessitate being put in the dungeon? And who could they rely on to get her into the right cell? As penalties were decided more by the mood of the sheriff than the words in a book, the question was particularly delicate.

In frustration Jessica had to let Will Scarlet, Friar Tuck, Marian, and Little John work on the plan without her help. She couldn't keep herself from throwing out suggestions of course. But these were met with laughter or scorn. She wasn't sure which she hated more.

The cold evening dew and the chill of night made her miserable. Oddly, no one else seemed bothered by the cold. Perhaps they were just used to it, or was it because they had on woolen undies and weren't telling? Or was it perhaps just because people of this time just didn't complain the way they did back in the twenty-first century?

Jessica was almost dozing when the group approached her with the plan.

"Now try and take thy rest," Marian said. "Thou seemeth weary as an October wasp."

Not quite sure what that meant, Jessica bunched up some leaves under a wool blanket and tried again to fall asleep.

The next morning they let her in on the plan. Jessica entered the village nervous as a feral cat but determined to play her part. She approached a thin man with what seemed a week's growth of beard and wearing a tunic made of a thick gray wool that did not seem to have been washed in many wearings. He was selling food and wares from a cart. Jessica introduced herself as she had been instructed.

"Good day, milord. I am called Jessica of… Hampshire, and I have been charged by some acquaintances with the planning of a great feast in honor of the return of their lord, one Robin of Locksley. It is said on report he shall returneth any day now and so I must procureth the meat and vegetables for the feast-eth."

Whether it was from the oddness of her accent or the invocation of the hereditary name of Robin Hood, the merchant stared hard at his customer. Clearly Little John had known who to send her to. The merchant sized her up without apology, glaring at her from head to toe as though to ask, Who is this? And did she have the money to pay for her goods? And did she know (as the Merry Men had informed her) that he had a haunch of venison under his cabbages? She removed a bag of coins to show she was quite willing to pay for what she needed. The merchant nodded to his wife, and she, who was, in the words of Little John, a good and loyal patriot when not selling illegal game for a hefty price, was off in a trice.

Jessica had not left the cart with her burlap bag filled with root vegetables and the venison haunch, when two guards approached her.

"Hold thy ground," said one.

"Oh, oh my. Yes, what is it, sir?" Jessica tried to sound innocent and surprised at the same time.

"Sir?" smirked the other guard. "Doth thou suppose him knight?"

"Give me no cleverness, girl," said the first. "Why hast thou purchased such a large portion of food?"

"It isn't against the law to buy food. I paid for it fair and square," Jess replied as the merchant squirmed.

"Truly spoken, but it doth be against the law to hold back sound answer to one of the sheriff's guard."

"Oh, well…" Jessica stammered. "I am preparing a welcome home feast, and my larder at home is quite empty."

"And whom shalt thou welcome?"

"Rr…, no one you would know. A friend hasteth been away and is just now returningeth to our land." Jessica smiled as she hefted the bag up and started to walk off.

"A friend of Locksley?"

The Merry Men were certainly right about the effect of uttering that name in Nottingham.

"The sheriff will want to speak with thee."

"But I haven't the time. So much to do. Perhaps another day?" Jessica started to walk off.

"Enough nonsense," growled the guard. Tossing the bag back to the shop keeper, he grabbed Jessica's arm and walked her off towards the castle.

Jessica noticed the merchant's wife smiling to her husband as, despite the Friar's warning, and although getting caught was essential to the plan, she tried to resist. But she gave up when the guard tightened his grip on her wrist until she grunted. Friar Tuck had warned her against the savagery of these men.

"Really, this is unnecessary," Jessica said as the guard pulled her under the portcullis of John's castle.

"Thy betters shall decide that which is necessary."

In a first floor room, Jessica recognized the sheriff, sitting on a high chair like a throne. He was dressed in red, black, and gold. He had a trimmed and pointed beard on his wide face. And he was much better fed than she remembered from their very brief encounter years ago. His glower was intimidating.

Behind him stood two flags. One she'd seen in a book. It was red and though it hung limp like the other, she knew it had three lions on it. It would have been the flag of the kingdom. But the other flag was one she hadn't seen before. It was green and seemed to have some pattern of blue and yellow on it. She couldn't quite tell what the pattern was, but she guessed this would be the flag of Nottingham. And what she noticed was that this flag stood higher than the flag of the realm. That probably meant something.

"Kneel, prisoner," the sheriff commanded in a voice much higher than Jessica would have suspected from such a large man.

It was time to launch into the act she'd worked up with the friar. She gulped, took a deep breath, and trusted the plan.

"Sure," she spread her arms with a theatrical bow and a "how's this?" expression just as Friar Tuck had told her to do.

The sheriff would not have met with such a provocative reaction to a command—not since the days of Robin himself. He leaned forward, put his elbow on his knee and his chin in his hand, and stared as though he were contemplating a move in a game.

"Can I get up now?" said Jessica.

When the sheriff said nothing, Jessica hopped up. Two guards rushed over to push her back down. She rolled her eyes. She hoped this was what Friar Tuck had meant when he told her to be as foreign as possible. She would have thought humility and contrition a better strategy for that. But when she'd said so that morning, the whole cave had laughed. "The sheriff doth honor weakness like any devil, as an opportunity to display his utmost cruelty."

"Really," said Jessica to the sheriff, "push the meek little prisoner down on the stone floor? Whatever happened to innocent until proven guilty?"

A puzzled expression flitted across the sheriff's face. Suppressing it, he continued to stare. Finally he said, "Surely we have heard such speech e'er now." And he seemed to be trying to remember when it was.

"I wouldn't know."

"Thou doth surely know 'tis death to support the outlaw Locksley in Nottingham, e'en to utter his name in the market."

"Do I look stupid? I beg your pardon. I'm not from around here. The truth is…Can I stand up? These stones are killing me."

The sheriff nodded his head once.

"Okay," Jessica inhaled deeply and was glad she'd taken that acting class in college. "Cards on the table, I'm walking through the woods and this guy in this green tunic thing hands me a big ole sack of money—more doubloons than I'd…"

"Doubloons?"

Jessica had no idea if she'd stepped into something with that. Was a doubloon something other than an old coin? She gulped. "Not actual doubloons. Good old English coin. Try to follow me here."

The sheriff continued to look suspicious. But that was good. At least Friar Tuck would have said so. Jessica was beginning to doubt the friar's assertion that the sheriff would find her too curious to torture or to release if she sounded as foreign and acted as insolent as possible. But what could she do? She kept it up: "Anyway, he tells me if I'll buy him this and that at the market, there's two more bags of money just as big waiting for me when I get back. Okay, I say, I'm in. I need money. I could just run off with the one bag and have this guy with a bow and arrow on my tail, or I can do this little favor and maybe get two bags, and if he's pulling my chain, well, I'm no worse off, right, so, 'deal,' I say. Only he says, 'Just whatever you do, don't say the name "Robin of Locksley."'"

The sheriff straightened up in his chair.

"I'm a bit of a contrarian, I have to say. This isn't the first time I've talked myself into trouble. So I ask myself, 'what could happen?' I want to see, so I say the name. Wow, freakin' unbelievable, ya know?"

The sheriff held up his hand. She knew he meant for her to stop. But she thought perhaps she should go on. She clearly had him intrigued. She found she could not do it, however. This man had not got this job by chance. He stared at her and a cold shiver went from her nape to her toes, and she found herself unable to speak. It was not witchcraft, it was fear—but it might as well have been witchcraft.

"Thou art not from Hampshire. But so. I confess I do not well understand thy poor imitation of our Saxon tongue. But it seemeth clear, thou hast not told all nor nearly all."

"God's truth," said Jessica.

"The man did say unto you he awaiteth the immanent return of Robin of Lockley. Did the man in green say when?"

"Not that I remember."

"Art thou sure?"

"Why would I lie? Like I give a rat's ass."

"I do wonder how many turns on the rack shall be needed to improve thy memory."

"Look, you want to break me. I'll tell you a secret. I come pre-broken. I've got nothing to hide. I'll tell you anything you want to know. So there's no point putting me on any rack. What's more, I work for the highest bidder. You want info on this Robin, this Locksley, two bags of gold and I'll find out what he had for breakfast last Thursday. Here's the deal: You give me the provisions you stole from me which I actually had all paid for, I bring 'em to the guy in green, invite myself for dinner and get him to spill the beans on whatever you need to know. Don't worry, I have ways. So you don't need any more talk about racks or dungeons."

"Who hath spake of any dungeon?"

"Isn't that what you guys do? Never mind. Sorry I brought it up. There's no reason in the world to put me in a dungeon. I hate confined spaces. You want me to help? Think it over. Give me a nice clean comfortable room for the night, anywhere in the castle. And I promise, I won't talk to a soul. I'm not dangerous. I got no beans of my own to spill about this Robin guy. I don't care a fig what's between him and you so long as I get my cut. Trust me, I won't put any ideas in anyone's heads. Just a secure room while you think it over. I'm sure the guy's gone back to his secret hideout today. But I'll bet I can find him tomorrow for you." And then she looked up at the flags. "Just think of how your reputation's gonna skyrocket when you bring this Locksley in."

"Sky rock it? What language doth thou speak, natively? Thine English hath been but poorly taught."

"We got a deal? I assume we got a deal."

"We shall consider of it." And then the sheriff glanced at his guards. "Toss her in the dungeon. And keep her far from the other prisoners."

Turns out Friar Tuck knew his stuff, all right. Jessica was shoved down the curved stone steps. The farther they went, the darker it became until she could not see the steps. Walking in the dark on uneven stones proved quite dangerous, and she slowed her pace. The guard gave her a rough push, which almost made her fall. She stumbled and nearly fell several more times as she tried to keep up with his long stride.

When they reached the bottom, the damp stench from within made Jessica gag as the guard pushed her along the corridor.

Soon they reached a cell along the back wall of the castle. Even in the dim light that came from the one window high overhead Jessica could see it was a filthy hovel filled with soiled straw and furnished with a single wooden bench.

"Is this the one? Is this the right cell?" she whispered. Friar Tuck had assured her they'd found and bribed the guard. But had they bribed the right one?

The guard made no sign that he understood her question, or that he had even heard her question, as he pushed her in.

Holding her dress up to avoid the rushes, brown and wet and smelling worse than any sewer, she made her way to the bench and sat while the guard shut the door with a loud clunk.

CHAPTER EIGHT

The Turtle and the Rabbit
by Doug Robbins

"THAT'S SUPPOSED TO BE the tortoise and the hare," said Debbie.

Gary smiled.

One fine day, as she sunned herself by the Pond, Turtle…

"The tortoise is a he," said Debbie.

…Turtle felt a crick in her neck. "Oh, dear," she thought slowly, "I have a crick in my neck." Turtle was a very happy turtle most of the time. But this crick in her neck was not at all pleasant. She fell into an unhappiness.

Turtle had fallen into an unhappiness before—once or twice about this or that. And she had learned that when she fell into an unhappiness, she could always find a way to climb back out.

She just had to figure out how.

She did this by thinking.

She was not a quick thinker. She sat, or perhaps she lay (it's hard to tell with a turtle) with her flat stomach on the cool, cushy moss, and waited for a thought to bubble up into her slow brain.

She waited, and waited, and waited.

And then she felt a something in her stomach, a something like a fish, swimming around, perhaps, or a butterfly beating its papery wings against the wall.

Or a bubble.

Yes, it was like a bubble, rising, pushing against the roof: a thought

76

was bubbling up from her stomach, and rising into her throat and floating past her mouth and past her eyes and into her brain, where thought-bubbles belong.

"Perhaps," the bubble said, "if I push my head out of my shell as far as it will go, I will feel the fresh air on my neck, and it will feel better."

So she pushed her long neck as far and as high as it would go— way up into the balmly breezes of the warm summer day.

"Turtles have short necks," said Debbie.

She imagined she was a giraffe reaching for the highest leaf on the tallest tree.

She felt a crick in her neck.

She pulled her long neck back down to earth.

It had not worked.

Turtle eased her neck back into her cozy shell. There she sat, or lay, and waited. And waited. And waited—for another bubble to bubble up into her little brain.

And sure enough another bubble built in her stomach and rose in her throat and lifted past her mouth and her eyes, just as she knew it would.

"Perhaps what you need is exercise," the bubble said.

"This is *not* how the story goes," Debbie crossed her arms and put her chin on her chest.

Gary glanced up from the book. The four children on cushions sat in a semicircle around his chair. Trisha had her fists under her chin and was smiling up at Gary as he turned the bright picture of the large turtle at the bottom of a deep hole. Jennie turned her head politely toward the page.

Caleb was boiling. As the picture was turned toward him, his eyebrows were nearly touching his nose. His nostrils were flared and his mouth was twitching like a caterpillar.

"It doesn't say the turtle is *in* a hole," said Debbie.

"That's a metaphor, Debbie," said Gary.

"You're not supposed to draw the metaphor," said Debbie.

"I wish I knew as many things as you do, Debbie."

"Sarcasm does not help the situation," said Debbie.

Across the bog from Turtle, Rabbit was doing her morning sprints. Fifty strides from the pine to the spruce, fifty strides from the spruce to the pine, fifty strides from the pine to the spruce, fifty strides from the spruce to the pine.

Rabbit was fast.

But Rabbit was bored.

"What I need," said Rabbit, "is someone to beat!"

"Rabbits," said Debbie, "aren't especially fast."

Caleb exploded. "Shut up, shut up, shut up, shut up."

Debbie tried to talk, but Jennie cut her off. "You're ruining it for *every*one."

"Caleb, we don't say, 'shut up,'" said Gary, mildly.

"She's a whiner," said Caleb.

"Mom won't let us be whiners," said Jennie.

Tricia giggled.

"Your mother's in a nuthouse," said Debbie.

"Your mother's dead," said Jennie.

"Shut up, shut up, shut up," said Caleb.

Gary closed the book.

With all his years of experience, Gary sometimes supposed he'd seen it all: every type of kid, every problem, every combination of personalities. Yet every time he dealt with a new group, he felt at moments like he was just starting out. "How do you correct Caleb for saying 'shut up' when you know the real problem is Debbie for provoking him?" he would later say to Gwen. "But of course that's the instinct."

"But you didn't," said Gwen.

"I *had* to."

Gwen tisked.

"Was I supposed to just pretend nothing was happening?"

"Isn't that your normal coping strategy?" Gwen asked.

Gary wanted to tell his wife that that was untrue. But that would be difficult to pull off at this moment because, if she pressed him, he'd have to admit that what he had actually done was to re-open the book and continue reading.

"Sarcasm will not help the situation," he said.

"Wait a minute," Debbie said as soon as Gary had resumed reading. "Does the rabbit win?"

Gary looked up over the top of the book. "What do you think would happen if a rabbit raced a turtle?" he asked after a long pause.

"This is a stupid book."

It did occur to Gary at that moment that this might be the reason Doug had had such a hard time placing this particular book. Of course the story had the proper twist at the end—turtle, who wisely cared nothing about winning foot races, lost the race by a mile, but she fixed the crick in her neck and proudly challenged rabbit to another race when she felt an itch in her back. It was the kind of twist Doug favored. It did not lead to the insupportable moral that slow and steady wins the race. (Slow and steady never won a sprint, for goodness' sake.) Nonetheless, it may be that *The Turtle and the Rabbit* was a little too down-to-earth. You don't want that in this kind of book. If the turtle wins, the readers will buy the story no matter how insupportable the message.

Had Doug's marriage trouble led to cynicism and cynicism to this particular story? Would Doug's professional career get back on track if his marriage could be fixed?

"Maybe you can give Doug your critique yourself when he comes home," Gary said to Debbie.

"Where is Doug?" asked Jennie.

Where indeed? Gary had been thinking and thinking and thinking—ever since he'd found *Lust for Life* in the magic room. If *Lust for Life* was Doug's book, then the best conclusion, perhaps, though it was hard to believe, was that Doug *had* managed the wardrobe magic. Maybe something in Van Gogh had put him in the right mood and then—poof! Maybe he wasn't even trying. Maybe he'd stumbled into fairyland when he thought he was just leaving the room. (It turned out his car was still in the garage.) But if he had somehow crossed over, where had he gone? And how could you go after him when he could be anywhere at all? But it had to be a story—not a painting. Gary looked down at the page. Turtle and Rabbit stood side by side on the starting line in the middle of the bog. Just beyond them stood a porcupine with a starter's pistol. Rabbit was cocked and ready to zoom. Turtle was still half in her shell. The porcupine, however, drew Gary's attention.

It had Doug's face.

"Well, there's a thought," he thought. Had he drawn Doug's face when he illustrated this book? Of course he had—almost certainly. Doug liked to have Gary draw his likeness onto one of the characters in each of his books. He called it his homage to Hitchcock. And they'd proved over and over again that trips to fairyland never changed the published stories. But didn't Doug's face also suggest a desire to enter into his own stories? Gary said to the children: "If you had a door that took you to a magical place, any place at all that you'd read about in a book, where would you go?"

They all thought about it.

"What if you could go into a world that you had imagined yourself—one of your own books?"

JESSICA WAS ALONE IN THE CELL. That was the only good thing—assuming it was the right cell. If there was a portal in here, no one would see her find it. The more she'd thought about it, the more she thought there had to be one.

But now that she was here, she was having a hard time holding onto that hope. The cell was almost dark enough inside to hide a door. The only light was what came from a single window high above her. But the room was small. How could there be a hidden door in such a small room?

A portal, even one as simple as a door frame, could hardly go unnoticed. The room was almost bare. And if they'd actually searched it, then wouldn't a portal have been found? There was no place in this cell where you could hide anything bigger than a shoe.

And she needed it to be here. As far as she knew from her own experience, although very often the doors would not get you from OzHouse to fairyland, the portals always worked from this side. They didn't always take you back to OzHouse, as she'd had to realize when she'd lost Buddy, but they always took you somewhere. (Gary said the somewhere was "home," but she wasn't so sure about that anymore either.) She didn't have a backup plan. She really did not expect the sheriff to trust her as a double agent. If not that, then the portal was the only way she had of getting out.

It was a terrible thought to have when you were actually locked inside.

The odor that rose from the slime of the decaying rushes never ceased. She'd never get used to it. And even worse than that were the sounds of the prisoners that crowded in from everywhere. Madmen and madwomen crying as if in pain, swearing incoherently. Saner prisoners yelled at one another and growled at the guards. Chains rattled like something in a horror movie. And from somewhere down in the depths of the castle Jessica heard terrific screams. The torture chamber. If she'd heard the screams yesterday, would she have dared put on that silly performance in front of the sheriff?

Of course she'd always known that the older you get the harsher the worlds the wardrobe drew you to. But she had never thought she'd be old enough for torture. And was it still certain the sheriff would not try to torture her? If there was no portal in this cell, and if the sheriff saw through her silly act, what would happen to her? Would they see something strange about her—her clothes, the material of her shoes, her untraceable accent—and in fear torture a confession out of her? And if they did, what could she possibly say to make the torture stop?

"Oh, man, Isabelle, you owe me for this," she murmured.

Jessica sat a long time on the bench, unable to make herself move; her feet were flat on the plank out of the slime, her arms were wrapped around her legs, her knees pulled up under her chin. She told herself she was waiting for her eyes to adjust to the dim room. Then she would have a look around. But as the horrible sounds rose and fell like waves in the dark, she became less and less inclined to move.

This was unlike any place the wardrobe had ever taken her to. What had Janey gone through in her life to make it possible for *her* to get here—ten years ago?

Her eyes never did adjust.

The high window was closed off with an iron grate. Up against it weeds grew. The small hole, open to the rain, Jessica realized, would probably allow direct sunlight in the room for a few hours no more than one or two days once or twice a year; most of every other day the room would be dim as twilight all day long. She told herself she would have to ignore the sounds of suffering she could not help and that she would have to ignore the smells that made her gag and she'd have to put her shoes on that floor and search.

Water quickly soaked through the cloth of her running shoes. It surrounded her feet and began to wick up her socks as she inched forward with her hand along the damp stones of the wall. Baby steps.

The cell was featureless. Aside from the window and the bench, there was nothing but walls made of large, stacked stones all around. She found four sets of iron cuffs dangling from chains on the wall. But that was it. The only "portal" was the door through which she'd entered. But she'd never heard of a magical portal coinciding with an ordinary door. And if that had been the portal she was looking for, she would have fallen into some other place when she'd crossed into the cell. She moved a second time around the room. Could the portal be hidden in the ceiling or the floor? Some sort of trap door? She'd never heard of such a thing. If she had to feel for a door under these soaked weeds, if she had to put her hands into the muck now soaking its way up her jeans hidden beneath her dress—well if she had to, she had to. But she might pass out from the stench.

After all, she was doing all this for Isabelle and for Amanda, even if they couldn't appreciate it. She lifted her wet shoes and they made a sucking sound. Searching the floor would be a last resort. It was hard to breathe.

She went back to the bench and stood upon it to catch her breath. Leaning her back against the damp, stone wall covered with niter, she stretched her neck toward the window grate for a breath of outside air.

To her surprise, she did catch a wiff. The air was just a little fresher. No, actually, it was much fresher than she'd expected it to be. The air in this corner of the room was not only surprisingly fresh, it seemed vaguely scented. The scent reminded her of something. She could not say what. It wasn't flowers or grass or anything that should have been coming in through the grate. It was more like cinnamon. And lavender. No, not lavender. Oranges. And it did not seem to be coming from the direction of the grate at all—but from the other side of the room, as though an air current were flowing from out of the wall, across the ceiling and out through the window.

But that must be a kind of olfactory illusion. She had to get closer to the window.

She could not reach the space even on tiptoes. She tried to pull herself up on the huge wooden rafters that held the ceiling. She put a foot in one of the steel rings that held a short, rusty chain to the wall. She grabbed hold of the corner of rock that stuck out from the wall and pulled herself up as though she was on a climbing wall at the gym. From there she reached one of the spars that held the structure up. Hauling her skirt up, she managed to pull on the spar and swing herself up high enough to look outside. There was a scrappy little garden between the dungeon and the outer wall of the castle. She saw nothing strange. But the smell grew stronger. But it wasn't a garden smell. It was as an indoor smell. But not a medieval indoor smell. More like—air freshener. Canned air freshener.

It smelled like OzHouse.

"Hold on, here, Jess," she said to herself. Perhaps the flower from which that scent was canned grew in that neglected garden. Yes, come to think of it, it was Beth's air freshener smell, and Beth was British.

But oranges were not.

Just then the sun crossed a crenellation in the outer castle wall and sent a beam directly through the window grate, illuminating the near corner of the room.

"Wow," Jessica said out loud. The sun only comes to this room once or twice a year, and this was the day and this was the hour—just when she'd been tossed in. What were the chances of that?

On the other hand, wasn't it really just the sort of thing that happened in these kinds of stories?

The beam of light revealed in that corner one more feature of this empty room. Jessica could not have seen it from the floor—a rectangle of stones situated just above the beam on which she sat. They were not really so different from all the other stones in the room, but they were smaller—and they made a rectangle that just might be a door.

Was it? She could not have reached that high on the wall when she'd circled the room. And no one searching for a tunnel would have climbed up here.

Jessica slithered across the beam as far as she could, but she was much too far away to reach the space. The only way to get there would be to jump. But what if it wasn't a door? Then she'd be throwing herself against a stone wall and she would fall uncontrollably onto the bench or the fetid floor. Which meant she'd not only be a fool, she'd be a fool in a lot of pain. Oh, but she had to do it. Not only did she have to find Buddy and save Izzy and Amanda, now she also had to find King Richard and Robin Hood and save all of England. And she probably would have to save Doug and Charlie too because if they'd managed to make it through the wardrobe, by now they'd probably got themselves up to their necks in trouble. Why was it always up to her to save everybody? She knew they always accused her of having this martyr complex that made her think it was her job to fix everything. But the truth was anything she didn't fix, didn't get fixed. It wasn't a complex. She really did not want to save everyone. She *had* to. Gwen certainly wasn't going to do it.

But how do you get the courage to throw yourself at a stone wall?

She took off one of her shoes—and threw that at the wall.

It disappeared. It was a door.

But it was a wall too. And it was a pretty good distance to jump. What if her eyes had played tricks on her. She sat a long time staring at the hard rectangle. She took off the other shoe and threw that.

And then she heard a key turn in the door and a voice come through it.

"His excellency the sheriff would speak with thee."

Well that was it. She stood up on the beam, steadied herself and then with all her strength dived head first into the rectangle of stones.

Her knees knocked against the casement stones as her arms pushed through the wall into empty air. She cried in pain as she scampered up the wall, half in both worlds, and pulled herself through until she fell, holding her bruised knees, onto the floor of the Narnia room.

"SO YOU DIDN'T ACTUALLY HAVE TO MAKE A DEAL with the devil at all," said Doug.

"I'm not sure I did make a deal. We were still negotiating terms." Charlie snapped a dead limb from a pine tree.

Doug laughed. "Man, see, I like this world. You can outsmart Beelzebub."

Charlie flourished the dead branch as though he was testing a foil. "You don't think you're overdoing the enjoyment thing a little?"

"You don't think this is a blast?"

"I think we've got the devil in our tale and on our tail. We can't count on endless rescues by strange Grimm creatures, you know. We're stuck in this weird world without a doorway home, and, I don't know, I don't have a clue anymore what I'm doing with my life."

"So what a great opportunity to figure it out."

Charlie's expression clearly conveyed how much Doug didn't get it. "Oh, and I hear your marriage is on the rocks. I'm kind of surprised at you. Gary told me you were a little down in the dumps."

"In that world maybe," Doug nodded as though he had some idea what direction the world of OzHouse was in. "Here, it's like a dream—without any of that death wish stuff that always spoils actual dreams." The shadow of a large bird with a hoarse, croaking call fluttered across their path. "I'll worry about my marriage when I wake up."

"This isn't quite like what you read in books, Doug. Time is passing in OzHouse at the same rate it's passing here."

Doug slowed his pace. "Really?"

Charlie nodded. "So if there's anything you were supposed to be doing right now, it's not getting done."

"I was supposed to call Beth. She's going to be pissed—and not in the British sense of that word." He looked ahead, he looked around. "In that case, maybe we *should* go back."

"We *can't* go back. The devil burned the door. Are you paying attention?"

"Then why did you bring it up? So in that case, listen, I can't do anything about it. I'll just have explain it to her when we do get back and hope she understands."

"*If*, Doug, *if* we ever get back."

"Well if we don't get back it kind of stops being a problem, doesn't it."

"That's it?"

"I refuse to be gloomy about something I can't change. In fairyland no less." And then he held out his right arm and pointed dead ahead and imitated a favorite moment in his favorite movie: "To Oz?" he said.

"You never know," said Charlie, and he almost found himself smiling.

"Do you really think that devil might come back for us?" Doug asked after a period of silence.

"Unless those six soldiers of fortune take care of him for us. What a weird bunch. But I wouldn't count on that."

"Why not? Didn't they defeat a kingdom, just the six of them? That one with the ice hat could freeze him, and the one that could shoot someone's tooth out two miles away, he could take him out with one bullet." Doug thought about this for a while. "In a comic book, they'd sure take care of him."

"If this were a comic book. If that weren't the devil. The devil's not easily daunted." Charlie had been intrigued by the story of the six soldiers at the Bodleian—a fun gang of heroes, fearless and innocent. They seemed somehow out of place even in Grimm. They could have been a great help in the search for Buddy. Whole armies could not stand in their way. But they had declined to help when Charlie asked—said they needed to help their friend who carried his leg around in his arms because when he put it on his slowest pace would leave a cheetah in the dust.

"Devil and all," the marksman had said, "might give him some trouble if he manages to catch him."

So Charlie and Doug had set out in the direction the men had pointed them in, toward the house of a cranky forester and his wife who sounded to them like this Rumpelstiltskin fellow Charlie had described, although they did not know the man personally and weren't sure they'd ever heard the name before. To get to the cabin, however, they'd have to cross through Grumbottem or go around it. Dressed as they were, said the dwarf, they might save time to take the long way and go around it.

Charlie's colorful shirts, jeans and running shoes had drawn attention before, and Doug wasn't dressed any better in his worn out Led Zeppelin T-shirt.

"You'll find a little castle there," said the marksman, "presided over by a prince of good reputation and his young princess, still known to some by her affectionate family nickname, Aschenputtel."

"Aschenputtel?" Charlie said. "You mean Cinderella?"

"Just don't call her that when the prince is in the room."

Charlie thought perhaps they'd try their luck in town after all.

It was late afternoon the next day when they finally made it to the outskirts of Grumbottem. The walking was getting more difficult by the hour on their unaccustomed legs, but Doug remained undiscouraged. He managed to keep his cheerfulness despite the mild ache, despite even the night in the open without pillow or blankets. The night had been warm enough and the sun was out in the day. This time of year, some cold nights could be expected. But he was sure they'd find shelter when they needed it. They'd seen no sign of people since they left the six soldiers of fortune. Now, here, outside the town wall some unprotected houses had been built. They were connected by narrow streets paved in cobblestone.

"I've been here before," said Charlie, and he looked around until he found the house that confirmed his impression. "That's where Cinderella lives—or used to."

Doug nodded and looked through the trees toward the town where a small hilltop castle could be seen in the distance. "Do they really live happily ever after in this world?"

The gates of the town were pretty unimpressive, as were the walls. This was not a wealthy place, and these were not the ramparts of Avignon. No, these were short stone walls anyone could climb with a homemade ladder. The gates were iron, short, narrow and entirely without ornament. There was none of the wrought work you'd expect of a medieval city wherein the prince showed off his power in all public works. And they were open and unguarded as well. Doug thought it was marvelous. Once again he wished he had a camera. He wanted to remember the look so Gary could sketch it. But Charlie was a little disappointed. Through the gates they saw a busy avenue of shops, the blacksmith, the cooper, the wheelwright, all advertised with miniature examples of their trade hanging above their doors.

Doug and Charlie had hardly passed through the gates when they heard a gang of angry voices. Down the widest of the narrow streets a small mob was moving, pushing a man before them. The man had a bag over his head. Every time he stood up, someone in the mob tossed him further in the direction of the gate, and he'd fall on the cobbles and cry out. He'd get up as quickly as he could, but by then the mob was ready to toss him further forward.

"Oh, my God," said Doug who instinctively took a step to help the man.

"I don't think so," said Charlie, grabbing Doug by the arm. "You want a bag over your head?" He pulled Doug quickly to the side.

The grumbling mob was not ten paces away. A burly man with a grizzled beard lifted the fallen man and pulled him toward the entrance to the village. "Ye be at the gate now, wizard. Hear me. Walk 100 paces at full stride, spin thrice, then ye may remove the sack. Take yourself then in whatever direction you face so long as it be not back here. If we see that face again within these gates we will spit it on a pike and show it on the walls as a warning to wizards everywhere." And then amid the cheers of the men and women in the mob, he flung the fellow hard onto the packed earth.

Doug shook Charlie off and moved to confront the mob, but Charlie grabbed his arm and pulled his startled companion with so much force, the two of them tumbled together behind the walls of the blacksmith shop.

"Do you want *your* head on a pike?" Charlie whispered.

"I'm just going to find out what he's done to deserve that. I'm sorry. I'm a democrat. I'm not into mob justice."

"Listen to me: when they put your head on a pike, they have to cut it off first."

"I'm not going to yell at them."

"Look at yourself. You've got rubber shoes on. You're wearing a Led Zeppelin T-shirt. They're a mob with a chip on their shoulder for wizards. Let it go."

"It's wrong."

"It works for them."

It occurred to Doug and Charlie at the same time that the clang of the blacksmith's hammer had ceased. And just then the door to the side of the building opened and the blacksmith himself filled the space. He looked a long time at the two oddly dressed strangers arguing in the alley. The blacksmith took a step into the alley, his huge torso blocking their exit to the street just as the mob was walking past.

"Is there a problem here, Richard Smith?"

"No problem," said the man without turning around. "Just a couple friends who have had a little too much ale for breakfast. Now, in you go," and he pointed to the door of his shop and nodded Doug and Charlie inside.

Once inside, the big man looked the pair over slowly up and down. He felt the material of Doug's T-shirt and then again the material of Charlie's loudly patterned Hawaiian shirt. He pressed a plastic button between his fingers then looked down at their shoes.

"Art thou from the Merica?" he asked.

BUDISTILTSKIN HAD NOT GONE TWENTY PACES when he reached his hand up to the sack and, with swollen fingers, started working on the knot beneath his chin. When he did not hear the mob behind him, he assumed they had disbanded. Not that he cared. They probably wouldn't venture past the gates if they saw him remove the bag, and even if they did, he had a lead of twenty paces. He could outrun them.

If he could get the knot undone.

CHAPTER NINE

Dear Doug and/or Charlie,

I ended up in Sherwood Forest, as in Robin Hood, and things there are a mess. Apparently a little girl named Janey had gone through the doorway years ago and really screwed up their world. Robin has been missing for years and so has King Richard. They all seemed to end up in a dungeon before they passed through a portal and now are God knows where. So now we have to find them, as this Janey seems to have come from OzHouse. And anyway, I promised. Once I settle this thing with Isabelle, I have to try to return them to Nottingham. It seems Glinda was right and our first trip has caused serious problems, and I could not live with myself knowing that people are suffering if my visit had anything to do with it, which maybe it did, even though it was not intentional.

I am going to check to be sure you are not still here at OzHouse, and then try my luck at getting back into the Fairy worlds, and try to find you or Buddy or just find a place safe for my sister and her kids.

If you read this, know that I am okay, and I am either off searching for you, or was unable to get through the portal and am now downstairs in the living room sulking, unless, of course I am rescuing my sister.

Text me,

Jessica

JESSICA PLACED THE NOTE on the table with the big book of signatures. She put her ear to the door. No one seemed to be in the hall. How awful if someone were to see her sneaking through the closet. Doug was on her side, but for all she knew Gwen or Gary might kick her out of the house for breaking the deal with Glinda. Then how could she save anyone? And, what was almost as bad, her shoes and her socks and pants were covered with dungeon muck, and she smelled like a sewer. She cleaned herself off as best she could with the dry parts of Maid Marian's tunic and practiced looking nonchalant. She would do her best to keep her distance from anyone out there until she could get to a bathroom. She left the tunic with the wimple and hat in the secret room. She'd have to find a time to wash them or toss them out later. But at least here no one would be able to smell them. She'd have left the sneakers and jeans behind too if she had any other pants or shoes. She slipped back through the secret door and crept to one of the guest rooms. Gwen and Beth had always kept a supply of clothes on hand for kids of all ages who might need them. They were pretty old, but maybe that was good. She took a quick shower but still felt even with her perfumed soap and toiletries she that there was a pungent odor bubbling around her. She stashed her jeans and socks. She slipped into a baggy white shirt and a long frumpy skirt and looked at herself in the mirror. She looked like someone practicing to be a homeless person, but Gwen would no doubt think she looked "artsy," and the look might help her pass in various fairylands better than anything else on hand, better certainly than a T-shirt and jeans. If only there were an extra pair of shoes. But there was no time to scrounge. She was in a hurry.

She texted Isabelle and ran through the house to check for Doug and Charlie. The place was deserted. She spied only a small child sitting on the couch in the Persian Room looking at a book; she smiled, said nothing, and moved on. In the kitchen Gary was slicing onions and Gwen was pouring oil in a frying pan. They smiled when they saw her.

"There you are," said Gary, seeming much happier to see her than he had any reason to be. "Is Doug with you? Where's Charlie?"

"Doug?" said Jessica. "Why would Doug be with me?"

"Oh, nice skirt," said Gwen. "Give us a hand?" She seemed to be assuming Jessica would be staying for supper.

"Huh? Oh, sure thing, Mrs. Robbins. But I... I'm not sure I remember where everything is."

"We haven't seen you all day."

"It's a big house. I forgot how big it was."

"Doug was supposed to..." Gary interrupted himself. "Never mind. You're all here. You're all safe. No one has wandered into..." and he paused again, "places they are not supposed to be."

"I certainly, I mean, isn't that supposed to be boarded up?"

"Perhaps you can help slice some vegetables." Gwen pointed at a bunch of celery with her knife.

"Yes, yes, of course," said Gary. "So of course you couldn't have gone in there, could you?"

Jessica smiled vaguely as she took the knife from Gwen and moved the celery to the farthest countertop and absently set to work.

"You having a nice visit with Charlie?" asked Gwen.

"Oh, yes," said Jessica. "But have you seen him recently? We, uh, we were out exploring in the woods. I love what you did with all the trails back there." Jessica assumed there would still be trails in the woods from years ago. "But I can't seem to find him now."

"Good luck putting a bell on Charlie," Gary laughed. "He might be in one of the workrooms or off drawing somewhere."

"I'm sure he'll turn up," Jessica said. So he and Doug really must have made it through the door after all. Good for Doug. "It's not important," she said. "I'm sure I'll bump into him soon enough. Did you get my message? Have you gotten ahold of my sister?" Jessica pulled out her phone. "She hasn't answered my texts. I mean I expected when I got back, I'd get a dozen all at once."

"Back?" said Gary.

"From the woods. You know, in cell phone range. But nothing."

"So she must be doing all right," Gwen said. "I'm sure she'll contact us if she gets into trouble. She's all right, isn't she?"

Gary darted a look at his wife.

Jessica remembered how Gwen always insisted people look out for themselves, even if that meant seeking the help they needed.

"She just needs a push sometimes," said Jessica.

Gwen only smiled.

That just went to show that the whole burden was still on her. But how do you do two things at once? Should she go after Doug and Charlie or after Izzy and Amanda? The most important thing was to help Izzy and Amanda, but what was the best way to do it? If Gary wasn't going to contact her, then she'd have to do it herself. But that might mean running down to Manchester and seeing her mother, which meant confronting her mother, and that was something she'd certainly put off if she could. On the other hand, maybe the best thing she could do for Isabelle and Amanda was still to go back through the closet and help Doug and Charlie look for Buddy. What were the chances those two could find that crazy dwarf without her help? Well, maybe Charlie could, but Doug would probably weigh him down. And anyway, weren't three people better than two in a search?

Still, she wished Isabelle would call or text or something.

"You look anxious," said Gwen. "Something wrong?"

Jessica put down the knife. "I think I better call my sister."

From the hallway, she heard Gwen commenting on a bad smell. Gary worried it might be the septic tank, he'd have a look as soon as he could. "But at least it's only Doug," he said, sounding relieved.

Jessica didn't know what that meant.

Isabelle still didn't answer her phone.

Jessica rushed up the stairs and back down to the secret room. No one was in the hallway, so she quickly ducked into the closet and fumbled in the back for the door.

She searched the room for a book of Grimms' fairytales. One of the easiest books to find in a place like this. Pulling an old volume with wonderful pen and ink illustrations, she sat in the well of the gump-couch across from the still reeking dungeon clothes and flipped through the pages.

"Could be worse," she sighed to herself. "At least it wasn't the world of Hans Christian Anderson. That dude was one weirdo." But then again, it must be hard being ugly and rejected by the all women you love. At least the Grimm brothers ended most of their tales sort of happily ever after. That's what she needed to focus on, happy endings.

With that thought in mind, she approached the doorway. With her eyes shut tight and the words "happy ending" on her lips, she stepped forward.

She felt the cold wind blow from behind as she opened her eyes to a quaint village street. The wardrobe had taken her much closer to civilization than usual, practically in the middle of a town in fact. But nothing the wardrobe did surprised her anymore. It was like a computer that way—always seeming to guess what you really want to do, rarely getting it right. She didn't recognize the place at all. Perhaps this little hamlet was not an important part of a fairytale. The portal door seemed to be part of a fence surrounding a small wooden cottage.

She ventured a few feet down the street. Tile roofs, cobblestone streets, horses, and wagons—could be a Grimm village. But which one?

BUDISTILTSKIN STARED BACK at the village, holding the rough burlap sack he'd pulled from his head. He had not followed the townsfolks' instructions, had neither walked far enough nor waited long enough before removing the sack, but, as he had expected, they had left the gate and returned to their own endeavors, and he was on his own.

The curse had stayed with him. Everywhere he went fire would not burn. The people had declared him a wizard—and almost revered him as such until they found he could not control the power. Then they feared for their lives. Taking the chance that he would be angry and smite them, as any evil wizard would, several men had jumped upon him, beat him to the ground and tied him with rough ropes.

Now Budistiltskin was at a loss. He couldn't return home until the curse was lifted, and if anyone knew of his condition they would chase him off as these people had done. He couldn't even go to his cousin Jack. His plan to apprentice himself to the furniture maker must be set aside until he could cure himself of this curse. He couldn't well stay in Jack's house or anyone else's. A houseguest who keeps putting out your fireplace and your candles and cookstove—it would be worse than having a guest who kept eating all your food.

A noise from beyond the hill drew his attention. A remarkable white coach was rattling toward him along the cobbles—remarkable because it was white, as white as an eggshell, because it was almost tall enough to stand in (the coach of a very rich person), because it was pulled by two identical white horses, and because it was here at all. In fact Buddy had rarely seen a coach before. Only the best people had them. Perhaps this was the prince. The oddest thing about it, which he noticed as it drew closer, was the coachman. He was dressed in black, with a tall black hat and a face so much in shadow he might have been nothing but an empty suit of clothes. Budistiltskin stepped back and prepared to bow. To his surprise, the coachman pulled upon the reigns and slowed the beasts.

Budy looked up as the curtain closed and opened again in the coach window. It was dimly lit inside but there was no mistaking the face that looked out at him. Large cold eyes glared out from the window.

"Oh, color my yoke purple—it *is* you? I was right, wasn't I? Of course I was."

"That would depend on who you believe me to be," replied the young man.

"That sounds like something *I* might say," harrumphed the white face. "You're that boy that came here years ago that had that irritating little girl looking for you. You're older, but I am an egg who doesn't forget a face, and I say you are he."

Buddy was amazed at the ability of Humpty Dumpty to recognize him after all these years. "Yes, I'm him."

"No," said the egg man, "*him* is something you certainly are not."

Budistiltskin shook his head in confusion, "But I am. I *am* him. I'm Budistiltskin."

"Nonsense. You may well be 'Budistiltskin,' as you say, and you may be *he,* but you are certainly not *him*. Or have we now exiled the predicate nominative along with everything else, launched it through a magical doorway perhaps, hmmm? Galumphing off with the Jabberwock, perhaps?"

"All right. I'll be he, if you like."

"It has nothing to do with what I *like*, young man."

"I *am* Budistiltskin. Isn't that what you are asking?"

"Don't change the subject."

"But that is…. What are you doing here? This isn't Mother Goose Land. How did even you get here? Are you allowed to be here?"

"Allowed? Allowed by whom? I am a free-range egg, am I not? Do as I please, go where I please. Moreover, I have an invitation from the prince of this hamlet to come to dine. I am well respected in many of the fairy worlds, you know."

Budy didn't feel his questions were being adequately answered. But there were more pressing matters. "As long as you are here, maybe you can help me?"

"That is decidedly *not* why I am here. Here to dine with the prince. Thought I made that clear," Humpty Dumpty sat back and pushed the little curtain back over the window.

Budy pretended not to notice. "I realize that is not why you came, but you did come, and you do know me, and I do need help."

The door opened. "Oh, all right then. Come in and tell me your problems, everyone always does, eventually," sighed the egg. "Perhaps the prince will extend you the courtesy of a seat at table, although it would stain his reputation to do so. Or better yet, perhaps I will tell the prince you are my footman."

"No, no, no. I cannot go into the village," the young man stammered.

"I'm sure you meant to say hamlet," said the egg almost to himself.

"I have just been thrown out at the gates. I have a curse on me and..."

Humpty Dumpty leapt to his spindly legs, "A curse! I allowed a cursed man in my coach? Out out out—"

"Relax, you ridiculous egg. It won't hurt *you*," said Budy.

"Ridiculous? Ridiculous? You call me a ridiculous egg, and yet you want my help? You insult me and curse me and yet you entreat my assistance? You may have a thing or two to learn about rhetoric, young man."

"I didn't mean to insult you. I'm sorry. But there is no curse on you. And my curse is not contagious—as far as I know. Somehow I have a spell on me that prevents fire from burning when I am near it. That's all it is." Budistiltskin placed his hands on Humpty Dumpty's shoulders and eased him back down on the seat.

"As far as you know? Hmm. Well, sounds safe enough I suppose. For me I mean. Pretty deadly for you, I'm afraid. No fire, you say? Never use the stuff myself. Bad for the lungs—and no picnic for the yoke either—nor the white now that I think of it, which, by the bye, I prefer to call the clear. Still, must make bath time interesting, especially this time of year. What was it? Insult a witch, did you? Caught stealing from a wizard, perhaps?"

"Nothing like that. I was home and a fire started, and I got frightened and wished it would go out, and it did. Boy, did it go out. Never had any magic in me before. Ma and Pa have tried to teach me magic for years, but nothing. Then this happened. I need to find a real magic worker to remove the spell or I can't go home."

"No, certainly not, not if we take that *à la lettre*. Won't be welcome anywhere else either, I'll wager," the egg said with a smirk.

"You know everyone, can you help me?" asked Budistiltskin.

"I don't know everyone. No one knows everyone. But I do know a great many people, not to mention dwarfs, eggs, and a few kings. Some know magic. The Blue Fairy comes to mind. And the witch..., ah, no, but she's dead right now. Snow White's stepmother, Cinderella's fairy godmother—or is it her dead mother the tree in this version? Always get those mixed up. Either way, she shouldn't be too far from here."

"The Blue Fairy? Oh, I bet she could help. I met her, sorta, years ago. Have any idea where I might find her?"

"Tough one to find. Only in one book, and a weird one at that. Her magic is odd, but her knowledge of magic is impressive." Humpty placed his fist under his mouth where his chin would have been if he'd had one. This gave him the appearance of thinking. "Still, it seems to me something more local, first. Crossing willy-nilly from one world to another—draws attention one doesn't always want if you know what I mean."

Budy did not know what he meant. But conversing with Humpty Dumpty was so much like going down rabbit holes, he decided he didn't want to know.

After a few moments of silence, the egg man made a decision. "I suppose I'll need an excuse to get away from the prince anyway," he said. "Yes, I know what you're thinking, 'but you just seemed so proud of the honor.' Yes, it is an honor to be invited to dine with a prince. But it is an honor one cannot refuse, which makes it not so absolutely unlike a curse. And this prince has—how shall it be said?—a certain reputation."

"A certain reputation?"

"Let's just say he doesn't order eggs to dinner out of boredom. Since I can't bring you into his castle, I shall make my visit as short as can be without insult to His Majesty or threat to myself, and return to this spot on the road, and then we'll see if I might recall how to find where some eleemosynary magic worker may be."

"What?"

"Look it up."

The coach stopped. Budy wanted to know how far the egg man was going to accompany him to find this eleeosomething magician. But he wouldn't answer Budy's question as he invited the young man out of his coach, saying, "by this door, please, not that one."

Budy decided he didn't need to know why the egg was so particular about doors. "I'll wait right here, Mr. Dumpty," he said as the coach pulled away.

"Mr. Dumpty… I like that." The egg sat back and closed his eyes and brushed the curtain over the window closed.

"WHAT DID YOU SAY?" asked Charlie.

"Are you from the Merica?"

Charlie and Doug looked at each other.

"I know we're dressed strangely," said Charlie.

"Aye," said Richard Smith, "and hast strange speech."

"Actually we're from…" Doug began, but Charlie cut him off.

"I'm sure you've never heard of where we're from," said Charlie.

Richard Smith was not convinced that was true.

"Thank you for helping us get free of the mob," said Charlie, "but we are in kind of a hurry."

Richard's imposing frame stood firmly between Doug and Charlie and the door. "Do not fear that I shall discover you to the prince," he said. "Do you deny you come from the Merica?"

"Well, actually..." said Doug. But Charlie grabbed his arm and squeezed it with such force that Doug decided he'd better find out what was bothering the young man before he said more.

"I must speak with you on a theme of great moment," Richard said.

"We are *quite* busy right now," Charlie said. "Perhaps another time?"

"'Twill be but short. If you will kindly meet me in the tavern anon, we might speak over a flagon of ale."

"Gary tells me you never turn down ale," said Doug.

"We are *really* in an *awful* hurry," Charlie said with gritted teeth.

"I shall pay for the ale. In truth, it shall take but a moment. Let me but bank my fire. The tavern is hard by, yonder, at the sign of the barrel."

"Works for me," said Doug.

"Okay, fine," said Charlie, "we'll meet you in the tavern but only for a few minutes."

The blacksmith rushed off to bank his fire. As soon as Doug and Charlie were in the street, Doug turned his feet toward the tavern.

"Where are you going?" asked Charlie.

"To the tavern."

"Don't be ridiculous." Charlie caught up to him.

"You don't want to see the inside of a medieval tavern? Raise a flagon of mead? I wonder if it's like *Beowulf*."

"You've seen what they do to wizards here. One thing I've learned in the Grimms' world is don't interfere, and don't trust anyone. Besides, it'll be dark before you know it and I'd just as soon not spend another night in the open when we are no closer to finding Rumpelstiltskin or Jessica or a way home."

"And I'll bet we can get some bread and cheese out of this Smith and perhaps a place to stay."

"Adventure starting to get to you?"

"Nothing a drink and a hunk of cheese couldn't solve, my friend."

"Listen, close, Dougy. 'Trust no one.' This guy's acting weird. I think he suspects us of something."

"He said he wouldn't turn us in."

"Which is exactly what he'd say if he was going to turn us in," Charlie huffed.

"Not that I know what it would mean to be turned in—I mean, for what? Wearing funny clothes?"

By this time they were just across from the sign of the barrel. They could see in through the window. The room was sparsely filled. There would be no way to remain inconspicuous in there. Doug stopped.

"He thinks we're from a place called 'Thumerica,'" he said. "But he must mean '*A*merica,' don't you think?"

"Don't be crazy," said Charlie, nodding Doug to keep walking.. "How could someone from a folk tale that is God knows how many centuries old possibly know about America, let alone infer that we are from there? There has got to be some obscure Grimm story set in some place called 'Thumerica.'"

Charlie grabbed Doug's shirt sleeve and pulled him along down a side street away from the tavern. As soon as they were out of sight, Doug said, "I've read every Grimm story there is. And I don't remember any such place."

"You've got a mob hunting for wizards and a random blacksmith pretending he knows who we are. My spidey sense is tingling."

"I thought you wanted to see Cinderella."

"Not as a prisoner of the royal guards. Besides, I doubt she'd even recognize me. It's too dangerous."

Doug crossed his arms and stared at Charlie.

"What?"

"I'm here to have an adventure. You seem to be here to avoid one. You're like a guy that goes to Paris and never leaves his hotel room. Is this how you acted all those times you sneaked through the closet? Marching through the forest staring at your feet? What are you here for if you don't want to have an adventure?"

"I've had my fill of adventures, thanks. I've had more than enough fairyland. I only came through the door to help Jessica. I'm here to find Buddy. That's it."

"Well, why not say 'hi' to your girlfriend on the way?"

"And then what? She's married. And she was never my girlfriend. So even if I wanted to be here, I just don't think that should be our focus right now. We've got Jessica, Isabelle, Amanda, and Buddy—lots of things higher on the list than visiting old flames that were never flames or doing the private errands of a crazy man."

"Is that friendly concern of just cold feet?"

"Whatever. Look, not only do we still have to find Rumpelstiltskin and a way home, *you* also have to get back to your wife while you still have one," said Charlie.

"There will be time for that."

"You don't know that."

"Well forgive me if I'm reluctant to charge into a hornet's nest."

But Charlie resumed walking and now Doug was struggling to keep up. Charlie found a gate that lead them back into the forest.

Outside the town, looking back over the wall, it was obvious that the walk around Grumbottem with its modest castle would be quite long. Twilight was upon them when the wall finally fell out of sight. They were hungry and tired. Still, Doug had resumed his high spirits, and Charlie was tired of chastising him.

"What I don't understand," said Doug, "is how you could *not* want to come through that door every chance you get. I mean I understand you might think there are real dangers."

"There *are* real dangers here."

"But that's not it, is it? That's not why you didn't want to come with us. You can't tell me you've had enough of this." He gestured to the woods.

"Yes, I can. I've had enough. I'm sorry. I didn't want to tell Gary, but that's what it is. That's what I learned in England. I'm stuck—as an artist and as a person. I'm stuck. And it's because of this place. I've spent my whole life here. When I wasn't physically here, I was thinking about it. When I couldn't go back through the door, I went to England to see the old world."

"England?"

"Ich spreche kein Deutsch. It's time for me to find new things."

"That's an awfully odd thing to say. I mean, you voluntarily came back to OzHouse after England. It's *Oz*House. Who goes to the woods to avoid nature?"

"Well, as for that, I'm also broke."

Doug looked at Charlie, then glanced off into the woods. They walked a ways in silence as the moon and the evening star appeared. "Do you suppose that wizard the townspeople evicted might have helped us?" Doug asked.

"Never a good idea to befriend a wizard that the locals hate. They're not all like the Wizard of Oz. Some are hell bent on proving their powers by hurting people. Forget about wizards. Look for the poor and lowly. They are far more likely to help us."

"You mean like Cinderella?"

"Shut up," said Charlie.

Doug laughed.

As they rounded a hill, they saw a small cottage. A steady stream of smoke rose from the chimney.

"Maybe these people are poor or lowly," said Doug.

"Huh? Oh, yeah, guess they would be. Perhaps they'll offer us a bite to eat. But don't be pushy, let's try some tact here."

"You sound like Beth."

The woman who answered Charlie's knock wore patched clothes and had her hair tightly hidden under a ragged cap.

"Good evening, Ma'am," Charlie smiled. She looked at these strangely dressed men and smiled politely back. "My friend and I are travelers from a faraway land, and seem to have lost our way."

"Very far away, I am sure," said the woman.

"No doubt you have noticed our clothes. Yes, they are odd. We, uh, we found these things and since our own clothes were worn beyond use by our travels, we borrowed them. Not quite the fashion we are used to either."

"Borrowed? Most likely stole. But they are the strangest bits of attire I have ever seen, so I doubt anyone would want them back. You folks in need of a drink of water?"

"Yes, Ma'am, that would be very nice. The road is dusty."

Doug was thrilled with the furnishings in the little home. It looked just as he would have expected in a fairytale, rustic but well built and very clean. Handspun fabric hung in the windows and a crocheted table runner was placed on the oak slabs that served as the main dining table. After the drink of water, the woman offered the travelers a trencher of bread and cheese.

Unfortunately, the woman knew nothing of anyone named Rumpelstiltskin. Had never even heard the strange name. And as for the cottage Charlie described, well, that could be any cottage in the forest, she told them. She could offer no help.

When Charlie mentioned heading off, the woman looked surprised.

"It is already dark. Not safe on the road after dark. I don't have any extra beds, but if you'll get a pallet from the shed you can sleep near the fire."

"A bit early for bed though," said Doug, though he was tired from walking.

"Night comes early this time of year," the woman said as she moved her chair from the center of the room.

Doug noticed there were no candles or lamps in the room, the only light came from the fireplace. People here must go to sleep when it gets dark and rise with the sun, which is really more sensible when you think about it he decided. With many thanks, he and Charlie headed out to the shed to find a pallet.

"Living up to your expectations?" Charlie asked.

"Well, they're not accommodations I would have preferred, but, yes, this place is great. And her accent is wonderful. I have to find a way to remember that for my next book."

Somewhere near, a wolf howled.

"Hurry up," called the woman from the doorway. "Didn't you hear that? The wolf is hungry tonight."

Without delay the two men carried a large pallet stuffed with straw across the yard and into the house.

"Wolves are an often maligned animal," Doug observed. "They are not so much the villain as the victim of human cruelty."

"Interesting belief you got there. But in the Forest of Grimm, we stay in when the wolf is hungry."

"Thank you very much for your kindness," Charlie said to the woman, making a face at Doug as he lay down.

"In these times we must all help each other. Keep the door well locked during the night, though you think this poor old wolf is misunderstood," she said as she entered her small bedroom and closed the door.

"Careful of the twenty-first century thinking, Doug. This is an old-fashioned fairytale. Wolves are not an endangered species."

"Okay, okay, I get the point. So what do I do if I have to go during the night? I'm no spring chicken, you know. This ol' bladder won't lie still eight hours in a row. No bathroom, I suppose?"

"Not for about 200 years, I'd guess. Go outside if you need to go."

"What about the wolf?" Doug asked.

"Let him find his own place to pee," Charlie smiled as he lay back down and closed his eyes.

CHAPTER TEN

Carte de Menu
Pour le repas du M. H. Dumpty, esquire
chez le très Charmant Prince de Grumbottem

SALADE: Salade du chef
LE COURSE PREMIER: Eier In Gruner Sosse
LE SECONDARIE: Svenska Turkiet Köttbullar med äggnudlar
LE DESERT: Lemon Custard

A WIDE PAINTED SMILE HUNG on Humpty Dumpty's face as he put down the menu and stared up at the prince.

"And is your lovely bride not to be joining us this evening?" asked the egg at last.

The prince took no notice. "Je suis sur que vous amierez tous," he said, snapping his fingers to call for the salad.

Humpty glanced back at the menu. "My Swedish is a little rusty."

"Quelle est dans un nom?" said the prince. "Est-ce-que vous voulez plusier vin?" The host held up the bottle.

"Oh, I may need a lot of that." Humpty Dumpty twirled the stem of his glass between his fingers.

"Je suis heureux que vous êtes venus me voir, Monsieur Dumpty," the prince's speech had a heavy German accent.

Humpty Dumpty scratched his shell. "You're happy that... what?"

He found French difficult enough when spoken with a French accent.

"...que vous êtes venus me voir, Monsieur."

Well, he might have been determined to be polite, but this was not going to work: "I'm not French, you know," he said.

"Non?" The prince looked startled. "Alors, vous êtes ... euh ... quoi, exactement?"

"Goose, I suppose. You did notice I was speaking an entirely different language, didn't you?"

"Hmmm?" the prince seemed to reflect back on the conversation. "Now that you mention it, I suppose you were. Too bad, really. Hoped I'd have a chance to lay out my rusty Français," the prince laughed. "How's your Danish, by the way?"

"Let's see, ah, windmill, sabotage—no, no, that's Dutch. No, I guess it's no better than my German."

"Wat schande. Doel, vielleicht spielt es keine Rolle."

Humpty Dumpty screwed up his mouth and wrinkled his brow and rolled his eyes. But it did no good. He had no idea what the prince was talking about. In fact he wasn't quite sure what language he was talking it in, and the prince could no more read the egg's confusion on his face than a blind man could. And yet the prince was looking straight at him.

"As I was saying," the prince tented his fingers, "I am so glad you agreed to come to visit me. I was worried. I'd heard you had a bad experience of Grimmsworld some years ago, and I feared you would not answer my invitation."

"Ha," he laughed, as though he'd had an option, "so you have heard of my little adventure?" Humpty Dumpty paused. "I admit it, I once foolishly followed a silly girl into your forest. Don't recall what possessed me to do that—quite horrendously out of character for me, I do say. But no matter. I'm sure I'll never run into that one again." He attempted a chuckle. The prince's expression did not change.

"And now I hear you are quite the traveler since those days. Indeed, the story I hear is that you have appeared in world after world, yes?"

Humpty Dumpty grew wary.

"Some even say," the prince went on, "there is a door somewhere in the vicinity of your Geese Land that was missed during what you might call the great destruction."

Humpty Dumpty stared ahead a moment without speaking. At last he chuckled, "Just a rumor, I'm sure." The egg man's laugh was nervous.

"Perhaps," said the prince. "Not that a cautious egg such as yourself would use such a door in a manner ill-advised or even reckless? After all, there's no way to control the doorway is there? I mean from all I've heard. it takes you where *it* wants, never where *you* want. You could end up where, I don't know, where egg-sucking dragons live."

Humpty Dumpty bristled. "Oh, I don't know. Not that I am saying there is such a door, but if there *were* I don't doubt there are some of us with better abilities to control it than others."

"How did you get *here,* by the way?"

Humpty Dumpty cleared his throat, forked aside a hardboiled egg, filled his mouth with lettuce and chewed, and smiled, and swallowed. "I'm sure you have heard of 'The Pumpkin Eater's Wife'?"

The prince shook his head.

"Oh, sure you have—little sequel to the rhyme?" But the prince gave a minute shake of his head. Humpty Dumpty improvised:

> *Peter, Peter Pumpkin eater*
> *Thought a pumpkin shell would keep her.*
> *And so he closed the door and locked it*
> *And kept the key in his own pocket.*
> *And easy as the stars went round*
> *He dreamt of things that come and go*
> *That kiss the wind or hit the ground*
> *And never thought of the window.*

The prince shook his head, "Not among your jauntier rhymes."

"Every door is a portal," Humpty Dumpty waved a finger like a teacher. "But not every portal is a door."

The prince smiled to hide his confusion. "Let me get to the point," he said. "Supposing there were such a portal, as you call it, and supposing there were a character who had the ability to control where it took him, might that character not be able to get—let's say *something*— to get something from another world and carry it into, say, this one, Mr. Egg?"

The prince raised his eyebrows. The flames on the candles dimmed; the fire in the fireplace shrunk as though it were afraid of something and wanted to hide, and the room grew cold. The prince's face became a mask of strange shadows designed to affright. Humpty Dumpty gripped the table and scanned the room. All this happened quickly. And then the candle flames grew tall again and the fire blazed. The mask fell from the prince's face.

"Must be an open window somewhere," the prince smiled.

Humpty Dumpty looked around. There were no windows to open. He tried unconvincingly to give back an equal smile to the prince. "If there were such a door that still worked," the egg finally said, "and if there were a gentleman of sufficient means who wished to use the door for… for riches or power, say," the egg went on, "I would split my shell to talk him out of it. Bad, bad things happened the last time. I think if there were such a person as you speak of and if he could travel as he wished between the worlds, he would be careful of where he put the doorways and would even take the trouble to insure no doorways were left behind him when he left."

"You misunderstand me, my friend." But the prince seemed to be contemplating new possibilities of such a doorway. "I must be frank. My new wife, God bless her, did not come without some, er, ah—let us call them blemishes."

"Blemishes?"

"She was a scullery wench, I knew that. I admit I was blinded, as it were, for a time, by her beauty, her dancing, her laughter, and those adorable golden shoes."

"Golden?"

Just then the sound of heavy slippers could be heard at the doorway. It was followed quickly by a voice saying, "O, there you are." And in swept the princess herself, the former Cinderella. Humpty Dumpty rose and smiled politely. "Heard you were coming," said the princess in reply as she plopped herself into a chair and put her feet up on the long table. And indeed her slippers were golden.

"Must have read the wrong version," muttered the egg man. And then he said in a louder voice, "That reminds me Princess Cinder..."

"Uh, uh, uh, my good egg," said the prince. "We do not use that name."

"Oh, lay off," said the princess. "Name's a name." Then she turned to Humpty Dumpty, looked him straight in the eye, "Call me what you like. No harm in a word. I used to hate it, I know. But now I'm a princess." And then, as though that subject were exhausted, she went on. "Oh, the day I've had. Don't have a clue why I let those dreadful sisters of mine come to live with us."

"Nor do I, my dear," the prince forced a smile.

"You'd think misfortune would've humbled them a little. But no. It's still, 'Cinderella this' and 'Cinderella that.' As though a princess didn't have anything better to do than help a blind woman pick out her clothes. But hey, I see you guys are busy."

"Business, my love," said the prince.

"Well nice to meet you, Mr. Dumpty. I do hope I get an invitation to your next dinner party, dear husband." The princess pulled her feet off the table.

"Yes, yes, no doubt. Certainly. In fact what I had wanted to say..."

"Oh, look at the time," said the princess, heading for the door.

"I believe Mr. Egg is trying to say something to you my dear," the prince called loudly.

"Well, why doesn't he speak up then?" said the princess. "What is it, sir?"

"Oh, I was just wondering. I have been looking to consult with a magical worker on a matter of some importance. I wonder if you might introduce me to your fairy godmother."

"My who? Oh, yes. Her. I'm afraid I haven't seen her in years and years."

"Oh?"

"Well, not since before the wedding, anyway. I used to meet her at my mother's grave. But once I got married..."

"... she stopped showing up?" Humpty Dumpty speculated.

"Actually, I stopped going. She may still be there for all I know. What use do I have for fairy godmothers when I have a kingdom? Anyway, tout à l'heure, boys."

She bowed in a way that was both awkward and perfunctory and then swept herself out of the room.

"You see what I mean," said the prince when she was gone. "Now I have read of a certain princess very different from my Cinder Princess, one so true she stirs all night from the prick of a little vegetable placed beneath a mountain of mattresses. And so, to the point: I want you to find this princess and to fetch her here so she can teach my Aschenputtel a thing or two about being a true princess."

"Ashen poodle?" Humpty Dumpty scratched his head.

"A much better name than Cinderella to my ears."

Humpty Dumpty made a number of comic gestures with his hands as he processed the great quantity of information that had just been tossed in his direction. Finally he just let it out: "You want me to kidnap a princess?"

"Call it what you like," said the prince.

At just that moment a servant ran in yelling something to the prince in rapid German. The prince sprang up, "Oh, ho, we are in for some fun. Come Mr. Dumpty, apparently a wolf is out of doors chasing a man."

"Budy."

"Come, let us join the chase."

Humpty Dumpty held up his hands, "These limbs were meant for other sport than chasing I'm afraid," and then he mumbled, "or kidnapping for that matter."

"As you wish," the prince headed to the door. "But consider my request. You will of course be richly rewarded. I will be in touch."

The prince ran out the door. Humpty Dumpty pushed his plate aside and went to the hallway so he could look out a window. It was very dark. He had stayed with the prince longer than he should have. Now very likely Budy was out there running from a wolf. But which one was the prince out to catch?

SOMETHING ABOUT THAT STRANGE new woman who was hanging about the house made Debbie put down her book and stare into the hallway. The woman had stuck her head into the Persian Room where *she* was trying to read a book. She'd looked around with her baggy clothes and wet hair and without saying a word walked away. That was rude. Debbie had been told by her social worker that there was something very unusual—"strange but probably not dangerous" were her exact words—about the people you find in this *Odd*house. Her social worker assured her that she would try to get her out of it as soon as possible. So Debbie had been prepared for oddness, though not quite for this much oddness, but she had not been prepared for rudeness. These people did not like rules. But rules are what give life order and make it meaningful. How many times had her mother told her that? These people were like her father. That's what her mother would have said. They *say* there are rules, but they don't follow them. They have supper any time between 5:15 and 8:00 o'clock at night, instead of at 5:45, which is the proper time for supper, just late enough to be hungry but not so late you won't have time for evening relaxation before bed—which is why it was the time she and her mother had always had supper. Her father had always ignored rules, and schedules, and common sense. Her father had left when Debbie was little. She had not seen him in a long time. No one even knew where he was. "Typical," her mother had said. "Off gallivanting." Debbie's memories didn't quite match her mother's descriptions. But mothers are always right. Debbie mostly remembered him laughing, playing games, and making toys. But her mother told her memories are unreliable. Her mother had talked about him a lot, had told her so many times about how he wouldn't come home from work sometimes until the supper was cold and wouldn't put his dirty clothes in the hamper but just threw them on the floor beside the bed so she had to clean up after him like a naughty child—oh, and he didn't cap the toothpaste, and didn't mow the lawn for weeks on end, and, well, he just did a thousand things like that. Her mother told her so many stories that Debbie felt like her own memories of sitting at the TV watching old cartoons or playing Pokémon card games her dad made up or playing "round-the-world" croquet, which was a game that went all the way around the house that they made up together—these were probably just made up memories. Those things didn't really happen. And the lesson her mother always drew was that if her father had just followed rules, if he'd had the common sense that God gave geese, he would have stayed.

Would that have kept her mother from getting sick? Would she still be alive? Maybe not. But it would have meant that when they took her mom away, Debbie wouldn't have to be alone—or be put with odd people that didn't understand rules. And now this new woman with wet hair sticks her head in the doorway and looks around and sees her very plainly reading a book on the couch and doesn't even say a polite hello.

Debbie listened down the hall to voices in the kitchen. This new woman was talking to Mr. and Mrs. Robbins. She couldn't quite hear what she was saying, but it sounded to Debbie as though she was trying not to help make supper. But when you are staying with someone in their house and they ask you to make supper, you should do that.

Debbie picked up her book again and tried to read the story of the fairy princess who was cursed with lightness and giggled way too much, but she could not stop thinking of the strange, rude, and really kind of smelly woman. Besides this book could not hold her interest: it was too much like the kind of books they had in this place. She'd sampled several. What was the point of books filled with dashing princes and giddy princesses? They weren't very American. And what was up with all the magic? Magic wasn't real. Yes, no wonder this house and this country were in trouble, which she assumed they were. We need believable, American stories. That's what her mother would have said. If people must read made-up stories why not read stories that would help them live their lives?

As she was thinking these things, the strange woman rushed by the doorway again and did not look back in. Debbie yelled, "Hey." But when the woman didn't come back, she ran after her. She followed her down the hall. She called out to her again, but the woman was calling someone on her cell phone and she was walking fast, and she was ignoring Debbie yelling "excuse me." By the time Debbie got upstairs, the woman had turned the corner and was running down the long front hallway. Debbie walked faster. She didn't run, because you're not supposed to run in a house. And then the woman did a very funny thing. Something that was certainly against the rules (some rules are unstated rules her mother told her, you just know them)—the woman opened a door and went into a closet. Like a little kid trying to hide from the grownups. Debbie was certainly going to have a word with this strange woman.

She opened the door to the closet.

No one was there. Just a bunch of coats.

Debbie backed up and looked both ways down the hallway. She looked to the left of the closet and to the right of the closet. There was no other door. There was no other place the woman could be. But she wasn't in the closet.

Just then the back of the closet opened, revealing, for just a second a very colorful place. And the woman came rushing toward her so that Debbie thought she was going to knock her off her feet. She put her arms in front of her face. And then Debbie blinked. And there was no one there. Just coats, fluttering.

THE HEADLIGHTS' BEAM travelled across the wall in the Library of Alexandria where Gwen was reading to Jennie and Caleb and Trisha. A car must have come up the driveway. Cars didn't just drive by OzHouse. If you saw headlights on the walls, someone was coming up the long driveway to the house to see them. Gwen called Gary on his cell (he was looking through the house for Debbie, who apparently didn't want to join in bedtime book club this evening), "Are we getting another child?" Gwen said into her phone.

"Oh, yeah, forgot to mention it. I got a call from DCYF. They had to take a girl from a dangerous situation. It was pretty sudden. It's just precautionary, I think."

"So we've got five kids now and no Beth, and where is Doug?"

"Yeah, business is booming. It's almost like old times."

Gwen gave the book to the children, and ran down to the back entrance. "Well, they're here," she said.

Gary gave up the search for Debbie for the moment and joined Gwen at the door where a police officer the Robbinses knew well was ringing the bell. She had a little girl clinging to her chest. They opened the door. The officer smiled.

"Her name's Amanda," she said.

CHILLED AND HALF ASLEEP, CHARLIE reached down for a blanket, but found none. It must have fallen onto the floor. The room was pitch dark. The numbers on his clock were not glowing. The power must have gone out. Drowsily, he reached up for the light switch. His arm went through the wall. Or rather, there was no wall. The wall was missing.

He bolted awake—and remembered where he was.

"Doug?" he whispered.

He reached over to where Doug was supposed to be. No Doug. And the place was cold. Charlie shivered terribly and reached around himself in the blackness to find a blanket. He'd fallen asleep so close to the fire that he hadn't needed the blanket the old woman had set aside for them. But what had happened to the fire? Even if it had died down, the coals should still be glowing. He couldn't even figure out what direction the fireplace was in. That's how dark it was. "Doug?" he whispered aloud again.

Still no answer.

Well this was strange, and a little frightening. Strange things do happen in Grimm, but nothing like this that he could recall had ever happened to him. He felt like a man who'd lost his body, who floated somewhere in dark space, an incorporeal consciousness like one might feel after death when the soul has no bodily organs and therefore cannot see. Had he been transported in his sleep to some other part of this dangerous world? He felt for the pallet. He exhaled in relief at the feel of the rough wood beneath his hand. All right, so he knew he was on a pallet in the middle of a room—unless, unless the pallet too had been magiced away to the middle of the woods—transported by some Grimm wizard. Or perhaps the devil. The devil was certainly out looking for him. Could the devil do such things? Perhaps he could. It was not out of the question.

Or was he dead? Is this what death is like?

No, he could not be dead. True, he couldn't see, but he still could feel. He did still have the uncomfortable pallet under him. He felt the floor beneath the pallet. So he was still in the room. So he was certainly *not* transported to the woods or floating in space. He touched his body to make sure he still had a body. It was there all right. He brought his finger so close to his eye he almost touched it. He pressed the bridge of his nose. But he still could not see the finger. Somewhere a wolf howled. So he could hear as well. He was just in a dark dark room.

"Douuuuug?" he whispered and kind of sang. Maybe this kind elderly woman was a cruel old hag. Maybe she'd eaten Doug.

The door creaked slowly open. Charlie sat as quiet as a cat—except that his heart beat loud enough for a predator to hear.

"Charlie," a voice whispered.

"Doug?"

The door eased closed.

"Say something so I can find the bed. My God, I've never seen anything as dark as this in my life."

"Where were you?"

"Where was I? Exactly where I told you I'd be. I'm a middle-aged white guy. I haven't slept all night in ten years."

"No wolves out there, I guess."

"I don't know. I'm pretty sure there was something moving. I wasn't going to find out what it was."

Charlie let out a sigh. His heart slowed. A shiver ran through him. "What's 'white' got to do with it?"

"Probably nothing, really. I'm no expert."

Doug fumbled his way to the pallet, groped for the blanket and spread it over them.

"What happened to the fire?" Charlie asked.

"It was burning when I left."

Charlie crawled off the pallet and went to where he now remembered the fireplace was. He reached in and bumped his hand on an andiron. There was no heat. He buried his hand in the ashes. Not even warm. He found dry logs partly burned. He could feel the charcoal as well as the wood. They were as cold as the floor.

"How long were you out there?"

"What?"

"Never mind, we need to get this fire started."

"In the dark?"

"You got any matches?"

"Who carries matches?"

"Oh, never mind," and a flame erupted in front of Charley's face.

"Why do you have matches?" asked Doug.

Charlie looked around by the dim light of the match for something to ignite.

A SMALL, WHITE BIRD, perched on a fence post, kept opening and closing its beak as though it were singing, but no sound could be heard. Perhaps that was a clue.

It's funny. Jessica used to think she knew exactly how the portal worked. Now, she was starting to think she had no idea how it worked. If there were rules (and there did still seem to be rules) the rules themselves seemed to constantly change. Or maybe they were just very very complicated. For one thing, it used to be she would enter a story any time or any place. Now it felt like the doorway would drop her off much closer to people and nearer the center of the action. Had the doorway changed? Or had she changed? Or was this just a random series of events that seemed like order? Perhaps it was, after all, too soon to tell, this being just her second trip through since she was a little girl. But still, it felt different. Maybe it changed because she was older, became more linear and less fantastical, the way dreams did. They say you can't fly in your dreams after a certain age—puberty was it? She hadn't flown in her dreams in years.

Well, wherever she was, this quaint little old-European looking town would not wait long to reveal itself to her.

A diligence clattered by. Jessica was always astonished by how natural such things felt when you were in a fairyland, as though she saw such things every day. And yet how strange it would be if such a contraption rattled by in America. A pretty ghastly looking man with a top hat and a very large nose stuck his head out the window and cast a look that Jessica could only interpret as disapproval. She must look like a penniless orphan to a man like that. Still, she was glad at her choice of clothing. This baggy shirt and a long skirt looked almost like they fit in this world.

"If I don't figure this out soon, it's straight back to OzHouse," she reminded herself as she reached the bottom of the street. To her left was a path that led down to a river. By the river were women gathering firewood. That too was probably a clue. But she only vaguely remembered the image. Was it Grimm? She kept walking. The path grew marshy and soon became a puddle of mud too wide to get around and certainly too deep to cross without getting her shoes wet. Clumps of muddy grass grew here and there like spots of hair on a mangy dog. That was probably a clue too, a clue, at least, that she'd gone as far as she was going to go. It was certainly time to turn back. She really didn't want to walk through the mud.

On the other hand, she looked down at her worse-than-muddy running shoes. Dirty as this mud was, it was probably cleaner than the unthinkable stuff already soaked and dried into these shoes from that dungeon. Walking through this mud puddle would, in fact, almost be like washing them, relatively speaking.

What a horrible thought.

But in she went. The day was warm. And she still did have to find Buddy—and help Izzy and Amanda. Love is a pain in the ass, she decided as she lifted her skirt and put her foot down into a spot she prayed was not as deep as it looked.

And in she sank. Down and down and down into the black, bubbling pool. It was like Alice in the Rabbit hole. But it was not Alice. This was not a rabbit hole. Oh, my God, she thought. She was pretty sure she knew where she was. And it was the worst possible story a person could wind up in. She thought all this, but she couldn't say it. She held her mouth tight to keep out first the muddy water and then the mud itself. In fact there was no doubt what world and what story she was in. It was the world of that weirdo—Andersen. She never should have thought his name back in the magic room: never, never, never. And it was the sickest story he ever wrote: "The Girl Who Trod on the Loaf."

This is just great, she thought as she held her breath on her way to where she was going, which was, of course, hell.

Hell, where that girl Inga or Inger—whatever it was—spent enough time for an innocent little girl to grow into an old old woman and die.

So much for hurrying back to OzHouse.

The thickening mud through which she sank coated her from head to foot and soaked into every shred of clothes from her sneakers to her underwear.

When she finally stopped and gasped and pushed the mud away from her face she found herself shivering in a dim, fire-lit room. She cleared what mud she could from her nose and eyes and spat it where it had pushed itself into her mouth and dug it with her pinkies from her ears. Then she looked around. In the distance of the great, fire-lit, cauldron-filled hall was a very large woman. Her shoulders rose and fell as she stirred one of what seemed to be an infinite number of huge vats. But what was in the vats? Jessica blew more mud from her nose. The stench. She should have left the mud in. The image of the marsh woman flooded back from the story like a bad memory—the marsh woman brewing vats of stench to scent the rotting grasses of the world. There was not a smell to match it anywhere in Jessica's experience. Sewers couldn't match it. Even the prison cell in Nottingham could not match it. It was worse than the smell of steeping, unflushed toilets, or wet outhouses baking in the sun—yes, worse even than if those outhouses had dead rats decomposing inside.

She put her mud-stained hand to her nose and gagged and heaved—and moved to run, but then she stood stock still. Through her flowing eyes she saw out of the vats of stench toads and fat frogs leaping. And all around her spiders were weaving webs that she had not noticed before, vast webs made visible by fetid water dripping off the fibers. "Oh, that man was sick," she whispered. She remembered, yes, Hans Christian Andersen used his stories to torture effigies of people who had hurt him in life. He imagined horrible punishments for them. And this Inga must have beaten his heart with a rolling pin, whoever she was. If Jessica ran to get away from the stench, she'd run right through these gigantic spider webs spotted with gigantic vibrating spiders hunting huge wingless flies.

And snakes. Dozens of snakes, white as bone and sliding up the firm ropes of the spider webs. Dozens and dozens. Snakes everywhere joined the frogs and the toads in the vats of stench and crawled with the spiders. Jessica held one hand over her face, plugging her nose, and the other over her throat as she trembled forward. The marsh woman turned and yelled across the room, "Hey, you there."

That was it. Jessica ran. She ran through spider webs, one after another. There was no climbing up through the mud to the surface, so she took the path she knew must lead her to hell, to the devil's oldemor—his great grandmother. Spiders clung to her. Frogs leaped into her hair. She nearly slipped for stepping on hard, round snakes under her soaked shoes, but she made it out, huffing. She made out of the reach of the reptiles and amphibians and spiders and into the dark corridors of hell.

Well, one good thing, the run warmed her, a little. But that lasted only for a moment. As soon as she stopped, the sweat she'd worked up made her all the colder. And there were spiders all over her clothes. She shook and flicked huge spiders off her clothes. But they clung to her fingers like June bugs so she had to pluck them off her clothes and throw them to the ground. It was awful, it was gross. But she'd been through a lot. She could handle it.

"So this is what happens when you don't care if you get your shoes wet," she said aloud. And she thought she heard a little laugh. But that only made her aware of the sad moan or hum echoing in the vast white frigid space. If it was hell, why was it cold?

The hallway was endless. It made her dizzy to look down it. And in the dim light she did not at first realize, it was full of people, nondescript gray souls milling anxiously about, grumbling and moaning. She looked away. To her left was a statue. Better to look at a statue than at the people wandering like zombies. The statue was a little girl, a filthy little girl. It was crawling with spiders and centipedes and beetles and wingless flies.

"What, no cockroaches?" But jokes could not lighten the mood in hell. Humor fell to the ground like lead.

And then she realized—and her eyes sank to the statue's foot. Sure enough, the girl was standing on a muddy loaf of bread. Jessica looked up at the eyes. And the eyes moved—first back and forth, then up and down, then all the way around and back. Then they stared down at Jessica. It was Inga or Inger. Jessica touched the cold leg. "If it's any help, I agree he was a little heavy handed with the punishment," she said to the statue. She remembered feeling annoyed at the thought that the poor pretty girl went to hell because she hadn't been corrected enough by grownups on earth. Jessica reached down to the loaf—which was still soft—and tore off a piece and lifted it to the mouth of the statue. The eyes still stared down—but with a look of anger not of gratitude, as though by her gesture Jessica were mocking the girl. The statue's mouth was solid and could not move. Only the eyes could move. The eyes in the skull did a summersault. "I don't think I can help you," said Jessica. And the eyes looked down in contempt. "But you'll be all right in the end. I'm sure you will." It was in the story. She'd eventually turn into a bird and fly out of hell. Maybe even soon.

A snake came out of nowhere and slithered around Jessica's neck and turned its face toward Jessica.

"Ewww," she yelled and swatted the thing and it sailed through the air. The hallway echoed with the sound of her voice below the steady moan, and the snake writhed through the air and plunked, still moving, on the floor and slithered through the crowd. Not one head in all the crowd turned toward her.

Jessica left the statue and followed the snake. What better guide to have in hell? She pushed her way through the dazed crowd of lost souls telling herself there were no undead in Hans Christian Andersen. As long as this story hadn't mixed with *Night of the Living Dead*, she was okay.

The snake slipped under a door. There was light coming from down there—and heat. She felt it on her ankles. She touched the door. It felt warm. Maybe that was a good sign.

"Heat in hell," she said to herself. Probably not a good sign, but she was so cold she opened the door slowly and just far enough to push herself inside. At the sight of the open door, the gray souls' eyes grew wide, and they moved to follow. But she shut the door behind her quick.

Was that the right thing to do? She had no idea.

But she moved slowly down this better-lighted, warmer hallway. It smelled like sulfur—but if that was the worst of it, things were improving.

And then she heard voices.

"I still don't see how you let them get away," it was an old woman's voice.

"I don't *let* them get away, Mormor. Somebody helped them."

"You're the devil and you expect me to believe *humans* tricked you? First three soldiers, and now two more? What will your grandmother say?"

"Suppose we don't tell her."

"My own daughter. You want me to keep secrets from my own daughter?"

"She's not like us, you know."

Jessica inched closer. The warmth was so inviting. And the two seemed so entangled in their conversation, she doubted they would notice her. From where she stood in the shadows, she saw the back of a man in a black, shining suit like patent leather. She did not see any part of the woman. Whenever the one she'd called the devil talked, Jessica heard a clacking sound. Whenever the woman spoke, it stopped.

"You've lost the soldiers," said the old woman. "You can forget about them. But you will go back and you will fulfill the terms of the bargain you struck with the other two, this Doug and this Charlie."

Jessica started at the sound of the names, but, expert traveler in fairylands, she did not make a sound. But the moment she started, from a fold of her skirt a large and particularly hideous frog dropped. Hitting the floor with a splat, it began to croak, or rather bark, like an asthmatic dog.

The devil in his suit of shiny black scales—or maybe that was his lizardy skin—was in the hallway so fast she did not see him appear. He was just there, standing before her like a statue, mouth open, eyes burning. Jessica froze. His thin black tail curled around his ankle. The devil said nothing. But he grabbed her from behind, bunching her shirt with her skin and carried her into the room so fast she barely had time to feel the pain before he dropped her.

Jessica scrambled up and backed against the wall.

"What is it?" said a very old woman, wrinkled, obese, with a hooked nose and ears the size of plates and the shape of the mushrooms that grow on the bark of dying trees. She was knitting a very long, red garment or scarf or some such thing. That was the source of the clacking sound. Although she glanced toward Jessica, her voice revealed no more interest than she'd have had over a dropped stitch.

The devil scratched his arm, "lunch, I'd say. Home delivery."

"Or a servant perhaps. I don't suppose you'll let this one get away." The old woman set aside her knitting and went to a huge trunk that creaked open on rusty hinges. She rifled through it until she came up with a long blue length of cloth.

"Jessica Holton," the devil's great grandmother announced.

Jessica froze.

The name meant nothing to the devil.

"Not one of ours—not yet anyway," she said.

Jessica grabbed her right hand in her left and squeezed until the bones hurt.

Now the devil was interested. He looked down at the girl silently staring.

Jessica remained still as a stone, moving only her eyes, listening carefully, as though she were hoping not to be seen, trying not to be frightened. Her best plan had been, since they had seemed to care no more for her than for a particle of dust, that they would forget she was there long enough for her to sneak away. But she had spotted no chance and she was too scared to move.

"That will change things," said the devil.

"What do you mean?" Jessica whispered.

"A soul must be given to me," said the devil. "I did not make the rules. I can't just take them."

"Who gives you these souls?"

"Whoever owns them," he said.

Well that made her feel just a little better. She assumed she owned her own soul and she was not going to give it to the devil.

"What do you want for yours?" asked the devil. He may have been joking.

"Oh, you're not going to negotiate, again," said his oldemor. "That's how you lose them."

"Oh, I don't think this will be a hard negotiation," said the devil. "She's already down here. She has no way back to the surface. No one down here will help her. It's just a matter of separating the body from the soul."

These are stories, Jessica told herself. She was not in a *real* hell. This was no *real* devil. There should be a way out. Stories end. Yes, but hadn't Suzy Bishop spent the last 20 years in Oz and Buddy the last 10 in the Grimms' Forest? And then, of course, there was Inga or Inger.

"Careful of that," said the hag. "They sometimes float."

"I know that." The devil was peevish.

"Oh, I've found it," said the old woman. And she tugged on the threads of the garment or scarf which Jessica now realized was—somehow—her life. There were still needles running through the top of it as if it were still being knitted. Now for the first time, she looked directly at Jessica. Then she turned to the devil.

"Ask her about her sister."

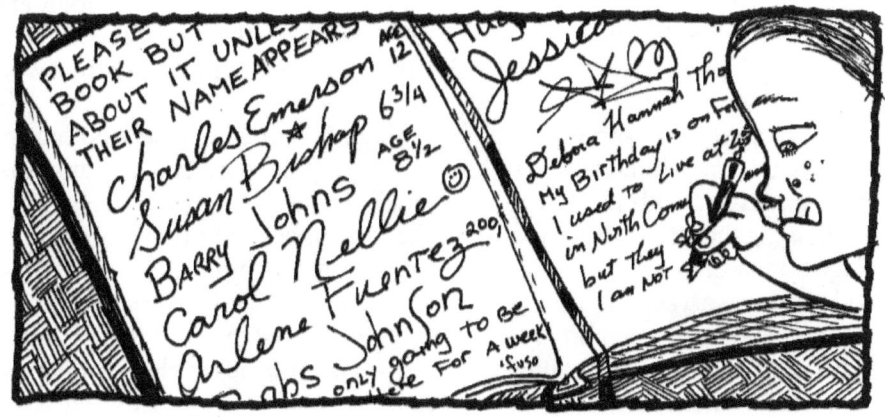

CHAPTER ELEVEN

Deborah Hannah Thomas· I am 9 years and 8 months old. My birth day is on Febuary 12ᵗʰ. I use to live at 234 Maple Street in North Conway New Hamshire, but they say I wont be living there any more. My mother is not coming back. I am not sure what else I am suppose to write on this page. Most people don't write much at all, just a name, but that is wrong if this is a recurd of people who have found this secrit room. Momma always said that secrits usually are not a good thing, but if it is part of a game, then I have to follow the rules. Rules must be followed. Even if games are frivalis.

DEBBIE HAD NO IDEA why anyone would put a secret room behind a closet. A closet is a place to store and organize your clothes. It is *not* a door. A door is a door. But she'd seen the back of the closet open as the strange woman rushed out, so she knew there was a room there. A room she entered on her knees crawling between the slats of wood at the back of the closet.

It was a small, bright room, filled with colored light that filtered through a colored window like a church window. The room was beautiful but had a very bad smell. The smell reminded her of the time her father's cat had brought a mouse and left it under the window where it sent such an odor into the hallway that her mother had to get rid of the cat. The room was stuffed with so many unusual things that Debbie put up with the smell. She could not keep from taking things off the shelves, toys to play with and books to flip through, very old books that were probably collectable.

Normally one should not touch things in someone else's collection without permission, Debbie thought as she replaced a silver oil lamp that was engraved with the words, "rub me" beside a small red glass bottle with a tag that said "drink me." But the Robbinses did say she could read any books or play with any item that was not behind glass, and while this room was secreted away behind a closet, it was *not* behind glass. She opened enameled boxes and found the sorts of things you might find in a fairytale: magic wands wrapped in velvet, bejeweled tiaras, and colorful masks. She looked at leather-bound books with elaborate watercolors of worlds she had never heard or dreamed of with names like Oogaboo and Erewhon. Magic and fairytale are for little kids, but she was intrigued; it reminded her, somehow, of her father—and no one was looking.

She continued to wonder where the strange lady might be who she knew had gone into the room and then seemed to vanish as she was rushing out. People do not vanish, that Debbie knew for sure, so perhaps there was a trap door or some other secret exit she had not noticed. She felt for seams in the walls or under the carpets but found no other exits. She had signed her name in the book as the rules on the top of the book directed, but the more she looked around the more she wished there was someone here who could answer the questions that were filling her head. Momma always answered her questions. She would stop whatever she was doing, no matter how busy she was, and would look directly at her and answer her questions. She used to say anyone who will not answer a child's questions is simply not civilized. Momma was very civilized.

She thought she'd like to let the other kids know about this room. But it said in the book you weren't supposed to mention the room to anyone whose name was not in it. That was the rule. And maybe that was okay. They'd probably just spoil it or get everyone in trouble for exploring a room they didn't have permission to enter. Besides, didn't Gwen say they were going to be leaving soon? Then it would be just her and those grownups in this giant house. And she'd need a place to get away from them.

Debbie spent time patting the golden mane on a larger-than-life-sized stuffed lion and picking up many of the very realistic plush animals that were placed around the room. Her mother had given her stuffed toys away when she was seven, explaining to her that they were baby toys, and she was a big girl. Momma was always right, but Debbie was very sorry when her teddy bears, baby dolls, and especially Flory the orange kangaroo had been given to one of her mother's friends who lived in Connecticut.

There was an hour glass on the floor with all its sand on the bottom, but there was no clock in this room, and Debbie was not wearing her watch, so she wasn't sure how long she had been exploring this secret place. She was, however, starting to suspect from her stomach that it was dinner time, and that she might even be late.

"I will have to come back here after dinner or maybe tomorrow," she said to herself. "If I had worn my watch I'd know if it was time to eat, but then these people have such a stupid way of scheduling things they might not have dinner ready for another hour." How she wished she was back home again with Momma and sensible routines. Traveling and seeing new things can be educational, but there is no place like home to feel safe and...

Debbie stopped talking to herself as it occurred to her that her home had not been very safe. Momma had gotten sick there, and Billy and Johnny Castillo who lived next door used to make fun of her and made her feel scared to go outside to play after her daddy left.

Removing a necklace made of bright green glass emeralds and faceted quartz crystals from a stand covered in black silk, Debbie sighed. She held it up to the colored light, sighed again, and then she placed it back just as she had found it. Then she left the secret room the way she had come in. The only way she could find. Later she would have to remember to come back and find the other exit that the lady had used.

Stepping through the boards, she easily slipped through the coats in the closet—and stopped suddenly. This was way too bright for the dingy, windowless hallway. And that was because she wasn't in the hallway. She wasn't even in OzHouse. She wasn't in *any* house.

She was standing on a walkway, a yellow brick walkway, with hundreds of flowers growing on each side and the bright sun overhead. She was facing, not too far away, a great wall made of green stone with a large roundy door that almost seemed to have a face—and it was smiling at her.

BUDISTILTSKIN HAD GROWN impatient waiting for Humpty Dumpty. He wasn't really sure he could trust the egg to return. His adopted father had taught him not to be too trusting of strangers, but his adopted mother had always shown such kindness to strangers that he'd often thought how nice it would be to be one and to bump into Sarastiltskin.

He waited almost two hours, being sure to stay hidden behind the low leaves of a chestnut tree until evening drew on. The moon emerged as a little sliver in the darkening sky. It would give barely enough light to see more than a few feet once the sun had fully set—far too little for comfort in the wild. Budy didn't want to move far from the town gate. At the same time, he didn't want any of the townspeople to discover him. He had no idea how far the story of the wizard had circulated. But finally his frustration got the better of him. He put his rucksack down—it was something the townspeople might recognize—and switched shirts. He hid the bag behind a bush and decided to sneak back into the town and find that ridiculous Humpty Dumpty.

It grew darker. Most of the people of this town had not seen his face, so if he kept away from fires, which he had to do anyway, maybe no one would notice him.

He waited till he saw a few shadows entering the gateway carrying large sacks that were probably filled with grain, and he joined their group, which dispersed almost as soon as it entered the gates, leaving him alone. But there was nothing unusual about that, as long as he walked purposefully, he'd be fine. "Always walk like you know where you're going, and no one will bother you," Rumpelstiltskin had often told him. No one questioned him as he headed toward the castle. Although he was sure he didn't stand out in any way, Budistiltskin could not help but feel people were looking at him.

The sun dipped further down past the horizon. More and more people were lighting fires and candles.

Humpty Dumpty's coach had rattled along the cobbles quickly; Budistiltskin, on the other hand, had to walk, and, staying clear of hearths or open fires, he took a long time to arrive at the castle. It was well past dark. He still had no plan to get inside to find the egg man. But he could wait here for him to emerge. He might not come out the front door (Budy didn't know how castle protocols worked) but he would have to drive by here in his carriage. Budy looked around but did not see the carriage. Torches on both sides of the large portcullis lit the walls of the castle.

If those flames died out, he would be noticed and, if the story of the fire-dousing wizard was out, he'd be arrested—or worse. Budy stood back and watched others enter the structure. He backed up until he was near the line of fruit trees that seemed to encircle the building. He was anxious, but at least he was alone—or so he thought.

And then a voice behind him spoke.

"My good fellow," said the deep voice, "is there a reason you do not wish to go into the castle? You *know* the prince welcomes all comers."

Startled, Budistiltskin turned and saw a large gray timber wolf with golden eyes emerge from behind an apple tree.

"No, no," he stammered. "I am waiting for a friend to come out.

That is all."

The wolf snickered. "Perhaps you might wish to hide farther back among the shelter of these trees. Trees provide excellent cover."

"I'm not hiding," Budistiltskin snapped. "Go about your business."

"This *is* my business," the wolf snorted. "It is time for my dinner."

Budistiltskin knew of the scheming ways of wolves. His father had taught him well. He reached for the dagger he always carried with him, and realized he'd left it in his rucksack back under the bushes. He gasped. He had faced wild beasts in his day, but never without a weapon. Compared to his adopted parents, Budy seemed tall and imposing, but next to a full grown wolf he did not feel big at all. The wolf knew it. The boy reached for a thick branch he saw lying on the ground, but the wolf was faster. Standing on the fallen limb, the wolf smiled and licked his chops.

"Are you going to make this difficult?" he asked. "I hate a difficult meal, gives me indigestion."

"I'll do more than that," the boy growled at the wolf.

"Big talk from a skinny human. I do not suppose you'll call for help though. Those guards could be here quickly, but you do not seem to want to be seen by them. Why is that?"

"You think I wouldn't yell to save my life?"

"Oh, go ahead," the wolf dared. "More choices for me."

"If I yell, they'll come running with their swords."

"I'll have you down in two bites, just like Red Riding Hood. You think they can catch me? Face it, you're stuck."

Budy was sure the wolf was bluffing. But he imagined the guards coming, torches ablaze, and those torches flickering out before they got close. And what help would the guards be then?

"Let's see what you're afraid of," said the wolf.

Budy took a step backward.

The wolf took a step forward. "Is it the guards, or the prince—or the big, bad wolf?" said the wolf. "You see, I know the prince's reputation. It is one even I could envy. If you are out here, skulking, you must be afraid of him. I don't know what you want. Is it a vision of his beautiful Aschenputtel?"

"Aschenputtel?" Budy knew that name, and the more common name of the princess as well. "Does Cinderella live here?"

The wolf let out a snort that might have been a laugh. "Oh, a clever pretense of ignorance. But it doesn't matter. You will not call for the help of the guards who, if they could save you from me, would then just drag you before the prince, your enemy, I'll guess. And that leaves us all alone here, just you and me." The wolf tilted his head and looked for a moment like a large friendly dog.

"I told you I am not hiding from the guards," Budy growled again. And then he bolted in the direction of the castle.

The wolf was stunned. But he recovered in a moment. "Too clever for my own good," he told himself as he watched his dinner run away.

No man can outrun a wolf in an open place, but Budy ran for his life. "Help, help," he cried. "Wolf! Wolf!" The guards drew their swords and almost as one they dashed towards the boy.

No one noticed the torches in the sconces on the wall fizzle out. The guards were watching the wolf. The wolf was watching both the guards and the boy. And Budistiltskin was breathlessly calling for help as he zigzagged across the grass and into the castle gate.

The wolf darted between the guards who stood stunned by the sudden darkness, and with all the daring recklessness for which his packmates praised and chided him, he avoided the well-armed guards and pursued his dinner into the castle.

The torches and candles died out one after another as Budy ran down the hallway. One by one the wolf passed by a string of guards as they fell into darkness. Budy felt the wolf pursuing him as he turned at every hallway and kept his eye out for a door back to the grounds.

People were shouting and jeering and ducking behind doors as the boy and the wolf ran past. A servant seeing the scramble from an upper window ran to tell the prince.

Budy made a sudden turn and ran on one side of the low wall that looked out on a garden while the wolf hurdled himself along the other side of the same well.

"Why are the sconces not lit?" shouted the prince.

"They had been my lord, but something has blown them out," a servant replied.

"The fire wizard has returned," yelled a guard across the courtyard.

"Relight the fires," yelled the Prince. "Catch the wizard and kill the wolf." That was all Budistiltskin heard as he at last found a door and, he hoped, lost the wolf, and left the castle.

Budy did not stop running until he was outside the city gates. He kept running, knowing the power of a wolf's nose. He ran past small homes and cottages where fires blazed in the windows. But he could not knock on the doors for help, for they would expect him to come inside, and *that* he could not do. He slowed when he could run no more, but he kept moving, walking for hours as the moon rose and clouds gathered to take away what little light it gave. Late in the night, he stopped by a home that was rather dark, and he peered through the window. If it were empty he might go inside, but he could see someone sleeping on the floor and as he watched, he saw the small fire in the fireplace go out.

Not knowing what else to do, and certain at least that he'd lost the wolf, he wound his way back between the trees and through a small stream to the place he had hidden his rucksack and decided he would have no choice but to wait there, his knife at the ready, and hope Humpty Dumpty hadn't already gone back to his wall.

JESSICA WAS IN HELL, guarded by a hag. She was frightened and confused and filthy. And now that the devil was gone, the room was quickly growing colder. She never imagined she'd be cold in Hell, but she was frozen to the bone. She had been in tight situations in fairylands before and had relied on her wits to save herself. But outwitting the devil was nothing she had ever had to do, and she could hardly keep from shaking in the presence of this bizarre creature who was, according to the weird mind of Hans Christian Andersen, his great grandmother.

How could the devil even have a grandmother or a great grandmother? Did he have a mother? Were any of his relatives married? This really did not make much sense at all. Was this supposed to be funny? Was Andersen making a joke? Jessica had studied the old fairytales in college. Like Charlie, she had been fascinated with them ever since her first encounter with OzHouse a decade ago. The Grimm brothers and Anderson especially piqued her curiosity. Not many people knew the tales that had not been cleaned up by cartoons. Now that she had experienced some of these tales, she was glad the cartoons she had watched as a child had been altered to make them have simple happy endings.

"I'm not sure what to call you exactly," she said to the old woman. "I seem to be here by mistake. I am not part of this story. I really don't think I have done anything to deserve Hell."

"Think harder." The woman sniffed at her. If Jessica had hoped the old woman would be a more sympathetic soul, she was very wrong. The devil enjoyed games of chance and often made deals; the old woman was bitter. She had no interest in helping and would do nothing to risk losing anyone. "No one ever does anything to *deserve* Hell," muttered the old woman. "That's what they all say. I say there's no one that doesn't. And here you are, and here you'll stay. Care for some tea?"

"I really can't stay," Jessica said after a brief silence. "Perhaps I could see your great grandson. So I could explain." Jessica's voice shook. She couldn't bring herself to say the word *devil*.

"He's a busy angel. He'll see you when he wants to. I suppose you'll want to make a deal?"

"A deal? Is that how I get out of this?" Jessica didn't recall Inga (or was it Inger?) making any deals with the devil. "Could you tell me where he went?"

"Told you, he's a busy one, many a soul to be dealt with," the ancient hag huffed. "He'll be back when he is good and ready, maybe tomorrow. Maybe a thousand years from tomorrow."

Jessica looked at the filthy pots and giant insects crawling about the tables and decided she wasn't really in a tea drinking place. Besides, she was fairly sure the woman wouldn't have given her any if she had wanted it. Her biggest fear was that time for the devil might not be the same as it was for her. What if he took weeks or months or years to return? What if the old woman was telling the truth? What if she was stuck here forever?

DEBBIE WAS STILL STANDING on the Yellow Brick Road trying to understand what had happened. She knew the story of the Wizard of Oz. She'd watched the movie with her father. And her mother had even let her watch it after he left—it was a classic and therefore acceptable entertainment. But it wasn't a real story. It was a dream or a fantasy or something, but not real. Now, however, she was standing outside the Emerald City itself and a beautiful rainbow was forming over the turrets of the castle. The sky was bright blue and the clouds were moving swiftly along as if caught in a great breeze. The air was crisp and smelled of wildflowers.

But it wasn't real.

With her hands on her hips Debbie frowned at it all. It was not possible. Perhaps it was a projection or a hologram. She would walk towards it and see for herself. Once she almost started skipping—the road seemed to make her do it—but then she caught herself and knew it would be terribly childish and she made herself walk calmly towards the great green doors.

"Hello," came a voice from above her.

She looked up and saw the rainbow was reaching towards her, and on the walkway of colors was a beautiful girl. Her long blonde hair flowed around her as if a fan was blowing it in every direction at once, but in slow motion. The girl, who looked older than Debbie but not much taller, hopped off the rainbow and glided silently the way a paper airplane moves down onto the grass.

"Who are you?" asked Debbie. Then remembering her manners, she added, "My name is Debbie Thomas."

"I am Polychrome, one of the daughters of the rainbow."

Debbie frowned and gave a small "humph" to show she did not believe such a thing.

"I have never had that response before," smiled Polychrome. "Are you on your way to the Emerald City?"

"I am walking towards that big door. I think it is a projection or something."

"A projection?" asked the dainty fairy.

"Well, it sure isn't the Emerald City, like in *The Wizard of Oz*. That is silly. We live in a real world, and there is no such place."

Polychrome put out her hand and took Debbie's and shook it, but then she didn't let it go. And Debbie didn't pull it back, which was strange, giving your hand to a stranger. But then she remembered the rule: when you are lost, find an adult that seems trustworthy and ask for help. That seemed to contradict the other rule about not talking to strangers. But sometimes the rules are different in an emergency. And when you're lost, it's an emergency. And the girl seemed odd, but not dangerous.

The girl started to dance toward the door, and she pulled Debbie along with her.

As they got closer, Debbie said, "It certainly looks solid. But they can do amazing things with CGI these days. Momma said, seeing isn't always believing anymore."

As they reached the large doors, one opened and Debbie heard cheerful music from the other side. A short fat man with a pointy moustache stood there smiling as they got closer.

"Hello," said Debbie, "my name is Debbie Thomas and this lady says her name is Polly Chrome," Debbie sighed, "though I'm sure that's not her real name. It doesn't sound much like a real name."

"It really is my name," smiled Polychrome.

"Not a proper name though. I mean it could be a nickname or something. But people are not named Polly Chrome. Girls have names like Lindsay or Tiffany, or Rebecca, or…"

"Or Deborah?" asked the fairy.

"Yes, that is a proper name. When introducing yourself you should use your Christian name," Debbie explained as if Polychrome were a small child.

"Your Christian name, like Rebecca?" Polychrome smirked.

"Yes," sighed Debbie.

Polychrome laughed lightly. "The Guardian of the Gates knows me," she smiled. "And he has always called me Polychrome. Would you prefer to call me Polly? Dorothy does that sometimes."

Debbie frowned a little as she thought, "Polly is more of a real name, I guess. Okay, I will call you Polly and you call me Debbie."

"And what is your name, sir?" Debbie asked the man with the funny mustache.

The Guardian appeared glad he was finally getting a word into the conversation. "I am the Royal Guardian of the Gates. When you know me better you may call me Thurbidore."

Debbie sighed again. She was about to explain that Thurbidore didn't sound like a real name either, but decided these people were so strange, maybe she should forget about that and find out where she was and what this place *really* was.

"Is this some kind of amusement park or something? I suppose those odd people in OzHouse might have created a special park that is only accessible through a secret room. Is this like Disneyworld or Universal Studios in Orlando, Florida? Is this where the woman went?"

"Do you know what she is talking about?" the Guardian asked the Rainbow's Daughter.

Polychrome shook her head, but the smile never left her face.

Debbie took a deep breath and smiled without showing her teeth. Being impatient was understandable. But *showing* impatience to strangers who may not know the right way to do things was not polite. She was sure she had solved the mystery of this "fairyland," but now the people were pretending it wasn't true.

"Look, I have questions," Debbie tried to hold her impatience still. "This cannot be Oz. That is just not possible. Oz is a fairyland. It's not a *real* place. It's not proper to play with people who are confused. This isn't Oz. So it must be something else. Is anyone going to tell me where I am?"

"If she has questions, someone must have answers," came a husky voice from behind the Guardian. "One cannot learn unless people are willing to explain things."

Debbie smiled. Finally someone was making sense. Her mother would approve of this stranger, whoever he was.

"Thank you. I have been trying to get an honest answer to my simple question, but everyone seems determined to play some silly game, and no one seems interested in helping me. That's rude, people should always help someone who is lost and certainly someone who is asking simple questions."

"I agree," said the Scarecrow as he slipped past the Guardian, bowed to Polychrome and held his white cotton glove out to shake Debbie's hand.

The girl froze. It must be a person in a costume of course. But it somehow didn't look like a person in a costume. His shape was lopsided and his legs bent at impossible angles. His face was a cotton sack. *That* could be a costume. But the eyes, nose, mouth and ears were painted on so that it did not seem possible that a person inside the costume could see out of it or talk without sounding muffled. Debbie looked for wires and someone holding the wires as the thing came forward with a kind of ambulation that was like the shuffling bounce of a marionette with its held-out hand.

Debbie bit her lip and tried not to fall backward. Older children don't do such things. Debbie reached for the outstretched hand and even squeezed his arm to be sure it wasn't just straw filled, that there was really a very flexible flesh-and-blood person hiding inside.

"And what is your name little girl?" asked the Scarecrow.

Debbie squeezed the cloth so tight she folded her fingers into her palms. She didn't feel any bones.

"D...D...Debbie Thomas," she tried to smile. She wanted to think it was a dream. But she had had dreams. And even though TV shows and books and movies try to make you believe that dreams and reality are easy to confuse, she knew they were not. *She* had never once confused them. "What's yours?" she replied the way she knew she was supposed to.

"I really have no name. I am just called Scarecrow or The Scarecrow. Isn't that odd? Everyone has a name, Nick, Scraps, Tik-Tok, Jack, even Toto, but not me."

"I really have no name either," came a deep voice from the other side of the door.

Debbie looked past the smiling Scarecrow and screamed.

CHAPTER TWELVE

ELIZABETH ROBBINS to   Oct 12
GWEN ROBBINS

Doesnt anyone over there answer a bloody phone anymore?
Yes Im a little frantic. Its one thing for Doug to blow off a call.
But surely he wouldve caught on by now. This is NOT my Doug.
Why is no one telling me whats going on? Why cant he call,
where is he, is he hurt, is he in the hospital, did he fall off the
roof? I told him hes too old to go clambering over roofs. What
the bloody hell is going on over there? Call me by tomorrow or
Im hopping a plane and you wont want to see me when I arrive.

                                      Love, Beth

On 10/11 7:44 PM, **Gwen Robbins** wrote:
Hope you're loving Spain. We all miss you. Lots of fun news,
wish I had time to fill you in.
Gwen

GWEN FOUND GARY IN HIS STUDIO and stuck her tablet between him and
his painting: "I called. Her phone's off."
    "This was sent yesterday."
    "I don't check my email for *one* day…."
    "She's probably on her way back."
    "You think?"

"And that means she paid top dollar for a last-minute ticket. That's not gonna go over well."

"Or, how about this: Where the hell is Doug?"

Gary put down his paint brush. "Beth's coming back, and the only children we have left are Debbie and Amanda, right?"

Gwen nodded. Trisha and Caleb and Jennie had all left within a few hours of each other, Trisha into a long-term foster home, Caleb and Jennie back to their parents' care.

"So she's not only going to be angry, she's not going to have any work to do. You know what she's like."

Gwen nodded again.

AT THE SOUND OF DEBBIE'S SCREAMS, the startled lion roared—which made Debbie scream all the louder and the Cowardly Lion roar all the more fiercely. Her screams shot out like a circle of sparks from a grinding machine; his roar exploded like a flame. Debbie's face went red, then brighter red, then white—and then she went silent as she crumbled to the ground as though she'd been shot, and the Cowardly Lion, pausing to breathe, heard the silence and grew quiet, sauntered up to the limp body of the little girl, and licked her face.

"People shouldn't scream like that," he said. "It frightens one so."

Everyone—Polychrome, the Guardian at the Gate (who decided it would be a long time before Debbie called him Thurbidore), and the famous Scarecrow—took their fingers from their ears and stared at Debbie.

"Maybe you should back up," said Polychrome to the lion, "in case she wakes."

The screams and the roars had startled a number of the citizens of the Emerald City. They came in a flutter of green through the open gate. When Debbie opened her eyes, she found herself at the bottom of an emerald cone with a thousand eyes.

"Is she all right?" said a voice.

"What curious clothes," said another.

"All those colors, it's like she doesn't know where she comes from."

"Or where she belongs."

The crowd was almost too thick for any light to penetrate—except through the hole at the very top where none of the people were tall enough to reach. Looking up at all those eyes, Debbie could not tell which face was talking. So she looked at the hole at the top of the crowd through fluttering eyes and said nothing.

"Do you think she screamed her voice plumb out of her body?" said someone.

"Quite likely," said someone else. "I recall my Uncle Tobey did that once. Didn't get it back for weeks."

"Perhaps we should look for it," said another voice. "Can't've got too far so quickly."

"Perhaps the Cowardly Lion took it."

"I'll wager he did just that."

And just then in the hole at the top of the cone another face appeared. It may have been the face of a giant. But then these other people seemed kind of short, so the person who owned the new face may just have been normal sized. It was a very shaggy face, Debbie could see that clearly. It was full of exquisite wrinkles and had a scattered beard and unkempt eyebrows and longish hair that instead of seeming uncombed seemed rather combed to look uncombed.

"Now, now, now," said a voice which could only be described as shaggy, "there seems to be a little girl in there. Back off good people and give her some room. She'll faint for lack of breath."

"Did that already," said a voice.

But the people thinned out, backing up and letting a course of fresh air insinuate itself into the space. The Shaggy Man knelt down and helped Debbie to sit. In his hand he held a glass of water which he offered to the girl.

"Is that your water," Debbie whispered, "because there could be germs in it."

The Shaggy Man smiled. "I drew it for you," he said.

"You didn't draw it," said Debbie. "It's not a picture. You got it from a faucet." And she took a polite sip, and then a little more. "Are you the one who rescued me from the lion?"

"You don't have to be rescued from this lion," said Polychrome, and Debbie turned to see the rainbow princess standing on the back of the lion—who was nearly as big as a horse—and then dancing onto his head. There was a big red bow fastened between the lion's ears. And it did not seem at all disturbed to have a girl dancing there.

"You must be very light," said Debbie.

"He's kind of a tame lion," said Polychrome.

"I prefer 'civilized,'" said the lion.

"Basically, he's a big coward," said the Shaggy Man.

"The real Cowardly Lion isn't really a lion," said Debbie. "He's a man in a costume. I've seen the movie. His name is Bert." But the sight of light-footed Polychrome in her flowing rainbow gown standing on the lion's head reassured Debbie that this lion, which clearly was a real lion, was not dangerous. It also helped that he could talk. And so when it was decided that they must bring the girl to Ozma and he offered her a ride on his back—she thought about it. But then she said, "I know the story about the little gingerbread boy."

Everyone looked at her with a serious and confused expression. No one else knew that story—except of course the Shaggy Man. He laughed.

Debbie walked.

"I believe Ozma is negotiating with Squire Fausvert," said the Guardian of the Gates.

"Squire Fausvert?" said the Shaggy Man.

"Yes, you recall," said the Guardian of the Gates, "the odd fellow they found sitting at Ozma's birthday table when everyone else had gone home."

Polychrome did not know the story of Squire Fausvert.

"An uninvited guest, wouldn't tell us where he was from or how he got here," the Guardian of the Gates went on. "He was sitting at the banquet table banging a cup and calling out in some foreign tongue."

"Oh, I had forgotten the name," interrupted the Shaggy Man. "But it wasn't really a foreign tongue. He was actually calling for a flagon of Rhenish."

"I don't know in what language that would not be foreign," said the Guardian of the Gates, and all the Ozites agreed. The Shaggy Man smiled benignly.

"Wasn't it the Wogglebug who gave him that name?"

"When he refused to tell us his own, yes, he did. Well, as I was saying," continued the Guardian of the Gates, "this odd person…"

But he was once again interrupted, this time by Debbie, "Excuse me, please, but I don't see how any of *you* could call anyone *odd*."

"Why is that?" said the Scarecrow.

Debbie pulled her lips into her mouth and stared at her shoes as she tried to think of a way to say what she meant that wasn't rude. But she could not think of any. So she finally said, "It isn't polite."

"I thought it was a compliment," said Polychrome.

"Certainly was intended that way," said Thurbidore.

"And…" said Debbie.

"Yes," said the Shaggy Man.

"Never mind," she said.

"Do you want to hear this story or don't you?" asked the Guardian of the Gates.

"I just wanted to know who Squire Fausvert was," said Polychrome.

"Apparently, he was the odd man who showed up after the party wearing the wrong shade of green who would not say his name or tell us where he came from or how he got here," said the Shaggy Man.

"—and who has only just learned that Ozma has the power to send him home," said the Guardian of the Gates. "And he now says he would like to negotiate for safe passage."

"Why would he have to negotiate?" asked the Scarecrow.

"No idea," said the Guardian of the Gates. "Ozma would be more than happy to grant such a trifling request. But he claims that that would be impossible. He said that where he comes from it is the height of presumption and ingratitude to accept favors without return—and some other such rubbish which put Ozma into a quandary for there is nothing the beggar has that she could possibly pretend was the equal of her favor."

"But you just said it was a trivial favor," said Debbie.

"Trivial? No. Trifling. It is trifling, but it won't seem so to Squire Fausvert. And even so, *trifling* is still more than *nothing*, which is precisely what Squire Fausvert has to offer. Ozma would have objected to his request, but you know how important it is to respect the customs of foreign lands."

"Maybe Ozma won't want to be disturbed," said Polychrome.

"Nonsense," said the Scarecrow. "I disturb the princess all the time."

"And yet not half as much as Scraps," said the Lion.

"True," said the Scarecrow. "No one is as disturbing as Scraps."

"Well, as for me, I must remain behind to guard the gate." The Guardian waved the others off to see the great and powerful princess of Oz.

It was not far from where they were to Ozma's palace. But the way led through some of the grandest parts of the most beautiful city in fairyland. Debbie, however, did not see the great wide boulevards of the glorious city, boulevards that rivaled the golden streets of the famous land of Eldorado. Nor did she see the emerald encrusted façades that put to shame the Taj Mahal on its most glorious day. She looked straight ahead at the back of the Shaggy Man who led the group and never turned her eyes to the left or to the right or up or down.

She also found the conversation increasingly silly and therefore did not listen any further to what Polychrome and the Scarecrow and the Cowardly Lion had to say to one another. She did not know that they were anxious to find out what adventure now awaited—as it seemed there was always a new adventure when someone from outside found her way into Oz. She did not hear Polychrome tell the Scarecrow it was too bad that Dorothy had gone home to Kansas after Ozma's birthday party, as she certainly would be instant friends with Debbie, an assertion that both the Scarecrow and the Lion doubted.

When they entered the grand throne room of Ozma's palace, the grandest room Debbie had ever entered, she did not see the impossibly high ceilings, the elaborate bas-relief on the walls displaying scenes like those on a medieval tapestry, the greatest scenes in the history of Oz. She did not see the flowers that fell in long colorful waterfalls twisted in lush vines from the balconies or the gold filigree on the massive columns that held up the ceiling of green glass.

She kept her eyes forward. She did not look to the left or the right. She did not look up or down. When they arrived in the throne room, she was looking at the piece of lint on the back of the Shaggy Man's coat until he moved aside, and then she was just looking.

When the Shaggy Man bowed and stepped aside, Polychrome saw, sitting in a throne of gold like a fairy in the blossom of a huge flower, a confident girl princess with a sweet, welcoming smile, her resplendent silk robe, ornamented in green, flowing left and right, the scepter of her authority lying comfortably across her knees, her hair done up with poppies to set off her caring eyes that stared at the supplicants.

Debbie saw a young girl in a pretty dress on a big chair.

Beside her on another chair sat a tall gentleman with a beard. That had to be Squire Fausvert, who clearly was dressed all in the wrong shade of green. The Scarecrow said hello.

Squire Fausvert rose and bowed.

"We're trying to find a way to send him home," said Ozma.

The squire just smiled.

"We've heard the talks have hit a snag," said the Shaggy Man.

"Aye, indeed, as doth so often be the case in such matters. Nothing beyond our powers, surely," Squire Fausvert added.

"As for that, I'd send him home in a minute if I knew where his home was."

"He sounds English," said Debbie.

Squire Fausvert cast a narrow-eyed look at Debbie. But she didn't see it.

"He insists before we can send him home, since he can't give us anything, he must do something to prove he is worthy of our favor. So you see we do have something more to talk about," said Ozma. "But as for now, please tell me who is this odd girl you have brought with you, Polychrome."

Debbie looked up now and stared at the princess, "I am not odd," she said. "I don't know why you people call normal things odd and odd things normal. *That* is odd. I would say *you* were odd, but it would not be nice."

Ozma laughed at this.

"This be an astounding speech to make to the face of a monarch," said Squire Fausvert.

"People mustn't lie," said Debbie.

"That certainly would make things easier," said Ozma. "One would always know whom to praise and whom to punish. And, if I must be honest, I must say, here in Oz when one is called 'odd,' one generally accepts it with a proper smile. And here in Oz you, I must say, are quite, quite odd, particularly so if you are normal."

"What is odd in Peoria is even in St. Paul," said the Shaggy Man.

Ozma laughed and waved her hands as though to clear the air of the fog of those words. "Yes, well, putting that aside, who might you be?"

Polychrome formally introduced the new arrival to the most charming, wise, and generous monarch ever to command a country. Debbie saw her smile, of course. You have to look at a person when you are being introduced. But Ozma's smile did not quite register; it did not elicit a corresponding smile from Debbie. Debbie's eyes were sad when Ozma said, "Is there some way we can be of service to you?"

Debbie stared at the princess then. She found herself looking first at the princess' elbow, but she brought her gaze up to her face. And she remembered her mother had always told her to stand up straight when you ask for something.

But then she looked at Lord Fausvert.

"I don't have anything to give you."

Ozma shook her head. "No one in the world has anything I need at the moment. That seems to be my problem today. It seems the one thing I don't have is something to need. And neither you nor Lord Fausvert can give me that. But if there is something you need that I have, it would make me happy to give it to you."

"Then I would be giving you happiness?"

"That would be an excellent trade."

Debbie pushed her shoulders back and dropped her hands straight at her side and she said, "I want to wake up."

Ozma did not laugh. No one laughed. The princess just flopped back into her throne like a toy that had suddenly lost a little bit of air. "Are you asleep?" she said.

"I don't feel asleep," said Debbie. "And I've never confused a dream with awake before. But perhaps that *can* happen—because I must be dreaming right now, because none of this is real. Lions don't talk, and no one's name is Polly Chrome, and you can't get from New Hampshire to a whole different country just by walking through a door. And no one could possibly think *I* am odd. I don't know when the dream started. Maybe the smelly room with the book is part of the dream. Maybe the strange woman is part of the dream. I may have fallen asleep reading *The Light Princess*. And then I met Polly Chrome. Dreams don't take you exactly where you were thinking of. I do want to wake up."

"This is a magic I have never done before," said Ozma.

Debbie sighed.

"But that does not mean it cannot be done." Ozma told Debbie to lie down on the green, satin couch near the door. "It's best to be lying down when you wake up," she said. And then she conferred with the Scarecrow and the Shaggy Man, and when they were done the three of them walked over to Debbie, lying awake on the couch.

"If you tell us everything you know about where you're sleeping, we can wake you up by means of the magic picture and the magic belt," said Ozma.

So Debbie told them about OzHouse in Cornish, New Hampshire, and she told them that her room was at the top of the stairs on Gwen and Gary's side of the house. The Shaggy Man knew where New Hampshire was. (Ozma told him he was so helpful, he would surely earn the right to live in the Emerald City as long as he liked.) And so it was not difficult for Ozma by the power of her magic to transport Debbie to her bed, where she soon found herself lying in the middle of the day on top of the blankets, and only a little confused—because she did not remember lying down or going to sleep. But there was only one possible explanation. She'd taken a nap (like a little kid) in the middle of the day and had the craziest dream any girl had ever had.

WITH THE RETURN OF THE DEVIL the room became warm again.

"Little update." The devil in his black lizard suit leaned back against the wall. "Your state has removed your niece from your sister. A real chip off the old block, that one."

Jessica went white. The devil's great grandmother, who had taken up her knitting needles again while the devil was gone, clicked away at her work.

"All problems can be fixed—for the right price. But the longer it takes, the less you get," the devil fixed his red eyes directly on Jessica. He looked like a man who was too old to look cool trying to look cool, his knee bent, his right foot flat against the wall behind him. "And just so that you know all the messes you have made, another child from the house has sneaked through your secret doorway. She's in Oz."

"You'll forget the loss of those soldiers in no time," the devil's oldemor hissed and clacked with glee.

"How do you know that?" Drops of sweat fell from Jessica's brow.

"Temper, temper," said the devil.

"How do you know it?" Jessica was surprised at her own bravery. But then again, this was just a story. Dangerous as it seemed, no story had ever done her any permanent damage as far as she could remember.

"I'm the devil."

"Oh, we have won her soul," his oldemor laughed.

"Not quite. But we will," said the devil.

"You're a *storybook* devil. You're not the *real* devil. I don't even believe in the real devil. And stories don't go into the real world. It can't happen. It's a one-way door. So how do you know? Unless you went to Oz, which I doubt." Oz didn't seem like the kind of place for a devil.

"True, that's one place I have no interest in at present. But you never know." The devil's face flashed the gleeful expression of a gambler with an unbeatable card. "Ah, but as for *your* world, there's so much you don't know. Isn't every brick and every stone and every cloud and every heart—hell," said the devil, "isn't reality itself, your world or mine, just a story in the end? Nothing if it isn't; nothing if it is. Why would it be any harder for me to go there than for you to come here?"

"Now, now," said Oldemor, "don't overplay your hand."

"Don't worry about me," the devil snapped.

"You always lose through smugness, sonny." She pointed with her needles. "Is that not how you lost your place to begin with—with *you know who*?"

The devil laughed.

"You don't see wizards and trolls and goblins running down the streets of Manchester. I'm not stupid. I don't believe you."

"And you think that if you don't see them they are not there?"

"You were invented by Hans Christian Andersen or, or the Grimm Brothers," Jessica stammered.

"Invented, collected, observed. Words, words, words," he scoffed.

"You're not *real*." She was trying to figure out whether a deal made with a fictional devil was a fictional deal.

"As you wish," said the devil, undisturbed. "By the way, I wanted to thank you for your note."

"My note?"

"It was on the floor." He pulled from somewhere in his clothes or conjured like a magician from the air a piece of paper which he laid on the table in front of her, "'Dear Doug and Charlie....'" he recited as she picked it up. It was her own note in her own handwriting. She felt a chill. "See, that note is the currency with which this fictional devil buys your actual soul. So, again, thank you."

Oldemor with a laugh resumed her knitting. "Classic, classic."

Jessica stared, speechless, inquisitive.

The devil smiled and nodded.

"You're real?" she whispered.

"Your distinction is tedious. I want your soul. What's your price?"

"It's not for sale," Jessica got a little more of her voice back.

Oldemor snickered. If she'd had liquid in her mouth it would've spurted.

"You're obnoxious," Jessica stared at the old creature.

"And you're food," the hag shot back through a crooked row of broken teeth. Halitosis added another flavor to the mélange of odors.

The devil moved forward and put his hands on the table. "Time to start the negotiation. You want three things. In ascending order, one: the recovery of Richard the Lion Hearted and Robin Hood." The devil pulled a small red stone and placed it on the table. "Two, the recovery of Doug Robbins and Charles Emerson." He laid a larger red stone beside the first. "And three, a permanent home for your degenerate sister and her doomed children." He laid a stone the size of his fist beside the other two. "Do I have it right?"

Jessica glanced from the stones to the devil. It would be best to find a way to trick this devil into letting her go without promising anything. But she could not think of any story in which a human outsmarted a devil. Moreover, she had no idea of her actual position here, whether to believe him, whether he was real—a devil or, worse, *the* devil. She didn't even know what it meant to sell your soul to the devil or whether if she did so she could buy it back. Confused, she acted brave: "I don't negotiate with devils."

"I can get you everything you want."

"I'll get it myself."

The devil chuckled. "You can't even get yourself out of hell. By the time you manage to see the sun again, Isabelle will be dead. Her children will be addicts on the run from the law, and you will look an awful lot like my oldemor."

Jessica crossed her arms and tried to stare the devil down.

"Listen," the devil roared. Fire shot from his hand; it passed like the jet of flame from some hideous engine of war just to the left of Jessica's head. She felt the heat singe her hair. It made the stone wall behind her glow bright red. She felt pain from the heat down her back. She let out a short scream as though she'd been punched. "I have other souls on my list. You want your sister to find a home in fairyland for her daughter and her unborn son, I can arrange that. Say the word and Amanda is the new daughter of the Stiltskins. They need a new child anyway."

"The child is mother to the woman," said Oldemor.

"I have no idea what that means," Jessica gathered her strength despite her fear and stared defiantly at the old woman. She was able to do so because she had understood two important things from what had just happened: first, that this devil was not going to harm her. He was part of a story that did not allow him to do so if she did not give him permission, which she was not about to do. And second, if he could somehow harm her, accidentally perhaps, he would lose. And he wouldn't risk that. So she was scared, but she was safe, even in hell. She crossed her arms again as though she were not frightened and turned again to the devil.

"It's a boy?" she said.

"All right." The devil doffed his anger like a garment he'd tried on that didn't fit and looked down at the stones he'd laid on the table. "I can't imagine Robin Hood and King Richard would mean much to you even if you knew the real stakes there. And so I withdraw that portion of the offer." He brushed the first stone onto the floor where it turned to dust and he picked up the second, "which leaves us with Doug Robbins and Charles Emerson." He rolled the stone in his hands and then displayed it between his thumb and index finger as though it were a portrait of the two men. "Take my deal right now or, for them too, you must abandon all hope. I know where they are. And they owe me. We have a deal. Speak now or they will not leave the Grimms' forest alive." The devil pulled the stone into his palm and hurled it hard at Jessica. She screamed involuntarily and tried to duck. The rock dissolved in the air leaving only sulfuric smoke to blow past her frightened head. And then the rock was back in the devil's hand. As though it was a cute, satanic yo-yo.

Everything this devil did told her she'd been right. And if the devil could not harm her, he could not harm Doug or Charlie either. At least not directly. As long as they didn't give him permission. And who would be so stupid?

Jessica straightened herself up again. "The devil is a liar," she tried not to reveal the shaking of her body in her voice.

"True enough. But unlike humans, I never break my contracts. I'd lose your soul."

Oldemor laughed. "You have not lost your touch after all."

"Show me where they are." Jessica hoped she sounded unintimidated.

"Too late. You are not in a Charles Dickens novel," said the devil. "They are gone, good as dead. Forget about them." He crushed the second rock in his fingers and let the dust and smoke fall and float. "But you can still save your wretched sister and her miserable children, can't you? And you are going to give yourself to me to save your sister. Because that's the kind of person you are."

Oldemor giggled at her knitting.

The devil picked up the large rock. Staring at it, he said, slowly and too calm. "What if you're wrong?" Then he looked hard at Jessica. "This is your only chance to save her. She could never get through that door on her own. You know that. And she would never let her children go there without her. You know that too."

And Jessica found that she did.

"I'd call it her one motherly virtue, if it were a virtue to doom your children out of loyalty."

Jessica fought the impulse to defend her sister. The devil couldn't hurt her. But he could save Isabelle. "Let me think about it," she said.

"No," he replied.

And then a look came over his face as though the stone had told him something. He rolled it once in his fingers. And as the stone melted into air, he turned, without a word, and he left so quickly the door did not fully close behind him.

Jessica's fear turned to confusion.

"He does that," said Oldemor, furiously knitting.

The room began to cool. "He wasn't finished." Jessica looked away. The sound of the clacking of the old creature's needles felt like beetles on Jessica's skin. That clacking was the only sound in the room. When she could stand to hear it no more she said, "Is that the life of a person you're knitting?"

The hag said nothing.

"Do you record what people have done or do you make them do things?"

But the ancient creature would not be engaged in conversation.

"Does he have the power to kill Doug and Charlie or just to strand them forever in Grimms' Forest? I don't think he does. I don't think he can help Isabelle either, and I don't think he even knows where Robin Hood and Richard are. Why would he screw with all those people's lives just to get my insignificant little soul?"

The needles clacked.

Jessica brushed dried mud from her arms and face.

The clack of the needles made it impossible to think. She needed to go somewhere. She backed slowly toward the door through which she'd come.

"Get back here," the corpulent hag yelled. But Jessica kept backing away and the old woman did not follow. Why had it not occurred to her until this moment just to leave? What was stopping her? She didn't know where she was going. She didn't have a plan. She just had to get away from this room and this thing with her needles. But as she walked, an idea occurred to her. Try something, anything, and see what happens. Do a Charlie. Go without a plan. In a moment she was in the long hall. Approaching the great big door that she'd come in by that marked the edge of the endless room where the gray souls wandered in the cold with the snakes and the spiders and the statue of Andersen's lost girl, she wondered what would happen if she opened it. What would happen if she left it open?

Souls poured in from the cold antechamber. That's what happened. In no time they filled hell's hallways like wandering zombies. Jessica backed up to the wall, but no one seemed to notice her. They merely continued down the hall toward what remained of the heat.

"Oh, she's let the dirt in," Oldemor's words echoed down the hall. The stream of gray souls might buy Jessica some time. They would be hard to wade through. But time for what? And what made her think anyone was chasing her?

Jessica found herself again at the statue of the girl on the ancient loaf of bread, the girl whose name she now remembered was Inge.

"This would be a good time to come back to life," said Jessica.

The statue started to cry. Hot tears ran over the girl's cheeks and fell onto Jessica's upturned face.

A commotion could be heard down the hallway. Gray souls were being pushed by some unseen force back through the hell mouth. Jessica grabbed the leg of the statue of Inge as though she needed support and looked around for any kind of exit. This antechamber seemed endless, dizzying. But no direction looked more promising than any other. Souls groaned as they were pushed back into the space.

And then there was nothing in Jessica's hand. She looked back where the statue had been—nothing there but the loaf, which had turned to stone, and a bird, a white tern, circling around her head. It flew quickly away, and then suddenly returned and circled Jessica again before flying off.

When it returned a second time, Jessica understood she was being asked to follow. But the bird nonetheless, to be sure, fluttered its wings rudely in her face.

"I get it, I get it," she said.

The bird led her down a hall and into a cavern through which a river flowed. Upon the river a small, long boat like a canoe or one of those boats they have in Venice was just landing. A tall, bearded man with a long pole waved to her to come. The little bird flew rapidly around the girl's head. Jessica tried to gently swat it away.

"I see him," she said, and she ran to the boat.

"Oh, am I glad to see you," said the man.

The bird flew once more close to her head and chirped loudly. "What do you want?" said Jessica.

With a huff, the bird landed on the top of the girl's head and stared at the man with the pole.

"Can you take me across?"

"Of course," said the man. "Climb aboard."

The bird twittered loudly as the man pushed off.

"Quite a talkative friend, you have there," said the boatman.

"If only I knew what she was saying," said Jessica. And she looked up. The boatman had an expression on his face that Jessica had never seen before. A smile so big and broad it went beyond happiness. She wished she knew what that was saying too. What lies beyond happiness? "Must be kind of boring, down here all alone? Get many passengers?"

"Oh, you'd be surprised," said the man.

"Surprised at how many or how few?"

But the man just smiled as though to wrap the ends of his mouth around to the back of his head.

"Been doing this a long time?" Jessica tried not to sound nervous as they crossed the half-way point of the river. It could not have been a very deep river if the boatman could navigate with just a pole.

"Years," said the man. "Years upon years." He must have realized how strange he looked because he used his hand to pull the smirk off his face. But the moment he let go, it sprung back like a balloon. It occurred to Jessica what lies beyond happiness. She decided she'd better not antagonize him. The bird on Jessica's head had grown quiet but continued to stare as though her eyes might burn a tattoo onto the old man's forehead. Her little feet gripped Jessica's hair until it hurt. When Jessica reached her hand up to pull the bird off, it pecked her hand. She left it there.

"Don't be nervous," said the man. "We're nearly across."

"I don't have any way to pay you," said Jessica.

"No payment necessary," he said, pausing the boat a short way from the shore. "In fact I have something for you." He tapped his pockets as though to find in which one the something was held. "If you would just take this pole for a moment." He leaned it toward her.

Jessica hesitated. She said, "Why did you say you were glad to see me?"

But the smiling man just held the pole for her to take. Fearing what a crazy man might do if she did not go along, she reached for it.

And the bird sprung. It darted straight at the eyes of the old man. The pole fell from his grip and went overboard as he swatted at the air. The bird pecked him once on the eye and he fell back. Then it charged straight at stunned Jessica. The girl fell out of the boat to avoid the angry bird and landed plunk in the river beside the boatman's lost pole. As she reached for the pole to give it back to the struggling boatman, the bird renewed its attack, and it occurred to Jessica that the quicker she got away the better. The water was shallow and warm, and the boatman could just as well get his own pole.

"Thank you," she yelled as she ran to the shore. The bird settled, calm and gentle, on her shoulder as soon as she stepped from the river.

"What was *that* all about?" Jessica asked aloud.

But the bird just chirped.

THE PROBLEM WAS NOT THE MOTHER, the problem was the environment, Gary and Gwen were informed. Isabelle had not been told that her mother's new boyfriend was forbidden by the terms of his parole to live in the same house with a child. The judge allowed Isabelle to follow Amanda to OzHouse the next morning. Gary got the call and drove to Manchester.

Now she and her daughter sat on the floor of the Wonderland Playroom putting colored shapes into colored holes of the same shape.

"Circah," said Amanda. And in it plopped.

"What's this?"

"Squayah." In it plopped.

"And what's this?"

"Squayah." In it did not plop.

"No, this is a square. *This* is a rectangle."

"Squayah," Amanda corrected her.

"And what's that?" Isabelle pointed to an abandoned toy.

"Cow."

"No, Amanda. That's an elephant."

"Cow," said Amanda.

"Okay, have it your way. It's a cow."

A voice at the doorway said, "You shouldn't teach her that an elephant is a cow. She'll be confused."

Isabelle looked up at the girl standing there, maybe eight or nine years old, a little chubby kid with short sparse hair that conformed to the shape of her skull.

"Even though technically it is a cow," the girl said. "A girl elephant is a cow, and a boy is a bull. But most people don't know that. So she'll still be confused."

"Really," said Isabelle.

"You should probably know that," said the girl. And if she had been tempted to say anything more on the subject, she decided against it. She walked into the room and collapsed like jelly on the floor, and started to cry. "I just had the strangest dream. I shouldn't tell you this. My mother would be mad. But I went into a room and I went through the door and I met a girl named Polly, and a bum, and a lion that thought he was the Cowardly Lion, but he was a real lion and he scared the crap outta me. Oh, never mind. I'm sorry." Debbie took a deep breath.

Isabelle did not go to her, did not put her arms around her. She just leaned back against the couch and watched quietly. Debbie got up to leave. But when she did, Isabelle said, "Why do you think it was a dream?"

And Debbie looked up as though this proved she was still dreaming. "It was a lion that talked."

"I see," said Isabelle. But she didn't seem to count this talking as evidence enough to prove the point.

"And…and…" but Debbie couldn't think of anything she'd seen more definitive than the talking lion. If this girl didn't accept a talking lion, what else was there? But then she thought of something, "and they sent me back with magic. But I never told them I was from today. So if it was magic, I would've been sent back to like 200 years ago or something, because that's a very old story and that's the America they know about."

"That's funny," said Isabelle.

"It's not one bit funny," said Debbie.

"Well you don't believe in magic, but you apparently know how it works. I think it's hilarious. You don't believe in magic worlds because you can't time travel in this one? You don't find that funny?"

"It *was a dream,*" said Debbie.

Isabelle looked around. Amanda was trying to force a circle into a star-shaped hole. Isabelle picked her unfrustrated daughter off the floor and turned to Debbie. "Come with me," she said.

"DEVIL'S ON THE MOVE," the voice came from the next room, a man's voice. Familiar.

"Contract must be due." That was the voice of the woman who had let them stay the night. Charlie hit Doug on the arm.

"I'm not asleep; I'm ignoring you."

The sun, level with the window, sprayed pink filament across the wooden walls of the cabin.

"He may be after the wizard who disrupted the prince's banquet last night—that one's warrant hath been cried from every crossroad in the village," said the man.

"Why would he want a wizard? A wizard would already be about the devil's business."

"If not the wizard then I say again, it must be he seeketh the two from The Merica."

"Get them from my house, Richard Smith. We have had too much of the devil about the place already."

Charlie hit Doug again.

"I get it, I get it," said Doug.

"We've got to get out of here." Charlie nodded toward the door.

Doug sat up wearily. "You've got a weird notion of hospitality, Chuck."

"You have no idea what that man wants."

"Nor do you." Doug pulled himself to his feet, and headed to the adjoining room ignoring Charlie's whispered curse. "Let's find out." He peeked through the open doorway. "Good morning, hostess, and good morning, Richard Smith, good morning from The Merica."

"You've brought the devil," said the woman without hesitation.

Charlie made a noise from the other room that may have been a snicker.

"You must be some magic worker that can laugh at the devil," the woman yelled through the door.

"Likely thou *hast* brought the devil," said Richard. "Though I do not say thou didst aim for it to be so. The dragon did circle Grumbottem twice before first light."

"I say these men are in cahoots with the wizard. Did you see my fire? Cold as any well."

"Can't explain the fire," said Doug. "But I do want to thank you for your kind hospitality. I only wish we had some way to show our appreciation."

"You can leave," said the woman.

Richard would not let them out the door, however, before they had changed into the rough tunics and hoods he'd brought with him. Richard fed Doug and Charlie a breakfast of spiced sausage, bread, and small beer that he pulled from a leather sack. Doug took the food eagerly, Charlie warily. Charlie thanked Richard for the clothes—which would be welcome for the warmth as much as for the concealment—and for the food, and he apologized for having to leave him again so quickly, but they were really on an important quest, he said, and...

"I used you civilly yestere'en, squire, when I did *request* thy company. But thou didst deceive me. Today, I must *require* you tarry with me a while."

"I really wish we could," said Charlie, "but we are really on an urgent quest to find this boy who may be able to...."

"Men from the Merica," Richard interrupted, "I do not ask. You shall tarry a time with me."

Charlie screwed up his mouth in a gesture of someone trying to solve a puzzle. And even Doug looked somewhat piqued by Richard's tone. But this Richard Smith was an imposing figure clearly accustomed to giving orders and having them obeyed.

"It burdeneth me to speak thus. But I must. Certain I need not threaten to deliver you to the wizard..."

"No, no, no. No wizards, please," said Charlie. "We need to find Buddy."

"...or inform the suspicious prince of your presence in his lands together with a wizard and dragon."

"I just don't think we can…"

"And concerning the dragon, I might be of some use in keeping you from his sight or placing you in it, as the need arises. I take no joy in speaking thus."

"We get it," said Doug.

"I have offered nothing," said Richard.

"We understand," said Charlie. "What do you want?"

BUDY WOKE UP SHIVERING. One would need a fire many a night this time of year. It was coming ever clearer how difficult it would be to get through the winter if he could not free himself from the curse. And he was no closer to doing that now than he had been on the day he'd left his home. Humpty Dumpty had promised to help him find the Blue Fairy. But Humpty Dumpty had not come back—or if he had come by it was while Budy was out fleeing the wolf. Surely the egg was on a wall in Wonderland or some other fairyland by now.

On the other hand, if, as the wolf had said, Cinderella lived here, maybe he didn't need the egg. He had met Cinderella years ago, soon after she married, when she still allowed herself the privilege of going places like an ordinary citizen, back when she'd been happy finally to be able to do the things her stepmother and sisters had forbidden her to do, things ordinary people do, like to go fairs. She might remember him.

But the townspeople had made his lack of welcome pretty clear. And if the wolf was right, and the prince was jealous of rivals, getting to Cinderella these days would be no easy task. Probably harder still if his little jog through the castle had got someone's attention.

Should he risk his life looking for the princess? Should he wander the woods in the faint hope of finding someone who could show him the way to the Blue Fairy? Or should he stay put and hope that Humpty Dumpty would keep his promise? Budy pulled his blanket tight around his shoulders. He would have called his prospects bleak, but he didn't want to sound optimistic. As he pulled his knees up under his chin, he saw a raven land on the leafy ground not ten feet away. There was a piece of paper tied to its leg.

DEBBIE DID NOT WANT TO SHOW ISABELLE THE ROOM. She preferred to believe there was no room. That she had not followed a young woman who had been rude to her or seen the woman crawl through the boards in the back of the closet and disappear and that she had not traveled to Oz. It was all part of the dream. But Isabelle insisted. And that was something Isabelle was good at.

"Jessica told me for ten years there was a secret she couldn't tell me about in this stupid house. Drove me flippin' crazy with not telling me about it. 'Oh, I wish I could tell you the about the secret and the room and the places you can go in that house.' 'So tell me already.' 'Oh, but I promised.' 'Like I'm gonna tell anyone, just tell me.' 'You would love it, Isabelle.' 'Okay, Jess, I'm not going to tell anyone.' 'Oh, but I just can't.'"

"You're telling me now," said Debbie.

The remark quieted Isabelle for just a moment.

"Yeah, well if she'd told me, I wouldn't be, would I? And this room you're talking about, that must be what she was talking about. So show it to me."

"You don't believe I really went to Oz."

"Of course not. Don't be stupid."

"You shouldn't call people stupid."

"Then don't act stupid. Where's the room?"

Debbie huffed and pointed down the hallway. Isabelle urged Debbie forward and dragged Amanda behind.

Just as they got to the wardrobe and opened the door a voice called behind them, "What are you girls doing?"

It was Gary. Gwen was beside him. They were coming down the hallway.

"Debbie said there's a room in there."

"There's no room in there," said Gary.

Gwen looked disgusted.

"See, I told you it was a dream."

"Do you mind if I just look?" said Isabelle.

"I really do," said Gary. "I'm sorry."

Isabelle stood by the open door. The coats had all been pushed aside revealing the painting of the lamppost that Gwen had put there years ago and the bolted boards that crossed it. But the back door was slightly ajar. Colored light came through the crack.

Gwen and Gary came up beside them.

"Debbie was scared," said Isabelle. "I wanted to show her it was nothing." She picked up Amanda and stood her in the wardrobe and straightened her clothes.

"What's the harm at this point?" said Gwen.

"What's the harm? I'm sorry. It's not a place for children."

Gwen screwed up her face to try to make sense of that remark. Isabelle let go of Amanda and turned to Gary. "Okay. It's just, Jessica used to tell me... That's a very pretty lamppost. Did you paint that? Look Amanda." Amanda climbed to the back of the wardrobe and reached for the painting—and opened the door.

"She's going to fall in," said Debbie.

Grabbing at her daughter, Isabelle got a face full of fur coat as the little girl slipped under the cross board and dropped into the magical room.

CHAPTER THIRTEEN

Dear Mama,

I wish I was sending you better news, but so far I have had no luck breaking the spell. My plan is to locate the Blue Fairy or Cinderella's Fairy Godmother or perhaps some other magical worker and ask for help in removing this curse. I know you and Poppa do not hold much for fairies, and I must admit I do not trust them all that much myself, but I am desperate. I have seen to a half a gaggle of witches since I left home, and they either tried to cheat me, eat me or just had no knowledge of this kind of spell.

I met with Humpty Dumpty yesterday—and before Poppa blows his stack about the <u>arrogant, useless</u> egg, let me tell you he did say he'd help me. Yes, I know, he probably has his own reasons, and I am still waiting for him to return. Big-headed as he is, he usually keeps his word if the stories can be believed, and I am trusting that he will help me find someone who can help me. He does seem to know people.

As the weather is getting chill, I am finding it harder to avoid fire. But I have survived so far and am determined to continue to do so. With luck on my side I will not be discovered and will find generous people to give me a barn to sleep in at night. I still have a few gold coins Poppa gave me in case the generous people I meet need a little persuasion. Cold stew and raw root vegetables are not a very satisfying meal but they are more to be desired than an empty stomach. I finished the meat pasties you packed into my rucksack a long time ago and look forward to coming home to your cooking before the first snowfall.

Please keep me covered with your good thoughts and prayers and any protection spells you know. I had a run in with the Big Bad Wolf once, and by keeping my head I managed to outsmart him, but I'd prefer to avoid him in the future as he has a long memory and a rotten temper.

I am sending Poppa's raven back to him. Thank him for his letter to me, I'm still not sure how Bandy found me in the wilderness around Grumbottem but I am sure glad he did. Any connection to home is really encouraging out here alone. Miss you both.

Love,
Budy

BUDY LEANED BACK against the smooth bark of a beech tree. The breeze was gentle and the smell of the woods was rich with moss and earth and decaying leaves. Tall ferns, their fronds edged with brown, swayed in patches of sunlight flickering through the foliage. He watched his father's raven fly off with the scroll tied to its leg and shaded his eyes as it flew in the direction of the sun. Although he had told his mother he was eating enough, in fact he'd had nothing to eat in over a day, and his stomach growled like an ogre with threats of how it would torture him if he didn't fill it soon. All the gold in the world wouldn't procure him a meal if people thought him a wicked wizard and were too afraid to be near him.

"That miserable egg better show up soon," he said aloud as he rearranged his rucksack and shoved it behind him in the small of his back.

"Doing the best I can, dear boy," came a voice from just beyond Budy's vision. He looked around to find where the words had come from—and then he saw the egg man strolling towards him, pushing through the hawthorn bushes. "These legs are simply not made for hikes in the woods. Why didn't you stay by the road where I left you?" Humpty pulled his pant leg free of a thorn.

"Too many people looking for me—and wolves too, and not the nice kind. I don't make many friends by killing their heat. I was afraid you wouldn't find me back here in the brush."

"Legs not much for hiking, but I still have a keen mind and sharp wits. Suspected that raven belonged to the Stilkskins, and I calculated the trajectory of its flight and discerned its taking off point." Humpty Dumpty sat noisily beside the boy on a pile of leaves and moss.

"Really?" asked Budy.

"No, you bumpkin, I asked around. Several forest animals said some guy was over this way muttering to himself. I assumed it would be you," a smug smile spread across the egg's face.

Budy was really not in the mood for any of the egg's nonsense. He wasn't quite sure which of the stories he'd just been told was the true one, or indeed if either was, but more talk was unlikely to settle the question, and, in truth, he really didn't care. He was tired, cold and hungry.

"You didn't happen to bring any food with you, did you?" he asked as he stood up.

Humpty Dumpty pursed his lips as he explained that he really didn't have any pockets to speak of, nothing roomier than you could stick a handkerchief in.

"But my coach is back by the road, so I suggest we get started trying to solve your mystery; I am an egg of my word, though Goose knows why I would bother to be that in a forest like this."

Budy could see the coach through the trees. "So you really just happened to notice me in the distance as you passed," said the boy, "isn't that right?"

The egg man did not seem to hear him.

The two tramped back to the carriage using whatever clear spots they could find among the thick growth of trees to make travel easier for the egg. Budy had studiously avoided well-worn paths to protect himself from the townspeople, but even a short hike was a bit daunting for the large egg. Humpty Dumpty was quick to point this out as Budy held back some ivy-covered branches to allow the egg to find a place to set his tender feet. Budy only considered letting go of the branch once, which, to his good credit, or perhaps his good upbringing, he did not do. Before long they reached the coach waiting on the side of the road. Budy opened the door and started to climb in.

"Door broken," yelled Humpty Dumpty at his heels. "Around to the other side, please."

"But…" he held the opened door open and looked back at the egg.

"Door broken," the egg repeated.

When Buddy put his foot on the first step Humpty Dumpty said, "When a person gives another person a free ride in his carriage that person should not question the door by which he enters." Buddy closed the door and walked around the carriage to the other side muttering too quietly for anyone to hear about the whims of arbitrary power.

Humpty Dumpty was in the carriage and sitting down when Buddy got in.

"I would have let you go first," Buddy said as he took his seat.

Humpty Dumpty just grinned.

"You got anything to eat in here?"

"There's an egg," said Humpty Dumpty in a low voice.

"Where?"

"Sitting across from you," he sighed. "Coachman, let us be off to the king's castle," Humpty Dumpty called out. And the coach jerked into movement.

"Back into Grumbottem? But I just got chased out of there."

"But *I* didn't. Anyway, we'll be long gone before the sun sets and the people start their cooking fires. Besides we are technically not going into Grumbottem but through it. We are going to the King's Castle—King Grisly Beard—not that silly prince's castle. And it's the fastest way."

"I thought we were going to find the fairy godmother or the Blue Fairy?"

"Hmm? No. Good as found. I squeezed the information out of Cinderella when I was dining with the prince. Not hard to do if you know the technique."

"Then why are we going to see the king?"

"First things first, my boy. Can't shirk a prince's quest, now, can I? Sure way to get yourself scrambled. No, no. Not good at all. Yes, one must get permission from a higher authority before one says no to a prince. And if that prince thinks I'm going to steal him a princess from that unpalatable Andersenland. No, no—must meet with the king, his father, first, then, sure as the sun rises over the crooked house on the equinox, we'll be after that fairy godmother, or the Blue Fairy if the fairy godmother cannot be found or if she cannot help us."

"You said you knew where she was."

"*Was,* indeed, *was.* We're looking for *is.* Might want to work on that attention span."

Budy found he had no energy to wander the paths of the conversation. He leaned back and kept his face away from the window. The seat was thickly cushioned to protect its owner from bumps on the rough roads, and although the trip was short, Budy fell asleep on the first soft bed he had felt for days.

When the coach pulled up to the castle, the egg let the boy sleep and made his way alone to see the king. He was not pleased to find 100 steps leading from the street to the main door of the palace, but not having the boy to complain to, he ascended silently. Or almost silently. He did mutter a bit as he grew tired climbing the wide, curving marble stairs, but no one heard him.

The egg man groaned as he reached hundredth step. He wiped his forehead with a small silk hanky that he kept in his vest pocket and breathed deeply. The two guards at the doorway stared down upon him. He stood about waist high on these giants, and they waited for him to speak or to try to enter the castle.

He held up a finger, gulped, took a breath, and finally spoke.

"Baron Ovum to see the king," he proclaimed with all the haughtiness he could slip into a huff.

"Is he expecting you?" asked one of the guards.

"Perhaps. He is the king. One might expect him to be on top of things in his own domain."

The guard raised an eyebrow and frowned.

"Come, come, my good man. I have just been with the prince his son and he has set me on a task that His Majesty will want to know of. I have urgent business to discuss with His Majesty. *Urgent* business."

The guard whispered something to the other guard, and then he slipped into the castle.

"Do you suppose he will take long?" asked Humpty Dumpty.

The guard didn't answer him.

AS SOON AS JESSICA LEFT THE BOATMAN BEHIND, the bird calmed down.

"I don't know if you're schizophrenic or if you just saved me from something," she said aloud, which made the bird twitter in a way that sounded a lot like a laugh. Jessica decided it was happy. She knew of course that the bird was really Inge, somehow—Inge freed from the curse at last. But despite all the fairyland adventures she had had, it was still hard to think of this bird as anything other than a bird. Perhaps that was because it could not talk. It lead her to a corridor that sloped upward to the light. First Jessica walked easily up it, sure the walk would be swift and safe. But as the ground became jagged with rocks and pebbles and the ceiling got lower and lower, she grew less sure. The bird would stop and tweet at her, and she'd continue faster. Escaping hell was going to be a bit harder than making it on time to her next class.

The air felt cooler as she climbed, but dry, and Jessica seemed to think she could see a pin prick of sunlight ahead. The ground became so acutely sloped that she needed to bend over and use her hands to keep her balance. Up she went with only a few glances behind to be sure she wasn't being followed. It had grown pitch black below. She could not see far enough to assure herself she was alone, but when she stopped to catch her breath she heard no one was scrabbling up the rocky incline.

"Can't imagine that fat old lady could make it up this path, but her great grandson," she still resisted calling him the devil, "he could probably make it easily enough." The bird was tweeting again.

"I'm coming, I'm coming."

On she climbed. Slipping on loose scree, she grabbed out with her hands and managed to grip a large lump of rock on the wall. Using it for purchase she pulled herself up onto firmer soil and continued towards the small speck of light that was thankfully growing larger and making the path easier to see.

She heard above her a coarse voice shouting. Tired as she was, Jessica decided instantly she would not take another break until she was on the surface again. The hole turned out to be almost big enough for her to walk through standing straight up, but she crouched and climbed through using one last bit of strength and rolled on her side, hot, sweaty, filthy, and exhausted. There seemed to be no one around. Whatever voice she'd heard was gone.

The bird tweeted once more and flew into the sky. Jessica watched it go until it vanished in the sun. Her eyes were still adjusting to the light, but she peered up hoping to see a sign that Inge had reached heaven, wondering what an Andersen version of heaven would be like.

"Thank you," she called to the small animal as it soared higher and higher. "I never would have known how to escape without you."

Not far away she could see a stream of quickly flowing water, and the sight of its clean ripples and its fresh smell urged her to get up and run.

As she removed her filthy clothes, she thought of how rarely anyone in a story strips naked to clean herself in a river without being spotted by someone. But she really desperately needed to get the sweat of the climb and the odors of hell cleaned away. She climbed into the bracing water, hoping this, whatever it was, was not that kind of story.

"Soap would be nice," she said out loud. But she would have to be happy with just getting most of this horrible muck and sweat off her with the current. The next fairytale she went to had better have clean clothes and a scented tub to wash in. These disgusting locations had no place in a children's book.

Once she had washed herself as clean as possible, and rinsed her hair at least three times, she returned to the bank. She looked at the pile of filthy clothes near the rock. She could smell them even at this distance. Well, there was only one thing to do. Looking around carefully, she darted out, staying low. She grabbed her clothes and hopped back in the river. So far so good. The good thing about fairy lands was there were vast tracts without any people in them at all. She soaked and wrung her clothes several times in the fast-moving water in the hopes of getting them if not dirt-free at least no longer stinking of the filth and sulfur of hell. The few small frogs and spiders she found in the folds of her skirt she flushed away with the water's flow.

She hated putting on wet clothes. No one had spotted her. And it occurred to her again as it had often before that when you are actually in a fairy land, many things happen that no writer would waste time putting down. But, still, she had tempted fate long enough. Well, if anyone did spot me, she could just say she was trying on the clothes she'd bought from the Emperor's tailors. She chuckled at her own joke.

As she left the bank, she heard singing. Turning back, she saw a round wooden boat floating in the stream with three people in it.

Hiding behind thick branches she watched as the tub floated by. The men were all in white, but one had a chef's hat and one seemed to have a soiled apron.

"Butcher, baker and candle stick maker," she said to herself as they bobbed past. So she must be in Mother Goose Land. But how could she be? How could she, an adult, make it into such a simple fairyland—the very one in which she'd lost Buddy so long ago? Would she ever understand magic?

"Just accept your good luck, Jessica," she whispered. Her plan was now obvious. She was going to find Humpty Dumpty's wall and ask the egg for help. He was, after all, the best traveler between tales she'd ever met. He wouldn't know about Gary or Doug, of course—unless she knew absolutely nothing about magic—but that egg seemed to know a lot for a creature who disdained walking and sat on a wall all day long. She was sure he would know or be able to find out how the Stiltskins had done as parents and if Buddy was really happy with this new life. He might also know how to get her home, now that there was no way back the way she came.

She left the shaded woods and found a field of grass and daisies where she enjoyed the feel of warm sunlight on her body. She wasn't exactly clean, and a bit of the pungency of hell still clung to her, but things were so much better here in this field that she could not help but feel happy.

On the far side of the field a young girl in a frilly dress was sitting on a small, three-legged stool. She was eating from a bowl, and seemed quite out of place in the middle of nowhere having her lunch. Jessica did not recognize the girl until she got close enough to see her bowl was filled with what seemed like watery cottage cheese.

"Did you fall in the river?" asked the girl as Jessica approached.

"What? Oh yeah, my clothes. Yes, I guess so."

"I don't recall a rhyme about anyone falling in a river, but I am not up on the latest, and truth be told, I'm not very well read."

"And you don't like spiders," Jessica added.

"What! Where? Is there a spider on me?" Miss Muffet starting slapping at her arms and legs and spilled some of her whey.

"No, no. I didn't say there was a spider on you," Jessica glanced at her clothes to be sure no spiders from hell were still on her. "You are really high strung aren't you?"

"I hate them," she said with a shudder. "Horrible things, too many legs."

"By the way, do you know which direction Humpy Dumpty's wall is in?"

"I'd squash 'em all if I could stand the thought of touching one. What? Humpty Dumpty? Yeah, nearer to town. Not so far from the road," the girl wiped a bit of the whey off her dress.

"Yes, but which way?"

"Over there," Miss Muffet pointed. "And take any spiders you brought with you."

"I REALLY DON'T THINK WE CAN HELP YOU," Doug said for the third or fourth time.

"Look, Mr. Smith, my friend, I have to say, is not enjoying himself here in your lovely world. I don't understand it. I've asked him to explain, but he's... well, he's having a hard time making sense of it. Now I would love to help you, but I think, under the circumstances, if we first do what we came here to do, and then once that's completed, I'm sure Charlie here will be in a much better mood..."

The blacksmith of Grumbottem let out a loud gust of air that made Doug think better of finishing this thought. "'Tis not a question any longer," he said sternly. "I did ask you once and you did lie to me and sneak away like thieves. Now 'tis *telling* I am about. You will stay and you will help. Methinks you feel your quest important, but I say to you, my fine men, it doth pale to mine." He pushed the two men ahead of him and strode swiftly behind making them walk faster than they would have liked.

Charlie turned to Doug, "Having a hard time? Really? I think I've been pretty clear."

Richard Smith growled.

"Okay, I get it," Charlie said over his shoulder. "We'll just have to find Buddy some other time, I guess"

Richard clapped the two on the shoulder, and they all slowed down. He said, "I know you are from the Merica. Your speech be so knotted, so like a vine that doth grow back upon itself that you could be from nowhere besides. Your former clothes had been less of substance than those of the poorest servant, and yet it is well made and not torn or threadbare. I did meet one from your country years ago and she did use witchery that did send me here."

"So you're not from here?" asked Charlie.

"'Tis truth thou speakest. 'Tis but ten year have I been in this land as I do log the time."

"Are you married? Do you have children here?" asked Charlie, as it occurred to him that in ten years his story could well have been altered.

"Truly, I am not of the marrying kind. I do keep to myself in search of Lord Locksley and do hope I might find the witch girl or the way she did use to bring me here."

Doug looked startled; he could do little but stare at Charlie, open mouthed. Charlie understood. He had told Doug over and over to keep their origins secret. The less these people knew about other worlds, the less likely they'd be looking to visit them. But Charlie himself did not mind the mixing of worlds. In fact he preferred it in his bones. But did he want to be responsible for the chaos of worlds he'd experienced the last time he'd been through the portal? Did he really want to do anything that would rouse the Sorceress of Oz? This man, however, seemed to know an awful lot about things already. And though he himself had railed against the way that Glinda the-so-called Good assumed she had authority over all fairylands, he did not wish to call her attention to his resumed travels by reconnecting all the severed pathways. He might just rather face the devil one more time.

Doug started to speak, but Charlie cut him off.

"Don't go jumping to any conclusions. I know it seems like this guy knows stuff, but we might be jumping the gun here."

"You see," Richard Smith tossed his auburn red hair as he stopped suddenly, "every time either one of thee doth speak, he doth show you to be not of this place. 'Twas the same with Janey. Young though she was, she did speak in riddles, like the witch that I have come to believe that she was. She did cast a spell on me and the Lord of Locksley, and though she did help us escape the dungeon, cruelly did she send me to this dreadful land and poor Robin to some other fateful place I know not, as I suppose."

"Robin of Locksley? Robin Hood?" asked Doug.

"Doth thou know of him? How doth thou? Be he safe?" Richard's voice revealed real concern.

"We know *of* him, but we have not seen him," said Doug. "But who is this Janey? I don't recall a witch child in Robin Hood. Do you, Charlie?"

Charlie shook his head. There had been so many different tales of Robin Hood, but none he could recall with a witch child.

Richard Smith led them back to his smithy as they spoke. Once inside they sat on small sturdy wooden stools, and Richard Smith, who stood almost six and a half foot tall, folded his long muscled arms and looked intently upon the two strangers.

"He does seem to know things," began Doug.

"I know, but think of the risk of screwing around with the worlds. You heard what happened last time."

"I think his world is already screwed up if he isn't in it."

Charlie kept recalling the words Glinda had used years before and the agreement he had reluctantly accepted.

"I thought you destroyed all the doorways," said Doug.

"They must have missed some."

"So there's still one out there somewhere to get us and him back."

"Small chance of that," said Richard. "No sooner did I arrive than I dismantled and burned it."

"You burned your own way back?"

"Think of it. I did not know I did land in this other world. And I did but just escape a deadly dungeon. Neither did I wish to return there nor leave a means for those there to seek after me."

Doug looked up at Richard Smith. "You said you escaped a dungeon? Who exactly are you? You someone important?"

"I hath not spoke my true name these ten years. I do fear what might befall if mine enemies ever did come to know what hath befallen me. But as it seemeth that no one in this place doth know my true name, nor is any man hard by just now..."

Doug and Charlie leaned forward as the man continued in a quieter voice.

"I be the Duke of Normandy, the Duke of Aquitaine, the Duke of Gascony, the Lord of Cyprus, the Count of Anjou, the Count of Maine, the Count of Nantes, and, best known of all, I am Richard, Coeur de Lion, of England."

"Richard the Lionhearted?" shouted Doug as both Charlie and the king grabbed him.

"Doth thou think I hath kept the name secret for all these years only to have it cried in the streets with the voice of a peddler?" Richard said through gritted teeth.

"We're not in the street," muttered Doug.

If Charlie or the king heard him they did not respond.

"This makes no sense," Charlie thought aloud. "King Richard went on the Crusades. He died in..." But perhaps it was not a good idea to tell a character in a story how he dies.

"Aye, I did go on the Crusades but I did not die there in despite of the rumors. I was on my way back to retake my throne when I was captured and put in the dungeon where I fell upon Lord Robin of Locksley."

"And some kid named Janey?" asked Doug.

"No, she was a human child when I did see her. No more than nine or ten year old. But a powerful witch she was to curse me this way. Now

I hath lived in a land where dragons fly over our very heads and witches and wizards boldly stalk the streets a-night."

"I think she must have come from OzHouse," said Charlie, though he did not recall anyone by the name of Janey.

The king jumped to his feet. "That be the cursed name. Ahs House in the Merica."

"I think we need to do some 'splainin around here," Doug said to Charlie.

Even Charlie had to admit the tales were sufficiently messed up by the intrusion of some child named Janey that no sharing of the facts could likely make things worse.

"GET HER OUT OF THERE," Gary and Gwen shouted together.

"Relax," said Isabelle with a smirk and a nod of her head. "She's right here." She pushed open the back of the wardrobe and peeked into the secret room. She leaned into the room between the slats and made a grab at Amanda.

"No," the toddler yelled.

"Stop being difficult," Isabelle shouted into the room.

"Just get her out of there," Gwen repeated.

"Okay, okay, it's not like she's going to break anything." Isabelle made another grab at her daughter.

"It's not that," Gary said sternly. "It's not safe in there. Get her out right now."

An odd, rank odor faintly wafted through the open door. But from what Isabelle could see, other than that, it seemed like a perfect playroom for a child. She didn't see how it could be unsafe. More likely the Robbinses didn't want Amanda near their precious the old toys, probably antiques, and pretty books. She managed to grab Amanda's foot and tried to pull her out.

"You shouldn't grab her feet," said Debbie who had remained quiet as long as she could. "You could make her fall."

Amanda fell. Loud screams echoed all the way down the hall.

"See, I told you." Debbie's voice could almost be heard over the crying child.

"She's fine," said Isabelle. "It's just for attention."

"She hit her head," said Gwen.

"All right, all right. You wanted her out of your damn room. I'm getting her out." Isabelle continued to reach into the room and shout back at the Robbinses at the same time.

"That's a bad word," said Debbie.

"You're gonna hear a lot more bad words in a minute if you don't shut up."

"Momma never told me to shut up. She said it was important to allow children to ask questions and to be a part of a conversation."

"Well she's dead now, so I'm telling you to shut your little mouth."

"Isabelle, what a horrible thing to say. I'm sure she didn't mean that, Debbie."

Though Gwen was shocked, Debbie didn't seem at all upset.

"We don't listen to negativity," she said. "It just means grownups are cranky. Everyone has their own problems."

Gary tried to calm things down, but Isabelle wasn't one for being calmed down when she was angry. She finally stopped muttering and cursing and pushed her whole body between the slats and into the room and grabbed up her child with both hands.

"Now you shut up too," she said as he hauled the toddler off the rug.

"Go in there and get them out," Gwen said to Gary.

"I could go Mrs. Robbins. I fit better," Debbie said.

"Thank you, Debbie, but Mr. Robbins can do it," Gary leaned into the closet.

"Is she all right?" he asked as he stood up in the Narnia room.

"She's fine. I am her mother. I think I know how to care for my own child." And she gave the baby a stern look and muttered comments about being quiet and that she was just making a fuss over nothing.

"Let's just get out of here, please," Gary said.

"Are you coming out?" Gwen called in.

Okay, okay keep your shirts on. What the hell is so special about this place that you want us out of it so bad? You don't actually think it's magic like that kid said I'm sure. Did something die in here? It smells like a toilet."

"I didn't say that," Debbie called in as Gwen held her from crawling back into the room.

"We'll explain it all as soon as we are out of here and back downstairs where it is safe," Gary said with a nervous glance and a sniff.

Isabelle saw his look and followed his gaze. She'd seen some book through the door but saw now that the room was full of them—old books and it was crowded with toys and furniture and games. This stuff was probably worth a fortune. Isabelle shook herself as though she were waking up from a dream. She said, "I'm sorry I was upset about Amanda," and under her breath she said, "no sense in killing the goose that laid the golden egg…"

As she crouched to leave the room, Gary grabbed her shoulder.

"Oh, no," he said.

Fearing he somehow knew what she was thinking, Isabelle turned and looked as innocent as she could. "What is wrong, Mr. Robbins?"

"I heard what you said. You can't quote anything before you leave this room."

"Excuse me? I didn't say anything," she said.

"Just wait a moment before you leave. Give yourself time to clear your mind," Gary said with a heavy sigh, "and fill your mind with, I don't know, cars, computers, garbage trucks."

"Garbage trucks? Yeah, you might want to find the source of that smell. But, really, I didn't have any ideas in my head, Mr. Robbins."

Gary glanced around the room again. It wasn't hard to find it now that he was looking, a wad of cloth and an old hat behind the couches. He picked it all up and made a face. Meanwhile Amanda crawled out of the room and Gwen was still calling in to Gary and Isabelle to hurry up out.

Gary held the clothing as far from his face as he could and took a breath. "Certainly. Think of garbage trucks. Now, I guess we can go."

One after the other Isabelle and Gary slipped through the small opening and through the closet and into the hallway.

"Now, close this door and let's go downstairs," Gwen said.

"Fine," said Isabelle. "Where's Amanda?"

"IS HE COMING OR NOT?" Humpty Dumpty huffed.

"The king is not going to come down and meet you at the door," grumbled the guard.

"I've been standing here for," he removed his pocket watch, "almost 15 minutes."

"You'll stand here as long as His Majesty deems it necessary, egg."

"Courtesy costs you nothing," Humpty Dumpty sighed. "Isn't there a waiting room with a chair or maybe a low wall?"

"You will get to sit in the waiting chamber if the king decides if he will be bothered to give you audience," the guard explained.

"A rather unfortunate custom you have here," Humpty said.

"It is our way," the guard smiled broadly.

Humpty Dumpty turned with an impulse to charge off in a huff. But he paused before taking a step. He stared down the long winding stairway he'd so recently struggled up, all one hundred steps, and thought he'd give the king another moment. Just then, the large oak door opened and the first guard returned.

CHAPTER FOURTEEN

They say in these clothes I am dashing
As the trim of my suit I am flashing.
An excellent cut
For my excellent strut,
In yellow and white I am smashing!

"LIMERICKS?" SAID JESSICA TO HERSELF. There were a number of them tacked in a row along the length of Humpty Dumpty's abandoned wall. Another one read,

> The Land of the Goose is a bore.
> There's so many worlds to explore.
> I'm going to Oz
> And staying because
> I happen to know there's a door.

This and several others seemed to serve to inform whoever might want informing where the egg man might be or might have been or might be going to be. He certainly was not where he was supposed to be, which was on this wall.

Jessica had had no trouble finding the wall once she found her own way to the village of Mother Goose proper, where all the famous houses were—the crooked house, Old King Cole's castle, and, of course, the Old Woman Who Lived in a Shoe's shoe house. That old woman's name was Hubbard. (Jessica noticed a surprising number of old women in Mother Goose Land.) She didn't find out if the Old Woman of the Shoe was the famous Mrs. Hubbard, Mother Hubbard. She hadn't gotten around to asking, although it did occur to her once she thought of it that both The Old Woman and Mother Hubbard were famously short on food. The Mrs. Hubbard she'd talked to tended to control the conversation. Jessica had gone to her house to ask directions to Humpty Dumpty's wall and had been invited in to tea, which politeness made her accept. But there had been no tea. And the place was overrun with children, just as you'd expect it to be. And if there was a dog, the dog would very likely have had no bone. But she had seen no dog. So whether this Mother Hubbard was *the* Mother Hubbard or perhaps *the* Mother Hubbard's sister or something, the truth was pretty plain: the Hubbards were not a wealthy people.

Jessica told her story to Mrs. Hubbard. When she got to the part where she tunneled up from hell, the old woman's eyes became bigger than the lenses of her glasses.

"Hell?" she exclaimed, "under Mother Goose Land?"

"I thought it was odd."

"Odd," the word shot out of the Old Woman's mouth. "I'll say it's odd. It's a great deal *more* than odd, it's practically unfathomable. If there's one place hell should *not* be, it is Mother Goose Land, now, isn't it?"

"Well, yes, I guess. But technically, it's not..."

"You *guess?*" Mrs. Hubbard would not be interrupted. "And that girl you mentioned who was turned into a bird, of course she should have come up in the same world she went down in, shouldn't she? Of course she should. You've changed her story."

"I?"

"Who else? You've done a very very bad thing."

Jessica wanted to blame Doug. But, as usual, she couldn't think of any way to pin this on anyone but herself. No one had forced her to come through the door again. In fact, it was her own idea to do so. "Yeah, but it never changes anything in the books, the stories I mean, if that's any help. We've confirmed it over and over again."

"Why would *that* be any help? Even if it's true, which I doubt. No, no, stories are always changing. Can't help that. But hell?—here?—in Mother Goose Land?" She couldn't get over it. "Where I actually live? To me, it's not a story, young woman. It's hell. In Mother Goose Land." She repeated the phrase as though the sounds needed repetition for the meaning to settle in. "If you think Old King Cole can stand up against the devil—no, no, no. Not with all the king's horses and all the king's men."

"But what makes you think the devil even *could* come to Mother Goose Land. *I* had a hard time getting here. And I'm much younger and nicer than him."

"'Than *he*,' deary. But you *did* get here. Nor do I see how you can call bringing hell to children's rhymes *nice*. And I'm sure the devil can get to any place hell has a mouth in. Don't you think so too? Of course you do. No, no, no, you will have to cover up that hell mouth. Fill it, fill it, fill it."

"I will?"

"Most absolutely, you will. You made it, you fix it."

"But I have to find Robin Hood, and I have to find King Richard, and I have to do what I came for. I have to find Buddy and..."

"And you have to fill in that hell mouth."

"But I didn't actually make it, not actually."

"Fill it, fill it, fill it." Mrs. Hubbard spilled her soup.

"You remember Buddy," Jessica tried to change the subject.

But Mrs. Hubbard had no recollection of anyone named Buddy.

"No," said Jessica, "I guess you wouldn't." Why would this frenetic woman remember one little boy who may have wandered by for a minute many years before?

But Mrs. Hubbard wasn't paying attention to anything Jessica was saying. "You must promise me you will fix this mistake you have so egregiously made. Promise me."

"All right, I promise." Jessica slapped herself on the forehead. "But first I have to find Humpty Dumpty."

"Humpty Dumpty? Why would you want to find him?"

"So he can help me."

"Help you? Ever met him? Find strangers? I don't think so. Fill a hell mouth? Not likely. Sound like Humpty Dumpty tasks to you? No, no. Unless you have in mind something for the benefit of Humpty Dumpty, or something in the line of a riddle or puzzle perhaps, there's very little hope of help from him. How could he help you anyway?"

"He knows things," she said. "And he has a good heart, really, under his hard shell."

"Good heart, nice girl? My, but you are full of pretty unproven conclusions. Remains to be seen, I say—Good heart! And as for knowing things, sure. I imagine. I've never really been able to tell for certain. He *says* things. Says them with great confidence, but as for whether he *knows* them, it never really seems to trump into his thinking, does it?"

When Jessica insisted, the Old Woman pointed her in the direction of Humpty Dumpty's wall. So Jessica left, without having had any tea but not without being reminded twice more of her promise to seal the hell mouth. She sauntered on down to the wall, where she found no egg. Just limericks lined up from left to right like targets for target practice. One read:

> An egg, he must get out and travel
> And explore from the pole to the navel.
> The world, it's so various,
> Its peoples hilarious,
> There's so many things to unravel.

And another one read:

> There once was an egg in fine trim
> Who had tea in the Forest of Grimm.
> He feasted on quince
> With a Jolly Old Prince
> And as for that Egg, I am—he!

"He?" If she'd had a pen, Jessica would have crossed it out and fixed it.

So it appeared Humpty Dumpty had taken to traveling about, and to more places than Wonderland. This was good news. If he really had gone to the Forest of Grimm, then surely he'd have looked up Buddy. But as Jessica read for more clues she also found other, contrary limericks that suggested the egg was not enjoying all this traveling and was no longer doing it:

> It's easily over, I'm done.
> This egg, it will no longer run
> Or scramble away
> In a second. I say:
> Short order is no longer fun!

And

> All this traveling isn't a joke.
> Soft shells are so easily broke.
> Getting pitched from a wall
> Is no free-for-all.
> And landing is hard on the yoke!

Apparently he'd met troubles in his travels and had given up on them. Which was just like him to do. But if he didn't like adventures, where was he? He'd have to be around here, somewhere.

Not far away, a man and a woman could be seen strolling slowly down the road, the woman moving one arm and waving one hand in animated conversation. They were close enough for Jessica to see that their bodies were bent and frail. The man might have wished to wave his arms as well, for he was talking just as loudly, but the one arm was occupied with a cane and the other was being held onto by the woman—whether to give or to receive support, Jessica couldn't tell. Though it was hard to make out the words, they were clearly arguing. "No," said the woman, as she drew into range, "you may not. It is locked up tight, and I alone have the key."

"But the doctor said I may." His voice was somewhat cloudy and yet surprisingly strong. "He said I may have meat. Much as I want."

"Meat," the woman coughed.

"Mutton specifically."

"Well, he didn't say you could have *my* meat." It seemed odd that the woman would speak with such ire and yet make no motion to release the Old Man's arm.

"Excuse me," said Jessica.

"I have lived on rice, gruel, and sago for so long, you can hardly imagine," said the man.

"And that is why you were always welcome in Exeter."

"And you always offered me meat," said the man.

"Because I knew you would not take it," said the woman.

"Excuse me," said Jessica a little louder. The pair seemed to have stopped deliberately before her but continued arguing as though she were not there.

"So I suggest you go that way back to Tobago, and I will go this way back to Exeter and either you give up this delusion of meat or hereafter we may be better strangers."

"Hello," said Jessica more loudly than she'd intended.

"Well, that was rude," said the old man.

"Well, I never," said the old woman.

"Never what?" said Jessica, who'd always wanted to hear the end of that sentence.

"Never heard that word spoken in that tone," said the woman. "What in the name of the Goose do you want?"

"I want to know where Humpty Dumpty is."

"Oh, you won't find him here on his wall," said the man. "Hasn't been here more time than it takes to stop and pace and tack another poem on, not for quite a long time, so they say."

"They do?"

"They do."

"Then why are *you* here?" said Jessica.

"To read the limericks of course," said the old man.

"One thing the two of us are particularly fond of is limericks," said The Old Woman from Exeter. "It's one of the things we have in common."

"Which is why we get along so well," said the man.

"We're limericks ourselves you know, both of us." She said this as though she were saying what sign of the zodiac they shared. "Which is another thing we have in common."

"Isn't that the same thing?" Jessica asked.

"We *like* limericks," said the man.

"And we *are* limericks," said the woman.

"Two things. Definitely two things."

"Where did you go to school?" the woman asked rhetorically. Jessica's silence and blank expression pushed the woman on. "Listen here,

> There dwelt an old woman at Exeter;
> When visitors came it sore vexed her,
> So for fear they should eat,
> She locked up all her meat,
> This stingy old woman of Exeter."

The woman smiled and bowed her head as she finished her lyric as though to her mind "stingy" was a compliment.

"And another thing we have in common is meat, the love of meat," said The Old Man from Tobago, with a distinct and pointed tone. "Here's mine,

> There was an old man of Tobago,
> Who lived on rice, gruel and sago
> Till, much to his bliss,
> His physician said this—
> To a leg, sir, of mutton you may go."

And he too nodded his head.

"What's the big attraction of meat?" asked Jessica.

Neither the old man nor the old woman had any interest in the question.

"How'd *you* get here anyway?" The old man sounded suspicious, as though anyone who belonged in Mother Goose Land would not have to be told his story.

"Never mind." The old woman let go the man's arm and began reading over the limericks. The old man hobbled over to join her.

"He traveled for a while but then got tired of it," Jessica observed, smiling broadly at her own cleverness. "So what I'm wondering is, where is he?"

"Pretty proud of those powers of deduction," the old man chuckled, clearly less than impressed himself as he leaned over the woman's arm and read the rhymes along with her.

"That's the problem with starting from text," the old woman said.

"True," said the old man.

"I'm sorry," said Jessica.

"As well you should be," said the old woman. "Much better to start from facts, don't you think?"

Jessica had no idea what they were talking about.

"You say he got tired of traveling. Could that be because you read the limericks from left to right?" said the old man.

"Never let the facts interfere with your reading," the old woman snickered.

"But if you would read from right to left," said the man, "you would see that what he got tired of was *sitting*."

"Now *that* is brilliant," said the old woman.

"And deserving of reward," said the old man. "I suggest meat."

"Except that when I said 'brilliant,'" the old woman rejoined, "what I meant was 'obvious.'"

"But," said the old man.

"Tobago," said the woman, "would be that way." And she pointed.

Jessica followed the woman's finger in the direction of Tobago. It was, it seemed, in the same direction as Mrs. Hubbard's shoe. This was made particularly apparent by the fact that Old Mrs. Hubbard herself was at that moment coming toward the three of them at Humpty Dumpty's wall, leading one of her children by the hand. The child was struggling to keep up, jogging, or rather being jogged along behind the Old Woman's voluminous dress by her no-nonsense stride.

"Excuse me, strange girl," said the Old Woman as soon as she got into earshot. "Leave something behind?"

"I'm sorry," yelled Jessica.

"Should be," said Mrs. Hubbard.

"Well, I never," said the woman from Exeter.

"Never what?" said Jessica.

"Never mind," said the woman.

"No, I don't suppose you do," said the old man from Tobago.

"This one is *not* mine," said Mrs. Hubbard. "Found her running around among the rest, but clearly not mine at all. And frankly I have enough. Not taking strays." The little girl remained hidden behind the woman's dress.

"I'm afraid I don't have any," said Jessica.

Just then the girl peered around the woman's knees. "Ahn Jessa," she said, wide mouthed.

Jessica leapt forward and scooped the girl, shaking her head as though to wake herself up as she did. "Amanda? How did you..."

"Goosh," said Amanda.

THE SOUND OF A CAR HORN penetrated the walls of OzHouse; it blew through the glass window of the Narnia room and through the open door of the closet.

"Where is Amanda?" Isabelle demanded. "You can't just let a little girl wander in a place like this. What is wrong with you people?"

The sound of the slamming of the front door travelled through the walls and subtly vibrated the floorboards under the feet of Gary and Gwen, Isabelle and Debbie.

"She never came through the closet," said Gwen. "She's still in the playroom."

But Isabelle had seen her climb up and out.

"Hello," came a voice up the stairwell and down the hall, a voice well known in OzHouse. "Where the bloody hell is everybody?"

"Oh, dear," said Gary.

"*She'll* find *us*," said Gwen when Gary was about to welcome the traveler home. "Amanda isn't in there? She has to be."

"'manda," Isabelle yelled. "'manda." She looked back through the wardrobe. "She came through the door. I *saw* her."

"I know where she is," said Debbie, quietly.

The sound of heavy steps climbed toward them from down the hall.

"I know where she is," Debbie repeated, a little more loudly.

"Where? Where the hell is she?" Isabelle raised her voice. "What did you do with her?"

"She disappeared."

"I know she disappeared."

The form of a woman in shadow filled the archway at the end of the hall. A heavy suitcase dropped to the floor with a thud.

"She's in Oz," said Debbie.

"Whose car is that in the driveway? Did someone sell the place and move out while I was gone?"

"Hey, Beth," said Gary.

"Did no one get my message? Why did no one get me at the airport? Why do you all have phones if you never turn them on? And where the hell is Doug?"

"What are you talking about?" Isabelle asked Debbie.

"I'll get her," said Debbie, and she climbed through the rack of coats into the secret room.

"Oh, no you don't," Gary chased after her.

"She's *not* in there," said Isabelle.

Gary followed Debbie into the room and back through the wardrobe. Gary fell into the hallway, hurting his knee. Debbie landed feet first in Oz.

"I'M SERIOUS," SAID CHARLIE, "it's the same thing. We're after the same thing. We need a way out of this world and back to our own just like you. And a doorway is the only way I know of to get there."

"Ah, but *my* doorway doth lead to Sherwood Forest."

"One doorway to both places, trust me."

Richard looked skeptical—intimidatingly so. Standing by his well-worn work table, he cast a long shadow on Charlie and Gary, who were seated on three-legged stools.

"Okay, it's hard to trust us right now," Charlie said. "I get that. But I still don't see how we can help you or you can help us. Our door was destroyed by the devil and yours was destroyed by yourself—meaning that unless there is still another door we don't know of, we are screwed."

"Screwed?" Richard twisted an imaginary tool in his hand.

"Stuck," said Charlie. "Trapped in Grimm."

"Never mind that," said Doug. "Minor detail. Tell him about Rumpel-stiltskin."

Charlie glowered at Doug.

"Rumpels…?" said Richard.

"…stiltskin."

"It's a wild theory. But if it pans out, perhaps…"

"Say on," said Richard.

"Thanks, Doug." Charlie proceeded reluctantly, "Okay. Rumpelstilt-skin is a guy—a magical dwarf—he seems to know a way to go between worlds without the door. I mean, he got a letter to Jessica, somehow, or his wife did, without using the door. So if we can find Buddy, he can lead us to Rumpelstiltskin, or if we find Rumpelstiltskin, he can lead us to Buddy, although that seems like kind of a side quest at this point, but we still have to do it or Jessica will never shut up, and since we are looking for Rumpelstiltskin anyway, why not? And maybe that will lead us out of here so Doug can reconcile with Beth, assuming he still wants to, and also satisfy Jessica so she doesn't come back and start all this fun all over again."

"He used to like visiting fairy lands," said Doug. "I think it's a hoot, myself."

"I never liked being *trapped* in fairy lands. And I don't like being chased by the devil. And I'm not a kid anymore. Might have mentioned that already. I don't go on roller coasters that much either."

"Didst thou say 'reconcile with his wife'?" asked Richard, and "'if he doth want to'? I know many a man unreconciled with his wife, but none that do find the state satisfactory."

"People sometimes grow apart," said Doug.

"But this is Beth," said Charlie.

"But as thou must be with her the rest of thy days…" said Richard.

"Why?" said Doug. "Why must I be with her the rest of my days? Maybe we're not the same people anymore."

"Didst this one not say thou wert married? Thou hast ta'en the vow, 'till death.' Is't not so in the Merica?"

"We wrote our own vows, actually," said Doug. "But, sure, that's the idea. You hope of course. You don't expect to grow apart. But," he exhaled, "these things happen."

"Buck up, man," said Richard.

"You sound like a country song," said Charlie.

"Maybe it was just the kids. I think that's most of what we had. And when they stopped sending us children, she kinda went away. She spends half the year in England with her parents. It's not unusual."

Richard laid his big hand on the table. "There be a portal from the Merica to England?"

"Not *your* England," Charlie laughed.

"Be there other Englands?"

"Well, no, I mean, there are other time… Well, yeah, I guess, because there's the real England and the fictional England."

"This man's Beth doth live in a fictional England? I must say, thou doth speak strangely."

"No, no, no. Hers is the…." but Charlie stopped again.

"In sooth, mine be not fictional," said Richard.

"Different times," Charlie grinned.

This satisfied Richard no better.

"Am I really to trust thee?" he was looking right at Charlie. "Should we find some such other door, as there may be, I say to thee now, if thou taketh me to this lawless, untimely, fictional the Merica, I shall see your real throats cut." King Richard pressed his finger so hard against the table it seemed it would collapse.

"What have you got against America?" said Doug

"Vows be broken in *my* England each day—each day that false King John, my hated brother, doth sit on her throne. That is certain. But it is a matter of some moment there. We make war over such things. In this unholy the Merica vows be held as light as skipping stones. This man's tired indifference to the breaking of his vow doth show me the Merica is more godless than the lands we have liberated for the Holy Church. I would not come to the Merica without an army."

"Wait a minute," said Doug.

"Maybe we should just worry about finding Rumpelstitlkin," said Charlie.

"Yes, yes, this Rumpel-silt-stin," said Richard. "I begin to think I have heard the name ere now."

A smile swept across Charlie's face. "...stiltskin," Doug smiled. And then to Charlie, "See, I told you we shouldn't have blown this guy off."

"So take us to him," Charlie laughed in an exhale of relief.

"Ah," said Richard. "If this be the same I know of, we do have no slight problem. Yes, as I do think, this Stiltskin be a hermit in the deep woods. Just where or how he appeareth, this I cannot say. Moreover, he doth hold his name guardedly—even in the tales. Most shadowy fellow, that. Many a story doth tell of his adventures, but as for finding him, well, many more have tried than have succeeded, if I do have him right."

Richard stood up to his full height. Suddenly all three were aware of something happening outside. Richard went to the window. "News," he said. And when he opened the window the sound of the town crier could be heard quite clearly—at the end of his declaration.

"...and the Prince orders therefore that all remain indoors until the dragon passes. Oyez-oyez."

High overhead, so high he looked hardly larger than an eagle scouting for prey, the black dragon circled.

DEBBIE RECOGNIZED THE PLACE IMMEDIATELY. Though she'd landed farther from the Yellow Brick Road than she had on her last trip, in among a stand of trees that she would have called "green birch" if there were such a thing (they looked just like the white birch trees of New Hampshire, but they were a fine emerald green), she could see the road down the hill not very far away. And once she was on the road, she could see the Emerald City. It couldn't be much more than a mile ahead of her, in the direction of the sun—which was setting or rising over the turrets of the city walls. When she got to the gates and knocked on the great door, she guessed the sun was setting, because she couldn't see it any more. The Guardian of the Gates opened a small door in the great big door and stepped out.

"May I call you Thurbidore yet? Or is it too soon?" she asked.

"Oh, much too soon. I never let strangers call me Thurbidore."

"I guess that's only polite," said Debbie, pleased to meet someone who had sensible rules and followed them. "We have just met."

"Oh, I'd say we have not yet quite met," said the guardian. "I am the Guardian of the Gates, pleased to make your acquaintance, Miss...ah..."

Debbie wrinkled up her lips and scratched her head. She was starting to doubt her initial impression. "Are you playing games with me?" Could his memory really be that bad? But no one could forget another person so quickly—it had been no more than one or two hours at most. And her last coming had been quite eventful. So he must be playing a trick on her. "It's not polite to play tricks on people," said Debbie.

"Oh, I quite agree. A nasty habit, never to be done except among the best of friends and then strictly in good fun. What may I do for you that is not like a trick, Miss... ah....?"

"That doesn't make sense," said Debbie.

"Oh, as for that, I beg, very politely, to differ. It makes the most perfect sense, from where I'm standing," said the guardian.

"Not the rule," said Debbie. "The rule makes sense. But we're not the best of friends, because if we were, I'd be calling you Thurbidore. And you *are* playing a trick on me. *That* doesn't make sense." Just when she'd become almost convinced that this world wasn't a dream after all, it started acting like a dream all over again. The whole day had been like a dream. And maybe it was a dream after all and she'd only thought she'd woken up before.

The guardian appeared ready to laugh. Then he appeared as though he wouldn't. "I see," he said, though he did not seem to see at all.

"I know that the Princess Ozma will be very surprised to see me again so soon," said Debbie. "But I do need to see her about a little girl named Amanda that is lost here in this land somewhere." On the possibility that the day wasn't a dream, it made good sense to do what she'd come to do. "And an older girl too, she also disappeared, a grownup girl named Jessica."

"Lost girls? With names." He gave Debbie a moment to let those last words sink in. But they didn't. "That does seem serious," he went on. "Ozma will certainly wish to know right way. Whom shall I say is calling?"

"I am."

The Guardian of the Gate put his hands on his hips. "I'm starting to believe you do not have a name." He bowed as he said it so as not to offend.

"Of course I have a name," said Debbie.

"Then I will need to borrow it from you for a while. I must pass it along to Ozma. She will need it before I can admit you. But I promise you I will give it back straight away."

Debbie put her hands on her hips. "So you *are* teasing me, Thurbidore."

"You are very free with *my* name, young girl, which I have never even offered you, and very stingy with your own. This is no way to get Ozma's help."

"I am not...." Debbie began, rising almost to anger, but she was interrupted by the Cowardly Lion who stuck his head through the door.

"What is all this roaring out here?" said the Lion. "A beast can hardly nap in peace."

Debbie had to take a deep breath not to be frightened again by the lion. "Thank goodness, you are here," she said. "The guardian won't let me in."

"This strange girl wishes to be announced to Ozma but won't divulge her name."

"Are you afraid of your name?" asked the Lion.

"You *know* my name. We've already met. I fainted right here, an hour ago, and the Shaggy Man woke me up and you took me to Oz and Polly Chrome danced on your head."

A smile curled the lips of the lion, a kind of a shy smile, as he shared a glance with the guardian.

"Come," said the Lion. "I will take you to Ozma."

Debbie was relieved finally to be recognized. But that relief lasted only as long as it took to be introduced, again, to Ozma. Ozma too pretended she'd never ever seen her before. Debbie explained again about the Shaggy man and fainting and the daughter of the rainbow, but Ozma just said, "The Shaggy Man has been wandering the back country of Oz for many years now. And I don't even remember the last time the Rainbow's Daughter came to visit us. Not this last 20 years that I know of. And I would know."

"You guys are just nuts," said Debbie. She knew perfectly well it was not the sort of thing you're supposed to say. But she was flustered, and it happened. "You all seemed so nice and so helpful, too. I was *just* here. And the Shaggy Man was here. And you sent me home from a dream. And you're not even twenty years old." Debbie shut her eyes tight and seemed on the point of tears. "Why are you playing tricks on me?" Then she turned to the Cowardly Lion and said, "Tell them to stop it."

The lion drew back a step from Debbie's anger.

"Stop what?" purred the lion.

"Pretending not to remember me. *You* remember me. Tell them..."

"I remember you..." said the lion, but it sounded like a question.

"You brought me to Ozma."

"You were disturbing my sleep and angering the Guardian of the Gates. I'm sorry. I've never seen you before," said the lion.

"You all acted very different when Lord Fossverr was here." Debbie pouted then sneered.

"Lord Fossverr?" said Ozma. "Oh, I *do* remember him. Lord Fausvert."

"Oh, yes" said the Cowardly Lion. "What ever happened to Sir Fausvert?"

"I suppose he wandered off looking for—oh, I remember, he was looking for his worthy adventure, his derring-do, something he could do to earn passage home," said Ozma.

"Why would he need that?" said the lion.

"I can't remember," said Ozma.

"I've heard the Shaggy Man say that people in other worlds have trouble accepting gifts. They have a need to pay for things," said the Cowardly Lion.

Ozma looked baffled. "I suppose he never found anything big enough to be worth the trip home. Anyway, we never saw him again. But if he's in Oz, I'm sure he's happy."

"You woke me up and sent me back to OzHouse," Debbie tried to get them back on topic.

"OzHouse," said Ozma. Clearly she'd heard that name before. "Do you come from that dreadful place?" Ozma rang a bell. "Did you come through a door?"

"How else would I get here? I have to find..." Ozma held up her hand to silence the intruder as Jellia Jamb entered the throne room.

"Do find Suzy Bishop for me, immediately," Ozma said to Jellia Jamb before turning back to Debbie. "This is terrible. Terrible. We had an agreement. Lion, find the Scarecrow and take him away to fetch Glinda." And then she turned to Debbie again. "Is that why you won't tell us your name?"

Debbie stared while a hundred expressions took turns on her face, as though her face could not find one that suited the situation. It was very strange. It was like having a hundred sets of clothes and nothing appropriate. "What is wrong with you people," she finally said. "An hour ago you were so friendly, and you all knew I came through the door, and no one said anything about any agreement about it."

Ozma got off her throne and came right down to Debbie and looked her in the eye as though searching for a clue whether to trust her or not.

"IF JILL SAYS TO JACK 'CLOSE THE DOOR' and Jack goes over and closes the door, has the communication been successful?"

"Yes," said Budy. "Obviously it has."

"Ah, ah, ah," said Humpty Dumpty.

"Not necessarily," said the king with the grizzled beard, strumming on a lyre.

"What?" said Budy. The king had ordered one of his servants to fetch Budy from the coach.

"I see where you're going, Your Majesty," said Humpty Dumpty.

"No, you don't," said Budy. "It doesn't make any sense. Jack did what Jill asked. The communication was obviously successful. How could you agree with him?"

"He *is* the king," said Humpty Dumpty.

"Precisely," said King Thrushbeard. "But in this case, I also happen to be right. Consider, my impetuous young man, if you can, the whole story." The king plucked three chords in quick succession. "Why has Jill told Jack to close the door?"

"Maybe she's cold. Maybe there's a wolf outside. What has that got to do with anything?"

"Oh, everything," said the king. "Jill may have had those reasons in mind. Or perhaps Jill just wanted to show Jack who was in charge. Maybe Jill wanted to reconcile with Jack after an argument and could think of nothing else to say. Or maybe she wanted to see how Jack would close the door in order to decide whether he was the kind of man she was willing to marry. You see, every word vibrates with many sounds." And he strummed the lyre for emphasis.

"I understand precisely," said the egg man.

"No, you don't," said Budy.

"Listen," and the king played a few bars of a tune as he spoke in a kind of musical cadence. He had a good singing voice.

> For ev-'ry-thing a person says
> there are a thousand things unsaid,
> someofwhich the speakermaywish
> to com-mun-i-cate
> buuuuuuut,
> which, may, ormaynot e-ver reach,
> the un-der-stand-ing of the spoken to.

And then he stopped strumming. "Is that clear?"

"As glass," said the egg man.

"Coated in bird poop," said Budy.

"Of course it's not clear. They're sentences. That's the point." And the king played a while on his lyre without speaking. Finally he looked up, "Would one of you please light the candles?"

"Oh, it's plenty bright in here, I think," said Humpty Dumpty nervously.

"No matches," said Budy.

"The truth is we do not and never can know if the communication has been successful. Neither can Jack. Neither can Jill. Hence it was *not* successful, since to be successful is *ipso facto* to know it has been successful."

"You're just thinking way too much," said Budy. "And why are we talking about this anyway?" The king had seemed quite friendly until Humpty Dumpty had divulged the prince's plans to him.

"Oh, I think he's doing precisely the proper degree of thinking," Humpty Dumpty smiled and kicked Budy under the table. "He *is* the king."

"Now as for what my son has asked you to do, I suggest we entertain the possibility that what he said was not precisely what he meant."

"I was just thinking you'd want to know," said Humpty Dumpty.

"So you've said," said the king, "although in fact you were just thinking I might save you the trouble of a visit to that world and a kidnapping."

"The thought had crossed my mind," said the egg man. "Of course if it is the royal pleasure…"

"To fetch the heroine of 'The Princess and the Pea' from that 'perversion of Grimm,' as you call it? And then to drag her into Grimms' actual Forest? I think not. It is not the royal pleasure."

Humpty Dumpty sighed a huge sigh of relief.

"That's not to say I won't make you do it," said the king, and he rang for a servant. "Somebody light these candles."

Humpty fidgeted.

"I have some experience with recalcitrant wives," said King Thrushbeard.

"Of course you do. Who doesn't know *that* story," said Humpty Dumpty.

"He doesn't," said the king, nodding to Budy.

Budy just smiled.

"But better I should let my wife tell it herself." And in the doorway as he said these words appeared the queen with a lighted candle. She was a tall woman with a warm, friendly face. A famous beauty in her youth, she carried herself as though all that beauty were still fresh, and she smiled in a way that made Budy in a moment believe it still was.

"My dear," said the king, "you are not a servant to be bringing light for the candles."

"Oh, I think a queen can bring fire as well as a servant if she chooses."

As she said this, she took a step into the room, and the candle went out. And the king laughed and the queen laughed and then Humpty Dumpty and Budy pretended to join in the mirth. "Well, I still think so," she said.

"Never mind," said the king. And he rang his bell for more candles as the queen sat down and told her story.

"When old Grizzly Beard here first came to court me, of course I made fun of him. I was young and highly sought after, and he was already turning gray. What was I to think?"

"You made fun of everyone, dear."

"Blame my father for that. As I was saying, this old man came with some presumption to marry me. I turned him down with all the rest. They left, and I considered I'd side-stepped a spear. My father saw it differently.

"'You've embarrassed me in front of every kingdom in the Grimmsworld,' he yelled."

"Every kingdom in Grimmsworld, dear?" said King Thrushbeard.

"Look, you've told this story for years. It's my turn now."

"Very well." The edge of the king's cheerfulness seemed to be growing a little dull.

"'So now I'm going to marry you to the next beggar who comes through that door,' said dear old dad."

The king looked as though he were going to interrupt again, but the queen quickly said, "You can ask him yourself." And then she continued, "Well guess who was the first 'beggar' through the door. It was old Grizzly Beard with his lyre pretending to be a minstrel. Clearly he and dad were in cahoots. I saw through it right away, but I played along. Long story short, he pretended to marry me." And then she shot a look at her husband before he could speak, "No, it was not a real marriage. That priest was a fake. Do you think I'd really have gone through with such a marriage? So anyway, he took me after the ceremony through his vast lands (he was looking better and better to me by the way at this point) and into a little hut, where he insisted I do an honest day's work for my bread. I played along. But I cut myself with the threads so I wouldn't have to sew and I cut myself with the yarn so I wouldn't have to spin. *Really,* I thought to myself, *you're married to a king, but you have to do manual labor? I don't think so.* When all else failed, he set me out to sell pots. And then he came along in another one of his clever disguises and smashed them just to 'teach me a lesson.' It was fine with me, I didn't want sell pots anyway.

"'You're pretty useless for earning money,' he said to me.

"'Well, you're not doing so hot for yourself, honey,' I said back. 'Just look at this hovel.'"

"I never once... And you certainly didn't..." the king huffed in the queen's direction.

"Well I certainly thought it."

"Well the point is that we eventually got married," said the king.

"Hey, *my* story, my dear." The queen's frown seemed genuine. "The point is he sold me to his own castle to help out in the kitchen. Naturally

177

I screwed that up as well, but I got plenty to eat. Then he picked me out of a line up at a ball. I acted shy. He revealed the whole plot. I said, 'Oh, my, what a lucky girl am I.' And he married me for real. And now I'm queen of this wonderful castle. And I don't sew, and I don't spin, and I don't cook." She grinned.

The king laughed. "Well, something like that," he said. "So you see, I have some experience with recalcitrant wives. And if my son has any hope of taming his Cinderella—his Aschenputtel rather—well, good luck to him. Once a princess, always a princess, I say."

"But she was really once a scullery…ouch." This time Budy stopped when Humpty Dumpty kicked him.

The king rolled his eyes and said nothing.

"Where is that fire?"

"I'm sure we have taken too much of the king's time already," said Humpty Dumpty. "So glad to have had this chance to make your acquaintance."

"Going?" said the king. "Where are you going?"

"Well, we have a fairy godmother to find, for one," said Humpty Dumpty. "Private business, of course."

"And as for the other affair?" said the king, but just then ten servants showed up at the door, all with burning candles. And behind them were two guards with drawn swords. Humpty Trembled. Budy frowned as the ten servants paraded through the door one after another, and as each one did, his candle went out. When the guards entered, the king nodded at Budy. "I think we've found our wizard," he said. "Arrest him."

CHAPTER FIFTEEN

PEOPLE, PLACES AND TIME ARE BEING REWRITTEN. A POWER OUTSIDE OF OZ MAY ONCE AGAIN BE WORKING ITS WAY INTO THE FABRIC OF OUR LAND. SUZY BISHOP, LORD LOCKSLEY OF NOTTINGHAM, AND DEBORAH THOMAS OF OZHOUSE ARE ALL CONNECTED TO THIS POTENTIAL DANGER.

GLINDA CLOSED THE GREAT BOOK and sighed. It had been a long time since the magical incident that had deposited all those doors in hidden places throughout Oz, threatening the land—so long that the great Sorceress had all but forgotten the people from OzHouse. Glinda had not fully trusted these outsiders, especially a young man named Charles Emerson, but as years passed without any contact with the mortals, she had relaxed and come to believe they were true to their word.

But that word "OzHouse" and Suzy's name mentioned in her magical book brought back all her mistrust. As for Lord Locksley, she had seen that name before too but had never connected him to the people of OzHouse. And as for Deborah Thomas, this name meant nothing at all to her.

Crimmy, Glinda's handmaiden, approached from behind and looked over the book. "The name Deborah Thomas doesn't sound Ozian, does it? Could she have been among these mortals from America who have invaded us in the past?"

"Not that I recall," said Glinda. "But if she is, her name would be in

179

here." It seemed a good place to start her investigation.

Using her most delicate magic, the ruby sorceress waved her hands over the book and repeated the name and waited. Slowly at first, the gossamer pages began to flip back over days, weeks, months, and then years. One year. Two. Five... Twenty... The leaves of the book turned faster. Glinda furrowed her brows and muttered, "Oh, dear." The book rustled through history as though it knew something was there but was unable to find any record of this girl. Fifty years ago... Seventy-five years ago... One hundred years ago—and the rustling pages slowed down.

The book stopped. Glinda leaned over the page.

"This makes no sense," she muttered to Crimmy. "I see here a mention of a Deborah Thomas being in the Emerald City, but how can this be the same person? Even if she had been a young girl then, one hundred and ten years have passed."

"Could she still be alive?" asked the girl.

Glinda reread the words in the great book but still found them hard to believe. This Deborah had been in Oz all those years ago. "Had she remained here, I could believe she had not aged, and so could be alive," mused the sorceress. "But it clearly states she was sent back home by Ozma less than an hour after she arrived—and not to any fairyland either, but to that blasted OzHouse, where people age rapidly. That would mean she would be around one hundred and twenty years old."

Crimmy shrugged. Glinda would have to travel to the Emerald City and ask Ozma if she could help fill in the gaps she could not fill in herself.

Although the Land of Oz is a world of great magic and power, things such as long-range communications and travel have never been much explored. It has always been believed in this fairy world that rapid communication and travel are the forerunners of the curse of "civilization"—to be avoided at all costs. Civilization may bring some good things, but it surely takes many more good things away. And no one in Oz was more sure of this than Glinda the Good. Magic always shrinks when confronted by advances in civilization. Death always comes with it as well. Witches and wizards become the things of folklore. But here in Oz, where everyone lives forever (if no accident befalls them), witches and wizards and magic of every kind are things of history. It would take Glinda many hours to reach the Emerald City by air on her swan chariot, and several days if she had chosen to go on foot. Glinda gathered a few important things and had her servants hitch up the swans.

When the sorceress arrived at the green gates leading to Ozma's palace it was early evening, and many of Ozma's finest counselors were gathered in one room. The sounds of so many opinionated friends discussing the events of the day was almost deafening. Glinda had no trouble following the sounds to the Throne Room.

Jellia Jamb did not even have a chance to inform Ozma of the sorceress's arrival before Glinda opened the door in the back of the room and approached her sovereign.

"Glinda, how soon you arrived. How did the Scarecrow reach you so quickly?"

"I have not seen the Scarecrow," said Glinda. "I have come to speak with you about something I learned in my magic book. It is a matter I had hoped not to ever have to discuss again."

Ozma frowned. "Does it concern those mortals from OzHouse?"

Glinda looked surprised but only for a moment. "Once again you have amazed me. How could you know about this without the Great Book of Knowledge?"

"I suppose it is because of me," Debbie cut in. "I am not sure who you are, but you act important, and I am guessing you are Ozma's mother. My mother used to talk to me like that sometimes when she wanted to talk about something that was very important."

Glinda smiled but only quickly before she calmly explained who she was. Debbie nodded as if she believed all she was being told, and then she told the sorceress her story.

"...so you see," Debbie finished, "I was here earlier today but everyone says they don't remember it. No one even remembers my name. I came here for something important. A baby went through the door and is lost in Oz somewhere."

Ozma shrugged her delicate shoulders and looked at Glinda. "No one in the Emerald City recalls having met this girl, but she seems sure she was here this morning. It's very strange."

"She was here," said Glinda with a frown. "But not this morning. She was here over 100 years ago."

Everyone went silent at this news.

Debbie's silence however was short lived. She placed her hands on her hips and fumed, "That's impossible, you silly people. I'm not even ten years old. No one could be that old. You would all be dead by now. I was *just* here. I spoke to you, and you, and you. Why don't you remember?"

"I do," said a voice entering the doorway that Glinda had opened. "Well, actually it was my sister, but I remember her telling me all about

181

it. I came down immediately when I heard the girl was back."

Into the large counsel chamber came a beautiful girl with long, thick blonde hair, and a rainbow silk dress that floated around her like a Ginger Rogers gown when she danced with Fred Astaire.

"Polly?" Debbie called out.

"Of a sort," the sky fairy laughed. "The Polychrome you knew was my sister. But we are all called Polychrome when we visit the earth. There are actually a dozen of us."

"I didn't know that," said Ozma.

"It has been the cause of much confusion," said Polychrome. "Most mortals forget us after we return to the sky, but the few that do not often don't know that they are probably seeing a different sister the next time they meet."

"None of this makes sense," Debbie huffed. "You aren't the Polly Chrome I met earlier today, you are her twin sister or something, but you are the only one who remembers me?"

"Not earlier today, my dear," Glinda said as she placed her gentle hand on Debbie's shoulder.

"And it's Polychrome, Debbie. One word," said Polychrome.

"It's true. You visited Oz almost 110 years ago," Glinda continued as though she had not been interrupted, "shortly after our dear Shaggy Man arrived on his first visit to Oz. How this is possible, I am not sure, but my book is never wrong, so it must have happened just that way."

"My father has an amazing memory, and he recognized you when you arrived in Oz. He sent me to help," said Polychrome. "I think Debbie needs to know that here in Oz no one ages or dies. So everyone is just as they were the last time she was here. Her last visit seems to have taken her to the Emerald City long ago, though for her it was just a few hours. I don't quite understand the magic of that, but we certainly cannot deny it is so. For she is still a young human child. Her being in Oz now causes no threat to us or anyone."

"My magic book says otherwise," Glinda cut in.

"Perhaps that is because it is *your* magic book," said Polychrome. "Or perhaps it is because of the fear that others from her world may follow now that she has somehow reopened the door."

"We owe you an apology," Ozma said. "It was so long ago none of us recalled your visit. But it seems you were here and I do now almost remember sending a girl home with the magic belt many many years ago."

Scraps, who had remained silent longer than anyone could recall, was twirling around the room between the pillars and humming a song she was in process of making up,

> Have a seat!
> Have something to eat!
> Our hospitality can't be beat!
> Try our cookies
> Oh, so sweet
> Heaven help us,
> Have a seat!

Debbie looked slightly horrified at the patchwork countenance of the woman singing. "That's not the Scarecrow, is it?"

"No. I am over here," came the husky voice of the man of straw. "That is Scraps, the Patchwork Girl. We have much in common, but we have much not in common too." His painted face seemed to beam with such a joyful smile, Debbie couldn't frown when she looked at him.

"You are back?" asked Scraps.

"Seems so. Lucky for us, we happened to see Glinda's swan chariot soon after we left the city. So we turned around and headed back. No need for an adventure in the middle of a mystery."

The great door opened a crack and a girl who looked to be about Debbie's age slipped in. "I was told Ozma wanted to see me," she said as she brushed her hair from her face.

"I might," Ozma replied, and then she introduced Suzy Bishop to Debbie, saying, "She is our first visitor from OzHouse. She's been here, must be about twenty years, isn't it?"

Suzy just smiled.

"But if what the sorceress tells us is true, as it surely must be, that would mean that Debbie is our first visitor from OzHouse," said the Scarecrow.

"Oh dear, that's right," said Ozma. "So you see, Suzy, we have a mystery to solve. And you might be the key."

Ozma explained to Suzy all they knew while Scraps continued to interrupt and toss small pillows into the air.

"You are not helping," Debbie said as Scraps began spinning in a circle.

"How do you know?" called the Patchwork Girl as she tried to balance on the back of a tall chair. "I might not be helping *you,* but I might be helping someone else."

Debbie grimaced at the stuffed woman. She was not acting like an adult, yet she was tall enough to be one. She was more like an unruly child, but no one in this crazy world seemed inclined to discipline her.

Suzy had an idea. "I am no expert on the magic that is in OzHouse, but as I have always understood it, people can enter a world they have been reading about or have been thinking about. Perhaps since the Oz books were written long ago and over a long period of time Debbie entered an earlier book the first time and arrived this time now."

Glinda nodded. "Of course. Very plausible anyway. My book said she had been here shortly after the Shaggy Man arrived for the *first* time in Oz. What for us was over 100 years, was for her an afternoon."

"Oh, dear I don't like that, not one bit," said the quick-witted Scarecrow. "That would mean our history is constantly changing. What happened yesterday this morning isn't what happened yesterday this afternoon."

"Why do you say that?" said Scraps.

"If this Debbie just entered Oz an hour ago her time, then it was only an hour ago Glinda's book first mentioned her. But at that time it slipped her name into the book a hundred years back. Don't you see, there was a time when everything happened, and this girl's name was not in the book. And then her name was in the book, and everything happened again, but now her name was in the book where it hadn't been before."

"I suppose it is so," said Ozma.

"And that matters how?" asked Scraps.

"Well if one little thing could change, everything could change— and we'd never know it."

"How marvelous," said Scraps.

"Marvelous? I find it quite disconcerting," said the Scarecrow.

"Oh, I don't know," said the princess, "if it's always been happening and no one's even noticed, I don't see how it could be disconcerting."

"How very, very fascinating," said Scraps.

"What if tomorrow someone comes on the day you were sprinkled with the power of life and steals the powder before you get sprinkled?" said the Scarecrow, "then you will never have been brought to life at all even though you will have lived a hundred years."

"Then I'm sure someone else will come along and sprinkle me again," said Scraps.

"But there's no guarantee of that," said the Scarecrow.

"Well if I never existed, I can't see how it could possibly bother me, Mr. Pin Brain."

Debbie exhaled audibly. She wanted everyone to get back on topic. She was the only one here who'd ever come through the door as far as she knew, and she didn't understand or care about whatever nonsense they were talking about. Since her little comment had got this talk started, she decided to say no more on the subject of doors and time. No, the real point was that Isabelle's daughter was lost somewhere in Oz, and she was too young to be on her own. It wasn't polite to interrupt grownups, but this was an emergency, and in an emergency the rules are different. "What about Amanda," she said very loud.

"Do you have any idea where this little girl might be?" asked the Cowardly Lion, as though that had been the conversation all along.

"I have no idea," Debbie replied. "I saw her go through the doorway and just knew she'd end up here. Back in OzHouse they seemed very confused by it all, though you'd think *they'd* know more about it than me."

"Perhaps we can find her in the magic picture," suggested the Scarecrow.

"Excellent idea," said Ozma with a broad smile. Within minutes a small group were in the hallway leading to Ozma's boudoir where the magic picture was hung. As the Scarecrow and the Patchwork Girl pulled back the drapes that covered the radium-framed picture, the Scarecrow explained its powers to Debbie. "When left to its own devices, the picture shows a pleasant scene of farmlands in the Munchkin Country, but when asked, it will show anyone anywhere in the world."

Debbie was skeptical. To prove it was true, the Scarecrow said to the picture, "Show me Jack Pumpkinhead of Oz." The blue field faded and in its place Debbie saw a tall, thin creature made of sticks and covered with rags. The figure had quite a large pumpkin for a head. At first it was standing in a field like a garden sculpture—but then it moved.

"Don't be frightened," said Glinda.

Debbie didn't know why she would be frightened. "That's interesting," she said. "I've never seen this movie."

"It's magic," said the Scarecrow. "Jack is really out in his field tending his pumpkins."

"I'm sure it's just satellites," said Debbie, "satellites, and cameras, and voice activation. But it is interesting. We mustn't pretend it's magic, however. We must be clear-headed about this."

Ozma sighed. She stood in front of the picture and was about to command the image to show the little girl they were looking for when she paused and looked at Debbie. "What was the child's name?" she asked.

"Oh, it's Amanda," Debbie said again.

"Right, Amanda. Amanda what?" asked Ozma.

"Just Amanda. I don't know her last name."

"I am afraid there could be many Amandas out there. It may take us quite some time to look at every image the picture would reveal of every Amanda."

"Show us Amanda," commanded Scraps.

"Is your Amanda about sixty years old with a gold tooth?" asked the Scarecrow.

"No," said Debbie with a touch of sarcasm that her mother would never have approved of.

"Then this is probably not her," the Scarecrow replied.

"Show us another Amanda," Scraps demanded as the image changed to a middle-aged woman near a windmill who was hanging out her laundry.

"This will take forever," Glinda said. "We will need to find this girl's full name if we wish to locate her."

"I don't know her name. Her mother's name was Isabelle, but that probably doesn't help much."

Glinda asked Suzy if she knew the child's last name, but of course Suzy had never met the baby or her mother.

While Ozma, Glinda, and the Scarecrow wracked their brains to come up with ways to find the toddler without the name, Scraps kept calling out to the magic picture to show them another Amanda. They saw a thin black woman standing in the sun in a savanna, they saw three blonde girls, none of whom was less than twenty years old, they saw a middle-aged woman in a wheelchair in what looked like a fishing village. None were the right Amanda.

Ozma pondered a few moments and then had a thought. While discussing possible ways to find the child, Glinda had said Robin of Locksley was also mentioned in her book, and although she did not know how he tied in to OzHouse, he might just, and so he should be spoken to.

"Show me Robin of Locksley," she commanded the magic picture.

The scene changed to a sturdy, young man chopping wood deep in the northern forests of Oz—the purple hue of the trees made that clear enough.

Using her magic belt, Ozma wished the Lord to the Emerald City.

"W...what is this?" cried Robin as he appeared in Ozma's room dropping his axe. Debbie was watching Scraps run through Amandas in the picture when he arrived.

"I am sorry, Robin, but there was no way to warn you I was about to bring you here. It has been many years, and I need to ask you some questions."

"Ozma, my liege." Robin bowed as he tried to clean his dirty hands on his rough-spun tunic.

"Am I the only one that finds it strange that guy is still in Oz?" asked Scraps without turning around.

"I have neither means nor cause to leave."

"Run home, save the world. I seem to remember some sort of plan like that."

Glinda smiled at the thought of Robin Hood trying to act out his life's plans in Oz, a land of no money.

"Ozma could have sent you home at any time," said the Scarecrow.

"It may be as you say. And there was a time I did eagerly pursue a course that would earn my passage. But to my shame, I did find myself drawn from my duties by the riches and the pleasures of your noble land. And then came a day when I must face the truth that either Richard did return and heal my land or my Merry Men had been overcome by false King John. I had no more cause for returning. In my world, all must have passed through to their eternal rest long since."

"As I understand it, they'd all be dead by now too," said the Patchwork Girl.

"I need to know your connection to OzHouse," Ozma declared.

"I know not the place, milady."

"Are you sure?"

"OzHouse," Robin said the word thoughtfully. "OzHouse? Oh. Perhaps. Ahz House. Yes. Now that I think on it, I do recall a girl Janey who did bespeak it and a book she did leave with Friar Tuck, but more than this I do not recall."

Glinda looked at Suzy.

"After my time I'm afraid," said the girl.

Debbie finally turned around to see who everyone was talking to. "Are you supposed to be Robin Hood?"

"'Tis no supposition, milady. I am in truth Lord Robin of Locksley."

"And that's Robin Hood, right?" Debbie's frown had returned.

"I have been so called," Robin smiled.

"Robin Hood doesn't belong in *The Wizard of Oz*. This story is totally silly. Someone is getting it all wrong."

Glinda nodded as sternness crossed her features. It made Suzy uncomfortable.

"I would like you to stay in the Emerald City while we sort out this confusion," Ozma stated. "I hope it won't be too much of an inconvenience to keep you from your new life."

"If your majesty doth need me, know that any untimeliness to me is small beside the privilege of being in thy service."

"Perhaps Debbie should return to OzHouse and find out this toddler's family name," the Scarecrow suggested. "It could save us a lot of time, and a child so young should not be running loose in Oz where she might get into trouble."

"Can you send me back again?" asked Debbie.

"I could," sighed Ozma. "But we really cannot leave portals open all over Oz. You should go back the way you came and have someone destroy the portal so no one else can use it."

"But we're in a hurry. A baby is lost in Oz. Something dreadful could happen." Debbie could not stand this calmness any longer.

"Pah," Glinda laughed. "If a baby is lost in Oz, it will come to no harm."

"As long as the Hungry Tiger doesn't find it," Scraps smirked.

"It can't grow old. It won't starve. It's probably in the house of some kind Quadling as we speak. And you can be sure, however tempted he might be, the Hungry Tiger would not eat it," Glinda smiled.

Debbie was still unconvinced. But as debating the question would just prolong the process, she went along. "I remember some weird birch trees that were green. I think I can find my way from there."

The Scarecrow led Debbie back outside and towards the great gates. Debbie waved at Thurbidore who smiled at her.

"My name is Deborah Thomas sir," she said as they passed him.

"Pleased to meet you miss, hope your visit was pleasant."

"Not sure about that. We still have to find Amanda, but we are all working hard. Many hands make light work, my mother used to say."

She and the Scarecrow walked along the pathway with Debbie looking left and right to find landmarks. Many times a person thinks she will recognize a place in the country only to discover so many trees, rocks and hillocks look alike.

"It wasn't very far, and I could see the city from where I entered," Debbie explained to the Scarecrow, who was feeling about, hoping to touch an invisible door frame or something that might lead him to the opening of the portal.

"WHERE IS MY BABY?" Isabelle screamed again.

"Oh, crap," Gary unfurled the odorous pile of cloth. Gwen grabbed hold of it.

"It's a dress," she said. "And a...a..."

"A hat."

"A hennin actually. It's a medieval hat."

"One of your costumes?"

"It's linen. No. I wouldn't make a costume out of linen."

"And it's filthy. And it stinks."

"Where is my baby?" Isabelle repeated every word distinctly and slowly.

"She's gone," said Gary. "It's happening again. Amanda and Debbie have gone through the portal. And they're not the first. Jessica must have gone already."

"And Charlie and Doug as well, I suppose," said Gwen.

"Are you serious? Are you trying to tell me my baby is lost in some magical hell hole? I'm going after her." Before Gary could stop her, Isabelle dashed back through the doorway. She could be heard yelling and cursing from inside the magic room, "She's not here. Where is she? Where could she go?"

"Just about anywhere," Gary sighed. Isabelle came back through the doorway into the hall where Gary and Gwen were arguing and frantically pacing and Beth was flinging her arms about and calling for Doug.

"What the hell is going on in this madhouse?" Isabelle demanded.

"Good question. Why is everyone up here in this hallway? Who's watching the children?" Beth rubbed her face and brushed back her hair.

"We have a lot of 'splainin' to do," Gary said with a nervous smile.

"A lot," said both Isabelle and Beth at the same time. Then Isabelle looked at Beth and added, "Who the hell are you anyway?"

CHAPTER SIXTEEN

Elizabeth Smith Robbins
Isabelle Rodriquez

TWENTY MINUTES AFTER SIGNING the book, Beth Robbins said, "Enough." She crawled through the closet for what must have been the two-dozenth time and met Isabelle once again in the hallway going in. "If you want to keep chasing your tail, that's up to you. It's your turn anyway. But for me, Doug can just as bloody well stay in storyland for all I care."

"So you do believe that's where he is?" Gwen and Gary had spent the afternoon trying to convince both Beth and Isabelle of the reality of the doorway—their best evidence being the dirty dress that had shown up mysteriously in the secret room.

"Of course not," Beth huffed. "Sure, you had me going there for a minute."

"A minute?" Gary called from inside the secret room. "That's a pretty long minute."

"Well, Gary, I suppose it's like you to play a joke on me with all that's going on. But how did you get Gwen to join in? And by the way, it didn't work. I'm still cheesed. Maybe if I just hadn't spent twenty hours flying from Madrid to London to South bloody Carolina to Boston…"

"Oh, my God, this is a joke?" said Isabelle. "My daughter's run away and you have me jumping back and forth through a closet? What kind of people are you?" She looked back and forth as though trying to figure out which way to go. "Amanda," she shouted. "Help me find her."

"That's what we're doing," said Gary. At least he'd confirmed what they'd always said: if you don't believe in fairyland, you can't use the door. And that's something very hard for an adult.

"You've been to fairyland, Gary, right? That's what you said. So if this isn't a joke, how come you're not jumping through the time warp with us, hmmm?" Beth asked.

"Because I might end up in Oz and have to face Glinda the 'Good.' And because I have no idea where Doug actually is. Do you know how many actual fairy worlds there are? And because the real problem is Amanda."

"So find her," Isabelle crawled out of the room into the hallway.

"As I've said already, we don't actually know that Amanda is in Oz. It would be like parachuting into the Rocky Mountains to find a child who was lost 'somewhere in North America.' It's not practical."

"What if you're wrong?" Beth asked.

"If she gets hurt, I'm going to sue the hell out of you people." Isabelle took off down the hallway still calling for her daughter.

"That apple didn't fall far from the tree, did it," said Beth.

Gwen stared at Beth.

Gary crawled out through the closet and stood beside his sister-in-law. An awkward moment passed between them.

"So how was Spain?"

Beth glared over her glasses. "Did you really think this was going to help?"

"What about the dress?" said Gary. "Certainly that is proof?"

"Apparently not," she said.

"But..."

"I don't want to hear any more about the dress." Beth went down the hall in the direction of her bedroom.

But the dress and hat *were* a clue. And more than just a clue to the reality of fairyland. They were a clue about where Jessica had gone—somewhere where they wear medieval clothes.

But how much help was that? A lot of these stories are very old: Cinderella, Sleeping Beauty, Robin Hood—could be so many.

"You should try to find her," Gwen said.

Gary's face ran through a number of expressions. He finally said, "It occurred to me that maybe Doug went into one of his own stories, too."

"Find someone," said Gwen. A rattling noise came through the closet. The sound of a girl's voice followed, mumbling words her mother would not have approved of.

"Was there someone else in there?"

Just then a little girl fell through the wardrobe onto the floor.

"Closet floors should be at floor level," said Debbie.

"OH, IT'S YOU," SAID HUMPTY DUMPTY.

Jessica was standing on Humpty Dumpty's wall, looking out over the land beyond. She was trying to remember the path she'd followed to the Grimms' Forest years ago. She spun around at the sound of the familiar voice, "Humpty Dumpty. I could hug you."

The egg man's eyes grew big and he threw both arms stiffly before him as though Jessica had already leapt from the wall and was charging at him with her hug unsheathed, "No, no, no, you could not. Egg shells were not designed for hugging."

"Oh, of course," said Jessica, plopping herself down on the wall, letting her feet dangle. "I'm just so so happy to see you. I've been trying to get here for such a long time."

"Pleased to see you as well. Now get off my wall."

"Really?" Jessica swung her legs back and forth. "You're really pleased to see me?"

"Well, no, since you ask, not a bit. Seemed like the polite thing to say. I don't know why you insist on trampling perfectly sanguine pleasantries with grubby little truth. But if you must, you must. No, I am not pleased at all. Your presence compels me to recollect that you were nothing but trouble the last time you came through—and you were a foot shorter then by the look of you—what are the chances you'll be a little ray of sunshine this time? And what in the name of the Goose are you doing on my wall anyway? Peering into the worlds beyond, I suspect. Did I not forbid that? Quite sure I did. Get down before you fall and break your shell."

"I don't know why I wanted to hug you," said Jessica.

"Who wouldn't? I'm adorable," said Humpty Dumpty.

"Dumpy," said Amanda. And the egg man recoiled at the voice of the unseen little girl sitting among the flowers at the foot of the wall.

He composed himself instantly.

"I see you've acquired some baggage since last we met. Adorable," he repeated, "I'm adorable. Just ask your daughter." He smiled down at Amanda and assumed the tone of a shopping-mall Santa, "Hey, little Jessica. How would you like a lollipop?"

Amanda jumped up and ran in a circle for no apparent reason.

"Her name's Amanda. And she's my niece."

"Just as well, fresh out of lollipops anyway." The egg man smirked. "But, if I may ask, not that I need to know this for anything but the satisfaction of my curiosity, what brings you to... No, no, no. On the other hand, I don't find myself half as curious as I had expected I'd be.

Couldn't care less. Make me privy to another one of your schemes, I just might be drawn in—drawn, split, and omeleted, I'm sure. Besides I'm a bit overwhelmed at the moment. No, indeed. Just stopped back to tack another limerick on the wall, grab my copy of Andersen, and head out on the most unintriguing and yet utterly unavoidable quest of all time. How do I get myself into these things?"

"I need you to help me find Buddy."

"On the other hand..." But Humpty Dumpty abandoned the sentence at that point. "Budy again, is it? Budistiltskin? Why come to me? You know where he is."

"I don't know how to get there."

"Well, doesn't matter, wouldn't find him if you did. He's not there. Just left him in fact," said Humpty Dumpty. "Just one 'd' now by the way."

"Really? Just B-u-d-y?"

"Oh, he's had more than a letter cursed away I can assure you."

"So if you know where he is, you can take me to him."

"Yes, to the first, no no no no no no, to the second," said the egg man. "Boy got himself into the dungeon, boy can get himself out. Plate's full at the moment. Think I said that already. Took all of my very considerable verbal skill to keep my fragile shell out of that dismal palace prison as it was. Think I want to try that again, do you? Think I want to climb up and down a hundred stone steps twice in one day, do you? Certainly not. I have other princesses to fry at the moment."

Jessica stood up and turned her gaze toward the Forest of Grimm. "So the question is, how do we get there? I think I see the path we took last time through the field behind this wall."

"JUST LOOK FOR A ROCK THAT LOOKS LIKE A HOUSE," said King Grisly Beard.

"Do you really think she'll help me?" asked Budy.

"Can't say. But I expect she *can* help you, which is more than I can do. And as for finding this Blue Fairy—well I must say, I've never even heard of her. And I don't see any chance of getting from here to wherever she is without that fool egg's help. He's the only one I know that can travel between the worlds. But having met him I would not count on anything that way. Bad news for the prince as well, I'm afraid."

After the king had relit the candles, he'd rethought the story he'd heard from his spies about the evil wizard of Grumbottem. Having met Budy and seen for himself how the fires had gone out, he decided that what he had here was not a wizard at all but a cursed boy, and so he decided not to throw him into his dungeon after all, at least not before hearing his side of the story. Budy sat on a cushioned chair in one room and the king sat on another just across the threshold of the arched doorway. At the far end of the king's room a fire and candles sputtered and burned low.

"I have met the Blue Fairy. I know she's real."

"I don't doubt that," said the king.

"What about the fairy godmother?" asked Budy.

"She's not *your* fairy godmother is she? Even if you could find her, I see no reason to think she'd help you."

"But the devil's grandmother?"

"I thought you'd read the stories."

"Well, maybe not *all* of them. I've read the ones with the people I've met. Except of course my father's."

"Rumple..."

"He would prefer you not say it, sir."

"Ah, well, yes. I can see why." He paused in his eyes tilted upward toward his bushy grey eyebrows. "Can see why he wouldn't want you to read it either if it says what I think I recall that it does."

"What do you mean?"

"Well, it's not for me to jump into family matters, is it? No, let's just say we all have fathers, and the less we know about them, the happier we all may be."

"Really?"

"My own gave me to a man that three times to kill me."

Budy wanted to say that that didn't mean we should be suspicious of all fathers. But he knew better than to contradict a king. Even a kind one. "So, as I said," he said instead, "I mostly know the stories of people I've met."

"Typical," said the king. "Read what you already know. What's the value in that? I've been wondering if we should institute schools—force people to read things they have absolutely no interest in and tell them it's good for them. What do you think?"

Budy thought he'd ignore the question. "I don't recall any story about the devil's grandmother. And, with all respect, sir, I don't see why a devil's grandmother would help me when a fairy godmother would not."

"Much kinder than you'd expect, given the pedigree," said the king. "But of course you'd have a much better chance if you had something in it to thwart her grandson—she loves that. She was a big help to me once, many years ago. She not only helped me secure the riches that guaranteed me a kingdom, but she helped get rid of my evil father-in-law."

"How did she do that?" Budy was still trying to figure out if a relative of the devil could really be trusted.

"No, no, never mind that. Late hour, long story." And then the king's face lit up. "That gives me an idea."

The king rang a bell and a servant came. He got instructions to retrieve a certain black case. Finding he had time, the king decided he would tell Budy the story of the three golden hairs after all and how retrieving them led his greedy father-in-law to become eternal punter on the river Styx. It was not a long story at all. But it did have a lot of action for a short tale. King Grisly Beard told Budy he was born poor and lucky. "Better to be lucky than to be rich sometimes," he said. The king at the time, Old King Charon, a frightened and selfish man grew afraid of a prophecy and tried repeatedly to have him killed. But each time he escaped. His third attempt sent him into hell itself on a quest of three golden hairs.

"Powerful hairs?" asked Budy.

"Not that I know of."

"Do they protect you or something?"

"Luck protects me," said the king. "May I go on?"

Budy nodded. The king told him how the devil's own grandmother plucked those hairs for him while the devil was sleeping and found out at the same time that should anyone take the pole from the punter of the river Styx, that person would have to take his place and ferry all comers for the rest of time—providing of course no one ever took the stick away from him. "But who would do that, you ask?" he said. "I'll tell you who would do that, Old King Charon, the greedy man whom I tricked with a promise of gold."

"Aren't you afraid someone will take the pole some day and he'll come back and recover his throne?"

But the king was not afraid. "Luck brought me here, and luck will keep me here. I'm not afraid of anything."

"Must be nice," said Budy.

The king's servant returned and handed him an ornate black case. "And these are those very hairs I spoke of." The king opened the box revealing three curly needles about four inches long and brighter than any gold Budy's father had ever spun from straw. "You take these to her with your story and she will know it is I who sent you."

"And then she'll help me with the curse?"

"Just make sure she gets to thwart her grandson in the process."

That was not encouraging.

The king raised his stein and looked at Budy. He must have noticed something in his expression. "Is there a problem?" he asked.

"You wouldn't happen to have a copy of those stories I could read? The ones that have this devil's grandmother in them. I think I would feel more confident if I had some idea what she was really like."

The king moved his hand slowly toward his bell. He laid a finger on the handle. And then he pulled it away. "I am afraid not," he said. "I would certainly help if I could. But I have no volume of the tales that does not include the tale of Rump... the tale of your father. And you are forbidden to read that tale."

"Not by you," Budy said.

"But I approve that particular interdiction. Anyway, you would not learn anything. Tales are tales and life is life."

"Well then, all the more reason not to forbid me," said Budy.

"And all the more reason not to allow you as well."

King Grisly Beard was starting to sound like Humpty Dumpty. Budy would have said so. But he had pushed the king as far as he dared already. He thanked him for the golden hairs. The conversation left him uneasy, although he wasn't quite sure why that was. By then it was very dark outside. But the king, to his surprise, had not offered him a bed. And that was just as well, he decided. Having barely escaped the dungeon, and having seen Humpty Dumpty all but hurled down the stone steps by the king's enthusiastic footmen, he was glad enough not to sleep in the castle. Not even the chill night air or the distant howls of wolves discouraged him. He had his blade in his hand, and there was just enough moonlight weaving down through the trees for him to make his way.

"NOW WE'RE JUST PLAIN LOST," said Charlie. He and Doug and King Richard had slipped out of Grumbottem under the shadow of the circling dragon and had been wandering about in the forest all day. Now and then, they stopped still at a glimpse of the dark shadow of the dragon crossing under the clouds. They had not seen it in hours, and now the sun was setting and the pink horizon could be seen over the mountains through the dark bars of the trees.

"Did I not tell thee 'twould be no easy task to find this Rumpelstiltskin?"

Doug rubbed his arms.

"A little cold there, Dougie?"

Doug smiled and snickered. In the fading light, his face looked eerie.

"It's gonna get colder before it gets warmer," said Charlie.

"Aye, to that."

A wolf howled. They stopped in their tracks.

Doug's face brightened again. "It just kills you that I'm enjoying this," he said.

"We're lost in the woods, at night, in the cold. There are wolves out there somewhere, and we have a dragon, who is also the devil, on our tails. We need a fire to drive off the wolves and the cold, but if we build one we'll attract the dragon who's really the devil. That's not something you're supposed to enjoy."

"Really? Isn't this what everything else in life is trying to be? Writing, work, marriage. It's all an adventure, Charlie. I've spent my life writing books so I could pretend to be doing exactly this. Now I'm doing it. And just think of the books I'm going to be able to write when we get back."

"*If* we get back. *If* we survive," said Charlie. "Those are real wolves. In fact they're not even just real wolves. They're Grimms' wolves, far more ferocious than anything you would ever see in 'the Merica.'"

"Better they be wolves than dragons," said Richard.

"Dead is dead," said Charlie.

"We *should* build a fire," said Doug.

"You're an idiot," Charlie said as nicely as he could.

The howling stopped. But they heard movement in the trees nearby. A gray streak passed through sight into shadow.

"It's circling," said Charlie.

"Back to back in a circle," said Richard.

The three scanned the woods on all sides. Richard unsheathed his sword.

"Shouldn't we stop talking?" Doug whispered.

But King Richard bellowed: "We see you." His voice echoed through the trees. "And we have arms." He swung his sword so it caught the light of the moon.

"Or maybe that," said Doug.

"You'll get no meal here tonight," the king's voice was confident.

The woods grew silent and still. The fading light contracted the circle of visible forest around them until they could hardly see beyond the nearest trees.

"Do we have to stand like this all night?" Doug whispered.

"Wouldn't *that* be an adventure," said Charlie.

And then with a thud a large gray wolf plopped himself down a few feet from Richard's sword and began slowly circling the three, growling as he did. His pulled-back lips revealed a thick line of gums. He stopped in front of Richard and huffed.

"Get him," said Doug.

"Oh, I don't think he's fast enough for that," said the wolf.

"Holy crap, a talking wolf," said Doug.

"Grimm," said Charlie.

"Go thy way, wolf. Thou canst not sup here this night."

"Why not? You're the only one with a sword. You may be the meatiest, but I'm not picky."

"One sword be sword enough."

"For one wolf, maybe," said the wolf. "But we hunt in packs." The wolf howled and five more wolves leapt into the circle. Four stopped at the leader's command but the fifth charged at Charlie. Charlie raised his arm to defend his face. King Richard swept this sword at the wolf. Charlie screamed and the wolf lay dead at his feet. But in that same moment all the wolves attacked. Richard swung his sword in a fury. "Do not run," he yelled. "That be their way of hunting."

The wolves backed off.

"Why did they stop?"

"My hand," Charlie screamed. "He got my hand."

Having failed in their direct assault, the wolves spread out to attack from all sides. They charged again. And once again King Richard swung his sword with a skill that astonished the wolves.

The wolves panted and withdrew a second time. Richard raised his sword and breathed hard.

"One more charge should do it," said the lead wolf.

But just then a fireball lit up the sky above their heads and the wolves scampered away in a fright.

"The dragon," said Doug. And everyone froze.

Nothing moved in the growing dark. And then a voice came to them from the woods, "Not a name I'm generally called." A light sprung up on the end of a stick revealing the frowning face of dwarf. "I want you to know, you all owe me for this."

"My hand," said Charlie. He was holding the end of his arm as tightly as he could, but he could not keep the blood from seeping out between his fingers. He raised his arm for everyone to see. "It's gone."

The dwarf said a word and flicked his torch at Charlie. A stream of fire sailed across the space between them. "Let go," the dwarf yelled. The fire touched Charlie's uninjured hand and for a moment he did let go of the bleeding stump at the end of his arm. The fired touched it. Charlie screamed again and fell to his knees. And then the bleeding stopped.

"And you'll owe me for that as well," said the dwarf.

BEFORE MORNING BROKE Budy figured out why the king's story unnerved him. He'd sent his own father-in-law to the river Styx on a pretense. How could Budy know he wasn't sending him to the devil's grandmother on a pretense—to appease the citizens of Grumbottem perhaps by getting rid of their wizard? And then he wondered why the king wouldn't let him read the stories about her—just after saying the thought he would like to establish schools. That seemed contradictory somehow. Would reading the book have shown him why he should avoid the devil's grandmother? Was he walking into a trap? But even if he was, *even if he knew he was*, would he stop? He had no trusty magic worker to help him, and he was running out of time.

The long rays of the morning sun sent spears of light among the trees of the forest before Budy managed to locate the stone that looked like a house. He'd searched for it all night in darkness that grew thicker and thicker as the moon disappeared. He would rather have slept. But he needed to move to stay warm. And if he went to sleep without a fire, he'd have no protection from wild animals. So he kept moving. He told himself that if he was moving in the right direction, something this big would be hard to miss. And he was right about that. Cold and tired, he stood before the two-story stone that he assumed was the house of the old hag—it had a door-shaped cutout where you'd expect a door to be. He was not sure he was ready to face the devil's grandmother. As he was thinking what to do, the stone moved. A door opened and a stooped old woman stepped out carrying a basket heaped with wilted flowers. A smell like perfume wafted out the door behind her as she straightened up, adjusted her spectacles and without a word looked Budy up and down. Budy started to speak, but the old woman held a chubby finger up toward his mouth. She sniffed the air.

"Woods," she said, "stone, castle, wolf, dwarf." She sniffed again. "Well, that's odd."

"I'm Budy..." he tried again, but her finger shot back up a second time.

"Awful free with your name for a Stiltskin," she said. "But why is there no trace of smoke about you? Never met a person in the whole of Grimm without charcoal and candle in the mix."

"You smell dwarf but not fire?"

"Not a trace. You're cursed."

"And how did you know...."

"Never mind that. What do you want?" She walked away as she asked this, either uninterested in his answer or inviting Budy to follow her as she shuffled toward the large flower garden at the back of her stone house. It was not a normal flower garden with plants decoratively arranged to please the eye and make the passerby say "wow." The flowers were planted in rows, like vegetables, and arranged by height: hyacinths in the east, canna lilies in the middle and marigolds in the west with many bright rows of seasonable and unseasonable blooms in between. She dumped the wilted flowers from her basket on a pile at the edge of the garden, and with a large and squeaky pair of scissors she cut, one by one, from several rows a number of plants, counting as she did so: "one, two; one two three; one, two; one, two, three, four, maybe five today; one, two, three...." She placed the cuttings in her basket until it seemed too full to carry. Budy did not interrupt her, and she did not repeat her question.

"You still here?" she said when she had finished. "Devil must be after you," she spoke as she walked back to the front of her house.

"Not that I know of."

"Then what do you want me for?" By then she was at the entrance, and it seemed as if she would enter and shut him out whether he spoke or not.

He opened the box with the three golden hairs. "The king sent me."

She let go the door and stared at Budy more intently than she had before. She sniffed again, looked for the first time at the three twisted hairs on the scrap of black silk in the ornate little box. "Come in," she said, taking the box from his hands and putting it into her basket.

As soon as they crossed the threshold, the old woman's stove went cold. "Oh, you do have a tale," she said. As she went around the room filling vase after vase with colorful and aromatic flowers, cutting arranging, watering, Budy told her everything he could.

"Rumpelstiltskin is the best fire worker in all of the forest," she filled a pause in Budy's tale. "If he cannot reverse the spell, I doubt it can be done."

"What about your grandson?"

"The devil? Even if this is within his power, which is more than I know, you'd have to trick him into it. And how would you do that?"

Budy had no idea.

And then a smile came across her face. "Ah, but perhaps I do," she said. "See that big stove over there, plenty big enough for a boy like you. You can hide."

"Excuse me?" The image of Hansel and Gretel flashed before him. "Who exactly are we trying to trick?"

"Oh, you people are always so suspicious. Do you want my help or not?" She sniffed the air. "The devil is on his way." She sniffed a hyacinth. "And he smells like hell. Once you are hidden, I will ask him about the curse. Simple as can be. If it is reversible, I'll get it out of him. I always do." And then she giggled as though her ordinary day had suddenly turned splendid.

Budy hesitated. "Couldn't I just hide under the bed?"

"He'd smell you."

Budy glanced around the room doubtfully for a better idea.

"Oh, even if I wanted to roast and eat you, the stove won't light as long as your cursed little self is in it, now will it? Nowhere else can you hide in this little room. Get in or get out."

Budy pushed aside the charred logs and squeezed himself into the cast iron stove that took up about half of one wall. There really was a good deal of space inside once you got through small opening where the logs went in. The old woman pushed his rucksack in behind him. If the devil's grandmother had wanted to trap him for her son to catch, this was of course the perfect place to do it, he realized. He just had to remind himself again that he had no choice. If he could not burn a fire, he would die. It was really that simple.

It was not long before he heard the front door grind open. He listened to them talk.

"I see your mood has not brightened much today," said the grandmother.

"Why do you keep it so cold in here? Light the stove," said the devil. Even angry, his voice had a pleasing tenor. "Here, I'll light it for you."

"I have something to show you first," said his grandmother.

The devil huffed. "Three more have eluded me," he said. Budy could hear footsteps growing closer then farther away. He pictured an angry devil busily pacing the room. "A girl from very hell itself, she just walked out. I knew I could not keep her against her will—but how did she figure that out? And then those two I found in the cornfield."

"What a shame. Have some… cold tea?"

"Why would I have *cold* tea?"

"How have they managed it, this Charlie and… Dore was it?"

"Doug. Douglas. Charles Emerson and Douglas Robbins. And now this Jessica Holton. She's a slippery little fish, but the men, two men in strange dress traveling alone in Grimms' forest. I do not know why they are so hard to find. They owe me—all three of them. They made a deal."

"Yes, I know how much you hate a broken deal. Isn't that what got you into trouble in the first place?"

"Must we bring that up?"

"No, of course not. What more is there to say? There we were in very heaven, you yourself the first in line until…"

The grandmother stopped midsentence. Budy wondered at the strategy of getting her grandson riled before asking for help.

The grandmother adopted a milder tone: "What if these three new cheaters have found your three golden hairs?"

"Then I would have no power over them. But I could still find them. But it's not possible in any case. If *I* cannot find those hairs, how could they? Why would you bring them up anyway?"

Wow, thought Budy. He'd had no idea what he was trading. Why had the king not told him? But even if he knew, of course he would still have traded them. The cold of winter is not the curse of the devil. Those hairs would have been no help in surviving that.

The grandmother laughed. "Perhaps I can help you to feel better," she said. She paused. It was a long pause. Budy heard steps and rustling sounds, but he could not imagine what was going on.

"You wanted to show me something? What's this," said the devil. "My...."

"Yes, it is. Your three golden hairs."

"How did you get them?"

"An ignorant boy brought them to me. Oh, no, mustn't grab. I'm sure you'll get them back eventually. Now as for the stove," said the grandmother, "the truth is, it seems to be cursed. I have tried all day to light it and it will not light."

"Oh," said the devil. "Have you checked the flue?"

"Clear as virgin's cheek. I'm sure it's cursed. Perhaps a word from you will get it going again."

Budy imagined he knew now why she'd stuffed him in the stove. As soon as the devil fixed the curse, the stove would light, and he'd be toast. Now he wished he'd kept those hairs. He felt around. In the back of the stove was a panel that slid left and right to allow the coals to be removed neatly. It slid easily.

"Sounds like there is something inside it," said the devil.

And that was the last thing Budy heard. The panel opened through the back wall of the stone house. Budy hit the ground running.

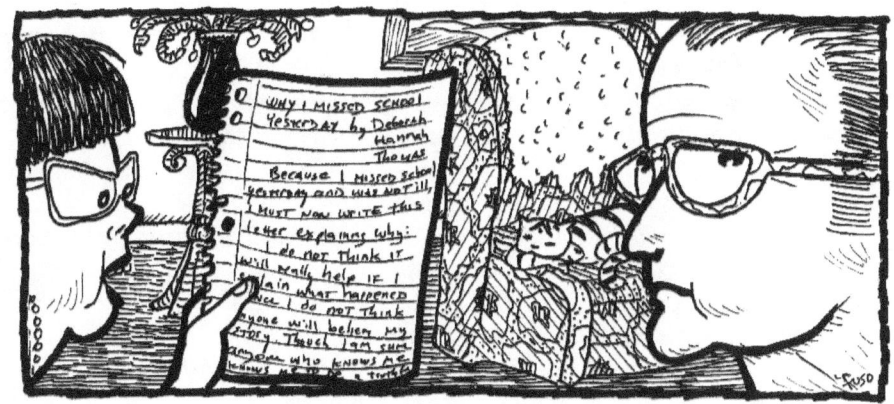

CHAPTER SEVENTEEN

Why I Missed School Yesterday
by Deborah Hannah Thomas

Because I missed school yesterday and was not ill, I must now write this letter explaining why.

I do not think it will really help if I explain what happened since I do not think anyone will believe my story and there are still things I don't understand because no one will tell me. Though I am sure anyone who knows me knows me to be a truthful girl who definitely knows it is wrong to tell lies. But Mrs. Robbins told me that I had to write this, so I am. She is sort of my guardian right now and Momma would have told me I have to obey her even when she tells me to do things that don't make sense like she does a lot.

When I woke up in my bedroom I thought for sure it had all been a dream, after all it was a ridiculous place with silly rules and a lot of very silly people. But then when I asked around I started to think that maybe it had been real, and then later I heard the Robbinses arguing with this lady up near the play room that's hidden behind a closet. I think that's from a book. They think it is fun to pretend things about books in this house. I don't know why. It was the same room I had been in before I was in the ridiculous place that was suppose to be the Wizard of Oz with yellow bricks and a big green castle which was suppose to be the Emerald City but didn't really look like it. It was like magic. I don't know how they did it. But we all know magic is fake. It's just sleight of hand and mirrors and things.

I know anyone reading this will think I am playing a nonsense game, but I am too old for that. I had thought at first that it was a joke or game I did not want to play but this is a true story. Maybe it was kind of real. But it was probably a stage with actors and a trap door that is very clever. It would maybe be fun if they didn't try to make you feel stupid by making you think it's real. Like Santa Claus.

When I heard that a baby had gone into the room and was missing I knew what must of happened. I went up there and went to find her. Her name was Amanda and she was the daughter of the lady who was shouting and using all kinds of naughty language.

What was really annoying was that when I did go through the door again, and returned to the place of talking animals and crazy people wearing weird clothes, everyone pretended they didn't remember me and told me a really dumb story (I almost said crappy but that's a bad word) that I was there 100 years ago even though I had been there just earlier that day. People who I had spoken to and spent actual time with said they didn't know me. How annoying was that? Even if it's part of a game, it isn't a fair game because they were all trying to trick me. They must think I'm really stupid.

But Momma said people who call you stupid are stupid. And that's all I have to say about that.

It is very confusing. Eventually Polly Chrome, she's suppose to be some kind of fairy or something though she doesn't have wings on her costume, even she explained it all and I had a chance to tell them that a baby was lost and they needed to help me find her. It seems their flat screen couldn't work because I didn't know Amanda's last name. Yeah, right. But I came home to find it out, and when I arrived in the room, everyone was standing around and they looked at me like they couldn't believe I was there. But that was just part of their stupid game because they built the house and must know how it works. I wanted to go back with the information, I guess her last name was Rodregus, though I am not sure of the spelling and my spellchecker isn't helping. But no one will let me back into the room, and now I have to write this.

"Is that all of it, Debbie?"

"Yes, Mrs. Robbins. All the important parts. There's a lot more details about a lion and the man called Thurbidore and stuff like that, but they don't really make a difference about why I missed school, and the more I put in the more trouble it will cause me if people want proof."

"They may want *proof*," said Gary. "But this isn't geometry. All we have in this world is *evidence*."

"What?" said Debbie.

"Never mind," said Gwen.

Gwen and Gary read the letter and then folded it over.

"Well," said Gwen, smiling, but her expression said, "I don't think we can let her pass this in to her teacher tomorrow."

Gary looked at his wife and with raised eyebrows said, "At least we know where she has been." He passed the letter to Beth.

"Not again. We can't start this nonsense all over again. Are you two sure you know what you're saying? I know we all heard this stuff years ago. We were younger and more naïve back in the day, but are we really buying into this again?" Beth's frown made her eyes seem dark.

"Who are you, Susan Pevensie. It's more than gossip to me," said Gary.

"You saw it yourself?" Beth said. "You keep saying that. But I tried for a bloody hour. It isn't real. And don't tell me you have more imagination than I do, because that's..."

"I was there, and now we know Debbie has been there... Oh, oh, Debbie? Did Doug go with you? Or Charlie?"

"No, Mr. Robbins. I went by myself."

Gary nodded, unsure of how to process the information. "Oh, by the way, did you happen to meet someone named Glinda the Good while you were there?"

"Yes, Mr. Robbins."

"Crap."

"That's a naughty word, Mr. Robbins."

"Yes, it was." He smiled weakly. "I'm sorry to say there may be a lot of naughty words spoken soon." Gary rubbed his face.

"What difference does it make whether she saw Glinda?" Gwen asked.

"Well I don't know exactly—besides of course the broken promise. But if she knows someone has been messing with the door—I mean she's a powerful and frankly pretty scary woman. Forget that ditz you saw in the movie."

"So you really think this little girl went to Oz?" Beth shook her head.

"I'm sure she did. But she shouldn't have. Like I said, Glinda will have a cow."

"A four horned cow?" asked Gwen.

"Yeah, and all four will be up my keister for breaking my promise of destroying the portal."

"Can I have something to eat?" asked Debbie. "I sort of missed dinner."

"Oh yes, of course you can." Gwen led Debbie down the hallway to the stairs.

"Isabelle will never find Amanda in OzHouse. You should tell her that."

"Maybe *you* should tell her that," said Gwen.

"Maybe I need to have a talk with Glinda."

BUDISTILTSKIN RAN AND RAN AND RAN. Without the protection of the three golden hairs, he wanted to get as far away from the devil as possible and as quick as he could.

He thought he heard the old woman laughing, but he was so far from the stone house she might have been coughing or choking.

"Hope she chokes good and hard," he grumbled. He should have known he couldn't trust any relative of that miserable Beelzebub. She had no intention of helping him, just wanted the three hairs to taunt her grandson with. She'd have cooked him in the stove as quick as that other witch cooked Hansel—or anyway as quick as she would have cooked him if Gretel hadn't rescued him. Good ol' Gretel. She'd saved Budy too, long ago.

Which reminded him, he was hungry.

He rummaged through his rucksack and managed to find a mealy crabapple.

Budy had put so much hope in this meeting that he really did not have another plan. King Grisly Beard or Thrush Beard or whatever he called himself—he seemed to think Cinderella's Fairy Godmother and the Blue Fairy would be dead ends, but then he seemed to think the devil's grandmother was a good possibility, so why trust him? Budy had come across the Blue Fairy only once and not for very long back when he'd stumbled upon Hansel and Gretel. He had no idea if she was generous or not. Not that it mattered now.

Maybe he could find her after all. This was a tough curse to break, and the Fairy Godmother might not even have the magic to handle it. If he could find Pinocchio, he might be able to help him find her. But how could he find that puppet?

Knowing who you are looking for is a promising place to start, knowing where to look is far better. Perhaps a soothsayer or fortune teller could direct him to Pinocchio. His father had often warned him to stay away from those kinds of people, as they were often dishonest and dangerous. This, however, was not the time to be cautious. The first snow would arrive within weeks.

Sometime later, as he was walking along a narrow road that led through the woods, he passed a man with a sackbarrow who was hauling large grain bags. Budy greeted the man. He learned that an old woman lived not far off this path and she was said to be one who could divine the future, if your coins were true. Remembering his father's advice about traveling to unknown places, he shifted the few gold coins he had to different places on his person and tried to stand tall and look as important as possible before he met the woman. He left the dirt path and headed into the trees.

The day was warm for this time of year, and the ground was soft from the fallen leaves. The path was well worn, but a few small logs crossed his way, and these he hopped over. As he walked he kept his eyes peeled for nuts or berries. The apple he had eaten was a distant memory. Keeping to the path, he moved along briskly and seeing how well worn it was gave him hope that many people came to the fortune teller for help, so she just might be trustworthy.

He came in sight of a small daub and waddle, thatched cottage between the tall elms. Sunlight was trailing down through the branches; it seemed like a peaceful, safe place. Still, Budy approached cautiously. Hadn't Hansel and Gretel met a witch at a candy house?

He knocked on the rough oak door. Almost before he finished knocking, the top half of the door opened and he was looking down at a wizened but kindly looking face.

"So glad you made it. I was almost starting to worry," she said. "I've been expecting you."

Budy was surprised and pleased, which must have shown on his face. "You were expecting me?"

"Wouldn't be very good at my job if I weren't, now, would I?"

"I suppose not," said Budy.

She opened the bottom half of the Dutch door, and Budistiltskin ambled in. The room was generously furnished with comfortable chairs and a colorful day bed with a garish patchwork quilt as a counterpane. The kitchen was spotless, and a large cast iron pot bubbling on the stove sent the comforting odor of roots and herbs through the place. He hoped she was a good enough fortune teller to feel his hunger and offer him some.

The bubbles died down to a simmer almost as soon as Budy crossed into the room.

The woman looked at her cook fire and then back at Budy. "And that is why you have come to see me," she said as though she'd known it all along. "You do know I am no witch nor a powerful caster of spells. Just a simple fortune teller who does her best to help those in need."

"I'm not looking for a cure from you," Budy began, "unless you happen to have one. I am looking to find someone who might be able to remove this curse, and I hope you can help me. It is very important."

"Can you pay?"

"I have gold." Budy put his palm over the sack dangling from his neck.

"Have a seat." The woman slid his chair under him. She put a hand on his shoulder. "Oh, dear." She pressed the other to the side of his jacket. "I feel that you are hungry. You have traveled many miles on little food. But you are too proud to ask."

Budy was impressed. "Yes, my father would not approve of entering a stranger's house and begging food."

"There is no need to beg," she said. "Now, tell me how the curse has befallen you?"

As he ate a bowl of half-cooked soup, Budy told her the tale with all the detail he could recall. At the mention of the family name, the fortune teller's grey bushy eyebrows rose high on her forehead.

"I have settled on finding the Blue Fairy, but I have no idea where she might be."

"Oh, I've heard of this Blue Fairy. She is from…" The old woman twisted her head in thought.

"She is friends with Pinocchio," Budy said.

"Yes, yes, yes. I know her well. Not easy to find, not the fairy, no, nor Lord Pinocchio," the woman said after some silence.

"Lord? Are you sure you are thinking of the same Pinocchio?"

"Oh, yes. Are there two? I sometimes forget that there are those who can only see the present."

"But he's a marionette. He's made out of wood. He becomes a lord?"

"As I say, not an easy one to find."

"Well, I know. But they did come here once. So perhaps—"

"During the great disturbance, yes." Her face lit up with understanding. "There was a great deal of crossing then. And there are those who got stuck in stories not their own at that time. But now—now there's no easy crossing over."

"So it's hopeless? You think it's hopeless."

"Nothing is hopeless when a man has gold," she pointed to the little pouch dangling from Budy's neck.

"I thought maybe you'd have a crystal ball or something to help you see things," said Budy.

"No ball of crystal will help you. But we have our minds—and books and maps, to find the place where the—the future Puppet Lord Pinocchio lives."

The old woman put her hand on her chin and turned her back to inspect her stock. She had shelves and shelves of dusty books and cupboards full of papers. She blew the dust away from the marble-edged volumes then slipped on a pair of spectacles. She read aloud from the books whose contents were of magic and rhymes and stories. The books led her to open vast maps with colored veins of roads and rivers which soon covered her large oak table.

Several hours were spent reading through books and scrolls and watching the fortune teller run her finger down the routes of many maps.

The way to Pinocchio would be long and treacherous, she said. After every stage of their deliberations, she brought out fresh sheets of parchment on which she copied a part of the journey. These she folded and labeled and set aside until they made a tidy stack. To the boy's delight she gave him a plate of cold meat and cheese to sustain him while she read through the papers and made corrections on her growing pile. Finally the woman gathered together and tied the maps in a bundle which she handled with a flourish to Budy. Complicated as it was, she assured him that these maps revealed the simplest route from her home to where the future Lord Pinocchio had last been known to live. Budy thanked her and started to rush out the door.

"She cleared her throat. Budy looked and saw a small wrinkled hand being held out for payment. He grabbed a gold coin from his pouch and handed it to her. It would be enough for the old woman to live on for many days, and more than her considerable work would have been worth to anyone with less at stake. Certainly his father would balk at giving so much gold for a few hours of study and a pile of maps. But she had treated him well, perhaps even saved his life. And though she seemed kind, she was a magic worker of some sort. It was better to be generous.

"Thanks again, should I pay you for the food as well?" he shouted as he was turned again to the woods.

"No need, happy to share my bounty with such a nice boy as you." She closed the door and smiled.

"OH, MY GOD, CHARLIE. Oh, my God." It was all Doug could manage to say as he watched Charlie hop up and down holding his bloody wrist, unable to speak.

"My hand, my friggin' hand," Charlie finally yelled. "He bit it off. How will I draw? How will I paint?" Words came flooding back.

"What can we do?" Doug asked.

We could look for my son," said the dwarf as if in reply. "Been gone too long." Rumpelstiltskin pulled on his grey beard. "He hasn't responded to my last three ravens."

"But my hand," Charlie screamed. "Does this answer your question Doug? Can we get hurt here? Can we be killed? Do bad things happen in fairyland?"

"Don't yell at me. Yell at the wolf. And don't worry. We'll fix this. We have to. It's just a story. We need to remain calm."

"Calm? Hard to do when you have a stump where your hand belongs." Charlie continued to hop about and squeeze his right wrist with his left hand. But then he let go and stared at the stump, which was scarred and red and irregular. "Funny thing is, it doesn't actually hurt. I would have thought it would hurt like a bastard, but it's just numb." He poked the soft, hairless skin.

"Small price for such a fight, I say," said Richard. "Forsooth, if thou be the stock of the Merica, 'tis good we drew not from thy land for the Holy Crusades. Many a subject of the realm would have rejoiced at so slight a loss to what he hath suffered at the hands of the infidel. And yet I stand amazed at thy forbearance for the hurt of it."

"Oh, that's my doing," said the dwarf. "When I stopped the bleeding I thought it might be worth more if I stopped the pain too."

"You did. It is. Thank you, I guess. It does help, somewhat. And as for fighting in any Crusades," Charlie flashed a sharp look at King Richard. He held his breath a moment. "Never mind. But just for the record, this adventure was not my idea."

Richard stroked his beard. Doug tried not to smile.

"So what do we do now?" Charlie asked.

"We find my boy," the dwarf said again. "Thought I made that clear."

"I mean about my hand," said Charlie.

"Not much to do about that. It's pretty much done as I can see. Let's check the western woods, shall we?"

"Can't we fix it?" asked Doug.

"The hand? Fixed already. No bleeding, no pain. These Grimms' wolves tend to swallow things whole. Hands, grandmas, riding hoods. Got a knife?"

Richard handed the dwarf a sharp dagger.

The little man slit open the wolf's stomach and out spilled his intestines, his stomach, and Charlie's hand. Doug heaved as the smell of the wolf's innards hit him.

"You'd need magic to replace this proper, pretty strong magic at that." The dwarf wiped wolf slime off the hand with a dark handkerchief he pulled from a pocket. Then he turned the limp appendage over in front of his eyes as though it were a chicken leg. "Bit clean through the bone." And then he dropped the hand into a small burlap sack he'd brought with him.

"We'll need ice," Charlie gasped.

"Why? You feeling warm? No ice around here till the snow falls."

"Not for me. For the hand to keep it fresh till we find a doctor."

"Don't worry about the hand. It'll keep just fine, if I know what I'm doing. Don't need ice, don't need a doctor. A good *magic* worker would be handy though," the dwarf smiled wide as he tied the bag up with a cord. "And they don't come cheap." He looked at each one of the men in turn. They all just stared back. The dwarf shrugged and threw the sack over his shoulder and started to walk.

The men immediately followed.

"We do seek a door 'twill take us home. I to the Sherwood Forest, and these to the craven Merica," King Richard said.

"That might have been what you *were* looking for. But as you all owe me and none seems otherwise able to pay, your quest has now become helping me find my son." As he said this the dwarf patted his pocket then reached his hand in and pulled out an object. The turned the object over and squeezed it in his palm. Doug almost started to argue with the dwarf when he noticed what the dwarf was holding.

"What's that?" he said.

"Oh, nothing. Thought it might be magic once. It is but a bauble from my son," he said. "Plas-tick was the name, I believe." He held it out for Doug to see but pulled it back when Doug reached for it. "Little statue, little green man in very curious clothing looking down a long stick. A sort of warrior it seems."

"Warrior?" said Richard. When he reached for the item, the dwarf let him take it. "'Tis a curious pose for a warrior." Richard rubbed the figure with his thumbs. "What stuff be this?"

Doug took the thing from Richard. "He's right. It's plastic. It's an army man," said Doug. "That's a plastic soldier—Chuck…"

Charlie grabbed the soldier awkwardly. "Oh, my God."

"Warriors in the Merica wage battle on their stomachs?"

"Your son," Doug said, "he wouldn't be Buddy Samson?"

"No. He would not," said the dwarf.

"But that's from…. So you're not Rumpel…," Doug started to say, but the dwarf reached up and placed his hand over his mouth to stop him.

"Let's keep names out of this, shall we? Never know who's listening."

Charlie took a hard look at the dwarf. "But it *is* him," he said. "I know you. I've met you. Your son is Buddy."

"Budi*stiltskin*," he whispered.

"We've been looking for you for days," said Doug.

"Many have tried," said the dwarf.

"We've met," Charlie repeated. "I told you this was him. Do, do you remember me?"

"I am indeed he—he to whom you owe much for two favors. One for ridding the woods of that wolf, and one sealing up your stump afterwards."

"No, no, we met ten years ago. I was in Oz with you when you first got Buddy."

The flame of his torch grew in the dwaf's hand. His eyebrows rose as he peered back at Charlie. "Oh? Well, yes. You would be the one had all the shrapnel stuck through his head." The dwarf reached his hand to his own eyebrow. "As I recall you weren't much help to me then. You and that girl with you who was hell bent on stealing my son back to her world and leaving me and my Sara barren as before."

"That was Jessica. I wasn't on her side. I tried to convince her to give him up. And besides, she's come to realize Buddy made the right decision."

"Wouldn't expect you to say anything else now that you need favors from me."

"So Buddy worked out all right as a son, did he?" asked Doug.

Rumpelstiltskin took the toy from Doug and resumed the hike. "Budi-stiltskin is the finest lad a parent would want. Bright, honest, and respectful. His mother and I have never had a moment's doubt that we did the right thing by him."

"That's kinda why we are here," Doug cut in. "Well, Charlie anyway. He was wondering how it had gone with the adoption. We have a situation back home, and Jessica, although she was apparently not your biggest supporter..."

Rumpel harrumphed at that line.

Doug continued, "her sister has a little girl, and another on the way, and she really isn't prepared to raise them, and we all started wondering how things had worked out for Buddy because maybe Isabelle, that's the sister, might consider finding someone here in your world to..."

"Hold thy tongue." King Richard put his hand on Doug's shoulder to stop him. "In the Merica they do this? They make changelings of their own children? They despise the marriage vows as well as the office of parentage?"

"No, no, of course not," said Doug.

"Thou hast come hither to trade a child to a dwarf?"

"I don't think we're explaining this right," Charlie said.

"Not all people are fit to be parents," said Doug.

"Oh, what sort of unholy place be this the Merica? It seemeth worse than the darkest place in all the pagan world."

"We're getting maybe a little off topic here," Charlie said. "We're just saying we all got pulled in to this drama of Jessica's, and well, that's sorta how we got here, or rather why we got here. And we heard that Rump..."

Rumpelstiltskin grunted.

"That the magical dwarf and his wife could send messages to our world. Jessica had gotten a letter from Buddy's new mother, and so we thought he, that is you," he turned his attention to the dwarf, "might also be able to help us find portals or some other means to get us all home."

"Wanting more favors from me, eh? Does anyone pay for anything where you come from?"

"And thus the trade? Another woman's children for passage home?"

"No," said Doug. But he didn't know exactly how to explain.

The four walked on in awkward silence, led by the dwarf. Darkness deepened. What moonlight there was did not penetrate the trees. Rumpel-stiltskin conjured more torches somehow and set them ablaze.

"Are we really looking for Buddy in the dark?" Doug asked.

"Oh, hey, you wanted an adventure," said Charlie.

"Best time to travel right now," said the dwarf. "I hear the dragon's been seen all over—as though he's looking for someone."

"I was just thinking how much more adventurous I'd feel after a good night's sleep," said Doug.

Rumpelstiltskin stopped in his tracks and spun around to look at the three wanderers. "You wouldn't happen to be on the run from the devil, would you?"

"No, no, course not," said Charlie.

"Dost mean to deceive our savior, thou of the Merica?"

"No harm, no harm at all, Richard Smith," said the dwarf, scanning each face. "Just need to know what I'm dealing with. You help me find Budy, I'll keep you clear the devil."

"You can do that?" said Charlie.

"Guess we'll have to see, now, won't we."

They once again resumed their walk. Doug wanted to know why they needed to look for Buddy. How did he get lost? Was this really a good place to raise a child if you couldn't keep track of them?

"Not lost. Just fleeing a curse. Not sure how it happened, but while trying to put out a fire he set in our home while Mama and I were away, he managed to cast a spell. Shocked us all. The boy has never shown any aptitude for magic. Nothing, not even a small transformation or cooking spell. But somehow when the fire broke out…"

"In your home?" asked Doug.

"Yeah, from the looks of the burn, half the floor and some of the wall scorched pretty bad. Must have been a pretty tidy inferno there for a while."

"You left him home alone and he set your house on fire?" Doug sounded like he was taking notes.

Charlie asked him what he was doing.

"Jessica will want to know this." He turned back to the dwarf, "he was in a fire before, you know. That's how his real family were killed."

"We are his *real* family."

"I'm sorry, I meant his birth mother, and his sisters."

"Had sisters, did he? He never said that I recall. Well, anyway, when he tried to put the fire out he somehow latched onto some deep magic, and not only did he put the fire out, but now no fire will burn near him. Can't survive without fire, so he set off to find someone to break the curse."

King Richard suddenly jumped into the conversation. "The Wizard of Grumbottem. They said he did put out fire."

"Not likely many with such an ailment. Grumbottem you say? Then that's where we are headed." With that Rumpel made a sharp turn due south.

"That was him? We were that close?" said Doug. "We could've touched him."

"But that would have cut off our adventure too early," said Charlie holding up his injured hand.

Doug sighed. "How do you know the way to Grumbottem?" Doug asked the dwarf.

"Maybe I am a magical dwarf from Grimms' Forest."

"Oh yeah, right."

"But what about my hand?" Charlie whined.

"Guess we'll keep it with us. Never know who you will meet on this kind of trip," the little man said with a small smile.

HUMPTY DUMPTY CROSSED HIS SPINDLY ARMS and frowned. He had told this foreign girl in the past not to look over his wall, and now she had clearly done just that and even spied out the path to Grimm.

"The point is," Jessica continued, "Amanda and I..." and then she abruptly turned to Amanda, "—by the way how did she ever find her way here? She couldn't have signed the book. And how did she get into the secret room?" And then a look of horror came over her face.

"What is it, child? I made it very clear, did I not, I have things to do—sad things, foolish things, things I'd shave my shell to avoid, but things nonetheless that must be done—and I cannot stand here until the cow lands waiting for you to skip to the end of your sentence."

"I'm sorry," said Jessica. "I was just thinking, Isabelle must have left my mother's place and gone back to OzHouse without my help. I didn't think she had it in her. And then she must have found the room and lost Amanda in the door. My God, she'll be frantic. It's like Buddy all over again, Amanda lost in Mother Goose Land, but there's no *me* there to find him. Do you suppose Isabelle is lost someplace horrible?"

"Him?" said Humpty Dumpty.

"I mean, we're talking Isabelle here. What if she's in a Stephen King novel? Do you suppose she's in *Cujo?*"

"Him?" the egg repeated.

"Well, I've already found *her.*" She pointed to Amanda.

"Oh, for the love of the Goose, it all comes flooding back. You know, I used to just sit on this wall for years and years, peaceful, content, friend to all who passed, no one pressing me into shell-shattering service in distant lands."

"Yes, yes, then I came along, ruined everything. I get that sometimes."

"Matter of fact you did. Whose idea of knight errant do you people think I am anyway? Do these arms say 'derring-do' to any creature of good sense?"

"Heroes come in all shapes and sizes."

"They do *not* come in the shape of eggs. Why must you always be fixing things?"

"Because things are always getting broken."

"I think we need to have a little more appreciation for loss and decay myself. Do you realize I am still fixing things *you* pushed off walls years and years ago—thought they'd died and then they sprung up again like weeds sprayed with vinegar. And let me tell you, unlike some people I could name, I'm not that fond of getting broken. Done it more often than you can count. So listen, I don't care how sorry you are for things that can't be helped."

"You need to help me find Buddy."

"One 'd,'" said the egg.

"Right, sorry."

"No one could ever say you're not persistent," said Humpty Dumpty.

"Thank you," said Jessica.

"Or obtuse. Okay. Listen, nuisance that you are, I'll make a deal with you. You like to fix things, you have strong young legs and a very thick shell—you help me, I'll help you. Yes, I think that will work. Fastest route back to this peaceful wall goes through you. And as for Jessica Junior here, I'm sure those creatures in OzHouse can wait another short while for one little girl. A little panic never hurt anyone."

Jessica finally hopped off the wall. "Works for me. *I* have to find Budy and the Stiltskins. *You* know where they are. I think we should do that first."

"SOMETHING IS DELAYING THE GIRL," sighed Ozma.

"It is certainly those meddlesome people of OzHouse," Glinda frowned. "Surely, they have interfered with Debbie's return. I should not have believed they would destroy that portal. Magic corrupts people."

"Not all of us," cut in Dorothy. "I owned the Nome King's belt for a while and when I left, I willingly gave it to Ozma."

"You are not an adult. For some reason children often lean towards goodness. But those people, even when they are trying to do what they believe is good, they interfere with things they don't understand and cause all kinds of trouble."

"There is nothing more we can do," Ozma began. "Until Debbie returns with the child's last name, we can never hope to find her. There must be thousands of Amandas even in Oz. It would be crazy to simply keep asking the Magic Picture to show us one after another until we find the right one."

At hearing this the Patchwork Girl leapt from her seat and spun around the room like a colorful top.

"Sounds like a royal command to me. Crazy is right smack in my wheelhouse." With a giggle, Scraps ran to the Magic Picture and started calling out to the framed image maker, "Show me Amanda," and then, "show me another Amanda." By the time a few dozen faces had appeared on the canvas, the other Ozites had left the room, but Scraps, who never tired, was just getting started.

CHAPTER EIGHTEEN

Dear Mrs. Henderson,
Please excuse Deborah for missing school yesterday.
She was not feeling well.
Gwen Robbins

"BETTER PUT THAT in a sealed envelope," Gary said.

"You're back already?" Gwen was startled. "What did Glinda say?"

"I couldn't get through. I tried for half an hour. I don't understand. I didn't have any trouble last time. Have I grown old? Have I lost my imagination?"

"You didn't want to see her, did you? Not really."

"No. But it wasn't just Oz. I couldn't get anywhere. I tried *The Rabbit and the Turtle*, Grimm, Pinocchio. Places I should be able to get to—some of them anyway."

"Andersen?"

"Don't be ridiculous. But Middle Earth. I tried that. I can't be too old for Middle Earth. How can you be too old for Middle Earth? No doing. Nothing. I'm pretty pissed."

"Maybe that's your problem."

"Doug made it, for God's sake. Doug."

DEBBIE FOUND ISABELLE in the Rip Van Winkle nursery.

"I don't know why you people won't help me find Amanda," Isabelle didn't turn to see who it was. "I'm just about to call the cops."

"I know where she is. And I know she's safe. You can't find her in OzHouse. But I know I can find her." Debbie's words got no reaction. "I don't want to go back. But I know I have to. I just wanted you to know, I can find her."

Isabelle turned around. "Where is she?" Her voice sounded like an accusation. "And don't tell me she's in fairyland."

"Her name is Rodriquez, right? Amanda Rodriquez? That's what Gwen said when she was telling me never to go into the room again."

"What difference does that make?"

"You have a different father than your sister. That's why you have a different name."

"Where is Amanda, you little twit?"

"It's understandable that people get angry when they're experiencing stress."

"Where is Amanda?"

"She's in Oz."

Isabelle said a bad word and stalked forward with her arm raised as though she were going to slap Debbie for lying. Debbie ran. Isabelle chased. Debbie wasn't very fast, but Isabelle was awkward and very pregnant. Debbie was much quicker on the stairs, but Isabelle almost caught her down the straight hallway. Debbie opened the door to the big closet and dived in.

"Get out here, you little twerp. Don't make me go in there after you."

"I can get her back. You don't have to chase me."

"There's no other way out," said Isabelle. "Come here."

Debbie said, "My father always wondered why Dorothy wanted to come home when she was in Oz. But I know why. I don't want to go back. But I will."

That just seemed to make Isabelle angrier. She yelled out a string of words like Debbie had not heard since her father left when she was a little girl. Everyone in the house must have heard her because there were sounds of people hurrying up the stairs. Debbie stared at Isabelle, just on the other side of the closet. Then she climbed through the slats across the back. Isabelle reached in to grab her. Debbie felt her hand on the back of her shirt, pulling.

And then no one was touching her.

"SHE'S GONE. SHE'S JUST GONE. SHE DISAPPEARED."

"Just like Amanda," said Gary.

"Right out of my hand."

"I think we need to calm down," said Gwen.

Isabelle put her hand on her stomach as though it hurt. And she sunk down onto the floor and started to cry.

BUDY LAID HIS MAPS ON A LARGE FLAT STONE. The stone marked the last step on his first map. His initial euphoria upon leaving the fortuneteller's house had started to fade the moment he realized all three of his gold coins were missing. The woman wasn't being nice. She helped him to a chair and fed him food so she could get close enough to him to fleece him. A person can steal from you while they're actually helping you, even if the helping is only a pretext for stealing. But not more than they have to. The discovery of the missing coins made him doubt the whole encounter. But on the other hand, she had put a lot of effort into studying those maps and those books. And she had given him a lot of stuff. The encounter was very expensive for him, but wouldn't he gladly pay more than even three gold coins for his life?

Of course he would. And maybe she had given him what he needed after all, like an honest con. But he still felt he'd been ripped off.

With a finger on the second map, he retraced a route from where he was over a river eastward past a spot dangerously close to a known wolf den. The third map would take him up past Rapunzel's empty tower to the sea by a fisherman's hut. Another map carried him through the village of the famous shoemaker near the castle of Briar Rose, and the final map sent him past the dank wilderness at the forest's edge. It was full of names he had never heard or read about. And in the corner of each map was a warning: "Before you pass, pay the toll of the troll of the bridge," and, "watch out for the witch who hoards the rings," and "several good people have never come back from here." Desperate as he was, the warnings meant nothing to him. He was far more troubled by the grimness of his situation. The Blue Fairy was the most powerful magic worker he knew of. But it would take him a long time to find the place of Pinocchio. And even if he did, the puppet might not be able to help him. And even if Pinocchio knew how to call the fairy, he'd still have to make it there before the icy cold of winter. Could he do that?

He'd have to. He'd just have to wrap himself in furs and do what he could to generate his own heat from eating all the heaviest foods he could find.

Budy looked over to the last map in his thick stack, the one on which the fortune teller had drawn the picture of the wooden puppet with a very long nose. What a funny looking puppet too, not quite as Budy remembered him. And that nose was easily twice as long as the wooden body. It pointed like an arrow. In fact there seemed to be an arrow at the end of it, pointing off the edge of the map. Was it pointing to the back of the map? Budy turned it over.

There was indeed something on the back. Text. Big block letters. Four sentences. The first said,

THE PUPPET BOY IS NOT OF GRIMM.

And the second said,

YOU CAN'T GET THERE WITHOUT A DOOR.

And the third one said,

I'VE SEARCHED FOR YEARS.

And the last one said,

THERE ISN'T ANY DOOR.

Budy wanted to run back, steal back his money, and tell the witch what she could do with her maps. But he guessed he'd learned his lesson for trusting a fortune teller, someone he'd never even heard of. And he had no time to waste. And was she even from Grimm? He'd never heard of her. Had she come through one of the doors back when there were doors everywhere, and she was trapped when the doors were all destroyed? What else could it mean?

"I guess you can feel angry at someone and sorry for them at the same time," he muttered.

Well, then, he thought, if the devil's grandmother was a bust, and the Blue Fairy was unattainable, that left just one faint hope: Cinderella's fairy godmother. But that meant returning to Grumbottem, where they'd threatened to cut off his head for being an evil wizard. Budy heaved a big sigh and looked around at the beautiful forest. The day was bright, but the air was cool. The leaves on the trees were turning beautiful colors. It was the kind of day when the woods were as refreshing as a cool drink. It made you glad you were alive. It made you want to stay that way. If this fairy godmother was his last hope, then so be it. If he had to risk losing his head to save it, well there actually could be worse things. Like freezing to death.

HUMPTY DUMPTY LED JESSICA and Amanda down the street, past the willow, and onto a path that Jessica remembered from all those years ago.

"The path to Grimm," said Jessica.

"Oh, better than that," said Humpty Dumpty. "The doorway to Grimm—or anywhere else."

He told her that although all the doorways were thought to have been destroyed, certainly one or two would have been missed. And as he knew where one of them was, he'd decided to rescue it. Not only that, he said, he'd learned through careful practice how to control it.

"No one can control it," said Jessica. "It takes you where and when it wants. I should know."

"Perhaps you should," he said. "But 'should' isn't 'do.' I have gone back and forth hundreds of times in the same day and catalogued the whats and the wheres and the hows until my shell almost turned purple." And then he said, as though talking to himself or perhaps answering someone who wasn't there: "The door magic is okay, as long as it's controlled. I think a little crossing of magic is not a problem, but then I've always been a character of many stories, haven't I? Of course, there is a value to integrity as well. All books should not be the same book, as I'm sure anyone would agree if one were so claudicant as to ask." Finally he said, as though remembering Jessica was still there listening, "It's a very simple thing to cross and recross as long as you refrain from the time-waste of exploring. I'll bet you never tried that."

Jessica had always been too curious of where she was to try anything like that.

"Curiosity, highly overrated. Once the meat is cooked, a good chef turns off the heat. And I—yes, I—am thoroughly boiled."

Jessica was hit by a dreadful thought: "But that means you've left hundreds of doorways—which was very foolish. What will Glinda say?"

"No, no, no. Did I not just thoroughly disavow precisely that, human girl? Do pay attention when an egg speaks. Not one doorway. Not only do I control where it goes. I take the doorway with me when I leave."

Jessica was visibly doubtful. "Yeah, but even if you *could* control it, that doesn't mean it will work for us as it works for you. We could end up back in OzHouse." And then it occurred to her that she and Amanda might be separated if they did get through the door. "I'd rather go around the door to get to Grimm, like last time."

"*Could* control it?"

"I still don't think you can control it."

"Your reasons."

"I just don't think you can. It can't be done."

"Girl from OzHouse, how can I tell you why you are wrong if you won't tell me why you think you are right?"

"I just don't think you can. And what do you care about reasons?"

"It will make you a better person to be correct on this essential question."

"So you think you're better than me because you prefer your opinion to mine?"

"That," said the egg "is illogical."

"But if it would make me a better person…"

"I do think I am a better egg than *I would be* if I had the wrong opinion on this important matter. But there are many parts to me: yoke, albumen, shell, not to mention arms, legs, hands, feet, facial features, and, of course, hat. It were erroneous to conclude too much from this one opinion."

"So you don't think you're better than me?"

"I wouldn't go that far. Facts are facts. But why I let myself be dragged into these 'adventures' with these insinuators and doubters I'll never know. Now, listen: we only *thought* we went around last time, my girl. One does not always know when one is stepping through a door what sort of door it may be. I'm afraid we have no choice but the obvious, which is whether or not to go at all. Mother Goose Land isn't the worst place for a little girl. I'm sure we could slip her in with the Old Woman. What's one more mouth to feed when you don't have any food anyway? Not exactly an expense."

Jessica was quite sure she remembered *not* going through any doorway last time when they went from Mother Goose to Grimm. But she was too concerned with the possibility of being separated from her niece to argue the point.

"My only concern," Humpty Dumpty went on, "is what happens if I show up in Grimm without that pea princess."

"Oh, I've met her. You don't want anything to do with *her,* " said Jessica. "But really, what if the door separates me and Amanda?"

"Can't recall the last time what I *wanted* was part of any equation that contained *you* as a variable. Now, listen," Humpty Dumpty said, "if she doesn't come with us to Grimm—which she will, I assure you—a child that age couldn't end up any place but *here* in M. G. Land or back where she belonged. Am I right?"

"I guess so."

"No guessing involved. It's like I'm talking to a wall."

Jessica knew he was right. Probably right, anyway. If they didn't end up back in OzHouse, Amanda would just walk through the door and end up just here, where she already was.

"You take her," said Jessica. "If she ends up with you in Grimm, fine. I'll come right after and hope for the best. If she ends up here, I'll still be here and we'll have to figure something out," although she had no idea what that would be. "If she disappears from both places, she's back in OzHouse. I'll doubt I'll have any trouble getting back there."

"If that plan were a colander," said the egg, "the spaghetti would pour right through it."

"I suppose you have a better one?"

"Couldn't easily have a worse now, could I?" Humpty Dumpty made a scoffing laugh. "You humans, you're not very trusting, are you?" He stopped in front of a stage coach. (Jessica called it a stage coach, the egg called it a diligence. But he had a history of getting words wrong.) "To Grimm," he said to the coachman—or rather to the seat where the coachman should have been sitting. The seat was empty. And there were no horses. Probably he was going to drive it himself, somehow, thought Jessica. But then why would he have told the "coachman" where to go? And why did he climb inside where the passengers belonged? Perhaps he'd been spending too much time with the Mad Hatter. Humpty held the door and she and Amanda trundled in.

"Is this supposed to take us to Grimm?" asked Jessica, sitting down.

"Supposed to?" asked the egg. "Already has." Jessica blinked twice and looked out the window. She did not see any sign of Mother Goose Land, not Humpty Dumpty's wall, or the castle of Old King Cole in the distance, or the shoe house where it should have been. Just woods. Grim, dark, foreboding woods. And then the coach started to move. She stuck her head out the window. There were horses, and someone was driving.

"You built the door into the coach?"

"Please," he said. "I delegate. These arms were never intended for the swinging of hammers."

It all worked, he told her, provided you knew which door to enter. Enter from the starboard side and you go through the magic door. The port door one was ordinary. "And that, I have come to understand," he continued, "is how we managed to get to Grimm together the last time. The doorway was the white gate. My first clue. Do you remember the white gate?"

She did not.

"With the snow just over the border, on that side but not this side?"

That sounded familiar.

"Well," the egg man exhaled, maintaining a note of condescension, "we made it through not because we focused our energy and thought real hard and tried our conscious best to get to Grimm but because it never occurred to us that we might not be crossing into Grimm. Not the penumbra of a doubt."

"And that's how you and I got here again just now? But I don't think I..." Jessica gave up on that sentence and said instead, "And how come

Amanda made it?"

"Because we brought her. Although I must say," Humpty Dumpty's tone become increasingly smug, "I wasn't *absolutely* sure that part would work."

Jessica made a face any cartoonist would love to draw before she huffed disapprovingly and said, "What makes you think your hat is part of you?"

RICHARD BROUGHT CHARLIE AND DOUG and the dwarf to his smithy. They had worked out along the way that if they could locate Budistiltskin, all their debts would be paid. But if Rumpelstiltskin found him first, they still owed him. The dwarf seemed particularly intrigued by their interest in Sarastiltskin's letter to Jessica. But he would never let on whether he knew how she'd sent it or whether there were to his knowledge any way of getting these people back where they belonged without a door. The king laid four small boards together on his work table and with a pencil drew a crude map of the town. Richard assigned each of them a quadrant of Grumbottem. When the map was made, he gave each the board on which his quadrant had been inscribed. If they followed his plan and the order of roads he laid out they would all meet at various intervals in the town square to confer on their progress.

Doug marveled at the military efficiency of the plan.

"'Tis but simple and as reason would have it," said the crusader.

They were to stay out of the open areas as much as possible in case the dragon returned. They'd be looking for anyone who might have information on the wizard they had cast from the town. Along their walk, Charlie and Doug had informed Rumpelstiltskin of the townspeople's threat to Budistiltskin's life should they find him in Grumbottem after dark.

"Cursed for a wizard because he cannot do magic? What a race." The dwarf was sure his son would not be in a place where his life had been threatened. But it was not unlikely that in his time here he'd talked to someone who might know something that would give them a hint of where he was going next. It was the last place they knew he'd been, and it was the best they could do. The Land of Grimm is a very large place to look for one boy.

Charlie was assigned the quadrant that included the castle. He found himself half hoping and half fearing he'd run into Cinderella. He'd avoided her thus far because his fear had overwhelmed his desire—fear she would not remember him or that she would remember him but not care that she did. He was very fond of his one memory of her and did not wish to have that ruined by a bad second visit. Still, he kept looking around.

Not that he'd do anything more than just look. He might even find himself turning around and walking the other way if he did see her. He would not go to the castle itself. He realized he was too much a coward for that. So really, he said to himself, there was no chance. Who was he kidding?

But of course he was in a fairytale. He ran into her almost immediately, in the shop of a chandler. He strolled in when he saw the candle maker through the window. He didn't notice the finely dressed customer with her back to him. So in he went and greeted the man. The chandler looked up and the customer turned around—and there she was, Cinderella herself, in a long blue dress, wearing a headscarf and a turquoise necklace. He recognized her at once. She hardly looked ten years older. She did not immediately recognize him. He could tell. She opened her mouth and raised her hand and pointed her finger as though she were about to upbraid him for presuming to interrupt her. But she stopped herself. "Speak again," she said.

Charlie did not find that command easy to obey. He made a face and took a breath and said, "My apologies, princess."

She looked at him several long seconds without speaking. She made herself tall, stiffening her back. "What happened to your hand?"

He hid it behind his back. "Big bad wolf."

"Show it to me." She had learned how to issue commands since becoming a princess.

He brought it out slowly as though he were showing a stolen object to the person he'd stolen it from. She stared at the stump several seconds before looking back at his face. "That will make it hard to use your compooter," she said.

A smile grew across Charlie's face, a great wide grin which he could not have dropped even if her royal person had ordered him to.

Cinderella however, seeing the grin, turned her back on him without further acknowledgement. She said to the chandler, "You will bring the candles personally to the back of the castle in the evening just before sunset and you will entrust them to no one but me."

She turned and stiffly walked toward the door. "I have no idea why you are grinning like a fool," she said sternly to Charlie as she passed him. And the grin fell like a stone from his face. "You may open the door for me, peasant."

Before she left the shop, she hesitated and said, without looking at Charlie, "No doubt that hand makes a beggar of you. I can give you nothing here. But there are alms to be had at the castle for those who ask."

Charlie bowed without a word and the princess left. The encounter left him numb—and angry. And sad.

"Well, did you come for some purpose or just to gawk like a halfwit at a princess?" said the chandler after a moment.

It was all the more urgent now that Charlie get home and put this dismal excursion behind him and never, any under circumstances, visit this Grimm world or any fairy world ever again. Indeed it was the last straw. He would not only never come back, he was certain now he would never again let fairyland be the subject matter for his art—if he ever did make more art with his right hand. It was time to grow up for real. To move on. He asked the chandler what he'd come to ask. He learned nothing very valuable from the old man. Yes, he'd heard of the wizard. He'd even been among the crowd who had driven him from Grumbottem. And he was glad he was gone.

"You are not that wizard's companion, I trust." It sounded like a challenge. It sounded dangerous.

"Huh," said Charlie. "Oh, no, we're not with him. Not a bit. Just making sure he's truly gone for good. One thing we don't need around here is wizards killing our tallow."

That made the chandler change his tone. "Not that he was so bad for business, in the end," he said brightly, inviting Charlie into friendship. "That very night the wizard cast a spell on all the candles in the castle." He pointed to a box of barely burned candles. "Half of them have to be replaced. They won't relight. That's why she was here. A real commoner princess, does castle business herself, in person."

The moment Charlie left the shop, he was caught. He felt a hand on his arm and then almost before he had time to panic two arms around his neck.

But he was not being captured. He was being hugged.

"My dear, Charles Emerson," said Cinderella, releasing him. And she stared at him until he felt awkward, staring back at her, eye to eye as though they were connected by invisible beams. "Let me see your hand again."

He held it up. "This is fresh," she said.

Charlie was finding it hard to respond. How could she be angry at him one moment and throwing her arms around him the next? He spoke cautiously, "Rumpelstiltskin has the hand in a bag. We're looking for a magic worker."

"Like the wizard who put out the fires?"

"No, that was Buddy. Remember him? He's the child I was looking for before. He's been here in Grimm all these years."

Cinderella looked around, took his good hand, and drew him into the shadowy side of the street. She pulled her scarf down even further over her forehead and they walked together talking quietly.

"You don't want to be seen with me," he said.

"You are a peasant, I am a princess. What I want doesn't matter. There are rules you can break and rules you cannot break. It can't be helped."

"That's why you acted that way in the chandler's shop," he said.

After a moment of silence, he told her about his quest, and she told him about her husband had concocted a plan, which she'd overheard, to humble her.

"You don't like your husband?" said Charlie.

"He's a good man. He's just a little addled in his thinking," she said. "Don't get me wrong, he's a charming enough prince most of the time. One could do worse, even in Grimm. But he's not terribly enlightened. Not like the Charlie Emerson I met all those years ago who drew all the strange and naughty pictures."

"You're not comparing me to Prince Charming?" They arrived at the back door of the castle. Cinderella invited him in.

He looked around as though she had forgotten they could be seen, as though he needed to protect her.

"We're at the castle now," said Cinderella. "Here I may do what I like without the town gossips gossiping. And I want you to meet my husband."

DEBBIE LANDED SMACK ON THE MARBLE FLOOR of Princess Ozma's throne room. Ozma was there, and Dorothy and the Scarecrow and Robin Hood and the Cowardly Lion and the Hungry Tiger and Suzy Bishop.

"Did you get the other name?" said Ozma.

"Rodriguez," she said. "Her sister's last name is Holton, but her sister has a different father. The baby's named Amanda Rodriguez." And they rushed to Ozma's chamber where they found Scraps asking for girls named Amanda in alphabetical order. She was still in the A's.

CHAPTER NINETEEN

Long-time DCYF head Fuller-Brinks leaving to seek public office

CONCORD—During his final days on the job, long-time head of The New Hampshire Department of Children Youth and Families, Colin Fuller-Brinks has been busy tying up loose ends.

While in his personal life he oversees the foundation of his new year-round cottage on Lake Winnipesauke, in Concord Fuller-Brinks has spent his time reshuffling the caseloads of a shrinking number of full-time staff and lobbying the Republican-led House for funds to hire another fifty case workers, according to his staff.

"There are simply too many children in need of help for the staff we have to cope," DCYF spokesperson Sandra Franklin told the Monitor from her office on Monday.

Recent layoffs and retirements at DCYF have left the office "severely short-staffed" according to Franklin. Fuller-Brinks, an avid hunter, has already put off his retirement twice due to a hiring freeze at the department. According to sources close to him, Fuller-Brinks announced his intention to run for the state legislature as a Republican.

"STOP RIGHT THERE," said Gary. "Brinks is finally leaving?"

"Apparently." Gwen lowered the paper.

"Who's taking over?"

Gwen looked through the article, "Someone named Maita Semgupta from Londonderry. Know her?"

"Wonder what that means for us."

"Fascinating," said Isabelle, folding her arms across her wide belly. "Now is someone going to tell me what you did to my daughter and that obnoxious Debbie?"

"We *have* told you and told you, again and again," Gary said. "As incredible as it sounds, magic is real, and they *are* in some fairyland, possibly Oz. We think they're safe."

Beth entered the kitchen and Gwen handed her the newspaper and pointed to the article as Isabelle continued to rant.

"Well, one bit of good news on a terrible day," said Beth. "I've always liked Maita. Good egg."

Gary smiled at his wife and sister-in-law. He looked as though he had something he wanted to say. He shifted his eyes toward Isabelle.

"You're just lucky I don't call the police," Isabelle yelled as she noisily pushed back her chair and stomped out of the kitchen. She continued ranting as she stalked down the hall and up the stairs.

Isabelle certainly didn't believe in *magic* doorways, but maybe there was a *secret* doorway or trap door in the room where her daughter had gone. And maybe that Debbie had been sent to watch her. She couldn't begin to fathom why this scheme would have been orchestrated by the freaks who ran this circus. But Jessica had always told her these people were weird. At least her daughter wasn't alone, wherever she was.

"Should we let her into the room?" Gwen asked as she and Gary and Beth followed Isabelle up the stairs.

"FYI," said Gary, "if she calls the cops and we do the whole Buddy thing again, you can forget ever getting more children."

"Good thing she's afraid of the police. But should we let her in the room?"

"I doubt we could stop her," Gary said.

Gwen ran ahead of the others.

Isabelle twisted her awkward body through the wardrobe and between the wooden slats and stood up the secret room. She moved furniture from the walls and even pulled back the throw rugs and slid books off the shelves.

Gwen crawled after Isabelle. "Do be careful. Many of those are first editions."

"Who gives a rat's ass? I want my daughter and I am going to find her."

Gary crawled through as well. Beth stood in the hallway and

watched. Books were landing everywhere, and tables loaded with delicate knickknacks were dumped onto the thick carpet.

"There are no secret doors." Gary grabbed Isabelle and held her a few seconds. With arms flailing she smacked his arms and then his cheek and he let go. She resumed rummaging through the room.

"You're going to break something." Gwen picked up a hand blown glass cat with a heart of pink glass inside that was fortunately still intact.

"So what? You gonna call the cops? Go ahead." Isabelle swept a raft of old books from a shelf. They made no emphatic thud when they hit the floor. She squinted and stared at Gwen.

Beth sighed and crawled through the wardrobe, muttering. Together with Gwen, she managed to make Isabelle sit down. They held her gently, like a young child throwing a tantrum, as she continued to berate and threaten them.

Gary rubbed his face. It was clear now if I hadn't been before that no one in the room was interested in involving the police. Eventually Isabelle calmed down. Her daughter was not in the room and there was only one way in or out.

"I need a drink," she muttered.

"Not in your condition," said Gary.

"I need a smoke," she said.

"*Not* in your condition," Gary repeated.

"The hell with my condition. I need a drink and I need a smoke and I need my daughter."

As Isabelle started to get up and head toward the slatted doorway she was pushed back. She would have fallen smack on the floor had not Beth and Gary been there to fall upon.

"What the...." Isabelle screamed as Debbie pulled herself up off the floor. "Debbie? Where did you come from? And where is Amanda?"

Debbie picked herself off the floor. Gary, Gwen, and Beth let out a collective sigh. "She's right here," said Debbie. "I told you."

And there she was, picking herself up off the thick carpet. She let out a giggle and held out her arms to her mother.

"I knew it," Isabelle screamed. "There *is* another door, isn't there? Where have you been?"

"We were in Oz."

"Yeah, right." Isabelle scooped up her daughter and carried her out of the room and back into the hallway.

"We were," said Debbie.

"We know that," said Gary. "But how did you find the baby?"

"No one listens to me. Momma used to listen to me, but no one else. I told you all that Amanda was in Oz. The people there said they could find her with the magic picture thing, but I needed her last name. I tried to tell you all this before."

"We weren't in a listening mood," Gwen said. "I'm sorry. But we're listening now."

Debbie frowned and then started to explain. "I thought the baby was in Oz, but they pretended she actually wasn't. The princess there used her tricks to show a movie of her in another land with that rude woman who was sitting with a giant Humpty Dumpty statue, and then the princess had this weird looking belt that she said made Amanda appear out of the picture, which was really a camera and a satellite of course I guess, and she must have come through a door when I wasn't looking and into the room with us. Then we both went back through door. They said it was magic. But of course it wasn't really magic."

"You've been to Oz," said Gary.

"Yes, Mr. Robbins, I know."

"And you saw Ozma use a magic belt."

"That is what she called it, Mr. Robbins."

"So why do you keep pretending magic isn't real? Why do you think the picture was a satellite?"

"Because we all know magic isn't real. Momma said."

"But you've seen it," Gwen said.

"Seeing is not always believing. We can't always... Momma wouldn't want me to say that magic is..." Debbie huffed. "It did seem kind of real."

"Maybe it was?" Gary suggested.

Debbie took a moment. Then she said, "Now I'm supposed to give the princess a secret symbol to tell her everything is okay. But I don't suppose there are any cameras in this room."

"What symbol?" Gary asked.

Debbie put her hands over her head and made an "O" shape with her thumbs and forefingers.

"Just thank God this is over," said Beth. "Let's plaster over this damn doorway once and for all."

"It's not over," said Gary.

"Why not? We bloody well got them back, right?"

"Yes, we did. But we still haven't heard from Charlie or Doug or

Jessica. They're probably all in there."

"I didn't see anyone from OzHouse in Oz," said Debbie, "except maybe some girl named Suzy but she said she left here a long time ago. And the rude girl in the... I was gonna say 'movie.' Makes no sense really. Things are all screwed up through that doorway. Momma would not approve of such a lack of discipline."

"Suzy?" said Beth and Gwen together.

"Yes, I think that was her name. I don't know if she told me her last name, but she said she came from OzHouse a long time ago. Though that's probably not true because she doesn't look much older than me, so she is probably lying or exaggerating, which Momma said is really the same thing."

"Let's get out of this room," said Beth.

"I told you I could find the baby and I did. I don't tell lies," Debbie said as she crawled out the doorway.

Gary, Beth, and Gwen followed Debbie into the hallway. They all climbed through and, in the hallway, Gary, Beth, and Gwen straightened their clothes. Debbie wasn't there.

"AMANDA," JESSICA CRIED.

"What about her?" said Humpty Dumpty. He was looking through the velvet curtain that covered the side window of the carriage.

"She's gone. She was sitting right here. Did your carriage send her somewhere? I knew this would happen."

"Surely you prevaricate, young lady. You did not *know* this was going to happen. We discussed the dangers of taking the child through a portal, but when we all arrived in Grimms' Forest safely neither of us suspected that the little one would just up and vanish. I do so hate when something completely unpredictable happens and someone presumes faux sapience, 'I knew this would happen,' when they could not possibly have the slightest inkling, and in fact what they mean is 'I feared something which I didn't have any idea of might happen and something which it is possible to describe thus did happen, so I was right.'"

"Will you shut up?"

"We'll never solve any mysteries if we remain quiet. Our best course is to collect the facts and pool our wisdom, the vast pool of mine and yours such as you may possess."

"We arrived here in Grimms' Forest safely..."

"I am fairly sure we already covered that," Humpty harrumphed

233

"I am merely trying to say if she were going to return to OzHouse or go to Mother Goose Land that would have happened when we arrived here. But she didn't. She was here on my lap, and then as we traveled down the path, she just vanished."

"Nice recap, but hardly sheds light on the problem."

"Try to be helpful, will you?"

"Whenever am I not? Now let us be logical, or as logical as a human can be."

"Stop insulting me and help," Jessica gritted her teeth.

"No need to be touchy. Okay, then. People do not just vanish. Fairies might, witches could, even a leprechaun has the power. But if she is human—she is one hundred percent human, is she not?"

"Of course," said Jessica. "She came from my world, where there are no fairies or witches. Well maybe witches but not like fairytale witches, the ones who use herbs and try to heal people. But no magic, not like here."

"You do jabber quite a pile of noisome nonsense, don't you? Now clearly *someone* is responsible. The carriage could have sent her home, but only if she had slipped through the doorway, which she could not have done; we would have seen it. We didn't ride through a lost portal did we?"

"I didn't see one."

"Nor did I," replied Humpty Dumpty. "Therefore someone else's magic is assuredly at work here."

"But whose?" Jessica asked.

"No idea, but we are almost to Grumbottem, and although I'd rather not meet up with the prince, we may need more help than most people can give us."

"And what does that mean?" asked Jessica.

"Not sure. Sounded better in my head than my mouth."

"YOU SEE THE PRINCE WAS HANDSOME and charming and kind and loving…"

Charlie was having a little trouble following Cinderella's train of thought as she led him this way and that way through the stone corridors of the castle. So many thoughts jostled in his brain that he wasn't sure he would be able to speak when he was asked to. He might say that the ache in his hand was distracting him, but it was not nearly as painful as he thought it should be. The real problem was that his feelings for

Cinderella were bubbling over again. He knew he could not let them be known or he might harm her marriage or find himself in the dungeon. As she rushed him along, the girl went on and on about what had been happening in her life since her "happily ever after" began.

"Could see how that would be hard to get used to," Charlie smiled.

"Let me finish. The little things I did that were so wrong for a royal but perfectly right for who I had been, well, at first they amused him."

"Such as?" Charlie cut her off again.

"Such as stopping to help a maid carry her bucket or giving a servant a hand setting the table or going out on my own to buy candles. At first it wasn't a problem, but then people in the castle began to talk and to laugh at me behind my back, and although *I* didn't care—it was nothing like what I had to endure after my father died—but when the prince heard of it, he was furious. He warned me to remember my place. But the place he expected me to remember, which was one I could not remember because, as I told him, I had never been in it before, was a place *above* everyone else. I am not comfortable with that."

"And?"

"And recently I found out that he had enlisted the services of a Lord Dumpty," Cinderella frowned.

"Humpty Dumpty?" Charlie stopped running alongside the princess and made her stop with him just below a burning sconce.

"Yes, in fact that's just who it was. He requested this lord to find another princess," Cinderella's eyes started to fill with water.

"That bastard," Charlie shouted, which made the princess wince and assure her old friend that his parents, the king and queen, had most certainly been married when the prince was born.

"No, I mean how dare he cheat on you with some floozy princess?"

"Cheat on me? Oh, no. That is not it at all. He wanted this other princess to teach me the niceties of my position, how to be a proper princess—as though there were some riddle in looking down your nose at people. They claim she is so delicate that she cannot sleep on twenty mattresses piled up one on another if so much as a pea is inserted under the bottom one."

"The Princess and the Pea," muttered Charlie.

"I think we shall have egg and pea soup if that Humpty Dumpty does as he has been commanded," her voice rose. "Can you imagine? Perhaps I could borrow your severed hand and stuff it under her mattress. Or perhaps suspend it from a string over the prince's bed. I do not want to be 'taught' how to be haughty or rude. I worked as a servant for too long to forget what it was like. A small kindness might mean a great deal to the girl scrubbing the steps or the young man carrying heavy loads of wood."

"I understand, I even sympathize. But what do you want from me?"

Cinderella pulled him by his remaining hand and they continued along the corridor. "I want the prince to meet you. I want him to see your odd ways, and unusual manner of speech."

"Why the hell would you want that?"

"I'm not quite sure I want him to hear the foul tongue, mind you. But I do want him to see that the world is a bigger place than just this puny kingdom. Customs may be different and yet still perfectly acceptable," Cinderella smiled.

"Bring in a ringer? Taste of his own medicine?"

"Pardon?"

By then they had arrived at the room where the prince was sitting.

"Yes? Come," said the prince when he heard the sound of the brass knocker on the thick, oak door.

"Your Majesty," Cinderella smiled. "Might we have a moment of your time?"

"Of course, wife. What did you want, and who is this?" The prince's eyebrow was raised as if he questioned the appearance of this stranger in his castle.

Cinderella approached her husband and kissed his cheek. Charlie did his best to bow properly, or at least as he had seen it done in movies.

"This is Charles Emerson. You may recall I mentioned having met him years ago before we were wed?"

"No. I do not think I do," said the prince.

"Really," said Charlie. "You've actually mentioned me to the prince?" He smiled.

"Well, you are from a far off land and..."

"Seems obvious by his accent and attire," mused the prince.

Charlie looked at the borrowed peasant clothes, which should not have looked the least bit foreign to the prince, and wondered what about him made him stand out.

"Oh, wait. Is this the one who paints obscene pictures?" asked the prince.

"I wish you to speak together, so you might learn of his land, which is very far away and very different in customs from what we know," the

236

princess explained.

"Wife," the prince's smile was forced, "I am the Prince of Grumbottem. Surely you're not suggesting I have things to learn. I am the standard of things. I am what others look to for learning. Tell me you did not rudely bring this foreign peasant before me to teach me how to be a prince?"

"What Cinderella means," Charlie began, but the prince slammed his fists on the arms of his chair and leapt to his feet.

"How dare you, peasant? I have forbidden that wretched name to be spoken in the realm. Or have you come from so far away that common courtesy isn't practiced in your land? You will address my wife as 'Her Majesty or as 'The Princess Aschenputtel.'"

"Woops, sorry. I wasn't thinking. When we met years ago, she wasn't those things yet."

"But she is now. Allowing commoners like yourself such liberties is what has caused us so much of our grief."

"Oh, yeah, right," Charlie was very much taken aback. "But don't those words mean sort of the same thing? Cinder? Ashes?"

The prince just glared.

"Sorry," said Charlie. "My bad. I guess that's why you are having the 'Princess and the Pea' princess brought here..."

Cinderella gasped.

"What did you say?" the prince demanded.

"Oh, God, I'm really making this worse. I just meant that," Charlie became tongue tied, which hadn't happened since he'd left London.

"The prince didn't know I knew that," the princess whispered.

"Perhaps we got off on the wrong foot," Charlie said.

"Speaking of limbs," said the angry prince, "I could not help but notice you're missing a hand," and then he paused with a look that would not tolerate interruption before he added, "a punishment for thieves in many a kingdom."

"What, this? No, no. It was bitten off by a wolf, despite Doug's comments about how mistreated and maligned the poor creatures are in my worl... uh, that is, my kingdom."

"Perhaps this isn't the best time to bother the prince. Let us go, Charles." Cinderella tugged his arm.

"Perhaps," said the prince with a glare.

Cinderella and Charlie made a move to the door.

"Slow down," the prince commanded. Charlie stopped dead in his tracks. "What do you know of the princess I sent the egg lord in search of?"

Before Cinderella could speak, Charlie regained a little of his usual bluster and quickly started his tale, "I am not just a visitor to your world, Your Highness."

"Your Majesty," Cinderella corrected.

"There's a difference? Of course there would be. Okay, let's start over. I am in fact a magical traveler from far away, and I have been visiting many of the kingdoms in your part of the world to learn of your ways and perhaps to teach you some of mine. Where I come from, we know much that happens here. We have books filled with your comings and goings. That is how I came to learn of your sending Humpty Dumpty on a quest to find the princess who cannot sleep on mattresses if a pea be buried deep beneath the layers, though the layers be twenty or more." At this point Charlie wished he knew the name of the princess from that story but all he could recall was a TV movie starring Carol Burnett he'd seen when he was very young.

The prince seemed both mollified and confused. His face held a frown as he crossed his arms. Just as he was about to speak, there came a rapping at the door and a tall, nervous servant peered in.

"Yes?" said the prince with hardly a look in the direction of the servant.

"Please excuse the intrusion, Majesty, but there are some people here to see you."

"And you couldn't tell I was already speaking with my wife and this foreigner?"

"Yes, of course, but one of the visitors is the egg,"

"Is he with a princess?" asked the Prince suddenly.

"Is he? She seems female. As for whether she is a princess, Majesty, it would not do for me to speculate. But if so, she is an odd one, Majesty," the servant said in a low voice.

"None of your insolence." And then he glanced over at Charlie and ordered a footman to escort the foreign peasant from the room. Cinderella turned to go with Charlie, but the prince called her back. She paused. She looked at Charlie, then back at her husband, then back at Charlie again.

"We shall deal further with that one when we have greater leisure," the prince said.

Cinderella waved Charlie out of the room and then went to sit beside her husband. As soon as Charlie was securely out the door, the prince turned to Cinderella. "Since you seem to know all about this visit, I need not explain."

"Yes, of course, my darling prince."

"You see, a princess has certain duties of state she must perform."

"I am aware," said Cinderella.

"When a member of a royal family from another realm appears…"

"Shut up, my love," Cinderella smiled. And then she yelled down to the guard the door, "Serve the egg while he's still fresh."

RICHARD WAS THE FIRST to spot the dragon, a black cross against the high clouds. No surprise of course, but a complication they did not want. On the first meeting at the town square, as they waited for Charlie, the king instructed Doug and the dwarf to walk from now on along the edge of the street as close to the houses as possible and use shadow for cover. When Charlie failed to show, Richard changed plans. Either the young man from the Merica had been detained on some suspicion (as could happen in this town) or he had discovered something. They must together trace their way back though the route Charlie would have taken, Richard on one street, Doug and the dwarf on a parallel street. They'd meet again at the castle steps on the other side.

"These good people will be on edge," Richard warned as they parted, "once they see that dragon cross their skies again. Thou were best to approach them carefully, one by one. They may think a stranger in league with the dark powers."

"I'd kind of like another close up of that dragon," said Doug after he and Rumpelstiltskin had parted from Richard.

"Oh, I doubt that extremely."

"Yeah, see, I want to be able to tell Gary about those amazing scales. You know, maybe while we're here, we should ask about that fairy godmother for Charlie. I'm really curious to see how he gets his hand back."

"I wouldn't put much stock in fairies if I were you."

"I wouldn't know about that," Doug said. "Of course, I am not sure I'd even know a fairy godmother if I bumped into her—doubt she looks anything like the Disney version. And as for the *Children's and Household Tales* there's got to be a thousand different drawings of that creature, no two alike. Would she have wings?"

"As usual I have no idea what you are babbling about. Perhaps you

239

should be quiet and follow my lead."

When they reached the end of the alleyway, they met half a dozen donkeys drinking at a trough, but no people were about. Doug looked behind as they scurried to the overhang of another building. They had not gone more than a few steps when a large shadow passed overhead.

Rumpelstiltskin looked up and muttered a word that must have been either a magic spell or a local obscenity. The shadow came from the dragon circling lower and peering down into its streets and alleys.

"And so you are in luck. Your dragon has returned indeed." Rumpelstiltskin pressed himself against a rain barrel.

"Not strictly speaking mine." Doug took a step out from the shadow of the eves to get a look. Quick as a snake, and with more strength than Doug would have imagined in that small frame, Rumpelstiltskin grabbed his arm and hauled him back into the shadow.

"Crowd the building," he said. "You may not value your life, but I value mine. Now stay close, and run when I do."

"He's very high up. You don't really think he can see us, do you?" Doug mused.

"Never bet against a dragon—or a devil. Finest eyesight of any creature."

"Never read that in the fairytales I recall." Doug followed close behind the dwarf and pressed against the side of a small stone structure. Perhaps some caution would be called for.

"What books are these you read?" said the dwarf. "All right then, we run to that cooperage back door just over there."

"Who are you hiding from?" The voice came from a window whose wooden shutters were just opening.

"Dragon," Doug pointed up.

"Keep your voice low," Rumpel cut in. "They also have keen hearing."

"I wouldn't worry about him," said the woman as she opened the shutter a little more. "He's been circling the town for days."

"So much for everyone being on edge," said Doug.

The dwarf stared a moment at the American and huffed.

"No, that dragon worried us at first. But it hasn't bothered anyone," the woman went on.

"He's not looking for you," Doug said and smiled.

Rumpelstiltskin smacked his own forehead. Before he could say a word, the woman shouted, "Is he looking for you? Are you his prey? Get out of our town before innocent people suffer."

"*We're* innocent people," Doug replied.

But the woman cried out, "Hey, everyone, I know why the dragon is here."

Rumpel pushed Doug into a slow jog so they might get away before the woman's cries drew a crowd.

"OH NO," SAID DEBBIE. "What is happening to me? This isn't right."

"Who are you?" asked the small boy beside her.

"What are you?" Debbie asked.

He told her his name. It sounded like "Bee N'oak Yo." He said, "I am a wooden puppet."

The small wooden creature stood almost to the girl's shoulder.

"I didn't want to get back to Oz."

"Oz? You're not in Oz. I was there once. You have to pass through magic portals and all kinds of stuff to get there."

Every time she had used the magic portal, it had taken her to Oz, sometimes in the past, sometimes in the present, but always Oz.

"I'm not in Oz? Then where am I?" she finally asked.

"Not exactly sure myself," said the puppet boy. "I live in the small town of Collodi, not far from here with my father, but I do not know the name of these woods."

"You have a father?" asked Debbie. "You look like a toy, and toys have makers but not fathers."

"Well *I* have a father. And one day when I have learned all my lessons I will be a real boy and make him very proud."

Debbie wasn't sure she knew what this wooden person was talking about, but her adventures in Oz had taught her that some ridiculous things could maybe be true even though they made no sense. Maybe her mother was wrong about some things.

"Can we get to Oz from here?" she asked. "I know people there who can help me, and I really don't belong here."

"Of course you can get to Oz from here. Easiest thing in the world," he exclaimed.

"What happened to your nose?" asked Debbie. "It got longer."

"Happens sometimes, not to worry. It gets better."

Debbie was suspecting that this living toy was not going to be very helpful. Suddenly she said. "What time is it?"

"I don't know," said the wooden boy. "The only clock is back in town, and we have no way to see it from here."

"I need to know when it is four o'clock. Ozma said she would look for me in her magic picture thing, and if I needed help she would rescue me."

"Ozma?" he said. "I met her once, she seemed nice, but she refused to help me with my problems. So I suspect she's actually quite mean."

"Your nose is bigger again," Debbie said. "It probably isn't polite to mention it, but you seem to have a…" She tried to think of her mother's word, "…an affliction. Oh, wait a minute. What did you say your name was? You don't look anything like him, but, oh wait, of course you said… did you mean like Pinocchio? Yes, you must have. You should pronounce your name more clearly."

Pinocchio raised his foot and pulled his arms back as though he was going to kick her very hard. But he apparently thought better of it and put his foot down and hung his head. "Actually it is very hard to get to Oz from here. And though I did meet Ozma I never asked her to help me," the wooden boy sounded sad.

"Hey, your nose is back to normal. Doesn't that mean you told me the truth?"

Pinocchio did not bother to explain. He simply started to walk back through the woods with a sad look to his slumped shoulders. Debbie followed him. She did not know what else to do.

CHAPTER TWENTY

Dear Mr. and Mrs. Robbins:

This letter is to inform you that Mr. Colin Fuller-Brinks will be retiring from the State of New Hampshire Department of Children, Youth, and Families after many years of dedicated service. I hope you will join us in wishing him well. As of October 1 your liaison will be Ms. Janice Cummins.

As you are well aware, there is a shortage of experienced foster care providers in your area, as there has been throughout the state for many years. You and your staff at OzHouse should be prepared for an influx of children that will be in need of temporary housing pursuant to their being placed in the New Hampshire Foster Care system.

We thank you for your many years of compassionate service to the needy children of New Hampshire, and we thank you in advance for continued willingness to see to their care. Please contact us if you have any questions.

Maita Semgupta
Interim Head of DCYF

"DIDN'T I SAY SO?" SAID GARY. "And look, I think Doug and Beth got the same letter. I knew it was him. It was that Fuller-Brinks character who was preventing the state from sending us more children. God knows what he'll do as a State Representative, but thankfully he won't be in our hair anymore."

"What makes you think he'll win?"

"BUT HOW WILL I KNOW WHEN IT'S FOUR O'CLOCK?"

"Doesn't matter," said Pinocchio. "Four o'clock in Oz isn't four o'clock in Collodi."

"Then how will I ever let Ozma know I'm not all right? I don't know how I even got here."

"You came through the door," he said.

"But how will I get back?"

"It's a *door*," he made a swinging motion with his wooden hand.

"I'm supposed to make the sign at four o'clock." Debbie put her hands over her head and made the "O" shape.

"Guess you're out of luck," he said.

"I have to stay here forever?"

"There are worse places."

A look of horror fell over Debbie's face.

"I remember the last time, there was a little boy," said Pinocchio, "—named Buster or something, I don't know. He *never* went back. And then there was another girl, daughter of a Bishop, I think, which is odd now that I think about it. They don't usually acknowledge their daughters. Anyway, she didn't go back either. What have you got to go back for?"

Debbie didn't know how to respond. What would her mother want her to say? She didn't know what she had to go back for. But at the same time, this place with talking puppets did not seem like a place where American children should live. You should live where you belong. Who knew at what strange hour people ate supper or went to bed in a world like this one. And she didn't want to get swallowed by a fish or turn into a donkey. In this world things like that can happen.

"Well?" the puppet said again, and then he repeated the question.

A cottage came into view, still a ways ahead. It seemed to be Pinocchio's destination.

"My mother died," she said. "Someone needs to put flowers on her grave on Mother's Day." She thought he'd laugh at her. It was the kind of thing that grown-ups think is sweet and sad, but someone like Pinocchio would probably think was silly—living your whole life where your mother died just so you could put flowers on her grave. And in fact Debbie had just thought of it. She hadn't been back to the grave since the funeral. She'd said it only because it was the only thing she could think of. But now that she'd said it, she thought it might be a good reason.

Pinocchio didn't laugh. "Funny you should say that," he said.

"Why is it funny?" she said. But he just kept walking. "Where are we going?"

"I want to show you something." He pointed at the cottage now just a little ways ahead.

"Hey, what about the Blue Fairy thing that floats down from a star. She could send me home, right? She brought you to life. She must have terrific power?"

"The Blue Fairy? Do you the mean the Girl with the Azure Hair. Can't imagine how she'd get to a star. But, well, that's what I wanted to show you."

They had arrived at the little cottage. Pinocchio pointed at the ground, at a marble plaque. It read,

HERE LIES
THE LOVELY FAIRY WITH AZURE HAIR
WHO DIED OF GRIEF
WHEN ABANDONED BY
HER LITTLE BROTHER PINOCCHIO

"She's dead," said Pinocchio, "just like your mother. I killed her." A tear slid down the wooden face.

"WHAT ARE THEY LOOKING AT?" asked Suzy.

"There seems to be something on the ground," said Ozma. "I can't tell what it is."

"I wish this thing had a microphone. I can't hear what they're saying," said Suzy.

Glinda was pacing. The Patchwork Girl was pacing as well, shadowing the sorceress.

"I don't think you should do that," said the Scarecrow.

"Why not?" said Scraps. "How else will I know what thoughts are bubbling around in her head? Besides, it's a lot of fun. You should do it with me."

"She's going to think you're making fun of her," said the Scarecrow.

"If there is one thing I take pride in making, it is fun. Fun, fun, fun. Making it, having it, spreading it around. Most people don't make nearly enough of it."

Glinda stopped pacing. Scraps kept on.

"What I don't understand," said the sorceress, "is how she got into that story with that miserable puppet. Did Gary Robbins put no

245

restrictions at all on the use of that portal?"

"We have no authority over what people do in the real world," said Suzy.

Glinda glared at the girl from America.

"Well, that's just what they call it," Suzy said.

"We may have no authority, but we do have influence, and we need to figure out how to wield it."

"I agree, something must be done," said Ozma.

"Ah, something," said Scraps. "That's my favorite thing of all. I say we swing from the chandelier by our feet."

THE PRINCE OF GRUMBOTTEM sent his soldiers to find the remaining foreigners: Doug Robbins and Richard Coeur de Lion, lately Richard Smith, of England. That business done, he called for Lord Dumpty and his companion to be admitted.

"Greetings to you, Lord Dumpty, and to you, Princess..." And then he paused. He stared Jessica up and down in her indelicate, unfussy, peasant clothes. "Is this the attire of a princess in your land?" he said.

"Yes, well, the thing is," Humpty Dumpty put his hands behind his back and peered up at the high ceiling of the throne room, "about the whole Princess and the Pea thing."

"This *is* the famous pea princess, is it not?"

"So as I was about to say," said Humpty Dumpty.

"Because if it is not, there's a pack of wolves outside that have an extraordinary fondness for deviled eggs."

"Ah, but you do see, Prince...," said the egg.

Jessica jumped in front of Humpty Dumpty. "Well," she spread her arms wide, "so sorry if I wasn't all scrubbed and dressed for a kidnapping when your Lord Dumpty here and his minions burst in on me. I told him, I said, just give me a minute to freshen up, slip into a fancy, gossamer, princess dress, shine up a new crown, dust on some make-up and put in a call to my armed guards before you grab me by the short hairs and haul my delicate arse down that rickety ladder of yours. You want to see my bruises? I got splinters from my soles to my spleen, Your Highness."

"Majesty."

"Whatever."

"Kidnap?" said the prince, sounding offended. "Did you say 'kidnap'? How dare he? He was enjoined to extend you a royal

246

invitation. I assure you, he will be..."

"Yeah, yeah, yeah. So he said. You think I didn't see right through that? Like a chick with my gentle tush is gonna willingly park it in a stage coach and bounce it all the way from Andersonland to Grumbottem? I got a black and blue the size of Denmark back here. I won't be sitting for weeks—not with twenty pillows under my derriere. Thank you so much, Your Meddling Highness."

"Majesty."

"Yeah, like I said, whatever."

"Princess, I swear, if I had known... But do not worry, I will see that the egg is appropriately punished. I'll have that insolent omelet hurled from the highest tower of the castle."

"Sir, if I may..." said Humpty Dumpty. But Jessica put her hand over his mouth and kept her attention on the prince.

"Hey, stop projecting, all right? I'm not buying it. Besides, the poor guy's fallen off enough walls already." She patted the egg on the top of his head. "Really, what could he do? You scared the yoke half out of him. And don't think my father the king's gonna take this little diplomatic *faux pas* of yours lying down. You couldn't send him enough mattresses. If he finds that door..."

"But princess," said the prince.

Cinderella had had enough. "Sit down, husband, please." The prince puffed up his chest and raised his imperial hand. But Cinderella was not intimidated: "Clearly the whole peacock thing's not working for you at the moment. Are you looking for a war? Sit down."

"Would that be between the two of you or his kingdom and mine?" Jessica asked.

"We'll let him stew about that," said Cinderella.

The prince plunked himself onto his throne.

Before Cinderella could say another word, shouting erupted from outside the throne room. "Lock and brace the doors," came a voice. "Stand fast. Gather all the water you can find. Get archers at the ready."

"What's going on," Cinderella yelled. A half dozen guards ran into the room pushing two men and a dwarf before them.

"Doug?" Jessica forgot everything and ran. "Rumpelstiltskin?"

"Quiet, you meddling girl. Throwing around people's names like breadsticks."

"You know this foreigner, princess?" said the prince. "How is it possible?"

"Your Majesty," said the captain of the soldiers, "we have found the men you sought and this dwarf who was among them. But it is worse than we feared. It is they who have called the dragon," the captain kept looking over his shoulder as he spoke, "and the Old Nick is giving chase. The doors may not stand fast against him."

Another soldier continued the report, "We have run down narrow roads to get here, too narrow for the dragon. But I fear he knows who we are and will be soon be upon us."

"Throw them out," said the prince. "If the dragon wants these men, let him have them."

"Prince, you can't," said Cinderella. "They'll be burned. They'll be killed."

King Richard, now on his feet, made a formal bow to the prince, "Thy Royal Majesty," he began slowly and calmly, bowing, his presence bringing calm to the room, pulling all eyes to himself, "being of them that know the ways and burdens of utmost power, though I do not appear as such in this journeyman garb..."

But he was able to say no more. A shadow and a sound like a blast furnace drew the attention of everyone to the large east window, a depiction in stained glass of the legendary victory of King Grisly Beard over the devil. The lead holding the glass boiled and turned to wisps of smoke as they watched. The many frames of colored glass shivered and crashed in shards on the granite floor, sending three of the prince's knights scurrying for safety.

At the sound of the crash, another half dozen knights entered from the door behind the throne with swords drawn. Charlie stepped back in behind them and stared up at the gaping hole where the window had been. There, framed by the casement, like a very large canary, the dragon perched. His head reached the pointed arch. His scales like burnished black leather were edged in a fiery orange glow. The whiskers on his snout twitched. Smoke, grey and white, rose from his nostrils as he slowly scanned the room. Charlie ran to Cinderella's side. King Richard placed himself between the princess and the dragon. He drew and raised the battle-tested sword he had concealed in his robes. Everyone else stared in frozen panic.

"I always hated that picture," the dragon huffed and the smell of smoke from old fires permeated the room. He extended his great black wings and glided down with a rustling sound.

Finding their legs, the prince's guards ran up the steps to the throne to shield His Majesty from the dragon's wrath. But the prince spread his arms to hold them back.

"What business do you have with me that you would come with such fury into my castle, Lord Dragon?"

"I don't think you want to pick a fight with me, Your Majesty." And the dragon blew a great plume of fire up at the high rafters of the room. "I could bring this whole thing down on your heads before you could say my name. I suggest you bow," he said. "Or better yet, kneel."

King Richard took a step forward, but the prince waved him off and continued without any sign of fear: "State your business, devil. I know you. State your business so I can deny you, and then shuffle back to hell where you belong." The prince walked boldly down the steps and right up to the creature.

The devil was clearly provoked. He blew fire again up into the rafters. Half the knights ran from the room. Others entered at the perimeter and knelt and drew their bows and waited for a signal from the prince. But he signaled them to stand down.

"It's true," said the dragon, "I have no business with you. That doesn't mean I will let you live. Collateral damage—it happens. Price you pay for sheltering my enemies." He pointed a sharp finger at Charlie. This drew Jessica's attention for the first time to her friend. She ran up and grabbed him by the arm. "We had a deal, Charles Emerson," the devil went on. "You have reneged. You promised me a name. What is it? Who betrays me?"

"Well, that's the thing," said Charlie. "I'm not absolutely sure we did have a deal. Weren't we still in the negotiation phase? As I recall, we never shook on it." Charlie raised his right arm.

The dragon glanced down. And for a moment it seemed the dragon almost laughed at the sight of Charlie's stump. Jessica gasped. "Is that not the arm of the man who has shaken my hand?"

"No, no, no. This was a...."

Jessica reached out for the stump.

"We had a deal. Your contract is due. Who is it that betrays me? Who is my next victim?" Flame spurted through the dragon's crooked teeth.

"Don't you think you should just tell him?" said Doug. "It won't change the books."

"Those are stories," said Charlie. "These are people."

"Not yet," said the prince. "You may not reveal anything without

249

terms."

"The terms are set," said the dragon. "They are these: he tells me what I want to know and I don't necessarily burn the castle to the ground. You don't think stone can burn? You haven't seen the heat I can throw."

"But I've been thinking about what you said," said Charlie. "If I tell you, I'm helping you damn people. I'm having second thoughts about that."

"Damn straight," said Jessica. "I should know. If you haven't made a deal, I don't think he can do anything. He needs a contract. He told me."

"He told you?" said Charlie.

"Long story," she said.

"Don't be deceived. I have all the contract I need."

But Jessica stared up at the devil. "He's not going to do anything that helps you pull people into that nasty place."

The devil smiled. "Jessica Holton. How I have missed you. I almost thought you'd got away. How's that sister of yours." He reached for her. At his current size he could have fit her in the palm of his hand. Jessica jumped behind the nearest stone pillar. The devil snickered and puffed up his chest to let everyone know the next blast of heat would not be for show.

"Okay, dragon," said the prince.

"Too late," said the dragon. "I'm not to be toyed with. Someone has to pay."

He pulled in more air and held his massive chest for a long moment. The prince ordered his men to ready their bows. Arrows flew from all over the room, from the guards kneeling by the door and from balconies high overhead where no one knew guards were stationed, arrows from bows and crossbows. They bounced off the dragon's fleshly armor like toys. The dragon pulled his chest full of air. His chest glowed with the heat. The smoky smell cleared from the room as the air grew warm. Everyone in the room cowered or screamed or ran for the doors. And then the dragon let go with fury.

A flame too small to ignite a twig oozed from his giant mouth. It was followed by a little plume of black smoke. A look of consternation fell across the devil's face. Immediately he drew in a breath that sucked the remaining air from the room. Again he blew with all his might in the direction of Jessica Holton who had stepped out from the pillar. The wind of his breath knocked her over. But there was no fire. The dragon coughed and cleared his throat. Wisps of smoke issued from his nostrils.

Behind the dragon, a voice cried out, "Hey, dad." Budistiltskin's head appeared over the jagged glass at the bottom of the broken window. He was smiling brightly at Rumpelstiltskin. "I thought that was you." He climbed gently over the broken glass and into the space, ignoring the dragon.

Rumpelstiltskin ran over to his son, "Beware, my son."

"No, I don't think so," said Budy.

Consternation filled the room. Budy walked over to the great beast and kicked him in the thigh. The devil seemed to be growing smaller.

"Oh, of course," said the dwarf. "Come in, come in. Never been so happy for a curse my whole long life. Ha, prince, princess, dragon, everyone, here is my cursed son, Budistiltskin."

The dragon continued to diminish, like a balloon that had been inflated too long, as the heat died inside him. He gasped. No one tried to stop him as he heaved for breath and stumbled to the window. Using what seemed like the end of his strength, he pulled himself onto the sill, ignoring the broken glass, and spread his wings. But he did not fly. He fell heavily, three stories, to the ground. He landed with a resonant crunch. Everyone ran to the window to watch the horrible, broken creature hobble into the street and out of view.

"Should we go after him, Your Majesty?" asked the captain.

"No," said the prince. "He is still the devil. Weak though he seems, he cannot be killed or captured. We will not provoke him further. Let him go. I think once we have dealt with these foreigners, we'll give him no more cause to come for us."

The prince motioned for all the foreigners to come to him. Before they could take a step, however, two more creatures appeared in the room. No one saw them enter. Two young girls. Two more foreigners.

"This isn't home," said one of them, "I want to go home."

"Soon enough," said the other.

"Who are you?" asked the prince.

"Well, thank goodness that dragon is gone," said the second girl, who introduced herself as Suzy. "We saw the whole thing. Glinda wouldn't let us interfere. She didn't even want us to come once he left, but the Princess Ozma overruled her. She's not much for interfering with the working of foreign lands. 'Just bad policy,' she said."

"Glinda?" said the prince.

"Oh, dear," said Charlie.

251

"Who is Glinda?" the prince said. "And who is Ozma? And who is this other girl beside you?"

"I'm Deborah Hannah Thomas, sir. And if I ever get back to OzHouse, you can be sure I will never under any circumstances go onto that horrible room again."

"I think it's high time for everyone to go home," said the prince. He kicked the shards of glass. "I have a mess to clean up."

"Not so fast," said Cinderella. She called for servants to escort everyone to private chambers to freshen up, to get a change of clothes and meet in the great hall for a proper royal feast of thanksgiving before sending them home. "It is a glorious day. We've banished a devil," she said to the room. And then she turned to the prince and said through a forced smile, "Hospitality, it is our royal duty, is it not? And besides, we still have some things to discuss."

PRINCESS ASCHENPUTTEL AND HER HUSBAND, The Charming Prince of Grumbottem, sat side by side at the head of the table as the guests filed in. First came Charles Emerson, who sat on the princess's right. Next was Doug Robbins, who sat across from Charles. They were followed by Jessica Holton, Suzy Bishop, Deborah Thomas, Richard the Lion Hearted, Lord Humpty Dumpty, Rumpelstiltskin, and, last of all, Budistiltskin, who sat beside Debbie. All the candles went out when Budy entered the room.

Everyone enjoyed a feast like none they had ever eaten: boar and venison and bread with honey butter, cabbages and potatoes and spinach and peas—all served with vinegar—and soups that were more onion than broth with leeks and carrots and a little more vinegar, and wine and mead and water and cheese, and no eggs anywhere. Everyone ate their fill.

To her relief, Jessica learned from Suzy what had happened to Amanda. Cinderella learned of the wonders of Oz. Charlie figured out how to push food onto his fork using the stump of his hand and a hunk of bread and Debbie decided she didn't mind onions if they were sweet onions and, out of politeness, she had to eat them. At one point Humpty Dumpty ripped off a hunk of bread from a large loaf and, looking over at Rumpelstiltskin, said, "I'm curious, my friend. I'm always interested in the customs of other lands. I would love to know under what particular circumstances your people throw breadsticks?"

"It's just an expression," the dwarf grumbled.

Half way through his soup, Doug said to Charlie, as he'd said so many times before, "If only I had my phone so I could get a picture of this."

"For Gary to draw?" said Charlie.

"Yes."

"You keep saying that," said Charlie. "You do realize I am an artist as well. I've been drawing this stuff for years. For my whole life. You don't need to save up your memories to hand them to Gary. Just look at my pictures."

That hadn't occurred to Doug. He started thinking about Charlie's paintings and sketches, what he could remember. "Yeah," he said, "actually, yeah. You have been drawing this stuff all along. Now that I've been here..."

"You shouldn't have to have come here to be able to see it. That's what my paintings are for."

"You still giving up on this subject?"

Charlie held up his stump.

"Well putting that aside..."

"You can't put it aside, Doug."

"But is *this* what you want to draw?"

Charlie glanced around the room, the timber supports were made from whole trees, the walls from stacked stones, the floor from planed pine boards two feet wide. And then there were the extraordinary stained glass windows, as rich in color and scene and design as anything you could find in Europe. And then there was Cinderella. Chuckling at something Humpty Dumpty had said, she laid her hand softly on the prince's arm and whispered in his ear. He laughed. She caught Charlie's eye and smiled.

"It's what I would have to draw if I could," he said to Doug, "till I get it out of my system. I guess I'm not there yet. Whether that's a blessing or a curse, I don't know."

At the end of the meal, the princess rose and, in a most official voice, announced: "I am led to understand from my good friend Charles Emerson that many of you have petitions to bring before the prince. It is our custom after a feast to honor petitions to the utmost of our means from all who grace our table."

"It is?" said the prince.

"Customs have to start somewhere," the princess quietly said. Resuming her official tone, she bid each guest speak in turn.

"I'd kind of like my hand back," said Charles.

Doug said, "I must tell you, princess, now that my glorious adventure has come to its close, my thoughts turn toward home and my dear English wife."

Charlie cast him a look. So did King Richard.

"I'm sure that's how you are supposed to talk at a royal feast in the land of Grimm," he shot back. And then he re-addressed their Royal Majesties, "In plain English, now that it's time to go home, I'd like my marriage fixed."

Jessica said, "I'd like to find a place for my sister and her children to live."

King Richard said, "I would like my kingdom restored."

Deborah said, "I'd like to go home."

Budy said, "I would like to have the curse revoked so I can go into business with my cousin Jack and not freeze to death."

Humpty Dumpty didn't know what to ask for. But neither did he want to be left out. So he said he might like an armored shell if wasn't too much trouble. But really, otherwise, he was just quite all right.

Rumpelstiltskin wanted his son to come home, at least for the holidays, after the curse was lifted. And Suzy remarked as politely as she could that she lived in Oz and couldn't possibly want anything at all.

The prince fidgeted. "You do realize, I'm not a magic worker. The only one of those wishes I can honor would be Suzy's."

Charlie, holding up his stump, stared at Doug. "See. It's real. It breaks, it stays broke."

But aside from that comment, there was a lot of cheerful chatter around the table. Everyone understood. No one really expected anything from a mere prince anyway, and really everyone was still so glad to have escaped the devil that they were content to take on their own problems themselves. Cinderella, however, was not finished.

"If the prince cannot help, I suggest we might help one another where we can," said the princess. "Some of those wishes can surely be granted. Rumpelstiltskin, I think you have a sack with a severed hand in it. You are a powerful magic worker. Could it be you can restore poor Charlie's hand?"

"For nothing?" said the dwarf.

"You could have helped me all along?" said Charlie.

"You could have asked."

Budy reached down and grabbed the sack with the hand and put it on the table. Rumpelstiltskin patted his son on the back, then turned to Charlie. "What'll you give me?"

"The fee of our eternal gratitude," said the princess with a laugh, "to which I will gladly add my good will, and, for you, dwarf who would be nameless," he snickered, "the continued possession of your house and your lands."

Rumpelstiltskin harrumphed and grunted. But he grabbed Charlie's stump and tied it to the hand with a cloth then uttered a spell, and when he pulled the cloth away, the hand was back, fixed, good as new.

"What did I tell you?" said Doug. "No permanent damage."

"This proves nothing," said Charlie, grabbing one thing after another with his repaired hand.

Doug smiled so wide it appeared he might pull a muscle.

"Wipe that smile off your face," said Charlie.

And everyone laughed.

"Now, what else can we do?" said the princess.

"Sending people home will be easy," said Suzy. "Ozma has already sent Lord Locksley home. She was tired of waiting for him to earn it. As soon as I give the signal, she'll send everyone home with the magic belt."

"Or Humpty Dumpty could...."

"Shhhh, child," the Egg Man laughed.

"Then, with Robin, I shall need no further help to restore my kingdom," said Richard.

"See, it's not so hard," said the princess. "As for Doug, I'm afraid you're on your own. There is no magic for a successful marriage. I should know." She grabbed her husband's hand and smiled. "And as for the egg, I don't think you would be who you are with an armored shell, so it's just as well we cannot help you."

"Just as well, indeed," said Humpty Dumpty. "Probably just sanction recklessness anyway now that I think of it."

"And that leaves us with Budistiltskin. I am afraid the spirit of my mother cannot help you with your curse. She could perhaps reverse it for a time. But at midnight her magic would wear off. It always does."

"What about the Blue Fairy?" said Budy. "Is it really impossible to get to her?"

"Sort of," said Debbie. "It's the Azure Girl actually. I know. But she's dead, like my Momma. I saw her grave."

"Then I'm doomed," said Budy.

255

"You can always go home with us," said Jessica. "OzHouse will welcome you back. I know it will."

"Of course we will," said Doug. "You can have Charlie's room."

"Hey!"

"Oh, right. You're staying. Now that you have your hand back. Well, there's always room for you, Budy," Doug said.

"But I'd have to leave my home," said Budy.

"Most people do when they grow up," said Jessica.

"And if you want to make furniture," said Charlie, "you'll love Gary's workshop."

Budy smiled sadly.

"What about Isabelle?" said Jessica. "I have a letter from Sarastiltskin that promises she will take her and her children. Clearly, Budy is happy here. That means Izzy might be happy too and Amanda and the baby."

The dwarf smiled. "My Sara has a soft spot for little ones, and a tough hide as well for their shrewish parents. Could be we can help out. On a trial basis. Worth a conversation."

"Could Ozma bring her here? I don't think she could ever get through the door."

"Not if Glinda has anything to say about it," said Charlie.

"Still, we could ask," said Suzy. "The princess is not Glinda."

"Well, then, that's that," said Cinderella. "I think it's time for dessert."

"What about me?" Deborah said meekly. "I want to go home."

"We're all going back," said Doug. "Ozma…"

"I don't want to go to OzHouse. I want to go home."

Everyone at the table looked blankly at the little girl who hovered over her empty plate. Silverware clinked. Cinderella exhaled audibly and looked as though she were about to speak, but no words came out.

"Well, you see," she finally said. But she had nothing to add to that opening. The silence grew. Debbie raised her eyes and looked around the room and then hung her head again over her empty plate.

Budistiltskin tugged his chair closer to the girl and put his arm around her.

CHAPTER TWENTY-ONE

Doug,

It is 3 AM and I have just woken up in our bed alone.
According to Gary and Gwen you have been gone a long time, and I
am afraid you are not coming back. We have been on some rocky roads
lately but I must tell you even if it will mean really hard work I think
we are worth it. I am putting this card in the secret Narnia room so it
will be as close to you as I can get it. Please come back. I have no idea
if you are in some glorious fantasy world or some dark nightmare. I
pray you are safe even though I haven't done much praying lately.
News is, we will be getting a lot more children, a group arrived today,
and I see that as a sign that things are going back to the right track.
All else aside, we need you. And I love you,

Beth

BETH EASED HER FEET into her soft slippers and quietly went up to the secret room. She so rarely went near the closet of fur coats that it felt odd to be down the hallway again so soon after the incident with Isabelle.

She crawled through the bottom of the cabinet just under the coats and sweaters and pushed through the back door. Inside she stood up and felt for the light switch. During the day enough sunlight came through the stained glass window that most people did not need a lamp, but the tiny sliver of a moon was not nearly bright enough for her to maneuver in the crowded room.

Once the electric sconces were turned on, she looked around the room and decided to put her card on the large gilt book that the children signed.

"I hope he gets this somehow or other," she said to herself half out loud. Then as she went to turn off the lights and crawl back out, she stopped and picked up the deluxe feather fountain pen and added a flourish and a heart to the signature she'd left in earlier in the book.

As she reached for the secret doors, she heard a rumble and immediately was pushed back by someone coming through into the room.

"Doug?" she called out.

"No, Mrs. Robbins. It's just me, Debbie."

"Debbie? What are you doing up? Where were you?"

"I thought I was going back to Oz, but I ended up is some other place with that snotty puppet, Pinocchio who couldn't even pronounce his own name properly. And then I went to a feast with Cinderella because Ozma sent me there. And then when they said I couldn't see Momma again, which I knew they would say, because, well, you know, I said I was tired, so they sent me home. So here I am."

"Ozma?" If Beth had any lingering doubts about the magic of the doorway, she gave them up at that moment. "So you did go to Oz?"

"Oh no. Like I said if you were listening, I was in the woods and then I was in a castle. But it's okay if you don't understand because everything was very particularly confusing. Momma never would have approved of it all. But I have had to learn to accept a certain amount of silliness. Grownups can make mistakes too."

"You didn't happen to see Doug did you?"

"Yes, Ma'am, I did. We had dinner together."

"Then he is all right?" Beth wiped a small tear that was forming in her eye. "Then where is he? Why didn't he come back with you? He does want to come back doesn't he?"

"I did not want to stay. But the grownups had some, how did they call it, loose ends to tie up. I believe Mr. Robbins was coming home with

258

Mr. Emerson, and Ms. Holton, but there was a problem with two other men. I don't remember everyone's name. There were a lot of people in the room, and no one went out of their way to introduce themselves to me. Momma would have said that was improper. I had a hard time following all the conversations. They said I could go home first, which I think I said already."

"Do you think we could go through and find them?"

"Back through the doorway? I don't think so, Mrs. Robbins. A bossy little girl named Suzy made me promise not to use the door again. She was about my age, but everyone talked to her like she was a grownup."

Beth gave a loud sigh. "Do you know what story you were in if it wasn't Oz?" she asked.

"No, Mrs. Robbins. It was a castle all filled with people from many different stories. Humpty Dumpty was there. But so was Cinderella, which I think I already said. I don't know what story it was. They were talking about a black dragon too, which my mother said was make-believe and not real, but they said it was real, and it was big and scary and mean. And I've seen so much that it's hard to be sure they were making it up. But, no one said what story it was from, and I didn't think to ask. Can we go to bed now? I am very tired."

Humpty Dumpty? Cinderella? Dragons? Beth wanted to try the doorway to find Doug, but she had already proven to herself that she was not the kind of person who could make it into fairylands, and even if she were, she wouldn't know which story to think about. "Of course, darling. Let's get you washed up and into bed. It is very late."

JESSICA HAD NEVER BEEN much for wearing dresses. But she was enjoying the yellow and pink gown that Cinderella had loaned her. She'd turned in front of great gold-framed mirror twice to sneak a look at herself from all sides. Pretending to be a princess isn't something she'd ever wanted to do before. But then, she'd never had the right kind of clothing. She might have complained in the past about girls wanting to be princesses, but perhaps what people should be complaining about was how we use the word. Cinderella knew how to be a princess. And every superhero needs a costume.

When Debbie complained that she wanted to leave, Jessica had risen from her seat to tell the girl to inform the people of OzHouse that the rest of them would be back very soon—in a few hours she imagined. Doug had said he was ready to go home at last. But now that he knew his return was imminent and guaranteed, he didn't mind lingering just a little longer to drink in the last details of fairyland, and even Charlie with his restored hand was obviously enjoying getting the texture of solid things that this world so richly afforded. He looked comfortable grabbing the arms of his polished oak chair.

When Jessica returned to her seat, she noticed a servant placing something under the cushion. When she sat down she jumped up and shouted, "Lord, Almighty!"

Everyone was startled, especially the prince, but as she swept the tiny pebble off her seat and let out a sigh as though she'd just avoided some danger, he sat back and sighed as well.

"Nice work," Humpty Dumpty mouthed from his end of the table. Jessica just smiled at him.

"Look at my hand," Charlie said again. "It's as good as new. No necrotic skin, no scar, no sign of any damage. Look, the fingers work just fine. Like nothing had ever happened to it. It's better than Luke Skywalker's. It's my actual hand."

The feast ended. Musicians were brought in. And there was dancing and singing and hours of royal entertainment until darkness fell. Through the broken window the moonlight shined. Doug leaned back in his chair with a smug smile. "The lack of candles may have to bring our evening and our adventure to its end. And so, to the problems at hand," he began, "no pun intended, Chuck."

King Richard spoke up, "It would seem that good Queen Ozma has already sent the child Deborah home. If she would do the same for me I would be forever in her debt."

"She won't want your debt," said Suzy. "Your gratitude is more than enough. This debt business kept Lord Locksley estranged from your world for years."

"My gratitude, then. I am sure there is much work for me to do back in my England. The country needs its king."

"Oh, that reminds me," said Jessica. "I promised to fix what Janey did. I need to help the Merry Men fix that hole in the dungeon."

"Thou dost forget," said Richard, "once the isle is in my grasp once again, I will know what do with this door. Surely no one from the true England shall visit the false in that way."

"But," said Jessica. But she could say no more. Suzy made some motions in the air that looked like magical gestures to everyone in the room and suddenly Richard was gone.

"That is quite a trick," said the dwarf.

"Sign language," she said.

"Be there any other kind of language?" he mumbled.

"Ozma and her friends have been standing by the Magic Picture this whole time," Suzy continued as though she had not heard him.

"Two down," said Humpty Dumpty as he pulled a linen napkin from under his chin. "Who will be next to leave us?" And he reached for a bowl of candied apples. "Is it getting cold in here, or is it just me?"

"It appears to be our turn," said Charlie, looking at Doug, "you, me, Jessica, and Budy."

"I don't want to go," said Budy.

Rumpelstiltskin rubbed his hand under has nose. "Oh, but sure you do, son, for a time. It's what you were planning at the start, was it not? Going off with your cousin, coming home to visit now and then. All children do it at some point. It's part of growing up."

"You'll like New Hampshire, Buddy," said Doug. "A lot of woods, plenty of good outdoor work to do. It's not necessarily so different from here."

"Don't forget to mention Wi-Fi," said Charlie.

"And you and Mama can come visit me there. There has to be one of those doors somewhere."

"I don't think it works that way," his father muttered. "Besides, a world without magic and me and your mama being almost 500 years old, might not be a pretty sight. We could send letters though, apparently, somehow."

"Do you know how to get letters to our world?" asked Jessica.

"No idea. But Mama, she is a bit of a hedge witch, knows a few nifty tricks, she does."

"Poppa," Budy called out.

"I thought you knew."

"Couldn't *she* find a way to fix this curse?"

"She'll never stop looking, son. But keep in mind even a curse can have a good side. You defeated the devil himself. Your mama will be so proud. My son beat sneaky Old Nick; even I can't say that. And I've never seen a curse didn't have an antidote," he said through gritted teeth. "Just got to find it is all. We will leave no stone unturned till we do."

Even Humpty Dumpty offered to check every book he entered to find a possible answer.

"So I guess it is time to go," Jessica announced. But just as Suzy raised her hands to signal Ozma, she reached out and grabbed her arm. "Oh, dear," she said. "I still have a hell mouth I promised to fill."

"Excuse me?" said Doug.

She quickly told the story of the promise Mrs. Hubbard had extorted from her.

Humpty Dumpty laughed. "Believe me, that woman's all jabber. I'm sure she's already forgotten about it."

"But I did promise," said Jessica.

"Did you dig it?" asked the egg.

"No," said Jessica.

"Then I hardly think you are responsible for it."

"But I promised," Jessica repeated, "I did promise."

"Oh, well then, that is something else. No worries. I know just where it is. I'll have one of the boys take care of it. I believe Tommy Tucker owes me a favor."

"Okay, that settles it," Doug announced. "I've had enough."

"You've had enough?" said Charlie.

"Yes, I think I have. Fairyland is wonderful, but, if I can say it out loud, I miss my wife, and I hope she misses me, and I want to get back. So, Suzy, if you will..."

"Glinda will be happy to hear you say that," Suzy smiled.

Budy kissed his grizzled old father, which almost embarrassed him in front of all the others, and wiped tears from his eyes. Rumpelstiltskin asked to be sent back to his cottage with his wife before Budy left. He didn't want to see his son leaving him, possibly forever. Suzy's hands waved in the air. Once his father was gone, Jessica put her arm around Budy. Suzy pointed at him and Doug, and Charlie, then waved her hands again. Doug and Charlie were already fading away as they thanked Cinderella and the Prince for their hospitality. Charlie felt a pang of jealousy watching the Prince hold her hand and seeing her smiling back at him.

"I do hope you will visit me again someday, Charles Emerson," she said.

Doug and Charlie and Budy disappeared before Charlie could speak. Jessica, to her surprise, remained behind.

"Do you want Ozma to send you back to Mother Goose Land?" Suzy asked Humpty Dumpty.

"No, I think not," said the pompous egg. If the Prince will have me as a guest a bit longer I think I might take a few days to recoup, a good vacation from my solitary life on the wall. Besides, I have my carriage outside. Can't leave that behind."

"Ah, excuse me," said Jessica.

"Milady?" said the prince, "I am sure you wish to return to your own kingdom, but I wonder if you might tarry a while."

Cinderella glared at her husband. "I am instructed enough," she said. "We just need to talk more between the two of us."

"No, no, of course. I have given up on that rash course. I mean to have the princess tarry merely as a companion," he said, "at least until her injuries heal. You have so few equals in Grumbottem with whom to spend time."

"Oh," said Jessica. "You still think…. No, no, no. God no. I could sleep on the back of a running horse. I'm from OzHouse like the rest. I'm not the princess."

"But the pebble on your seat," said the Prince.

"Pretty clever, huh? My name is Jessica Holton. I thought you knew, somehow. I just happened to arrive with Humpty Dumpty." And then she looked at Suzy. "I belong with those guys. I need to go home."

The prince cast a look at Humpty Dumpty.

"Maybe I will cut my visit short, after all," said the egg as he pushed back his chair.

The prince glared a moment and then laughed. "This has been a time of great learning for all of us, and the truth is the best teacher of all."

"Truth, dear husband, is an excellent instructor if only more of us would listen when it speaks." Humpty Dumpty bowed and scurried toward the door, and in another moment Jessica too was gone. And that left only Suzy.

"My work is done here," she said and curtsied as though she'd done it her whole life. And Ozma wished her back to Oz.

"ARE YOU SURE I don't have to go to school today?" Debbie asked. "I am not sick, I don't even have a fever. Momma never let me stay home unless I had a fever."

"You didn't get enough sleep last night," Beth explained. "That's a bit like being sick."

"Yeah, you need time to get over the jet lag," added Gary.

"What's jet lag?" asked Debbie as she dipped her toast into the soft boiled egg.

"It's what you experience when you hop around fairy worlds all

263

night long," Gary said as he sat down with a mug of coffee for himself and placed a small glass of juice before Debbie.

"Besides, I'll bet you'll want to be here to meet the children," Gwen explained.

"What children? Oops sorry, I shouldn't talk with my mouth full."

"We're getting some new arrivals. Six actually," Gary smiled. "Seems like old times."

"And we have another reason for you to stay home from school today," added Gwen. "We had a call this morning. It's why we woke you up."

"That's very early for a call. People shouldn't call so early you know," Debbie chimed in.

"It was your dad," Gary said. He waited to see her reaction.

"My dad? No, that's not possible. He's lost."

"They found him. He's coming here today to see you. He wants to know if you'd like to live with him again. I know the rules will be very different than when you lived with your mom, but…"

"There won't be any rules," said Debbie. "Daddy never liked rules. My mom used to hate that, but I've seen a lot of unusual places without rules and I think I can handle it now."

"He will be so happy. He was a bit afraid you wouldn't want to see him," Gwen said.

"Daddy? Daddy is never afraid. He is the bravest man in the world. He invents games no one has ever heard of."

They heard a bumping sound.

"Is that daddy?"

"No, I don't think so. It sounds like it's coming from upstairs," said Gary as Beth jumped up in expectation and ran up the long staircase.

She almost reached the top when she was grabbed by Doug holding a small white card and laughing and crying at the same time. They kissed so many times that Debbie felt uncomfortable and went to her room to choose what to wear for her dad's visit.

Isabelle opened the door to the room she was staying in and shouted, "Jess, you're back. And look, Amanda is back too."

"We have so much to talk about," said Jessica.

"Any of you want breakfast?" asked Gwen.

"Just ate dinner," Charlie smiled. "But, what the heck, sure, I'm in."

As they re-entered the long kitchen they used when the house was full, Doug was trying to explain all that had happened as quickly as he could.

"Weren't you frightened?" asked Gwen. "I mean wolves and dragons and god knows what else."

"Keep in mind, dear, wolves are terribly maligned animals. They aren't the monsters the fairy tales made them to be."

Charlie was waving his reattached hand about as he drank a cup of Gwen's coffee, but Doug ignored him and continued. "But the most important thing to remember," Doug stated as if he were concluding a lecture, "is it's a fairytale. Whatever happens can be fixed or undone. No real harm."

"That's just not true, Doug. You know that's not true," Charlie jumped in.

"Seems true to me. Can you prove it isn't?"

Charlie looked confused for the first time since he and Doug had gone through the door. ""Because if it doesn't change you, what's the point?"

Doug took a moment to think that through. "Maybe," he said. "Maybe there's still more to learn about fairylands. Are you sure you've had enough?"

"No," said Charlie. "No, I'm not sure at all." He raised his hand and turned it in front of his eyes. "I just don't know," he said.

"So what do we do with the doorway?" asked Gwen. "Should we seal it?"

"Not yet," said Charlie. "We couldn't do that to Buddy."

"Buddy?" said Gwen. "Buddy Samson?"

"He's still in the secret room."

CHAPTER TWENTY–TWO

*On the third day the messenger came back again, and said,
I have not been able to find a single new name, but as I
came to a high mountain at the end of the forest, where the
fox and the hare bid each other good night, there I saw a
little house, and before the house a fire was burning, and
round about the fire quite a ridiculous little man was
jumping, he hopped upon one leg, and shouted*

> *to-day I bake, to-morrow brew,*
> *the next day I will have the child.*
> *Ha, glad am I that no one knew*
> *that Rumpelstiltskin I am styled.*

*You may imagine how glad the queen was when she heard
the name. And when soon afterwards the little man came
in, and asked, "Now, mistress queen, what is my name?"*
At first she said, "is your name Conrad?"
"No."
"Is your name Harry?"
"No."
"Perhaps your name is Rumpelstiltskin?"
*The devil has told you that! The devil has told you that,
cried the little man, and in his anger he plunged his right
foot so deep into the earth that his whole leg went in, and*

266

then in rage he pulled at his left leg so hard with both hands that he tore himself in two.

HE CLOSED THE BOOK WITH A SHUDDER.

He had remained in the magic room when everyone else went into the hallway. He needed time. He had to do this slowly. He knew already it would take time to adjust to living in this world again. It would not be easy. His memory of it was as vague as a dream. Everything around him already looked strange: the carpeted floor, the straight walls without timber beams or any visible support for the ceiling. He did not remember how much rooms in this world were like boxes. And the extravagant collection of knickknacks and toys, cloth, stuffed toys that seemed as real as the illustrations he'd seen in books. And the books. Books everywhere, along all the walls. What a strangely rich and claustrophobic world this one must be. Memories were coming back of this house, and this room—the head of deer or something almost looked familiar. And that book where you signed your name beside the two couches roped together. They looked familiar too. Was being in this world going to stir up the embers of memory he'd thought were dead? Somewhere in his memory was his mother. His other mother. Yes, he thought he remembered her, and the fire that killed her. Did he really have to spend the rest of his life in this place of sad memories? He didn't want to think about that.

He walked around the room some more. He was unfamiliar with most of the items in the room. But he was fascinated by the electric lights. No flame, but heat and light. The heat felt good, as though it were taking away a deeper cold than he had known he felt—until he burnt his fingers trying to touch the bulb. At least it did not go out.

He turned his attention to the books. There were so many books, and he had seen so few growing up in Grimms' Forest. But how did anyone have time to read so many books or have the wealth to hoard them? Not even the prince of Grumbottem himself would have a library like this one. He ran his fingers along the bindings and read the titles. A few were familiar, although most were strange.

There were several anthologies with the name Hans Christian Anderson on them. He'd never heard this name that he could recall. There was one bright, heavy volume called *Classic Fairy Tales*. He opened it, excited by the ornate, full color images, rich as a painting in the palace of the prince. But he didn't know most of the stories he was looking at. Then he saw *Mother Goose*. That seemed familiar, well, a little bit. He leaned on the couch and flipped through some pages until

267

he saw Humpty Dumpty.

The picture was bright and colorful, but it did not do the egg justice. He would be furious at how foppish the artist had made him look. Then he flipped a few more pages and saw *The Old Woman Who Lived in a Shoe*. Now why did that seem important? Had he met her? He almost thought he had. She had a very pretty face, not really like an old woman at all. He ran his finger over the picture. But he didn't know why.

He put the book down when he spotted a small thin book with a brightly colored cover. *Rumpelstiltskin!* His eyes grew wide. He grabbed the book and walked near the electric light. Finally he'd find out why his father never wanted the story in his house.

The first few pages were of a king and a miller's daughter. He had never met them. Then he flipped a few pages and saw a gnarled little dwarf with a shifty face and cruel eyes.

Who was this supposed to be? It didn't look anything like his dad. Then he flipped through the pages to look at all the pictures. Was that decrepit dwarf really supposed to be his father? If that was the sort of picture they drew, no doubt they had the events and the character all wrong as well. Then he read the tale.

His father had told him the story was a lie. And Rapunzel and Red Riding Hood had laughed at their own stories. And the pictures showed that whoever illustrated this book knew nothing of the world of Grimm. But the story disturbed him still. He didn't believe it for a moment. He was glad his father had not allowed it in his house. He was half sorry he'd read it. If that's the sort of thing you read in the books of this world. if all these books were so false, he would not enjoy reading any of them. But worse than that, how could he get along with the people of this world, if this is how they thought? Or, worse still, what if the stories weren't so terribly false? Don't people always get their own story wrong? Maybe this was what happened. Maybe Riding Hood and Rapunzel didn't remember or didn't want to remember things the way they really happened. That witch who had given him the maps—she told a rollicking good story of who she was and what she did. And none of it was true.

"I have a lot to learn in this world," Budy said, "if I have to stay."

Facing a wolf in the wilds of the Grimms' Forest with just his rucksack and his knife would be nothing compared to tussling with the unknown dangers of a place like this.

"Hey, Buddy come down here," Charlie called down the hall.

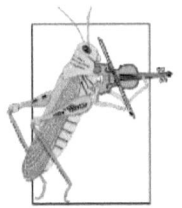

.